Edwin Waugh

Tufts of Heather

Edwin Waugh

Tufts of Heather

ISBN/EAN: 9783743394865

Manufactured in Europe, USA, Canada, Australia, Japa

Cover: Foto ©Andreas Hilbeck / pixelio.de

Manufactured and distributed by brebook publishing software (www.brebook.com)

Edwin Waugh

Tufts of Heather

Tufts of Heather.

By EDWIN WAUGH.

MANCHESTER
John Heywood, Deansgate and Ridgefield; John Dale
and 11, Paternoster Buildings, London.
1881

CONTENTS.

The Old Fiddler.

CHAPTER I.

The traveller stops and gazes round and round,
O'er all the scenes that animate his heart
With mirth and music. E'en the mendicant,
Bowbent with age, that on the old gray stone
Sole sitting, suns him in the public way,
Feels his heart leap as to himself he sings.

MICHAEL BRUCE.

T was not quite eleven in the forenoon as Lobden Ben sauntered along the road towards the head of the clough, near Healey Hall, as happy as the summer day. And right well did that jolly-hearted besommaker harmonise with the scene around him. He was a healthy, hardy, comely fellow, just in his prime,—as clean as a new pin, and dressed in his holiday clothes, freaked with such bits of rustic prettiness as his little garden and his native fields afforded. He looked like "a man of cheerful yesterdays," and hopeful future.

Embroidered was he, as it were a mead,
All full of freshé flowers, white and red,
Singing he was or fluting all the day :
He was as fresh as is the month of May.

The day was hot, and Ben was idle, and, as it still wanted more than an hour of noon, he paced the road with a slow,

1

wandering gait. His hat was thrown back from his broad forehead, and in his right hand he carelessly swung a green branch, as he chanted aloud,—

> Be merry while it's day, my lads,
>   'Twill soon be set o' sun ;
> An' fate will have her way, my lads,
>   Let a mon do what he con !
>   What he con !
>   Let a mon do what he con !

Then, wiping his moist forehead, he lounged onward in silence for a few yards. But he was too glad-hearted to be silent long, and, according to his wont when thus wandering alone, he began again to interweave the quiet thoughts that played about his mind with quaint threads of the minstrel memories of days gone by. Like a fitful bird in the summer woods, he chanted as he went,—now this, now that ; but nothing long,—

> I'm quite content, I do not care,
>   This world may wag for me ;
> When fuss an' fret wur o' my fare,
>   I geet no greawnd to see.
> So, when away my carin' went
>   I ceawnted cost, an' wur content.

And then, after another moment's silence, another fragment flitted across his thoughts, and he trolled forth,—

> And she did laurel wear !
> And she-e did laurel wear !

Ben's voice rang loud and clear in that quiet scene, where the rich repose of summer noontide seemed to steep every thing in drowsy delight. Haymakers were at work upon the hill-sides, spreading out the damp grass which had been cut before the previous day's rain ; and, now and then, a cheery laugh, or the cadence of some snatch of old country song, came sailing on the sunny air, softened by distance ; but Ben had all the highway to himself, and the man and his melody lent a charm to the landscape, as he wandered on, chanting "like tipsy jollity that reels with tossing head." The birds eyed him curiously from the trees as he went lounging by, with the rosy sprig nodding in his hat at every footstep, and the green branch swinging in his hand ; and they seemed to listen intently to his lay, till some dreamy pause of silent thought stole in upon the fitful strain, and then they gushed forth into wilder music than before, as if they had suddenly discovered an old friend, and were delighted to find any human creature astir in the gay green world as happy as themselves.

He was approaching the head of the clough, called " The Thrutch," the most picturesque part of the road, and ten minutes' walk would have brought him up to Healey Hall ; but, though afraid of being too late for his appointment with the colonel, he was too shy a man to wish to be too soon in such an unusual place ; and, therefore, he began to linger, and look about for a place where he might rest and cool himself during the intervening time. Seeing a bush of ripe "heps " that overhung the pathway, he climbed the prickly hedge, and began to pluck them, like a truant school-boy whiling away the sunny hours, and as he put them, one by one, into his pocket, he sang,—

> An' still the burden o' my song,
> Shall be, to great an' smo',
> For hee and low, for weak an' strong,
> Good government is o' !

Here he suddenly leaped down from the hedge-side, and seating himself upon the bank, he began to look at his hand, into which a great thorn had penetrated; and, as he examined the bleeding finger, he kept quietly repeating the last line,—

Good government is o' !

over and over again, until, with the help of his pocket-knife blade, he had extracted the thorn. Then, rising lazily to his feet again, he sauntered on, and sang,—

For I never,—no, never,—no, nev-er,—
Shall see my love more !

Go from my window, love, go,
Go from my window, my dear ;
The wind and the rain
Will drive you back again,
You cannot be lodgéd here.

Begone my juggy, my puggy.
Begone my love, my dear :
The weather is warm,
'Twill do thee no harm,
Thou cannot be lodgéd here.

Ben walked so near to the hedge-side, for the sake of the shade afforded by the overhanging bushes, that his face came in contact with a spider's web, fine as the down of a midge's wing. He halted, and wiped away the ruins of the delicate rosace from his cheek; and even this trifling incident seemed, unconsciously, to change the tone and direction of his wandering fancy, for he burst forth with an old ditty, of another tune :—

Come, ye young men, come along,
With your music, dance, and song ;
Bring your lasses in your hands.
For 'tis that which love commands ;
 Then to the Maypole hie away,
 For it is now a holiday !

It is the sweetest of the year,
For the violets now appear ;
Now the rose receives its birth.
And the primrose decks the earth ;
 Come to the Maypole, come away,
 For it is now a holiday.

Here each bachelor may choose
One that will not faith abuse ;
Nor pay with coy disdain
Love that should be loved again ;
 Come to the Maypole, come away,
 For it is now a holiday.

And when you well reckoned have
What kisses your sweethearts gave ;
Take them back again, and more,
It will never make them poor.
 Come to the Maypole, come away.
 For it is now a holiday !

When you thus have spent the time,
Till the day be past its prime ;
To your beds repair at night,
And dream there of your heart's delight.
 Then to the Maypole hie away,
 For it is now a holiday !

Here, spying a well at a little distance, on the other side of the road, he muttered to himself, "Hello, let's sup!" and away he went lounging across towards it. Laying his hat on

the green bank, he knelt down upon the edge of the well ;
and, as he bent down to drink, the reflection of his face
rose up in the water to meet him. Ben paused to contem-
plate the sight, and groping at his sore nose, which still bore
marks of the old fiddler's heel, he said, "Come, it does look
a bit better; but it's hardly fit to be sin yet. They'n be
sure to ax me abeawt it up at th' ho', yon. Well, I's be
like to poo through as weel as I con ; for I cannot go beawt
it, that's sartin. It would do weel enough to go a-fuddlin'
wi', but it's noan fit for a parlour. I wish I could wear
eawr Betty's a day or two till this gets mended. Hoo's a
angel of a nose compar't wi' mine. Come," continued he,
caressing it once more, "I'll poo tho through, owd lad, as
weel as I con." Then, seeing his holiday clothes, and the
posy in his button-hole, reflected in the water, he cried,
"Hello, Benjamin ! what's up at yo're so fine to-day ? Yo're
like th' better side cawt ! Are yo beawn to a weddin' or
summat ? I'll tell yo what, maister, yo're gettin' new things
fast ! Has sombry laft yo some brass latly, or summat, at
there's o' this fancy-wark agate ? . . . Posies an' o' !
Eh, dear ! There'll be no touchin' yo wi' a pike-fork in a
bit. . . . 'Ston fur!' said Simon o' Twitter's ! 'Ston
fur ! I never talk to poor folk when I've these clooas on !
Ston fur ! I'm busy wi' th' quality. Co' to-morn, when th'
brass is done ! . . . Well, come, here's luck, owd lad !"
And dipping his mouth into the well, he took a long drink ;
then rising slowly, and with half-shut eyes, he gave a sigh
of satisfaction, wiped his mouth with his napkin, brushed
the dust carefully from his knees, donned his rose-wreathed
hat, re-arranged the posy in his button-hole, and taking up

the green branch, he lounged back to the shady side of the road again, singing,—

> For I nev-er.—no-o, nev-er,—no never,
> Shall see my love more!

"Nawe, nor I never shall," said Ben, with a sigh. "Eh, hoo wur a bonny lass, wur Jenny. God bless her! Eawr Betty's forgetten o' abeawt it, neaw. But hoo use't to ding me up wi't a bit, sometimes, when we wur cwortin."

> My lodging it is on the cold ground,
> And oh, very hard is my fare ;
> But that which grieves me more, love,
> Is the coldness of my dear.
> Yet still he cried, "Oh turn, love,
> I prythee, love, turn to me ;
> For thou art the only girl, love,
> That art adored by me."

> With a garland of straw I'll crown thee, love,
> And marry thee with a rush-ring ;
> Thy frozen heart shall melt with love,
> So merrily I will sing,
> Yet still he cried, "Oh turn, love," &c.

> But if thou will harden thy heart, love,
> And be deaf to my pitiful moan,
> Then I must endure the smart, love,
> And shiver in straw all alone.
> Yet still he cried, "Oh turn, love," &c.

"Hello ; what's comin' neaw!" said Ben, staring down the road. It was a handsome, well-dressed, and well-mounted horseman, who came riding hastily along. As soon as he had got within a few yards of Ben, he pulled up, and inquired how far he was from the village of Whitworth.

"Oh, three-quarters of a mile, happen," said Ben. "Th' first heawses yo come'n to. Turn up at th' reet hond amung th' heawses, an' yo'n be i'th midst on't, i' two minutes. I've just come fro' thither mysel."

"Do you think Dr. James will be at home?" inquired the rider.

"Sure to be," replied Ben. "He's seldom off, except when he's oather huntin' or shootin'; an' then he doesn't go far fro' whoam. Well, yigh; he gwos into th' Red Lion a bit of a neet, after he's done "

"What kind of a place is the Red Lion?" inquired the horseman.

"Oh, the best shop i' Whit'orth, if yo wanten to put up. I know th' folk 'at keeps it, very weel. Th' landlady's an owd friend o' my wife's. I left my wife theer this forenoon. They'n a rare good stable, too."

"Thank you!" said the rider, and flinging a shilling towards Ben, he galloped off.

"Yon's moor money nor wit, I deawt," said Ben, looking after the disappearing horseman. Then, walking up to where the shilling lay, he looked down at it, and said, "Well, I never expected that, as heaw. . . . He met (might) ha' gan it one decently, beawt flingin' it o'th floor. . . . But it's no use lettin' it lie theer. It'll come in for summat (somewhat) better nor mendin' th' hee-road wi'."

Then he pocketed the shilling, and went on singing,—

> Green grow the leaves on the hawthorn tree;
> Green grow the leaves on the hawthorn tree;
> They hangle, an' they jangle,
> An' they cannot well agree,
> While the tenor o' my song goes merrilie,
> Merrilee!
> Merrilie-ee!
> While the tenor o' my song goes merrilee!

"I wish I'd axed yon chap what time it wur," said Ben. Then, after walking thoughtfully on a few paces, he burst out again in a fresh direction.

There wur an owd fellow coom o'er the lea,
   An' it's oh, I'll not have him!
     He coom o'er the lea,
     A-cwortin to me,
   Wi' his owd gray beart new-shorn.

My mother hoo tow'd me to oppen him th' door.
   An' it's oh, I'll not have him!
     I oppen't him th' door,
     An' he fell upo' th' floor,
   Wi' his owd gray beart new-shorn.

My mother hoo bade me set him a stoo.
   An' it's oh, I'll not have him!
     I set him a stoo,
     An' he looked like a foo,
   Wi' his owd gray beart new-shorn.

   .   .   .   .   .

My mother hoo towd me to cut him some bread.
   An' it's oh, I'll not have him!
     I cut him some bread,
     An' threw't at his head,
   An' his owd gray beart new-shorn.

My mother hoo towd me to leet him to bed.
   An' it's oh, I'll not have him!
     I let him to bed,
     An' he're very near deeod,
   Wi' his owd gray beart new-shorn.

   .   .   .   .   .

My mother hoo towd me to take him to church
   An' it's oh, I'll not have him!
     I took him to church,
     An' I left him i'th lurch,
   Wi' his owd gray beart new-shorn.

When Ben had ended the ditty, he wiped the moisture from his forehead again, and muttered to himself, " 'Eh, it's warm, God bless yo,' as th' owd woman said when they axed hur heaw hoo liked th' thin broth. I wonder what o'clock it is. Hardly eleven, bith' day, I think. Twelve's my time ; an' I'll go noan afore, as heaw th' cat jumps. I may no 'ceawnt o' bein' catechise't bi folk,—quality or no quality. Th' owd kurnul's sure to be theer,—an' happen a parson or two. I wish this nose o' mine wur reet; they're sich chaps for readin' folk fro yed to fuut. . . . An' then, they're sure to begin abeawt yon bit o'th jackass o' mine bein' wund up into th' mill chamber. Rare gam' for 'em, that'll be. It'll last my life-time, that jackass dooment. Sarve me reet, too,—leather-yed. I could ha' laugh't rarely if onybody else had done it but me. But th' laughin's o' upo' one side, this time, like th' handle of a can. Ne'er mind ; it'll be somebry else's turn th' next. . . . Th' most o' folk are fain to see other folk make foo's o' theirsels. It's th' way o'th world. . . . An', by th' mon, if a poor lad happens to be born wi' a hair-shorn lip, or his yure a bit cauve-lick't, he's sure to be punce't for't, oather by one bowster-yed or another,—though he's no moor to do wi't nor he has wi' makin' moonleet. There's a deeol o' feaw flytin' i' this cote,—that they co'n a world. . . . But then, I wur a jumpt-up foo abeawt that jackass-do,—there's no gettin' off that. Well,—come,—I's happen larn some-time. It's a lung lone 'at's never a turn. . . . But I's catch it, when I get to th' ho'. If it isn't mention't i'th parlour, it'll be mention't i'th kitchen. Th' sarvants are ten times war nor th' tother. But, never mind, every mon

mun do his do, while th' time's up. 'Come on!' said
Kempy; 'we're noan freeten't o' frogs! Folk 'at's boggart-
fear't han nobbut a feaw life.' 'Forrad, lads!' cried Tickle-
but; 'yo'r wark's i'th front on yo!' . . . I'll face up at
twelve,—but not a minute afore,—that's sattle't. An' there's
an hour to do on, yet. Come, I'll keawer me deawn, an'
pike a two-thre o' these heps."

Taking a few of the red hips from his pocket, he was just
preparing to seat himself upon the hedge, when, glancing
along the road, he spied somebody sitting in a shady place,
close by the wayside. "Hello," said Ben; "what's yon?
Somebry sittin' bi th' roadside, as snug as a button, wi' o'th
world to theirsel'. I wonder who it is. A tramp o' some
mak, I dar say. Come, I'll have a look at 'em, as heaw."
And away he went lazily onward, chanting,—

> Han yo sin my love, my love, my love;
> Han yo sin my love, lookin' for me?
> A cock't hat, an' a fither, an' buckskin breeches;
> An a bonny breet buckle at oather knee!

As Ben drew nearer, he began to recognise some features
of the person he had seen from the distance, and, stopping
suddenly, his eyes began to glisten, and, raising his hands,
he cried, "By th' mass; I believe it's Dan o' Tootler's, th'
owd fiddler! Eh, if it's him! Come, that'll do!" And
then he strode forward more briskly, singing,—

> Robin Lilter's here again;
> Here again, here again!
> Robin Lilter's here again,
> Wi' th' merry bit o' timber!

It was, indeed, Dan o' Tootler's, a blind fiddler, well known all over the country side. His native spot was a wild moorland fold, near to the foot of Brown Wardle Hill, at the north-eastern end of the vale of the Roch ; but he was a great wanderer ; and his wide acquaintance with old melodies, especially those peculiar to the north of England, as well as his remarkable power as a performer upon the violin, made him a favourite guest wherever he went. At wakes, and weddings, and churn-suppers, or any country holiday, his was a well-known and welcome face, in every country nook between Blackstone Edge and the bleak ridge of Rooley Moor ; and even far beyond that great dividing line,—in the hills and dales of Rossendale Forest, and amongst the lonely folds of Ribblesdale, up to the great end of Pendle, many a merry heart leaped with joy at the mention of blind Dan o' Tootler's, and his fiddle. There the minstrel sat, upon an old tree root, which had been left by the wayside, sunning himself, and crooning a quaint tune, with his blind eyes turned upward to the summer sky. He was called "Owd Dan" wherever he went ; but this was meant more as an acknowledgement of kindly acquaintance than as indicating the decrepitude of age ; for he was not yet sixty, and he was a happy-hearted and remarkably hale man for his years. He was humbly clad, but all was clean and whole from head to toe ; and even the clumsy, unconcealed patches upon his clothing, here and there, were indicative of wholesome thrift, and showed that, though poor, he was not severely so, and also that, in his lowly estate, he was kindly cared for. His son, a chubby lad of nine years old, whose business was to lead him by the hand,

had wandered into a field, hard by, to gather flowers, always
keeping within call, whilst the old man rested himself; and
as the blind fiddler sat there, with his face up-turned, and
quietly swaying his body to and fro, to the measure of an old
tune, which he was crooning dreamily to himself, there was
something very touching in the placid helplessness which
pervaded his well-cut features. Indeed, there is often a
strange heaven of peaceful expression in a blind man's face;
as if the loss of sight, which deprives life of so many
pleasures, had taken away also some of its troubles; and
the mute, pleading eloquence,—the plaintive quietude—that
dwells in a sightless countenance, moves the heart more
than strength, more than beauty ever can; as if helplessness itself was surrounded by an angelic atmosphere, more
potent for its defence than any merely physical protection
could be.

The fiddler was on his way to the house of an old friend,
who farmed a large tract of land upon the edge of the
moors, near the town of Bacup. Indeed, the minstrel and
the farmer were distant relatives, bearing the same name,
apart from the personal attachment which bound them to
each other; and, according to a custom long established
between the two, the fiddler had been specially invited, quite
as much in the character of a guest as of an itinerant
musician, to enliven the rustic gathering which thronged the
old house at the Nine Oaks' Farm at the annual churn-
supper, as the feast of the hay-harvest is called in South
Lancashire. The churn-supper at Nine Oaks was famous
all over the Forest of Rossendale, no less on account of the
number of the guests and the bounty of the cheer, than on

account of the presence of a minstrel so well known and so
universally welcome as Dan o' Tootlers was in those days.
He had already walked many a rough moorland mile, and,
having still several miles further to go, the old man had sat
himself down in this shady nook of the road to rest a little
while. The loss of sight had made the fiddler's hearing
more acute than is common to those whose senses are all in
full play; and in the all-pervading stillness of the scene,
where nothing seemed astir but the songs of wild birds, his
quick ear caught the sounds of Ben's footsteps approaching
from the distance.

"Husht!" said he, as if talking to the birds around him;
"husht! there's somebry comin'!" Then, catching the
tones of Ben's voice as he came singing on, a quiet smile
crept over the old man's up-turned face, as he rubbed his
hands and said, "Come, I know who that is! . . .
Husht! Let him goo on again! . . . Ay; it's him.
Lobden Ben, for a creawn!" As Ben drew near, the
fiddler cried out, with his smiling countenance still turned
sunward, "Hello, Ben, owd lad! Is that thee? Heaw
arto gettin' on amung yon yirth-bobs (tufts of heather) upo'
Lobden Moor?"

"Eh,—Dan o' Tootlers,—owd dog!" cried Ben, running
up, and catching the fiddler by the hand. "God bless thy
owd tweedlin' soul! Wheerever arto wanderin to, wi' thoose
bonny bits o' cat-bant o' thine?"

"Oh, a bit fur up, Rossenda' gate on," replied the fiddler,
"I'm beawn to a churn-supper, at the Nine Oaks."

"Th' dule theaw art!" cried Ben. "Eh, thae will
tickle yon owd clinkert shoon o' theirs up, aboon a

bit! By th' maskins, I wish I're beawn witho', owd brid!"

"An', by the good Katty, I wish thae *wur*, owd crayter!" replied the fiddler. "But I'm i' good time, yet. Come, keawer tho deawn a bit."

"I'm i' good time, too," answered Ben. "I've aboon an hour o' mi honds."

"Well; come thi ways, an' have a keawer, then," continued the fiddler, shifting, to make room for Ben upon the old tree root. "Keawer tho deawn. Th' moon's had mony a reawnd sin I let on tho afore. An' wheer arto for when tho sets off again, like,—conto tell? Or, thae'rt like wayter in a bruck,—noan tickle if thae can keep gooin'."

"Yelley Ho's (Healey Hall) th' first shop I have to play for, as soon as th' time comes," replied Ben.

"What, owd Kurnul (Colonel) Cherrick's?" said the fiddler.

"Ay."

"Why, thae'rt noan so fur off theer, now, arto?" replied the fiddler.

"I can yer th' dogs barkin' i'th yard, fro' here," answered Ben.

"Come, that'll do!" said old Dan, rubbing his hands; "that'll do!"

"He wants me to goo up to th' top o' Blacks'n Edge wi' him an' some friends of his, this afternoon," continued Ben.

"Oh, ay!" replied the fiddler. "There'll be fine doin's thae'll see. He's a rare owd cock, is th' kurnul. Yo'n be nought short, if he's theer. But yon be pinch't for time, winnot yo? I'd ha' started i'th mornin'."

"Well, thae knows," replied Ben, "I go bi orders. Twelve o'clock's my time ; an' I's go noan afore."

"Shootin', I guess?" inquired the fiddler.

"Nay ; I know nought what they're after," answered Ben. "It's reet to me, as what it is ; though I like to see a bit o' good spwort, for o' that. But twelve o'clock's my time ; an' it wants an hour yet."

"Well, then," said the fiddler, "thae'rt i' no peighl. So come an' sit tho deawn, an' let's have a bit o' talk. I'll be sunken if I'm not gooin' meawldy for th' want o' somebry to fratch wi' ! Come an' sit tho deawn."

"I'm willin'," said Ben, giving the old man a friendly slap on the shoulder, as he sat down beside him on the tree root. "Hutch up a bit. .   . Well, an' heaw arto gettin' on, Dan, owd lad ? "

"Oh, pecort (pert), lad ; pecort as a pynot (a magpie)," replied the old fiddler, smiling.

"That's reet," said Ben, "I like to yer o' folk doin' weel, particilar fiddlers,—they'n so mich fancy-wark abeawt 'em.

A mon 'at plays a fiddle weel,
Shold never awse (attempt) to dee.

I'll tell tho what, Dan ! "

"Well."

"It's a fine day, an' we'n plenty o' time on er honds ; an' it's a good while sin we let o' one another afore ; an' there isn't a wick soul i'th sect nobbut thee an' me."

"Well ; an' what bi that ? "

"Why. thae met trate a body to a bit of a do upo' that friskin'-stick o' thine.   Come, strike up ! "

"Well," replied Dan, drawing his fiddle from the bag; "I've nought again *that* noather."

"Good again!" cried Ben. "What arto beawn to give us, owd brid?"

"Aught 'at ever thae's a mind, Ben," answered the fiddler, as he rosined his bow.

"Well, let's have a good owd minor, then," said Ben.

"Agreed on," replied the fiddler. "But I'll tell tho what, Ben."

"Well."

"I'm just thinkin' 'at I could like to yer thee tootle one o' thoose bits o' ditties o' thine, th' first."

"So be it, then," said Ben. "What's it to be?"

"Try 'Chad'ick o' Chad'ick Ho'!'"

"I don't know it through," said Ben.

"Let's ha' 'Fair Ellen o' Ratcliffe,' then," continued the fiddler.

"Oh, it's so lung," replied Ben. "Thae'll have us agate o' yeawlin' till mornin'."

"Well," said the fiddler, "sing 'Bowd Byron an' his men,' then; or else 'Iron Cap o' Bernshaw Tower.'"

"Oh, I couldn't get through 'em i' time, mon," replied Ben. "I could happen manage 'Tuttlin' Tummy,' or 'Skudler o' Buckstones,' or 'Th' Piper o' Wardle.'"

"Doesto know 'Thungin' Robin?'" inquired the fiddler.

"Nawe."

"Or, 'Dark Rondle o' Sceawt Scar,'" continued the fiddler.

"I don't know that, noather," replied Ben.

"Well 'Cowd Simeon,' then," continued old Dan.

3

"Eh, nawe," said Ben.   "It's to hee,—it's to hee !   By th' mon, Dan, where I know one thae knows twenty."

"Well, I'll tell tho what," said Dan ; "try 'The Flowers o' Joy.'   That's short enough ; an' a bonny thing too."

> Full oft the sweetest flowers of joy,
> From the soil of sorrow spring.

" Here, here," said Ben, doffing his hat, and stroking his hair aside.   " I'll try one."

"Well, get agate," said Dan, beginning to tweedle on his fiddle.   "Get agate, an' I'll put an odd note or two in as thae gwos on.   Eh, Ben, I wish I could sing like thee !—

> Bowd Buckley o'er the wild hills rode,
>   A darin' dance to tread ;
> Wi' twenty-four o'th starkest lads
>   That ever Rachda' bred.

Come, get agate, Ben ; or else I'll start mysel'."

The fiddler's little lad, hearing the noise, had come out from the field, with his hand full of posies ; and he was now standing by his father's side, holding the lap of his coat, and gazing at Ben with wondering eyes.

"Come, Ben ; what is it ? " said the fiddler.

" 'The girl I left behind me,'" replied Ben.

" Brast off, then," replied the fiddler.

> I'm onely since I crossed the hill,
>   An' o'er th' moor an' valley ;
> Such heavy thoughts my heart do fill
>   Since partin' wi' my Sally.

I seek no more the fine an' gay,
　For they do but remind me
How swift the hours did pass away
　With the girl I left behind me.

Oh! ne'er shall I forget the night,—
　The stars were bright above me,
An' gently lent their silver light,
　When first she vow'd to love me.
But now I'm bound unto the camp,
　I pray that heaven may guide me,
An' send me safely back again
　To the girl I left behind me.

Had I the art to sing her praise,
　With all the skill of Homer,
One theme alone should fill my lays,
　The charms of my true lover.
Then, let the night be e'r so dark,
　Or e'er so wet an' windy,
I pray kind heaven may send me back
　To the girl I've left behind me.

Her golden hair in ringlets fair,
　Her eyes like diamonds shining,
Her slender waist, her carriage chaste,
　May leave the swain repining.
Ye gods above! oh, hear my prayer,
　To my true love to bind me,
And send me safely back again
　To the girl I've left behind me.

The bee shall honey taste no more,
　The dove become a ranger,
The rolling waves shall cease to roar,
　Ere I shall seek to change her.
The vows we've register'd above
　Shall ever cheer and bind me,
In constancy to her I love,—
　The girl I've left behind me.

My mind for her shall still retain,
  In sleeping or in waking,
Until I see my love again,
  For whom my heart is breaking.
If ever I return that way,
  And she should not decline me,
How gladly will I live and stay
  With the girl I've left behind me.

"Weel chanted, owd lad!" cried the fiddler, slapping
Ben on the back heartily. "Weel chanted. It's a bonny
owd thing, to this day. An', eh, I'll tell tho what, Ben,
there's many a poor sodiur lad has sung that wi' a achin'
heart when he's bin far away fro' whoam, an' little chance
o' comin' back again."

"Eh, ay," replied Ben; "I know summat abeawt that.
Eawr Bill wur kilt at th' stormin' o' Badajos. Thae knows
Moses Whistler, th' white-limer?"

"Sure, I do."

"Well, eawr Bill an' him listed together," said Ben.

"Oh, ay?" said the fiddler.

"Ay," continued Ben, looking thoughtfully round.
"Moses has getten whoam again, lam't for life; but eawr
Bill, poor lad, he's lyin' somewheer abeawt Badajos, quiet
enough,—what there is laft on him."

"Well," replied the fiddler, "my young'st brother, eawr
Joe,—a finer lad, nor a better-hearted, never stept shoe-
leather,—he deed, wi' Nelson, at Trafalgar. Eh, I thought
my mother would ha' brokken her heart! He're like th'
nestle-cock at eawr heawse. . . . I don't know heaw it
wur, but he would be a sailor, lung afore he'd ever set een
upo' salt wayter. . . . Poor Joe!"

"Ay, it's so, sometimes, for sure," said Ben, in a dreamy tone. "Th' last time 'at I yerd 'Th' Girl I left behind me' wur at 'Th' Amen Corner,' i' Rachda'. It wur one o'th leet horse, a fine yung chap as ever I clapt een on. He'd come upo' furlough, a-seein' his relations; an' when he geet to Rachda' he fund 'em o' laid by i'th churchyard, th' owd sweetheart an' o'. An' th' lad look't lost,—quite lost,—as he sit theer i'th nook bi hissel', as still as a meawse. But nought 'ud fit these tother but he mut (must) tak' his turn, an' sing 'Th' Girl I left behind me.' Well, I tell tho, he tried, an' I never yerd it better sung sin I're born o' mi mother. But when he'd getten abeawt th' hauve gate through, he brasts eawt a-cryin', an', by th' mon, he sets us o' agate,—th' drunkenest foo' i'th hole, they're o' cryin' at once. There weren't a dry face i'th spot. Owd Bill Hollan', th' butcher, wur theer, but he couldn't ston it. He had to goo eawt. Eh, heaw that lad did cry! . . . But, come, let's drop it, for God's sake. . . . Here, it's thy turn, Dan. Strike up summat or another."

"Agreed on," said the fiddler, drawing his sleeve across his eyes, and then shouldering his instrument. "Agreed on; what mun us have?"

"Try 'Remember the Poor,'" said Ben.

"Well done, Ben!" said the fiddler. "That's a fine owd minor tune!"

"It's nought else," replied Ben. "Brast off!"

The old man began to arrange the pegs of the instrument, and, as he tried the strings, one after another, and then in unison, he muttered affectionately to his fiddle, as if it was a living thing. "Neaw, owd lad," said he, as he screwed

first one peg, then another, and tweedled over little fits of
wailing prelude, to get the tones he wanted. "Neaw, owd
lad, this is a nice job for tho. Just thee talk to 'em a bit,
i'th owd fashion. Thae can do it if thae's a mind, I know.
We'n had mony a happy day together,—thee an' me,—
ha'not we, owd brid? Ay, an' we'n ha' mony another, if
God spares er lives.   .   .   .   Neaw, mind thi hits ! .   .   .
' Remember the Poor,' thae says, Ben ? "

    " Well, we'n see what we can do," continued the fiddler.
Then he quietly began the plaintive old forest tune, and, as
the beautiful wail rose upon the air, it seemed to hush the
wild birds around, and fill the summer noontide with a
sweet sadness. The rindle of water, dribbling into the well
hard by, subdued its silvery tinkle, and the very trees
and hedges seemed to stand still and listen, as if spell-
bound by the old man's touching lay. Ben was so moved
that he could not help taking up the melting strain, and so
they played and sang the tender old ditty together, till tears
began to trickle down their cheeks ; and when the song was
ended, and the last soft cadence was dying out upon the
woods in the clough, they sat silent together for a minute
or two.

CHAPTER II.

Oft seated 'neath some spreading oak,
To rapturous strains his soul awoke ;
Whilst listening hinds would drop the spade
Forgetful of their hardy trade ;
And peeping maidens raised the latch,
The minstrel's melting lay to catch ;
And the lone brook that crept along,
Bore on its breast the fiddler's song.

THE LAY OF THE POOR FIDDLER.

"HAT'S a nice thing," said Ben, drawing the sleeve of his coat across his eyes.

"Ay, it is," replied the old fiddler. " Gi' me thi hont, Ben ; I con play for thee wi' some'at like comfort. But, eh, mon, it hurts me.—it hurts me to play for folk at's no feelin'. There's nobry knows nought abeawt music if they ha'not a heart i' their inside. But, th' most o' folk, neaw a-days, are like as if they'd bin made cawt o' button-tops an' scaplins, put together cowd. . . . But, gi me thi hont, Ben, lad ! Thae knows what things belungs."

And they shook hands together, whilst the tears stood gleaming in the old fiddler's blind eyes.

The little lad was still standing by his father's side, gazing, wonderingly, first at one, then at the other.

" Billy," said the fiddler, "go thi ways an' play tho i'th feelt again a bit. I'll shout when I want tho."

.   .   .   .   .

"Dan," said Ben, groping in his pocket, "hasto had ony dinner?"

"Nawe," replied the fiddler, "but cawr Billy has a bit in a hankitcher somewheer."

"Wilto have a bit o' mine?" continued Ben.

"What hasto getten?" inquired the fiddler.

"Green-sauce-cake an' cheese," replied Ben.

"Ay, an' good, too," answered the fiddler. "Come, I'll have a bite wi' tho."

"Ben," said the old man, "hasto sin 'Duck-fuut' lately?"

"What. Tummy o' Doddle's?"

"Ay," replied Dan. "They co'n him 'Duck-fuut,' for a bye-name, dunnot they?"

"I thought his bye-name had bin 'Whelp,'" said Ben.

"Well," replied the fiddler, "I've yerd him co'd both 'Whelp' an' 'Duck-fuut.' It's thoose 'at doesn't like him at co's him 'Whelp,' I dar say."

"Well, but," continued Ben, "it's same chap that I mecon. It's lung Tummy, th' ceawnter singer, isn't it?"

"Sure it is," replied the fiddler.

"Eh, I connot tell when I seed him last," said Ben. "I believe it wur one Sunday forenoon, up at Ash'oth Chapel, soon after Kesmass. An' what dost think he did?"

"Nay, I know not," replied the fiddler. "Some'at quare, for a creawn."

"Well, thae knows, they'n no organ up at Ash'oth Chapel ; they'n nought nobbut th' singers, an' a bass fiddle. an' a little fiddle, an' a piccolo, an' sometimes a bazzoon,— that's when Billy Diggle's th' solid side cawt. Tim o' Yeawler's plays th' bass fiddle. Well, that forenoon, owd Nobbler, th' clark, ga' th' hymn eawt,—' Let us sing to the praise and glory of God, th' fourteent' hymn.' Then there wur a deeod stop for a minute or two, an' folk wur wonderin' that th' singers didn't start o' their wark. An' just as they began o' turnin' reawnd, to see what wur to do, up rose ' Duck-fuut,'—two yards hee,—i'th singin' pew,—sich a sect ! He'd a thick red wool muffatee reawnd his neck ; an' he'd two o'th primest black een i'th front of his face 'at ever thae seed,—for he'd bin to a fuut-bo' match, th' day afore, an' it had finish't up wi' a battle. Well, up that figure rose i'th singin' pew,—six fuut o'th quarest-lookin' stuff 'at ever stoode i' that spot,—an' he sheawted deawn to th' clark, ' Heigh, Bobby ! doesto yer ?' Owd Bob happen't to be blowin' his nose at th' time, an' didn't just catch him, so ' Duck-fuut ' sang cawt again, ' Doesto yer, Nobbler ?' Th' owd clark jumpt, an' dropt his hankitcher, when he yerd that word ' Nobbler,' an' he stare't at th' singin' pew, an' said, ' What's up ?' ' Well,' cried ' Duck-fuut,' lookin' deawn at him, ' yo mun stop a minute or two ; owd Tum's brokken a streng. Sit yo still a bit. I'll gi' yo th' item when we're ready.' "

"Just favvours him !" said the fiddler.

"A bit like him, for sure," said Ben. "But he geet th' bag for that."

"Sarve him reet," replied the fiddler. "But he never

4

wur very breet. I can remember 'em tellin' on him gooin'
to Rachda' rushbearin' when he wur a little lad, an' he
happened to see a chap i'th street playin' a trombone.
He'd never sin a trombone player in his life afore, so he
stood a while, watchin' this chap play. At th' last he
turn't to his faither, an' he said, ' See yo, faither, at yon
chap 'at's playin' yon brass thing; he connot get it th' reet
length, as what he does.'"

"By th' mon," said Ben, "he's as ill as owd Nukkin, 'at
went up Knowe Hill a-meetin' a sheawer o' rain."

"I yerd on him bein' at a rent-supper, once," continued
the fiddler, "an' when th' supper wur o'er, th' cheermon
code for 'order!' An' when he'd getten 'em still, he said,
'There is no parsons here, is there?' 'Nawe.' 'Well; I
could like to yer some on yo say 'Grace,' after sich a supper
as we'n had to-neet. Here, Duck-fuut, thee try thi hond,—
thae'rt a church-singer.' Then up jumped 'Duck-fuut' in a
minute, an' he cried cawt, 'Thank God 'at there's nobry
brawsen!'"

Here Ben began to feel a little compunction, remember-
ing how often he had laid himself open to ridicule. And,
wondering within himself whether the old man had heard of
his foolish freak with the jackass, which was now the talk of
the whole country-side, he silently determined to seize the
opportunity of turning the conversation into a different
direction.

"Dan," said Ben, "I've a good mind to gi' tho another
bit of a ditty."

"Do, Ben, do,—God bless tho!" said the old man,
shouldering his fiddle once more.

"Here goes!" said Ben,—

The day was spent, the moon shone bright,
   The village clock struck eight,
Young Mary hastened with delight,
   Unto the garden gate.
But what was there that made her sad ?
The gate was there but not the lad ;
Which made poor Mary say and sigh,
" Was ever poor girl so sad as I ? "

She traced the garden here and there,
   The village clock struck nine,
Which made poor Mary sigh, and say,
   " You sha'n't, you sha'n't be mine.
You promised to meet me at the gate at eight,
You never shall keep me nor make me wait ;
For I'll let all such creatures see,
They never shall make a fool of me ! "

She traced the garden here and there,
   The village clock struck ten ;
Young William caught her in his arms,
   No more to part again.
For he'd been to buy the ring that day,
And O! he had been a long, long way ;—
Then, how could Mary so cruel prove,
To banish the lad she so dear did love ?

Up with the morning sun they rose,
   To the church they went away,
And all the village joyful were,
   Upon the wedding-day.
Now, in a cot, by a river side,
William and Mary both reside ;
And she blesses the night that she did wait
For her absent swain, at the garden gate.

" Bravo, Ben !" cried the fiddler. "Thae mends !"

> Bravo, bravo, very well sung,
> Jolly companions, every one !

He then quietly began to play the air of the quaint old country song,—

> My owd wife, hoo's a good owd crayter :
> My owd wife, hoo's a good owd soul !

But before he had quite drawn out the last note of the second bar, Ben laid his hand upon his shoulder and said, " Dan, owd lad, we'n o'th world to ersels (ourselves), yet. There isn't a wick soul i'th sect. Let's have a doance ! These toes o' mine are ram-jam full o' flutterment ! Strike up ' The Flowers of Edinburgh,' or else, ' The Devil Rove his Shirt !' There's a bit o' nice hard greawnd i'th front on tho here, 'at looks as if it'd bide thumpin'. Strike up, owd brid ! ' The Flowers of Edinburgh.' I'll fuut it ! Just thee heatken my feet, neaw ! Brast off ! There's nobry comin'."

" Howd !" said Dan. " Howd a minute, till I get my strengs reet !"

Then he twisted and tweedled a minute or two, and when he had got his instrument into tune, he tapped upon the back of it with his fiddle-stick.

" Nae then, Ben," said he, " arto ready ? "

" Crash off !" replied Ben.

And at it they went, ding-dong.

Ben, though unusually strong-built for his height was a lithe-footed, and,—what is called in the country,—a " lark-heeled lad," a good runner, and a capital dancer of the dances common to his own country-side.

The fiddler's quick ear followed Ben's footsteps with glee.

"Go it, my lad!" cried he. "Go it, Ben, owd dog! Weel fuuted! By th' mon, weel fuuted! Rare time, Ben, owd brid,—rare time! Welt at it! Theighur! By th' mass, thae'rt makin' that bit o' floor talk like a Christian! Capital races! . . . Go thi ways, Ben, my lad! Dee when tho will,—thae'rt a glitterin' jewel!"

There they were, "with all the world to themselves,"— Ben dancing in the sun, with the posies in his hat, nodding to the tune; and the blithe old fiddler, with his smiling face upturned, frisking his gleeful elbow, and his whole body moving restlessly to the beat of the dancer's feet, whilst the fiddler's lad, with his hands full of wild flowers, leaned through a gap in the hedge, gazing upon the scene with mingled astonishment and delight.

"Stop! stop!" cried the fiddler, ending the tune with a soft wailing cadence. "Stop, an' rosin! Tak thi woint. Ben. Thae's done weel this time reawnd. Eh, if thou'd had a brewheawse-dur or summat to caper on, it would ha' made it sing! Come, sit tho deawn, owd lad!"

"It's warm wark, Dan," said Ben, wiping his forehead. "I wish we'd summat to sup. I'm as dry as soot."

"Eh," said the fiddler, "I wish thae'd a quart o'th best ale 'at ever wur brewed i' this world, i'th front on tho just neaw, fair singin' for tho to scawk at it! God bless thi heart! Thae's a fuut like a angel, Ben, an', by th' mon, thae'rt as lennock as a snig! Gi' mo thi hont! That bit o'th heart o' thine followed th' music, or else thae could ne'er ha' stricken sich time as that! Thae can doance both leet an' shade, owd brid! It does my heart good to yer a doancer touch th' tender bits of a tune with a soft fuut!

Oh, it makes me feel as fain as a cat in a tripe shop!
Come an' sit tho deawn upo' this tree-root. Eh, it would ha'
seawnded weel if it had bin a wood floor! Let's stop an'
rosin. Gi' me thi hont, lad! . . . I'll tell tho what,
Ben, 'thou's some music in tho,' as owd Swatter said
when th' jackass eat his tune-book. Thou has, owd lad!
'God bless thoose hoofs o' thine!' as Tuner said when th'
lon'lort brought him two keaw-heels to his supper. Come,
sit tho deawn. By th' mon, that's warm't me up!"

"Ay, an' it's warm't me up, too, primely," replied Ben,
taking his seat by the side of the old man.

It is a remarkable thing, that blind people,—even those
that have been born blind,—often speak of the appearance
of persons, and places, and things, as if they had actually
seen them. Whether this is merely an imitative manner of
speech in their case, or it may be accounted for by the
unusual acuteness of the senses still left to them, and the
keener attention to the reports of those who can see, aided
by the shaping power of imagination, which must be greatly
stimulated by the loss of sight, it is not easy to decide.
But the result is often so. And so it was with old Dan,
the fiddler.

"An' wheer is it 'at yo're off to this afternoon, Ben?"
said the old man.

"Top o' Blacks'n Edge," replied Ben.

"Well, yo couldn't have a nicer day for th' job," said the
fiddler. . . "I guess thae never wur i' Turvin Cloof, Ben?"

"Never. I know nought mich abeawt that country-
side," answered Ben.

"Eh, it's one o'th wildest nooks 'at ever I set een on,"

replied the fiddler. "I know o' that country-side, deawn as far as Ripponden,—hill an' dale, wood an' wayter stid, hamil (hamlet), an' roadside heawse. . . . Yo'n co' at th' White House, at th' top o'th Edge, I guess?"

"I dar say we sha'n," replied Ben. "There is nowheer else to co' at up theer."

"Nawe, there isn't," said the fiddler. "It's a wild country up theer, for sure. I've bin frost-bitten mony a time crossin' thoose tops. . . . Hasto ever bin to Robin Hood Bed?"

"Oh, ay," replied Ben, "three or four times. It's a fine lump o' rock, is that."

"Ay, it is," said the fiddler. "It stons upo' th' edge o'th moor-side, as if it own't everything within sect, an' that's no little."

"Nawe, by th' mon, it isn't so," answered Ben. "They can see across Lancashire an' Cheshire into Wales, fro' th' top o' Robin Hood Bed."

"Ay, they con," said the fiddler. "Let's see, I guess thae wouldn't know th' owd folk 'at kept th' White Heawse afore Joe Faulkner went to't."

"Nawe," replied Ben, "that wur afore my time."

"Eh," continued the fiddler, "I once yerd a bit of a tale at th' White Heawse. But heaw arto for time, Ben?"

"Oh, I've aboon hauve an heawer yet," replied Ben.

"Come, that'll do," said the fiddler. "This tale'll just do to put a two-three minutes on, while we're restin' us. . . . It wur one afternoon, i'th depth o' winter,——

But perhaps the old fiddler's story had better begin another chapter.

CHAPTER III.

How she did wish, with useless tears,
To have again about her ears
The voices that were gone.
                    WILLIAM BARNES.

Her lonely heart was breaking,
And crazéd was her mind;
She sighed, and wandered, seeking
A face she could not find.
                    ANON.

"IT wur i'th depth o' winter, an' th' snow lee thick upo' th' greawnd. This lad o' mine an' me,— we'd bin deawn at Mytholmroyd; an' late on i'th afternoon, we set off up through Turvin Cloof, to get to th' White Heawse, at th' top o' Blacks'n Edge. An' a wild an' lonely cloof it is, partickilar i' winter time. Th' road wur terrible dree, an' hard to travel; for it wur rough, an' sometimes very steep; an' here an' theer, wheer rindles o' wayter had run o'er it fro' th' hill side, th' keen frost had made it as slippy as a lookin'-glass. It wur as mich as I could do to keep my feet; an' thae may depend we didn't get forrud so very fast. I wur fain to sit me deawn neaw an' then, an' eawr Billy started o' cryin',—for th' lad thought we'rn lost, an' done for, sure enough,—when it geet th' edge o' dark, an' nought but th' wild cloof abeawt us; and it made

me rayther for-think (regret) ever settin' eawt. But I
cheer't him as weel as I could; for, thae knows, th'
lad wur o' that I had to depend on. Well, we geet forrud
o' somehcaw, bit by bit, but dark overtook us lung afore
we geet to th' top end o'th cloof, an' we'd o' th' wild
oppen moor-side to tramp at after, afore we coom to
th' White Heawse, at th' top o'th Edge. An' th' wynt blew
so keen that it welly (well-nigh) flayed (fleeced, stript) th'
skin off my face; an' eawr Billy cried. poor lad,—he cried,—
but I believe he cried moor because he wur freetent o' me
foin', than he did for hissel'; for every time that I slipt, or
gav' a bit of a clunter again a stone, he brast eawt again, as
if his heart wur breighkin'. An' he tremble't fro' yed to
fuut, an' he kept tellin me to tak care, an he gript my hond,
as tight as deeoth. An' he'd a hard job, had th' lad, that
day; for, bi what he said, bi th' time we geet to oppen moor-
side it had getten as dark as a fox's meawth, an' he could
hardly see th' gate afore us. But eawr Billy's made o' good
stuff,—God bless him!—an' I don't know what I could do
beawt him. . . . Well, at th' lung-length we geet to th'
White Heawse, fair stagged up, an' as starv't as otters,—for
th' north wynt blew as keen across that hill as if it had bin
full o' razors. I wur some fain for us to creep into shelter,
I con tell tho. But, afore many minutes wur o'er, eawr
Billy an' me wur comfortably keawert (cowered, seated) hi
a roarin' fire i'th kitchen, chatterin' together as if we'd live't
amung roses, an' etten nought but lamb an' sallet, ever
sin we were born. An' th' londlord an' his wife wur as
good as goose-skins to us. They're two very daycent folk,
I con tell tho. Th' owd lass, hoo set us a rare baggin' eawt

5

afore we'd bin mony minutes i'th heawse, an' we fell to't wi'
good heart, thae may depend. . . . An' th' woint went
whistlin' an' yeawlin' reawnd that heawse as if o'th witches
between theer an' th' big end o' Pendle had bin frozen eawt
o' their holes, an' wur ridin' reawnd upo' th' storm, like a
boggart-hunt i'th air. I yerd it o'th time; for, thae knows,
I've a keen ear for sich like things. But theer we wur,
snugly heawse't for th' neet; for they wouldn't yer on us
gooin' a fuut fur, till mornin'; an' to tell tho th' truth, I wur
fain on't. . . . There wur five or six moor i'th kitchen,—
a gam-keeper, an' two delph-chaps, an' three or four moor,
'at looked like hawkers; they'd bin deawn Ripponden road
on, an' they'd dropt in, one after another, as they'rn makin'
th' best o' their gate whoam again; an', in a bit, we wur as
thick as if we'd every one bin mates together fro' chylt-little
(child-little). An' nought would suit these chaps but I mut
(must) give 'em a touch upo' th' fiddle. So I played, first
one thing, then another,—an' we'rn o' as comfortable as
crickets,—nobbut one on 'em,—he'd rayther a three-nook't
mak of a temper. But, I took no notice on him, for he'd
had to mich to drink upo' th' road, afore he geet to th'
White Heawse. . . . Bi this time, th' moon wur up;
but th' sky wur o'erkest (over-cast), an' thick snow wur
drivin', white an' wild, across th' top o'th Edge. . . .
Well, I're agate o' playin' 'Roslin Castle,' an' th' folk i'th
kitchen wur as whist as mice, for they seem't a bit taen wi'
th' tune; an' weel they met (might), for it's as bonny a
minor as ever tremble't fro' fiddle-streng. . . . Well, I
wur up to th' een i' this fine owd tune, an' th' heawse wur
as still as a chapel, when o' at once, we wur startle't wi' a

clatterin' o' feet eawtside, an' then th' dur flew open, an' a
chap coom runnin' into th' kitchen, o' in a cowd sweat, wi'
a face as white as milk, an' shakin' till his teeth fair chatter't
i' his yed. 'God bless us o'!' cried th' lon'lady, 'whatever's
th' matter!' But th' chap wur clen done up, an' he thrut
(threw) hissel' into a cheer, an' theer he sit, speechless,
an' pantin' an' tremblin' fro' yed to fuut, like a hunted hare.
O' th' heawse wur terrified, for they could noather make top
nor tail on him, an' they thought th' felly (fellow) wur deein.
In a bit he gasped cawt for 'em to let him sup o' wayter'
an' he said that he'd 'sin summat.' Well, when this drunken
hawker yerd him say that, he began a-laughin', an' makin'
o' maks o' gam on him; but these two keepers soon stopped
him, for they threaten't mich an' moor that if he didn't
howd his din they'd throw him cawt at th' dur-hole; so he
kept his tongue between his teeth, like a good lad. . . .
Well, as soon as this chap had getten reawnd, he set to, an'
towd his tale. . . . It seemed that he'd bin to th' owd
hamil (hamlet) o' Sawrby (Sowerby), a-seein' an uncle of his
that wur just at th' last; an' he'd stopt theer, bi th' bed-side
till th' owd mon had drawn away; an' then he'd come'd
back i'th dim moonleet, across th' wild moor, that skirts by
th' top end o' Turvin Cloof. An' when he'd getten abeawt
a mile off th' White Heawse, as he wur feightin' on through
th' drivin' snow, o' at once he seed a tall figure of a mon,
wi' summat like a far cap on his yed, travellin' on abeawt
twenty yards afore him, but he couldn't yer th' seawnd of a
fuutstep. He co'd cawt to him, for he thought he could
like company, but still this tall figure travell't on, an' not a
word nor th' seawnd of a fuutstep; an' though th' keen woint

wur blowin' so strong across th' moor, he said it never
seemed to stir this traveller's clooas (clothes), an' he began
to think it very strange.   But when it geet close to th'
owd division-stone, between Yorkshire an' Lancashire,
he said this tall figure stopt, and seemed to stare deawn
towards th' White Heawse, an' as he drew nearer up to it
he sheawted again, an' then, he said, it turn't slowly
reawnd, an' he could see streaks o' blood fro th' for-yed,
deawn a lung white face ; an' then th' whole thing began
a-meltin' away into th' moonleet, an' it seemed to float
across th' road, an' o'er th' moor, i'th direction o' Robin
Hood Bed.   An', wi' that, he took to his heels, like a red-
shank, an' never stopt till he geet to th' inside o' th'
White House kitchen. . . .   Well, when he'd towd his
tale, they made him a bed up, an' he laft us to ersels (ourselves), for he wur quite done o'er, an' he durstn't go eawt
again that neet. . . .   As soon as he'd gone, some on
'em i'th kitchen rekon't that they'd never sin no ghosts ;
but, evenly, if there wur ghosts o' folk theirsels, they
couldn't see heaw there could be ghosts o' folk's clooas,—
fur caps an' sich like.   But these two keepers wur very
quiet, an' as soon as th' chap had done his tale, one on 'em
whisper't to th' other, 'He's sin Breawn Dick !'   An',
whether they believ't i' ghosts or not, they couldn't get one
o'th lot to goo eawt o'th heawse that neet, so they had to
find 'em quarters till mornin'.   They wanted no moor
music, an' as soon as these hawkers wur gone to bed, we
crope together, reawnd th' fire, an' I yerd th' tale abeawt
'Breawn Dick,' an' it wur this :—

    "It seems that lung afore Joe Faulkner coom to th'

White Hearse, it wur kept bi an owd widow woman. Hoo'd buried her husband fro' th' same hearse; but hoo kept it on, for hoo'd two or three good owd sarvants abeawt her; an' hoo'd an only son,—a fine, strappin', swipper (active) young fellow, th' pickter of his feyther, an' th' very leet o'th owd woman's ee. Well, it seems that this lad,—bein' th' nestle-cock,—had bin very much marred when he wur yung both by feyther an' mother. They'd letten him have his own way, an' he grew up very yed-strung an' maisterful. An' at after his feyther deed, he becoom quite a terror to th' country-side, for he took to neet-huntin', an' he geet connected wi' a lot o' desperate hee-way robbers, that prowl't abeawt th' Edge at that time o'th day. Some on 'em coom eawt o' Turvin Cloof, an' some fro' th' Tunshill, another fro' Booth Deighn (Dean),—but th' warst o'th lot wur 'Iron Jack,' that kept th' owd alehearse, at 'Th' Buckstones,'—wheer th' gang stable't their horses under th' hearse. Th' owd woman's son wur known bi th' name o' 'Breawn Dick o' Blacks'n Edge.' . . . Well, I believe there wur mony a feaw deed done upo' th' moorlan' roads i' thoose days. Mony a traveller wur stopt an' robbed, an' mony a lonely hearse wur brokken into, an' stript; an' neaw an' then, folk disappeared fro' th' road, an' never wur yerd on again. News o' these things kept comin' into th' White Hearse, but th' owd lon'lady little dreamt that her own lad had a hond i' 'em. Well, that gang wur not brokken into for years an' years. 'Breawn Dick' use't to be oft away fro' whoam, sometimes two or three days together; but his mother could never get to know wheer he'd bin; for he wur very close-temper't, an' very seldom oppen't his meawth to onybody. . . . But at last there coom a lung an' weary day. A whole week flitted by, an' he never darken't his mother's dur. An' th' lonely woman began o' mournin' for her son; for, to th' end of her days, he wur th' leet of her ee, an' hoo couldn't see a faut in him; but, when folk began to ax wheer Dick wur, hoo cried, an' said, 'Nay, there's no accountin' for cawr Richard. He comes an' he gwos, just as th' fit taks him, an' I noather know wheer he's gooin', nor what he's after, nor when I mun see him again, nor wheer he's bin, when he gets back. I wish he _would_ stop moor a-whoam, for I feel so lonely.' But still, day after day, an' week after week went by, an' he never coom; an' th' owd woman began o' lookin' wizzen't an' weary, for hoo wur frettin' her heart cawt, neet an' day. At last it began to be clear to everybody that th' poor owd crayter's senses wur givin' way, for hoo would have two candles set i'th window every neet, so that he could see th' heawse i'th dark; an' when th' wynt shook th' dur after hoo'd getten to bed, hoo'd come deawn an' oppen th' dur an' look into th' dark, an' hoo'd say, 'Richard, wheerever hasto bin, lad? Come thi ways in, eawt o'th cowd,—thae'll be starve't to deeoth! Thi supper's i'th oon!'—for hoo kept his supper ready for him, neet bi neet, week after week. But still, he never coom. At last, hoo geet worse an' worse, an' hoo began o' axin' every stranger 'at entered th' heawse, if they'd sin Richard, an' hoo kept turnin' to th' sarvants, an' sayin', 'Han yo sin aught of cawr Richard?' An' hoo began o' wanderin' up an' deawn th' road, an' cryin' cawt for him across th' wild moor, as if he wur a little lad that had gwon an arrand, an' wur lingerin' bi th' way.

But still, week after week went by. an' 'Breawn Dick' never
darken't his mother's dur. . . . At last, one wild neet,
when o'th heawse wur dark, except th' two candles hoo kept
brunnin' i'th window to leet him whoam, there wur three men
coom shuffling up to th' dur, carryin' another that had bin
shot, an' wur fast hastenin' to his end. When th' owd
woman yerd th' knock hoo wur comin' deawn th' stairs,
cryin', 'Richard, wheerever hasto bin?' but th' sarvants
kept her back, an' pacified her as weel as they could. But
th' rest o'th heawse wur astir that neet, for this chap that
had bin shot wur bleedin' to deeoth. He proved to be
'Iron Jack,' a noted neet-hunter, an' one o' this gang o'
robbers that had done sich depredation upo' th' moor-
roads. An' they saddle't a horse, an' th' hostler rode deawn
to Littlebruf (Littleborough) for th' parson an' th' doctor,
an' they geet up to th' White Heawse a very light (few)
minutes afore he drew away (drew his last breath). . . .
It turned eawt that 'Iron Jack' an' another o'th gang had
stopt these three men upo' th' hee-road, an' threaten't 'em
wi' loaded pistols, if they didn't give up what they had.
Well. they fought for it. One o' these travellers wur a
desperate strung chap, an' he gript 'Iron Jack.' Jack fired
at him, an' just grazed th' tip of his ear, an' then, as they
wur wrostlin', mon to mon, for their lives, tother robber
fired, but he missed his mark, an' shot 'Iron Jack,' an' when
he seed Jack drop, he took to his heels up th' moor-side.
An' then these three travellers carried Jack into th' White
Heawse, to dee. . . . When th' parson an' th' doctor
geet to his bed-side, he hadn't mony minutes' life in him;
but he made a terrible confession afore he drew away. I

don't know heaw mony murders an' robberies he'd had a
hond in, but amung other things, he said that five o'th gang
had robbed a farm heawse, up at 'Th' Whittaker,' an' then
they'd taen up th' dark moor-side, to th' little cave i'th
bottom o' 'Robin Hood Bed,' an' theer they divided what
they'd taen, bi lantron-leet.   Well, to make a lung tale
short, it seems they fell cawt abeawt their spoil, an' one on
'em shot 'Breawn Dick' through th' yed, an' they buried him
abeawt forty yards below Robin Hood Bed. . . .   Well,
when he towd his terrible tale, they tried to get th' names
o'th gang fro' him, but they couldn't.   He gaspt an' moaned
to his last, beawt utterin' another word.   That wur th' end
o' 'Iron Jack, o' Buckstones,' an' it wur th' end o'th gang,
too ; for they wur soon brokken into after that. . . .   Well,
they fun th' body, as he towd 'em, sure enough ; an' it wur
taen up, an' 'Breawn Dick' wur buried i' Ripponden Churchyard, close to th' yew-tree hedge. An' th' owd woman followed
him to his grave, witheawt a word, an' witheawt a tear in her
ee.   Th' White Heawse had to goo into other honds ; for th'
poor owd crayter wur getten quite dateless (disordered in
mind), an' hoo wur takken to live wi' some relations not
far fro' Ripponden.   But, though hoo wur harmless,—
rain or fair, they couldn't keep her in, an' they had to send
a lad wi' her, for hoo would goo an' sit bi th' side of his
grave, an' sing to him, as if he'd bin in his cradle.   An'
one cowd day this lad left her, an' went a-playin' him a bit,
an' when he coom back to tak her whoam, he fund her
lyin' across her son's grave, as still as a stone."

CHAPTER IV.

Is this thi own yure, or a wig?

BEDFLOCK.

HEN the fiddler's tale was ended, Ben and the old man sat in silent thought for a few minutes ; and then, being both deeply imbued with superstitious feeling, they were beginning to talk about the old halls and other places in the district which had the reputation of being haunted by supernatural beings, when Ben announced the approach of a stranger, from the direction of Rochdale.

" Hollo, Dan," said he, "there's summat comin' at last."

"What's it like?" said the fiddler.

" Nay, I can hardly tell yet," replied Ben.

" Is it a mon or a woman?" inquired the fiddler.

"It should be a mon, o' some mak'," answered Ben, "for, as far as I can see, it's getten breeches on."

" It may be a woman for that matter," replied the fiddler ; "they wear'n breeches, sometimes. I don't know heaw it is at yor heawse, Ben, but it is so at eawrs."

" Eawr Betty may wear what hoo's a mind for me," said Ben.

" Weel, an' thae'rt reet, lad," replied the fiddler. " We getten better through when they letten 'em have a bit o' their own road."

" Besides, hoo's moor wit nor me, i' some things," continued Ben, still keeping his eye on the advancing stranger.

6

"I dar say hoo has," replied the fiddler. "I dar say hoo has, lad. An' it's weel 'at thae can tak it so."

"Oh, I'll al'ays give in to a reet thing, as wheer it comes fro'," said Ben.

"That'll do, owd lad," replied the fiddler. "My mother use't to say that onybody that had ony sense met (might) larn fro' a foo. . . . But which gate is this thing comin', wi' breeches on?"

"Fro' Rachda' side," answered Ben. "It's a poor tramp. o' some mak', bi th' look on him. . . . By th' mon, it's Owd Skudler, I believe."

"Skudler? Skudler?" said the old fiddler. "What does he do?"

"Well, I connot tell what he is bi trade," answered Ben. "I can hardly tell what he is, he's so mony jobs; but I think he's keaw-jobbin' just neaw, bi th' look on him; for he's a cauve-stick in his hond, as lung as a clooas-prop. An' I know he does a bit for th' butchers neaw an' then; an' he use't to be a mak (make, kind) of an odd lad abeawt th' slaughter-heawse, at th' top o'th Bull Broo, i' Rachda'."

"Oh, I know him!" cried the fiddler. "He's better known bi th' name o' 'Boot-jack.'"

"I never knowed him bi nought nobbut Skudler," replied Ben.

"Then, I guess thae never yeard heaw he geet 'Boot-jack' for a bye-name," said the old man.

"Nawe; I don't know that ever I did," replied Ben.

"Well, thae knows, abeawt ten year sin, this Skudler wur a sort of a sarvant mon for owd Clement Royds, at th'

Failinge; an' one time, when he're off wi' th' family, i'th
south of Englan', they put up at an inn for th' neet. Well,
it seems that Skudler geet to mich drink i'th heawse. wi'
one an' another on 'em ; an' when it wur gettin' late on, th'
owd lad geet wander't into a grand reawm, wheer there wur
two or three travellers set drinkin' their glass, afore goin' to
bed. Well, one o' these travellers rang th' bell, an' towd th'
waiter to bring him a glass o' brandy an' a boot-jack, an'
owd Skudler stare't at this traveller fro' yed to fuut, for he
thought he're beawn to ha' th' boot-jack to his supper. At
last, Skudler rang th' bell, an' when th' waiter coom, he
said, ' Here, bring *me* a glass o' brandy, an' a boot-jack, too !
If that mon con height (eat) a boot-jack, 1 con !' That's
heaw he geet th' name o' ' Boot-jack !' But he geet
th' bag fro' Clement's, at after, through bein' to fond o'
drink."

"Husht, husht!" said Ben. "Here he comes ! Neaw,
Skudler, owd lad, is that thee?"

"Hello, Ben !" said Skudler. "Heaw arto?"

"Oh, as nice as ninepence," replied Ben. "Heaw arto
gettin' on, Skud?"

"Just middlin'," said Skudler. Then recognizing the old
fiddler, he continued, "Hello, Dan, owd lad, art thou theer,
too?"

"Aye, I'm here ; I'm here," replied the old man. "Thae
sees, I keep turnin' up again,—like Clegg Ho' Boggart."

"An' nought but reet, noather," said Skudler. "Nought
but reet, noather, owd lad !" Then, turning towards Ben,
he whispered, as he pushed his fingers through his unkempt
hair, "Eh, I am some ill, to-day, Ben."

"Thae looks rayther wild," replied Ben. "What's th' matter, owd mon?"

"I wur wrostlin' th' champion, again, yesterday," answered Skudler.

"Th' champion?" said Ben.

"Ay, th' champion," replied Skudler. "An' he geet me deawn again."

"What champion?" inquired Ben.

"I're drinkin', mon; I're drinkin'!" replied Skudler. "I geet too mich drink! That's o'!"

"Aye, aye," said the old man; "that's th' champion, reet enough! He's deawn't mony a better chap nor thee, Skudler. An' he'll deawn mony another, yet."

"I dar say he will," replied Skudler. "I dar say he will, if they dunnot let him alone. . . . But, beside that," continued he, "I've been ill trouble't wi' th' worms, this day or two back."

"Worms!" cried Ben. "I con tell tho heaw to cure th' worms, owd lad!"

"Let's be yerrin' (hearing), then," replied Skudler; "for they dun punish me,—to some gauge!"

"Well," answered Ben, "thae knows th' Hauve Moon, i'th Black-wayter, at Rachda'?"

"Ay, weel enough," replied Skudler.

"Well, then; co theer, as soon as tho gets back," continued Ben, "an' sup three pints o' their sour ale. An' if it doesn't kill th' worms, it'll kill thee."

"Oather'll do!" cried the old fiddler, rubbing his hands. "Oather'll do! But come an' sit tho deawn a minute or two, Skudler."

"Well," replied Skudler, "I've nought again that, noather. I wur al'ays a good hond at sittin'. If onybody wur to look at my breeches, they'd find that they wear'n cawt i'th sittin'-quarter th' first of onywheer. My mother use't to say that I wur just reet build for sittin' dnck-eggs."

"Well," said the old fiddler, laughing, "an' it would be a nice quiet job, too; for onybody that would gi' their mind to't. But, I deawt thae'd never stick to't lung enough to mak' a fortin cawt on't. . . . But, wheer arto for, lad; wheer arto for?"

"Well," replied Skudler, "I'm beawn as fur as th' Thistley Bonk Farm, for a wye-cauve, for Tummy Glen, th' butcher, at Rachda'. Yo known Jem at th' Thistley Bonk, dunnot yo, Dan?"

"Aye, aye," said the old fiddler, "I know th' whole seed, breed, an' generation. There's seventeen yards o' brothers on 'em, an' they're two sisters that are aboon five fuut eleven a-piece. Their mother's just prick-mete their dur-hole full, to an inch, an' hoo has to bend deawn, an' come cawt sideways. An' then, Jem had an aint (aunt),—his aint Sally,—hoo wur so tall that hoo couldn't for shame stretch hersel'!"

"There's a deeol o' stuff wasted i' makin' folk sich a length as that, too," replied Skudler.

"Well, I don't think it's a useful size for wark, mysel," said the fiddler.

"It depends upo' th' build, an' what sort o' wark they han to do," said Ben.

"It be reet enough for lamp-leeters an' white-limers, an' sich like," continued Skudler.

"Well, aye," said the fiddler, "it would save summat i' ladders, happen."

" Aught fresh deawn i' Rachda'," said Ben, addressing Skudler.

"Well," replied Skudler, "there's bin a bit o' damage done, here an' theer, bi thunner an' leetenin', yesterday."

" I say, Dan," said Ben, addressing the old fiddler, "thae'll remember that greight woint-storm 'at happen't i'th last back-end (autumn)."

" I should think I do," answered the old man; "it blew part o'th slate off cawr heawse. It *wur* a storm, wur that! Slate-stones, an' windows, an' shutters flew up an' deawn, like pigeons."

"Well," continued Ben, "that day I wur sit in a alehcawse kitchen, at Rachda', an' folk kept comin' in wi' news o' this damage an' that damage, —when, just as we'rn sit reawnd th' fire talkin' together abeawt th' storm, a chimbley, belungin' th' next heawse, coom crash deawn, an' part on't fell through th' kitchen-slate wheer we wur sittin'. But, by th' mon, there wur some scutterin' abeawt i' that hole. Well, while they'rn agate o' sidin' th' dirt, an' breck an' stuff, that had fo'n through, there wur a strange chap coom in, fro' some-wheer abeawt Castleton Moor, an' when he seed this rubbish lyin' upo' th' floor, he said, " What, yo'n had a bit of a touch o' this woint, I see. But, eh, by th' mass," said he, "it's bin a deeol war (worse) wi' us! I wur in a heawse at Castleton Moor, this forenoon, an' it blew th' window slap eawt ; an' in abeawt two minutes at after, th' woint brought another window wap into th' same place,—an' it just fitted,—to a yure (hair) "

"Nea then, Ben," said Skudler, "thae's done it at last."

"Aye," said the fiddler, "I think he's polish't that tale off middlin' weel."

"Yo han it as I had it," replied Ben. "But I thought at that time, that if this chap had said mich moor o' that mak, he'd ha' bin agate o' lyin'."

"Well, come," said Skudler, rising to his feet, "I mun be off."

So they bade him "good day!" and away he went, to fetch his wye-calf.

And, after a few minutes' further chat together, the old blind fiddler whistled his lad from the next field, and, taking his fiddle-bag under his arm, he shook hands with Ben, and went his way towards Bacup, with his face up-turned to the sky, and holding his little lad by the hand.

"Theer he gwos!" said Ben, looking up the road after the old fiddler. "There he gwos,—like a good un, as he is! Good luck go witho, owd crayter, for thae'rt one o'th better end o' God Almighty's childer!" and when he had watched the old man out of sight, he said, as he turned his face the other way, "It's time for me to be hutchin' a bit nar (nearer) Yelley Ho! It connot be so fur off noon."

As he went singing up the road towards the hall, under the thick-leaved shade, through which the strong sunshine stole here and there, freaking the highway with streaks of gold, he met a stout old farmer descending the road, and dressed in his best, as if he was on his way to a cattle fair.

When they drew near, Ben stopt, and asked the old man
what o'clock it was.

"It's close upo' puddin'-time, if my stomach's aught to go
by," said the old man, eyeing Ben all over as he pulled a
large, old-fashioned silver watch out of his fob. "It'll be
within a light (few) minutes o' noon, I'll be bund. But I'll
look at this silver turnip o' mine, as soon as I can get it
cawt." And, as he tugged at the chain, he continued.
"What, I guess thae'rt hungry? Thae's rayther a twelve
o'clock mak of a look, lad."

"Yo'n sided some beef i' yo'r time, too, maister; bith'
look on yo," replied Ben.

"Well, lad," said the old man, looking at his watch, "I've
done middlin', for sure. . . . Let's see, I'm rayther of
oather fast; but it wants abeawt five minutes o' twelve, bi
Rachda' (by Rochdale Church clock)."

"Thank yo!" replied Ben. "Good day!"

"Good day to thee!" answered the old man, taking his
stick from the hedge side again, and trudging sturdily down
the road. When he had got a few yards off, he turned
round, and cried out to Ben, "Heigh, my lad!"

"Nea then!" said Ben, looking back.

"I've bin towd yo'n had some lumber done abeawt here
yesterday, bi thunner an' leetenin'. Hasto yerd aught?"

"Well, ay," replied Ben. "There's bin four keaws kilt
up i'th White Hill pastur', here; an' it's knocked th' gable-
eend of a heawse in, up Facit road on."

"So I've bin towd," said the farmer. "An' I yer there's
bin a woman kilt deawn at Shay Cloof, yon."

"Nay, sure," replied Ben. "Dun yo know who it is?"

"Well, I did yer th' name," said the old man, "but it's slipped mi mind. But I deawt we's yer o' moor, yet; for I don't know 'at I con recollect a heavier storm, i' *my* time."

"Nawe, nor me noather," replied Ben. "But it's takken up nicely."

"It has," said the old man. "Han yo mich hay cawt, abeawt here?"

"Oh, nawe," replied Ben. "Very light (very little)."

"Come, that's better," said the farmer. "Well, good day to tho!"

"Good day," answered Ben.

And then the old man went his way, and Ben was left loitering about under the shade of the trees, waiting for the stroke of twelve.

"Come," said he, rubbing his hands, "they connot say that I'm too lat *this* time! I'll walk in just to th' minute, like clock-wark! That'll stop their meawths, I should think. . . . It wants abeawt four minutes, yet," continued he, groping at his sore nose. "I'll watch till it strikes." He was close to the yard door, and as he paced to and fro in front of it, he straightened his clothing, and trimmed his posy, and tied his kerchief afresh, with nervous fingers; for he was naturally shy and sensitive. There was a well by the wayside, a few yards off, and going up to it, he bent down to examine the reflection of his face in the water, and when he had looked himself well over, and had given another finishing touch to his kerchief, he said, "Come, I think I's do!" Then walking back, he halted at the yard door, and peeping through the lock-hole, said, "I wonder wheer that dog is?" The last word had hardly left his

7

mouth, when the great clock in the hall kitchen began to
strike the hour of twelve, and the kitchen-door being wide
open, the sound of each stroke came with a solemn,
measured pause between, clear and sonorous, into the noontide air of that still and shady spot. Ben's heart beat
quicker and quicker as he counted the strokes ; and, laying
his hand upon the latch, he said, as he told the eleventh,
" Neaw for't ! Th' next is a finisher !"

CHAPTER V.

Oh thou, who dost these pointers see,
    And hear'st the chiming hour,
Say,—do I tell the time to thee,
    And tell thee nothing more ?
I bid thee mark life's little day
    By strokes of duty done ;
A clock may stop at any time,—
    But time will travel on.
                        THE CHURCH CLOCK.

HE clock in Healey Hall kitchen had not struck
three times before the solemn monitor in the
gray tower of St. Chad's began to boom forth its
mid-day warning along the winding river, telling the inhabitants of the good old town of Rochdale that it was now
" high twelve,"—the ancient dinner-time in the valleys of
the north ; and, at the first stroke, the hungry workman
dropt his half-filled spade, and hurried homewards,—from
labour to refreshment. . . . From hoary steeples, and

from lordly towers,—in cottage and in hall, throughout our
English land, the hour of noon was pealing,—from clocks of
all kinds, and of different tempers of tone,—some solemn,
some gay; some too fast, some lagging in the rearward of
the sun; some musical and sweet as the ring of silver
cymbals, others dull as the stroke of a cobbler's hammer
upon a leather sole; some wheezy, asthmatic, and irregular,—
some funereal and measured as a passing-bell; others
tripping forth the tale with brisk precision, with the strokes
treading on each other's heels, as if they, too, were hungry,
and in a hurry to get done, and go to dinner. . . . The
captive school-boy had long been pining for this blessed
hour of his release. Oft had he glanced at the window of
his prison-house, and watched the slow-moving sunbeams,
streaking the dusty floor with bars of gold, which seemed as
if they had stolen in with the special intent to fret his heart,
and beguile his thoughts into the open summer day. Long
before the fingers of the clock had met at the striking mark,
he had rubbed his hands, and whispered to the right and
left that it was nearly dinner-time; and as the lazy pointers
drew nearer to the hour of his enfranchisement, he had
slyly grasped his cap, and gathered himself together, like a
greyhound straining upon the slip, for a sudden rush into
the open air, the moment the first stroke came. Dinner-
time! Oh, welcome hour to the healthy, the hungry, and
the well-to-do! Oh, welcome hour to the happy-hearted
school-boy, newly freed from the tether of his taskful time,
and with a bountiful board to run to! Oh, glad hour to
those careless young lordlings of life, who dream no more
than the well-fed fledgling that anything but plenty and

pleasure is theirs, by natural right of inheritance! . . . But the poor, the forlorn, and the houseless,—what of these? The little pinched student, with the iron teeth of penury preying upon his vitals,—the pale lad, whose scraps of learning are purchased by careful parings from his scanty meals, and who creeps homeward at noon with melancholy heart, because he knows that famine awaits him there, like a lean wolf whetting its teeth upon bones,—the child of a joyless life, whose days are all in shadow,—what of him? What is dinner-time to the poor mother, trembling as the hour approaches when her young brood will clamour for meat in vain; and when they will gaze into her pale face, with wondering eyes, trying to read how it is that the rest of the world have food, and they have none? Oh, the sadness of that mother's heart! Oh, the strange thoughts of that hunger-bitten child! . . . This is the hour when perspiring cooks are hard at work in rich men's houses, preparing ingenious dainties for educated palates, amidst a sickly atmosphere of savoury fumes! This is the hour, too, when famished wanderers stop to sniff the aroma of steaming kitchens, and gaze, with wolfish eyes, through cook's-shop windows! This is the hour when the happy cottager's family gather round their simple meal, promptly spread; and when poor men's slatternly gossips exclaim, as the clock strikes, "Eh, dear o' me! why, it's dinner-time, an' th' fire's out!" This is the hour when many a keen appetite clears the scanty board before it is half satisfied; and when rich meals are spread for vitiated epicures, who can find no pleasure therein.

The shadow upon the sun-dial in front of Healey Hall

had glided by the mark of noon, silent and sure as the finger
of fate. The last stroke had boomed from the gray tower of
St. Chad's; and the old chimes were beginning to trickle
forth the silvery tones of "Life let us cherish,"—the melody
for the day,—marking the time, here and there, with a kind
of tottering irregularity, like the shaky treble of an aged
minstrel's song. Just before the last stroke of twelve came
from the clock in the kitchen of the hall, Ben laid his hand
upon the latch of the yard-door and said, "Neaw for't! Th'
next is a finisher!" The sound was still ringing upon the
air when he lifted the latch; and, after he had looked carefully round, to see where the dog was, he entered the yard.
The fat cook stood in the open doorway, with her arms
a-kimbo, and her face glowing with the heat of the kitchen
fire.

"Come," said she, smiling, "thae's hit it middlin' weel
this time, Ben."

"What time is it?" replied Ben, looking as innocent as
if he had never heard the clock strike.

"Just gwon twelve," replied the cook. "It's a good job
thae'rt here; I expect him ringin' for tho every minute; he's
so partickilar abeawt folk bein' to their time. Come forrud."

But she had little need to invite him to come forward;
for, though Ben was giving the kennel as wide a berth as
possible, the dog, which had been watching his motions,
sprang out to the full length of his chain, and at the sound
Ben darted at the doorway, right into the cook's arms,
nearly upsetting both himself and her.

"God bless mi life, lad!" said she, "whatever arto
doin'? Thae's knock't breath eawt on me!"

"It's that dog," replied Ben, wiping his forehead, and looking back into the yard.

"Dog be hanged," said she. "Th' dog wants nought wi' thee, mon."

"Oh, doesn't it," replied Ben. "What did it come cawt o' that shap (shape, manner) for then?"

"Why, becose it sees thae'rt soft, mon; that's o'," said the cook.

"Oh, well," replied Ben. "Soft or not soft, I thought I'd better be comin' forrud, cawt o'th road."

"Thae'd no need to come with sich a ber," said the cook, wiping her hot face, and straightening her dress. "But go thi ways in, an' sit deawn, till I get my wynt; for thae's welly (well-nigh) kilt me."

Ben laid his hat upon the kitchen dresser, and sat down, and he had scarcely got settled in his seat before the colonel's bell tingled in the parlour.

"Theer," said the cook. "I towd tho. He's yerd th' dog barkin'; an' he's ringin' to see if thou'rt com'd."

One of the servants went to answer the bell, and returning almost immediately, she said, "Th' kurnul says that Ben's to get his dinner, an' he'll ring for him in a bit."

"Come, I'll look after that," said the cook, "if he has knock't th' woint cawt on me."

The colonel's bell rung again, and when the servant returned, she said that he had sent word that Ben could take time with his dinner, as Dr. Skelton didn't intend to start for more than an hour yet.

So Ben sat down, and enjoyed his noontide meal in pleasant chat with the servants in the kitchen.

CHAPTER VI.

'Fore God. you have a goodly dwelling and a rich.
                                                    HENRY THE FIFTH.

N the great wainscotted parlour of Healey Hall, Colonel Chadwick's ancient friend, Doctor Skelton, sat alone, reading a quaintly-bound volume of the *Spectator.*

Doctor Skelton was a native of Gloucestershire, and a justice of the peace of that county; and had come to Healey Hall, accompanied by his maiden sister, on a visit to his old college friend; according to annual custom, of fifty years' standing. The doctor was a curious, bookish man, naturally dreamy, and of a speculative turn of mind; and a man of varied acquirements. And yet he was sound-hearted, and clear-headed in all practical affairs of life. Apart from his own profession, of which he was an eminent member in those days, he was a learned man, in some of, what may be called, the by-ways of learning. Amongst the rest, archæology was one of his pet studies. His manners, however, were, in a worldly sense, so void of ornament and complacency, so evidently contemptuous of bald customs and little pleasing seemings, that to a superficial observer he appeared cynical and cold; and sometimes even absolutely rude. But, like the pine-apple, in spite of his prickly rind, the old gentleman was wonderfully sweet at the core. His

life had been curiously chequered; and he might, indeed,
be reckoned as one whose career had a specialty in it. The
strange events, and painful struggles of his youth had
tinged his character with melancholy; and some frowning
events had thrown his early days into shadow, so dark and
impenetrable, that it seemed endless.   Many a sad experience had dropt the plummet of his thoughts below the
level of custom; but he had taken the lesson of life with
such a tractable spirit that his mind had become elevated
thereby.   He had indeed "suffered persecution and learnt
mercy."   And yet, though tender-hearted as a woman, and
privately generous to a fault, he might be accounted a
crotchety man; for, though time had healed his wounds,
the scars were visible still.

Colonel Chadwick was a Tory of the old school; and,
though the doctor and he were far asunder in their political
views. there were so many points of affinity in their characters,
that they had been drawn together by natural attraction
when young; and, as years rolled on, quiet observation of
each other's strokes of character had insensibly endeared
them more and more.   They had learned to admire each
other's sincerity, and truthfulness, and independence of
mind; and now they were inalienably attached to each
other.   "What a strange fellow that Skelton o' mine is,"
the colonel would sometimes say to himself.   "How
thorough, how genial, how crotchety, and yet how really
good-hearted and wise !—except for his politics.   He has a
a thousand bits of quaint wisdom stowed away in odd nooks
of that queer brain of his, where other men have at best
only cold piles of mouldy platitude !"

Doctor Skelton was a great reader, and he had a wise leaning to the old and famous books, that have proved their vitality. He sat that day, with spectacles on nose, reading a quaintly-bound volume of the *Spectator*. He was quietly poring over the fine essay on "Novelty," No. 626,—an essay thoroughly in unison with the tone of his own mind, when his friend entered the room with a letter in his hand.

"This is a bad world, Skelton," said the colonel, shaking the letter in his hand, as he flung himself into a chair,—"a miserable world. By Jove! it's enough to make one willing to go to the lower regions a while. till things get settled upon a different footing,—it is, upon my soul!"

"What, Chadwick," said the doctor, raising his spectacles, "are *you* railing at the incomprehensible, too? Why, you talk of the government of the world as if it was a ball of thread that you had measured off, and found to be a few yards short of what you expected,—and bad stuff withal."

"Well," replied the colonel, sighing, "Heaven forgive me, if I'm irreverent; but I say again, it's a bad world,— and I'm sick of it!"

"Why, Chadwick, my good fellow, what's the matter *now?*" said the doctor, closing his book and rubbing his spectacles.

"Oh,—nothing,"—replied the colonel, "nothing new. Only an ungrateful rascal of a friend. Read that!" continued he, handing the letter to the doctor, "read that!"

8

When the doctor had read the letter, he gave a quiet whistle. " Phew ! "—

> Blow, blow thou winter wind,
> Thou art not so unkind
> As man's ingratitude.

" Well, this is *something* certainly," continued he.

> Freeze, freeze thou bitter sky,
> Thou dost not bite so nigh,
>   As benefits forgot ;
> Though thou the waters warp,
> Thy sting is not so sharp
>   As friend remember'd not.

" But you'll get over this, Chadwick,—you'll get over *this !*"

> Heigho ! sing heigho, unto the green holly !
> Most friendship is feigning, most loving is folly,
>   Then heigho, the holly !
>   This life is most jolly !

" You've seen worse things than this in your time, Chadwick. Take it quietly, my friend. It'll do you good," said the doctor, handing back the letter, and taking up his book again.

" Do me good !" cried the colonel, striking the table. " D——n the fellow ! I tell you, it makes me sick of life to see such villainy, Skelton. It does, upon my soul !"

" Ah, Chadwick," replied the old doctor, "you remember Shakspere's lines :—

> Sweet are the uses of adversity,
> Which, like the toad, ugly and venomous,
> Wears yet a precious jewel in his head.

"Oh, yes; I remember," said the colonel, "I remember that, and many another thing of the same kind. But, when a man's got the toothache, he *will* pull wry faces, in spite of all you can say. And Shakspere, and you, may preach till doomsday; but you cannot preach away the abominable fact,—you cannot make black ingratitude pleasing to the human heart."

"It's not a bad thing, Chadwick, that helps one to bear their crosses like a man. I never saw you so moved before. What, you're like a child crying because it has too much salt in its porridge."

"Oh, yes; I know," replied the colonel, bitterly. "I know how easy it is for one to bear anybody else's troubles. Pelt me with passages from the book of Job, my friend! . . . It's not the property, Skelton; it's not the property. I could bear that,—well enough,—though it's not pleasant. But it breaks down one's faith in human nature; that's the worst of it. It makes one a worse man,— it hardens one's heart, Skelton ; and that's a great calamity. . . . It's a sad world, my friend ; it's a sad world ! Ask me no more questions about it, for heaven's sake. You remember the proverb, Skelton, 'Whether it's the stone that hits the pitcher, or the pitcher that hits the stone, it's all the same to the pitcher.' I would not have cared if——. But here," continued he, tearing the letter to pieces, and flinging it into the fire; "I'm making too much of this! 'Perish the record!' as one of your favourite play-wrights say. 'Perish the record!' and, perish the remembrance, too ; for I will mention it no more!"

And he rose to his feet, and paced the room to and fro,

struggling to smother his excited feelings; whilst the doctor, seeing his friend so much moved, gave a quiet sigh, and opened his book again, and read on, or seemed to read on, in silence.

At last, the colonel took his hat, and walked out into the garden.

The doctor silently watched him out; then, laying down his book, he, too, rose, and paced the room, thoughtfully, muttering to himself, "What a fine fellow that Chadwick is! He always was! And he always will be! It's a sad thing! But that heart of his is too genial,—too forgiving,—to trail any lasting feeling of resentment about the world! He will soon be himself again, and able to look upon this unhappy event as he looks back upon yesterday's storm, which has left the air clearer, and the sky brighter than ever, to-day!"

.   .   .   .   .   .

After about a quarter of an hour's absence, the colonel entered the room again; and, though he began to walk to and fro, as before, he was evidently in a calmer mood. The doctor had resumed his book; and, in a few minutes, the colonel took a chair, and, after a quiet sigh of preparatory relief, he entered into conversation with the doctor once more.

"Skelton," said he; "what do you think of our reverend friend, Henley, after his last freak?"

The old doctor was glad to join in any theme which he thought likely to divert the thoughts of his friend, and relieve the pent-up bitterness which he knew was still scalding his heart.

"Well, Chadwick," replied the doctor, laying down his

book again, " I think he's a very indifferent specimen of the
cloth,—not the kind of man to do honour to his calling,
certainly."

" Well," replied the colonel, " I suppose he's only a
human creature,—he's only a man after all,—as you say,
sometimes."

" Nay, nay," said the doctor, " if he *was* a man, he would
do; if he had even sufficient humility to remember, now
and then, that he was, in some sort, a human being ' of like
passions' with ourselves.—he would be passable. But the
truth is, Chadwick, he's a precious sneak, wearing the
disguise of a lofty office. It was a mistake, Chadwick, it
was a mistake! He should never have entered a pulpit!
Such fellows bring evil tongues upon religion itself!"

" So proud, too," said the colonel.

" Proud!" replied the doctor, " yes; proud as Lucifer!
Proud! aye! and of all the prides that afflict poor humanity,
spiritual pride is the most beguiling, and the worst to cure!
Talk of that rare virtue, true humility! Oh, Chadwick; if
the crust was taken off that fellow, the rest would be
unendurable. Humility, forsooth! Lord help us all,—for
we're all tarred with the same stick, more or less! But the
creatures that I have seen stalking about this planet, as if
each had a consecrated wall built round him, and he alone
were admitted within the pale of the redeemed! And when
they *do* lift their chins over the paling, and condescend to
bestow a look of ' mitigated regard' upon the unregenerate
wretches outside, they do it with an air of ineffable contempt
for the whole human race. I hate such fellows, Chadwick.
. . . And then, they talk and walk as if they were in the

habit of taking wine with the Creator of the universe, in
some sly vestry; where they held council together as to
what was to be done with the miserable mass of mankind.
Heaven save me from any irreverent feeling for what is
truly reverend! But I say again, I hate such fellows! I'd
rather have a wholesome sinner than a sham saint any
day."

"Stop, stop, Skelton," said the colonel. "Why, you're
getting worse than ever!"

"Worse! Nay, nay, Chadwick," replied the doctor; "a
man of my age seldom gets much worse. His virtues and
his vices have culminated, long before that. Men's sins
change, as years roll on,—true enough,—mine have done so,
I know; but I can't get worse than I have been; 'No, no,'
says the Frenchman, 'that can't be!'—as that fine old sea-
song of yours has it. . . . And then, we old fellows
sometimes deceive ourselves with the idea that, as age
creeps on, we are leaving our sins, when it is only our sins
that are leaving us. But, what do *you* know about sin
Chadwick? You're all right; my stainless paragon of the
elected few!"

"Why, Skelton; this is worse still!" said the colonel.

"Nay, nay," replied the doctor. "It this be anything, it
is one of my poor virtues."

"You're a sad fellow, Skelton," said the colonel; "but
you may as well pass the bottle, for all that."

"Well," replied the doctor, pausing an instant, and then
heaving an involuntary sigh, 'that's true enough. I am
sad enough, sometimes, Chadwick,—God knows."

The colonel saw in an instant that he had touched a

wrong chord, and, when he had filled his glass, he assumed
a jovial tone, and, stretching out his hand, he said, "We
know one another, Skelton ; we know one another, old boy !
I am proud of you ! Give us your hand ! The worst thing
about you is that you are such an infernal Jacobin."

The shade passed from the doctor's countenance in an
instant, and he bristled up at once.

" Jacobin !" cried he, sitting upright in his chair.

" Now you're off again," said the colonel, leaning back in
his chair, and smiling. "You're off again! Well, 'Let her
went,' as the Welshman said."

" Jacobin !" continued the doctor. "Why, Chadwick,
I'll bet odds you don't know what you're talking about. But,
if you mean that I am a reformer, let me remind you that
wherever reform is impossible, revolution is certain. The
whole course of history shows it . . . . But what do
such fellows as you care about history ? You read it as a
painful duty, at school ; and perhaps you may remember
some scattered fragments, sufficient for a little disjointed
table-talk with folks of your own way of thinking : but you
never digest it, no more than a cat could digest the
wheels of a watch. Reform ! Why the whole course
of Nature is incessant reform ! You might as well try to
stop the rain from falling, with a pitch-fork, as try to stop
the progress of reform ! But what the devil's the use of
talking to such an unchangeable fogey as you, Chadwick !
When you were made, the politics were made for you at the
same time. The same old programme from father to son,
from father to son—world without end."

" Whatever is venerable and just, Skelton," replied the

colonel, "cannot be defended too long.   Our ancient
institutions in church and state ——"

" Yes," continued the doctor, interrupting him ; "and you
pin your politics down to your acres, too ; for you absolutely
make the unthinking land into an engine for the control of
thinking men !   Your acres make laws for your people !
Oh,—if the fields of England think,—the fields of England
that have been so often soaked with the blood of the
brave,—if they think at all, I wonder what they think of
that !   I can imagine the beautiful meadow-grasses having
great fun amongst themselves with the idea of their
having more power in Parliament than the perspiring lout
who sings as he whets the scythe that is to cut them down !'

Here, the doctor's deaf old maiden sister entered the
room, with her ear trumpet in her hand seeing that her
brother was in the midst of one of his old flights, she said,
as the colonel courteously rose to receive her, " Politics
again, I'll be bound !   But you know him, colonel.   I've
heard it all before.   After the training I have gone through,
I think I should be able to represent the county in the
Liberal interest, colonel, but for this deafness of mine."

" Humph ! " said the doctor, giving a grunt ; " we've
plenty of old women in parliament already, Mary."

These words were spoken in too low a tone for Miss
Skelton to catch them.

" A little friendly tilting-match, Miss Skelton," said the
colonel, speaking into her ear trumpet, as he placed a chair
for the ancient maiden ; "a little friendly tilting-match.   Be
seated, pray."

"No, thank you, colonel," replied Miss Skelton.   " I

merely came for a volume I had left behind me," continued
she, taking up a book from the table. " I have presided at
your tournaments before, colonel. These faded eyes of
mine could rain no new influence upon such familiar knights.
I will leave you to tilt it out alone."

The colonel bowed and escorted her to the door; and
when he had taken his seat again, the doctor resumed the
same strain.

" I'll tell you what it is, Chadwick," said he ; " you remind
me of a passage in Smollett's translation of ' Don Quixote '—
which, by the way. is the best translation of all, in my
opinion. The passage runs thus : " ' The king is my cock,'
quoth Sancho. ' It is plain,' said Don Quixote, ' that thou
art an arrant bumpkin, and one of those who always cry,
Long live the emperor !' "

" And why not cry. ' Long live the emperor ! " replied the
colonel. " Loyalty is a noble virtue."

" Loyalty !" cried the doctor. " Let your kings be loyal
to the people, then ! They are human creatures, I suppose.
Let them acknowledge the common dignity of human
nature !"

" Dignity of the devil !" replied the colonel, warmly.

" Yes," replied the doctor ; "and the devil has a kind of
dignity about him, too ; if all be true that Milton says of
him. . . . Did you ever read Milton's ' Tenure of
Kings,' Chadwick ? "

" No," replied the colonel, with emphasis, "nor I don't
intend."

" I dare say not," said the doctor. " Did you ever read
his ' Liberty of Unlicensed Printing ? "

9

"Liberty of the devil! I say again," cried the colonel; "no, I have not read it! nor I never will,—'*Deo Volenti!*'"

"Hollo, Chadwick," replied the doctor; "you've managed to save that fragment from the wreck of your school-Latin, I see."

"Yes,—Latin, said the colonel. "And I'll say the same thing in any language under heaven, Skelton,—if I can only muster words."

"I'm sorry for you, Chadwick," replied the doctor. "And yet I like you,—at least for one thing."

"And pray, what's that?"

"Because you're such a—fool!"

"Well,—thank you."

"Oh, you're welcome—as the flowers in May."

"I tell you again, Skelton," said the colonel, "I hate Milton,—and you know why."

"Hush!" replied the doctor, raising his hand.

"What's the matter, now?" said the colonel.

"Don't let the winds of heaven hear you say that," replied the doctor.

"Why?"

"Perhaps they mightn't like it."

"Rubbish!" replied the colonel. "The winds of heaven are as much mine as ever they were Milton's!"

"Aye," says the doctor, "that comes of the all-pervading goodness of the great scheme, Chadwick. The Creator of the world is kinder to us than we are to one another."

"I'll stick to my text, Skelton," continued the colonel; "I hate that canting, rhyming, republican rebel, for his share in the mar——"

" Never mind it, Chadwick, never mind it ; I know all
about it," replied the doctor. . . . " Well, let us drop it.
I see it's a bad case. ' He who will not be advised, neither
can he be helped.' Come, let us change the subject."

" With all my heart, Skelton," said the colonel, " with all
my heart ! You know we never agree about these things.
Confound it ; what an old fool I am ! Well, come, fill up ;
and let us talk of something else."

" Agreed," said the doctor, pulling out his watch ; " what's
the time ? Why, it's near one o'clock."

" Yes," replied the colonel, looking at his own watch ;
" you'll have to leave here in half an hour. George will
have the drag at the door exactly at the time. I suppose
Ben can ride behind with you ? "

" Certainly," said the doctor ; " where is he ? "

" Oh, the lad's all right," replied the colonel ; " he's in
the care of my cook ; and they have a neighbourly liking
for one another."

" Oh, by the bye," said the doctor, " Mary said she
should like to see the hero of this donkey-story that amused
her so much. Couldn't we get him into the parlour for a
few minutes ? "

" Of course," replied the colonel. " But stop ; hadn't
we better have Miss Skelton in first ? "

" Fetch her, Chadwick ; fetch her ! She'll be delighted,"
said the doctor.

Away went the gallant colonel, returning in two or three
minutes, chatting and laughing with Miss Skelton, as he led
her into the parlour.

When they were all comfortably seated, the colonel

rang the bell, and told the servant to send Ben into the
parlour.

Ben entered the room in a shy and awkward manner, as
usual; but the kind-hearted old colonel entered so freely
into conversation with him in the native vernacular, that his
embarrassment began to subside at once; and the doctor
and his sister, with true courtesy, began to chat with him in
such a frank and simple way that, in a few minutes, Ben was
almost as much at ease with his genteel companions as if they
had been cottage neighbours all their lives.   At last the ice
got so thoroughly melted that the colonel ventured to ask
Ben to sing a song for Miss Skelton.   This request rather
staggered the poor fellow at first; but, being earnestly
pressed, especially by the lady herself, he consented to sing
a favourite country song, called "Cupid's Garden."   The
great difficulty was, however, that he had to bend down and
sing into the end of the ancient maiden's ear-trumpet, which
confused him very much, for he was sensible of the
absurdity of the situation.   He could see, too, that the
humourous old lady was enjoying the fun of the thing.   But
he encountered the difficulty like a man.   He struggled
through the first verse, bent down with his mouth at the
end of the ear-trumpet; and with big drops of perspiration
rolling from his forehead, and with the old lady's dark eyes
fixed intently upon his own.   He got to the end of that,
and then he stopped to take breath, and to wipe his face.
He began the second; and he had nearly fought through it,
under the same circumstances, when he suddenly stopped,
and, drawing his sleeve across his forehead, he reared himself upright, and said, " By th' mon, aw connot ston this !'

at which the doctor and the colonel laughed "till the girdle rang," as the Scotch say. The old lady had not heard what he said ; but when she saw the sudden burst of mirth from her brother and the colonel, she inquired what was the matter ; and when they had told her what he had said, the quaint damsel laughed, and laughed again, till the tears stood glistening in her eyes. Then laying her hand upon Ben's broad shoulder, she thanked him, and said she was only astonished that he had done so well under the circumstances. "Eh, God bless yo, mistress," said he, "if there'd bin nobody lookin' aw could ha' sung ten times better nor that for yo !" At which they all burst out again, till Ben began to wonder what on earth he had said to move them to so much merriment. But he had won their hearts by his frankness and the simplicity of his demeanour; and as Burns says, in "The Twa Dogs,"

> They were unco pack an' thick thegither,

till the servant knocked at the parlour-door, and said that the vehicle was ready.

In a few minutes after that they were all mounted, and away they went. A pleasant ride of four miles brought them to the little village of Littleborough, at the foot of Blackstone Edge. The way thence to "Th' White House," at the top of that wild ridge, is a winding road, about two miles and a half in length. The heavy rain of the previous day had left it slushy, and it was difficult for wheel-carriages to travel. But, about half-past two on that glorious summer afternoon, they dismounted at the door of the old hostlery, on the top of the Edge.

There the learned doctor met with his learned friends, and they wandered about the wild moorland ridge that divides the counties of York and Lancaster,—from one point of interest to another. The feature of the scene that had special attraction for that learned company was, however, the remarkably fine relic of the Roman roads of Britain, which climbs to the summit of Blackstone, from the Little-borough side, and then winds along the moors to Slack, the ancient Cambodunum of the Romans. In that well-preserved remnant of the Roman road, they found so much to examine, and to trace, and to speculate upon, that it was unanimously resolved that the whole company should pay a second visit to the scene on the following day. There was all the greater reason for this, as they found, on meeting together, that each had some pet point of interest, which had not been sufficiently considered in the general scheme of the day's trip,—the ruined entrenchments thrown up during the Cromwell wars; the Druidical stones upon the lofty mountain track, called "The Wilderness;" the ancient halls of the district; and certain remarkable geological features of the scene. These things, together with the stress laid upon the matter by certain hospitable local gentlemen, of archæological tendencies, induced the assembled *savants* to resolve upon a second visit to the scene. However, they spent a pleasant and instructive day together, and when twilight began to dusk the evening air—

> Each took aff his several way.
> Resolved to meet some ither day.

Jannock.

CHAPTER I.

Oh, so drowsy! in a daze,
Sweating 'mid the golden haze,
With its smithy like an eye,
Glaring bloodshot at the sky ;
And its one white row of street,
Carpeted so green and sweet,
And the loungers, smoking still,
Over gate and window-sill,
Nothing coming, nothing going —
Landrail craking, one cock crowing ;
Few things moving up and down,
All things drowsy.

DROWSIETOWN.

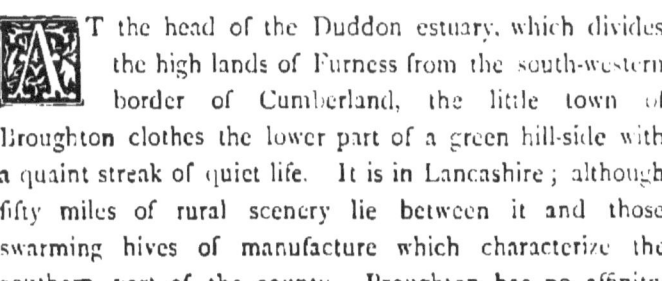

T the head of the Duddon estuary, which divides
the high lands of Furness from the south-western
border of Cumberland, the little town of
Broughton clothes the lower part of a green hill-side with
a quaint streak of quiet life. It is in Lancashire ; although
fifty miles of rural scenery lie between it and those
swarming hives of manufacture which characterize the
southern part of the county. Broughton has no affinity,

either in appearance or in habit, with that weltering sea of
restless toil. Its antique gables and leaf-strewn paths
belong to the pastoral hills of a secluded land ; and its way
of life smacks of the far-back olden time. Long before
Saxon Harold fell at Hastings, it nestled on that woodland slope, watching, with sleepy eyes, the ebb and flow of
the western waves. The voices of nature have sung its
nightly lullaby for a thousand years. Its thoughts are in the
direction of crops ; and its trade hath been in cattle all its
days. The green country laps it round with fruitful leas
and rustling boskage ; and a little way from its gardened
skirts, the charcoal-burner rears his conical hut of wicker-
work in the woods, even to this day. From outlying
pastures the low of kine comes up into the market place
upon the evening air ; and patches of wildwood, and
orchard trees, gush over its rootlets, here and there, with
feathered minstrels upon every bough. It never heard the
cry of the news-boy, nor the ring of a factory bell ; and
cheap trips have not found it out. . . . In the heart of
a varied paradise it dozes upon the mountain side—a land
of bloomy hill and dale—lush pastures, and clear streams,
wild waving woods, rich fields of grain, and mountain-slopes
that swarm with cattle, even to the rugged tops, where the
heather-flower tinges the wilderness with purple hue, and
the rowan-tree rustles in the wind among the ruins of
Druidical temples. And, here and there, in nooks of
verdant shade, the scattered homesteads of a sturdy race
adorn the pleasant land with nests of rural life. In front of
the town lie the far-spreading sands, over which " majestic
Duddon glides on in silence with unfettered sway ;" and,

from behind the hill, upon which it reposes, romantic
Cumberland stretches away northward, with its lakes and
mountains. About seven miles westward, along the north
shore of the estuary, that gloomy sentinel of the hills, Black
Coomb,—

> To far-travelled storms of sea and land,
> A favourite spot of tournament and war,

boldly overfrowns the heaving sea. Near the foot of that
mountain's southern steep, in a scene of quiet natural
beauty, nestle the ancient church and hamlet of Millom,
and the ruins of Millom Castle, once the feudal stronghold
of the Huddleston family. South of Broughton lies a great
tract of picturesque country, rich in story and antique
remains. First come the hills and dales of Furness—sweet
sequestered Furness,—with its quaint hamlets ; its old halls
and churches : its relics of the ancient Celtic race ; its
ruined castles and monastic remains : Dalton tower ;
Gleaston castle ; the ragged mass of Peel castle, on its wild
islet, near the shore ; and the magnificent ruins of Furness
Abbey, deep-bosomed in their cloistral glen. Looking
farther south, beyond old Ulpha's pleasant Saxon town, the
sands of the Leven spread out into wide Morecambe bay,
whose waters lave the site of many an ancient hamlet. On
the west, the blue waves of the Irish channel close the
scene ; on the east, the eye wanders from the thick woods
of Holker up to Humphrey Head and wild Hampsfell,
between which rests the grey town of Cartmel, and its noble
priory church, with the hills rising in craggy ridges behind.
Still farther south, we pass by balmy, flower-embroidered
"Grange," and by the little island paradise of "Holme,"–

10

we cross the " Keir," and we cross the " Kent," to where
the round top of "Arnside Knot" throws its shadow upon
the mouldering pile of Arnside Tower,—grey chieftain of its
solitary vale.   Over secluded Silverdale, and Wharton's
barren crag, we wander still, to where the towers of " time-
honoured Lancaster" crown the historic steep, at whose foot
flow the pleasant waters of the river Lune, "that to old
Loncaster his name doth lend." Beyond this, the blue fells
of Bleasdale bound the southern view ; and, in the south-
west, the landscape dies away upon the wide green level of
the Fylde.   Such is the view from the top of the hill which
rises up from Broughton town. . . . About a mile north-
west of Broughton, the river Duddon, after rushing through
a wooded gorge, flows over the widening sands, into the
Irish sea.   Leaving the shepherd and his flock upon the
mountain side, it descends from its stormy birth-place in
many a wild leap; in moody freaks, and elfish water-
pranks,—in gentle windings, and little falls, and lingering
pools where the sunbeams love to bathe, the limpid stream
comes down into the valley which its beauty makes so
glad,—

> And through the wilderness a passage cleaves,
> Attended but by its own voice, save when
> The clouds and the fowls of the air pursue its way.

About fifteen miles from its source, " cloud-born Duddon"
meets the teeming tide of the estuary, near Broughton town ;
and, thenceforth, like a child dying in its unsullied loveliness,
it mingles again with the mysterious sea.   Broughton sees
the sweet farewell of Duddon's charmed stream. . . . At
the head of the town stands the grey tower of the Broughtons,

of Broughton, among its ancient trees. Here, in Saxon times, dwelt the lordly thanes who ruled over the little hamlet at the foot of the hill. Mr. West, in his "Antiquities of Furness," says of the Broughtons, of Broughton, "This was an Anglo-Saxon family, of high antiquity, in whose possession the manor of Broughton had remained from time immemorial, and whose chief seat was at Broughton, till the reign of Henry the Seventh." It seems that then their vast possessions passed into the hands of the Stanley family; and a turn of obscurity came to the proud old Broughtons ; for, thenceforth, they almost entirely disappear from the page of history. Such, however, were the ancient lords of Broughton; and such is the picturesque setting of the little rural gem,— the drowsy hamlet on the mountain side, which is the scene of the following story.

CHAP. II.

Then first they ate the white puddings,
And then they ate the black. oh,
An' muckle the guidwife thocht to hersel',
But deil a word she spak, oh.
THE BARRIN O'TH DOOR.

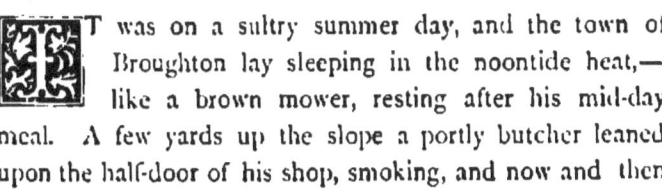T was on a sultry summer day, and the town of Broughton lay sleeping in the noontide heat,— like a brown mower, resting after his mid-day meal. A few yards up the slope a portly butcher leaned upon the half-door of his shop, smoking, and now and then

wiping his forehead with the sleeve of his shirt, whilst
watching the clumsy gambols of two harrier whelps at play
in the street : pigeons were croodling and strutting about on
the pavement and on the roofs of the houses, and sparrows
were chirping blithely all around. Apart from these a
slumbrous stillness filled the air ; save that by fits one could
hear a drowsy rustle of trees, and now and then faint sounds
of rustic glee came from outlying fields where the haymakers were at work. Even the sleepy monotone of the
river "Little," northward of the town, seemed to lend a
somnolent tincture to the dreaminess of that sultry summer
noon. Broughton had dined, and was evidently disposed
to dose away an hour or two of the meridian heat before it
meddled with business again. . . . The clock was just
upon the stroke of one as a solitary traveller, with a knapsack on his back, and clad in the garb of a holiday wanderer,
walked into the "King's Head," at the foot of the Market
Place. His tall, lithe figure, was a rare combination of ease
and strength ; his frank, intelligent face was browned with
the sun, and his double-soled boots were white with the
dust of country roads. He was a man of manly mould, and
near the prime of life ; his countenance beamed with good-
nature, and with the inborn gladness of a quiet mind ; and
there was a breezy rustle of natural grace and freedom about
him from top to toe. Many an unpremeditated smile, many
a dreamy sigh had that happy wanderer awakened on his
way. As he entered the inn, with a sprig of laburnum nodding from the brim of his felt hat, the bird in the cage at
the door-way burst into a fit of melodious glee that rang all
over the market place, as if, by some fine instinct, it felt that

a genial nature was near. There was not a single customer
in the house ; there was not a sound but the singing of the
bird at the door, and a quiet stir of folk in the kitchen at
the rear. All around was steeped in the drowsiness of
summer noon, and the strong sunshine seemed to slumber
on the street. A fine glow pervaded the old inn ; the sun
was high over the roof, but the front rooms were in shade,
and it was pleasant to look forth from the windows into the
sunlit street. Turning into the parlour, at the right-hand
side of the lobby, our traveller glanced around with con-
tented eyes, as he unloosed the straps of his knapsack.
Flinging his burden down, he stretched his limbs, and rang
the bell ; and then he sat down by the window, quietly
crooning Moore's song—" There is not in the wide world a
valley so sweet," as he looked up the slope towards the grey
tower at the head of the town.

The door was opened by a rustic-looking servant lass, who
came in wiping her mouth with her apron ; for she had just
risen from her dinner in the kitchen.

" Bring me a pint of your best ale," said he ; " and—here,
stop !—can I have some dinner ? "

" I'll go an' see," said she ; and giving her mouth another
wipe, she closed the door behind her.

" Well, what is it ? " said the landlady, setting her hands
on her hips, as the girl entered the kitchen.

" There's a gentleman i' th' parlour as wants to know if
he can hev some dinner."

" Dinner !" said the old landlord, who was seated in the
corner smoking. " Why, dang it, I doubt ye'll hev a
scrammle to find him yan to-day. Is he a gentleman,
saysto ? "

" Aye," said the lass ; "an' I'm to tak him a pint o't' best ale."

" Varra well, then," said the landlady, "tak him a pint o't' best yal ; but I'm thinkin' about t' dinner. What like chap is he ? Dista knaw him ?"

" Nay," replied the lass, " I dinnot knaw as I knaw him. He disn't belang this countra-side, I think. But he's a varra canny-like man bi t' look on him !"

" Well, that's a capper, hooiver !" said the landlord. " Canny or not canny he mun hev his dinner. But what, it's t' wrang day for us ; we han nowt to set afore him but ham an' eggs, an' caud beef, an' sic like ; an' if he's yan o' these tickle-stomack't chaps, he'll mebbe not care for that. . . . . " Matty, lass," continued he, addressing the landlady, " what canto do for him ? He'll not like to dine off o' what we'n bin thwittlin at, one's sartin sewer. We're in a bonny pickle ! Couldto shap owt ? What, it'll be a sham an' a bizen (a shame, forby a sin), if we connot find him a menseful bit of a dinner."

" Bless my life, Adam," replied the landlady, " how thou talks, to be sewer ; an' a goose daan at t' fire, reight afore thi e'en theere. What ! he can dine off o' that, if he can wait a bit ; if he connot wait, he mun tak what there is— there's nowt else for't. But I should think he'd like t' goose. Lord bless us and save us—what—gentle or simple, he's not aboon eatin' a bit o' goose, belike ! An' then, we'n tarts, an' cheese, an' a cowd saddle o' mutton i' th' aumry (pantry) yon, at's never bin cut intill. What can a man want ? Good gracious ! What, we're never so hard put tull't 'at we cannot scrammle a bit o' dinner togidder, sewer-ly."

"Well, aye; as thou says, lass," replied the landlord, "he can dine off o't' goose, if he'll wait a bit; an' not a bad thing for a hungry chap to pike at, nawther. . . . . . Sally, gan thi ways, an' tell him: an' tak him his yal! What! t' lad 'll be as dry as a bakin-spittle, I'll awarnd ye! . . . . An' tell him we'n some prime cheese, an' sic like, to be gooin' on wi' if he's onyways keen set! Noo, gan thi' ways wi' t' yal, an' let him wesh his neck a bit!" And away she went.

By this time our friend in the parlour had lit his pipe, and was leaning upon the open window, listening to the bird at the door, and drinking in the peaceful beauty of the scene. Hearing the door open, he turned round.

" Ah," said he. " About the dinner. Well? "

" Please sir, t' missis says there's a goose at t' fire; an' if ye can wait a bit ye can dine off o' that."

" A goose!" cried he. " Stars and garters, what a feast! Good; tell your mistress that I'll wait for the goose!"

" Please, sir, she said I was to ask if ye would have some bread an' cheese for a bitin'-on ? "

" For a what? "

" For a bitin'-on till t' goose is ready."

" Ah, I see. Bread and cheese! . . . No, tell her that nothing shall come between me and that noble bird— except this," said he, laying hold of the pewter pint, " except this !"

> Talk of the nectar that sparkled for Helen,
> Her cup was a fiction, but this is reality.

and he took a hearty pull at the bright bicker, " with beaded bubbles winking on the brim."

The landlady stood in the middle of the floor when the girl returned to the kitchen. Her round face was glowing with heat, her hands were white with flour, and her snowy cap-strings hung negligently about her shoulders.

" Well," said she, " what says he ? "

" He says t' goose 'll do."

" Canny man," said the landlord, charging his pipe afresh, "canny man; he's sensible to t' last—come frae where he will."

" He'll wait, then ? " continued the landlady.

" Yes," replied the lass, " he'll wait for t' goose."

" Varra well," said the landlady, "an' will he hev ony bread an' cheese ? "

" No, he says he'll hev nowt at o' till t' goose is ready— except his yal."

" Well, come, now," said the landlord, "I call that good again. He'll hev nowt at o' till t' goose is ready—except his yal. Varry good; I should ha' said t' same mysen. That lad's bin born o' t' merry side o' t' blanket, I'll awarnd ye. I begin to tak tull him!"

" Do haud thi tung, thoo madlin', I pritho," said the landlady.

" He's a varra funny man by t' look on him," said the girl, " an' he's dry, too."

" Aye, aye ; he's dry enough. I uphaud him," said the landlord. " Well, come, we can find some'at at'll suit *that* complaint, if he happens to be taen bad."

" Thoo can, hooiver," said the landlady. Then, turning to the girl, she continued, " Come, Sally, stir thi shanks ! Thoo knaws what a mess we're in. We're leet-handed thoo knaws ; there's nowt but thee an' me for't. Come, stir tho, do! an' market day to-morn, too. Clear that table, an' get this place sided up, while I look after this man's dinner."

"Aye, lass," said the landlord, "get t' lad his dinner. He's a clipper, I'll uphaud him."

"Adam," said she, "if I wur thee, I'd gan down to t' meadow, an' see what's goin' on."

"Well," replied he, "I don't knaw whether thoo would or not: but, as I don't happen to be thee, I think I shall bide where I am a bit langer."

And Adam lit his pipe at the fire again.

CHAPTER III.

The patch is kind; but he is a huge feeder.
SHAKESPEARE.

HE cloth was laid in the parlour, with the usual accompaniments of a good dinner, in that bountiful old country inn, where stint, and extortion, and dirt, and disorder, were equally unknown; and, with the natural taste which characterised the comely dame who "ruled the roast," and everything else under the roof of the old King's Head, a tuft of meadow-grasses, mingled with wild flowers, adorned the board. Everything was in its

I I

place, and everything was sweet and clean as dew upon a
budding rose. With a light hand, she had given the last
finishing touch to the graces of that tempting spread. The
traveller's wine was beaming, like liquid amber, in a quaint
cut-glass decanter ; and nothing now was wanting but the
main element of the feast. The place of honour was still
left vacant for that savoury bird : and the hungry traveller,
excited by the dainty preparations before him, sat with
quivering nostril, sniffing the coming banquet from afar.
. . . The goose lay dished upon the table in the kitchen,
ready to be carried in ; and when the landlady had washed
her hands, and straightened her hair, and arranged her cap,
so as to "mak hersen fit to be sin," she said, as she laid
hold of the dish, "Now, Sally, gan thi ways afore me, an'
oppen t' door. Yon man 'll be quite famished."

" Away wi' ye," said the landlord ; "if he's deein', that
brid'll bring him to. T' smell on't maks my teeth shoot
watter."

Away went the girl, and away sailed the landlady after
her, with the dish in her hands, and the white strings of her
cap streaming behind her broad shoulders.

Laying her dish down in its place, she said, as she glanced
at the table, "There, sir ; I think it's all right. I dare say
ye'll be able to manage now."

" Ah, thank you," replied he, planting himself in front of
the goose. "I shall be all right . . But,—here,—have I
the whole table to myself ? "

" Well,—yes," said she. " You see, we hev nae company
in to-day. Now, if it had been to-morrow, you would hev
had plenty o' folk to sit down with, as its market-day."

"Oh, thank you," replied he. "I think I shall agree very well with the company that's before me."

"I'm very glad, sir," said the landlady; "an' I hope that it'll agree with you. . . . An' now, if there's anything that ye want, if ye'll be kind enough to touch that bell, we'll attend to ye."

"All right, thank you," replied he.

The door closed quietly behind her; and he was alone, with the goose.

.   .   .   .   .   .

Our traveller rubbed his hands gleefully, as his eyes wandered over the table; and, laying hold of the carving-knife, he said, "Come on, sir; what shall I give you? A leg: or a wing: or a slice of the breast? or all three? Say the word,—your servant is here! . . . Ah," continued he. as he helped himself to the goose, "what manner of man am I that fortune should pet me, and pat me on the shoulder so? No matter, 'Take the good the gods provide thee,'—and--be thankful." And, straightway, he fell to, with right good will, like a man of hearty mould and hungry mood; and, for a while, there was no sound in the room but the music of that bold trencher-man's knife and fork in ceaseless play.

When he had eaten his fill, he sat down by the window, sighing a grateful "Non nobis," and looking back at the table, now and then, as if afraid that he might repent not having eaten more of that noble bird, when far away, on the morrow. He was a generous man, and he was in a merry mood; and there was, withal, a touch of Bohemian dash in his nature, that impelled him, by fits, to indulge in a bountiful

frisk that over-leaped the cast-iron palings of conventional
prudence. And in such holiday humour was he that day, as
he sat musing by the open window, with eyes that wandered,
now into the sunny street, now back again to the relics of
the feast upon the table.

Now, in that part of merry England, at the time of our
story, gipsies were not an unusual sight. In summer time,
these dusky wanderers might be seen encamped upon the
commons, or on the sprawling borders of some quiet road,
beneath a sheltering hedge, with the wild bird, the mole, the
weazle, and the field-mouse for their only neighbours ; or
lounging, with furtive grace, among the bustle of some
country fair, plying the hereditary arts of their race, as
tinkers, besom-makers, musicians, beggars, and fortune-
tellers ; or creeping along some lonely rustic way, in slow,
nomadic trail, towards another camping-ground. Gipsies
were a familiar sight in that green nook of the bonny north.
From the great rural plain of the Fylde, on the west coast
of Lancashire, up to the wild hills and beautiful vales of the
Scottish border, gipsies were well known. . . . And who
are these children of the wilderness, roving "homeless,
ragged, and tanned, under the changeful sky," as free as the
wild bird that flits at will from bough to bough ; and despising
alike the trammels and the comforts of settled life? These
tawny, trinketted aliens, clad in gaudy tatters,—so poor and
yet so proud,—found amongst all peoples of the earth, yet
belonging to none and, among all changes of climes and
nations clinging with such tenacity to the habits, and the
language, and the superstitions of their forefathers—who are
they? Whence come these ragged, landless, vagabond

lordlings of the waste,—these wild-eyed dwellers in tents,
gliding about the solitudes of the land, like half-tamed
panthers; and streaking the conventional web of western
civilisation with a wierd thread of lurid hue? What burning
tract of Egypt, or of Hindostan, was the ancient home of
this mysterious race of restless outlaws? Their name indicates an Egyptian origin. This supposition, however, has
been proved by careful inquirers to be an error—an error
probably encouraged by gipsies themselves—because Egypt
was, above all lands, the land of soothsayers and diviners.
Neither in manners, nor in language, are they Egyptians.
Both beforetime and now, they have been, and are still
looked upon as a foreign people by the natives of the land
of Pharoah. Those who are curious enough to delve into
the works of the learned on the subject will find that by
evidence of affinity in language, and by remarkable similarity
in arts, pursuits, and customs, it is proved that these people
are descendants of the ancient Pariars, or Suders of India,
the lowest caste of Hindoos—and, probably, from those
Pariars who fled westward in thousands, during the mur-
derous ravages of Timour Beg, in 1408,—which corresponds
with the time of the first appearance of gipsies in Europe.
. . . But, to my tale.

Whilst our hero leaned upon the window-sill, watching the
sleepy motions of the little town, a tall, swarthy man, with
Asiatic countenance, and dark, piercing eyes, in which the
fire of youth was blended with the cunning of age, came
lounging up from the lowmost part of the town. A long
black ringlet hung down each side of his face; and his limbs
indicated a remarkable combination of strength and agility.

In one hand he bore a rude ashen staff, and in the other hand a coarsely woven mat of rush-work. Glancing stealthily from side to side, he wandered by, off at the house-end, and out of sight. He was soon followed by another proud vagabond, of similar aspect, clad in a long tattered cloak, and a slouched hat, which half concealed his face. He carried a soldering-iron in his hand ; a well-worn leather apron was twisted about his loins : and a tinker's budget hung from his shoulder. A little behind him a ricketty cart came slowly up, drawn by a wild-looking, unkempt pony, and partly covered by a rude tarpaulin shade, from between the folds of which a swarm of dusky urchins and aged crones, peeped out at the town as they went by. The living freight of the cart was mingled with tent gear, rush mats, cooking utensils, wicker-work, and other simple stuff, the sole property of these migratory denizens of the wild. A graceful slip of a lad, bare-headed, and bare-footed, walked on one side of the pony's head ; and on the other, a tall middle-aged woman, with glittering rings in her ears, and dressed in gaudy-coloured clothing, much worn, and faded by constant exposure to the weather. A red kerchief, tied in a fluttering knot at the side of the temples, was her only head dress ; from under which, straggling elf-locks stole down, as black and as glossy as a raven's wing. She must have been singularly beautiful when young, for she was beautiful still. But the bright piquancy of the gipsy matron's countenance was tempered with something of sadness which touched the heart of the susceptible traveller as he leaned upon the window-sill that day.

Leaving the side of the cart, she came close under

the window, and, looking up with a pensive smile, she said,
" God bless your honour's bonny face : there's good fortune
before ye !"

"Oh, yes," replied he, laughing, and dropping a shilling
into her palm, "I know all about it. God bless you !
.   .   Are those your children in the cart ? "

" Four of them, your honour," she replied.

"Wait a minute," said he.

He glanced quickly up and down the road. There was
nobody about, and the cart had stopped just in front of the
window. He ran to the table, and bringing the dish with
the remainder of the goose upon it to the window, he said,
" Now, hold your apron. Hold it tight !"

Darting away to the cart, she dragged out a dingy tartan
shawl, and taking one end firmly between her teeth, and two
corners in her hands, she held it under the window whilst
he emptied the entire contents of the dish into it.

" There," said he. "get out of sight as fast as you can !"

The gravy dripped through the shawl to the ground, but
in an instant. the whole reeking mess was huddled into the
cart, and she whispered to the lad to " Drive on,—quick !"

He watched them off at the house-end, and when he had
set the empty dish down upon the table, he quietly closed
the window, and sat down, laughing heartily to himself.

He waited a few minutes, and then. after lighting his pipe,
he rang the bell.

" Now for it," said he, assuming a serious look, and taking
his seat at the table again, in front of the empty dish.
" Now for it !" he repeated as the girl opened the door.

" Did ye ring, sir? "

"You may clear away the things," replied he, stroking his beard,—"I've finished."

"Yes, sir," said the girl; and, coming up to the table, her eyes fell upon the empty dish. . . . For an instant, she gazed upon the dish, with a bewildered countenance; she took up a plate, and laid it down again—her eyes still rivetted upon the dish. Then, dropping a fork to the floor, she gave a sly glance under the table, and another into the fire-grate; and then, rising from the floor and looking at our hero with well-opened eyes, she said, "Did ye say that ye'd finished, sir?"

"Yes," replied he, watching her movements, as he trimmed his pipe with his finger, "Yes,—you may clear the table."

"Clear the table," muttered the girl to herself, laying hold of the dish, and setting it down again. "Clear the table,— yes, sir," continued she, in a confused tone; and she was hurrying away, empty-handed, when he stopped her.

"And, here, let me know what I have to pay."

"What you have to pay? Yes, sir." And she gave another scared look at him from the door-way as she hurried out.

CHAPTER IV.

An' as they watched their dinner fly,
  They fluttered to an' fro,
An' then broke out into a cry.—
  Eh, mam, he'll heyt it o'!
          THE WIMBERRY CAKE.

UR landlord was sitting alone, when Sally entered the kitchen, with a run ; and, lifting her hands, cried out, " It's all gone ! "

" What's all gone ? "

" T' goose ! "

" Art thoo all gone ? "

" I tell ye, he's etten it all,—bones an' all ! "

The old man paused,—and looked earnestly at the girl ; and then he laid his pipe down upon the table, and pushing his fingers through his hair he gave a quiet whistle.

" Well," said he, taking up his pipe again. " All that I hev to say is,— that if I happen to be wick an' hearty, when that man dees,—I sall be glad to go to his berrin',—with my best claes on,—whether I'm axed or not ! . . . Didto say 'bones an' all ? "

" I said bones an' all ! " replied Sally.

" Why then," continued Adam, " Good Lord deliver him, say I ! . . . But,—bones an' all ! Dang it ; thoo mun be lying ! Arto reet i' thi yed, thinksto ? "

12

" It's true, I tell ye ! . . . An' he says I'm to clear t' table."

" Clear t' table, eh ! I' godlin, he's done a good stroke at that, hissen ! Oh ! but thoo mun be wrang, lass. A whole goose ! an' a pummer, too ! I'll never believe 'at he's put hissen aatside o' that brid !"

" Well," replied Sally, " I've nowt nae mair to say. T' dish is yon for ye to look at."

" Oh," said the landlord, " t' dish *is* yon, is it ? Well, come ; that mends it a bit."

" Aye, it's yon," replied she, " an' he wants to know what he has to pay."

" Aye, bi th' mass, an' weel he may," answered he. . . . " An' so, he wants to knaw what he has to pay, does he ? It's a wonder, I'm sure ; for he's had nowt worth talkin' about. . . . Well, thou'd better call o' t' mistress,— thou's knocked me clean ower."

Just then the landlady came in from the pantry.

" Oh, thou'rt theer, arto ? " said Adam. " Well, thou'rt nobbut just i' time. If thou'd stopt a bit longer everythin would ha' bin i' wrack an' ruin."

" Whatever's t' matter, now ? " said she.

" Matter enough," replied he. " Doesto hear what shoo says ? "

" What is it ? "

" He's etten all t' goose ! "

" Who hes ? "

" Yon divulskin i' t' parlour."

" I nivver heard the like."

" Nor me nawther."

"It's quite ta'en my breath."

"An' mine, too. . . . An' he wants to knaw what he has to pay."

"Pay?"

"Aye, lass, that's what *I* said—pay! . . . Well, what thinksto?"

"Think! I knaw nowt what to think. It caps me completely. . . . What yan can't charge him t' same as anudder man?"

"Well, I sud think *not*, mysen. I don't know anudder man as could ha' done same trick. I consider him a varra remarkable sort of a person, as who his fadder was. I' tho charges him at all, thoo should charge him at t' rate o' five or six other men. . . . But I'm inclin't to let him hev it for nowt, if he'll go away quietly, wi' what he's getten. . . . Tell him we'n fayver i' t' house,—that'll tak him off."

"I wish he'd go," said the landlady.

"I could like to hev a look at t' divul," continued the landlord. "He sartinly has a most serious twist.'

"Oh, but I *cannot* believe it!" said the landlady.

"Well," said Sally, in a sulky tone, "ye can see for yersen."

"See!" cried the landlord; "bi th' mass, we's see nae mair o' t' goose, I doubt. But, here," continued he, addressing the servant, "didto notice ony difference about t' fit of his waistcoat after he'd hed his bit o' dinner?"

"Nay; I don't knaw that I see'd ony difference," replied Sally.

"Well, then," said Adam, "he must hev a terrible cavity somewhere in his inside."

"He must be varra howle (hollow) when he's hungry,"
said the landlady.

"Howle!" said Adam; "why, he'll be like a two-legged
drum about t' middle o' t' forenoon!"

"An' I should think," continued the landlady, "that he'll
be sairly troubled wi wind o' t' stomach just afore meal-
times."

"No doubt," replied Adam; "but then, thou sees, he's
an add-fashioned way o' drivin' t' wind out by fillin' t'
gap up."

"I wonder hoo he gets his livin'?" said the landlady.

"Aye, an' so do I," said Adam; "for that lad's livin' 'll
bide some gettin'. . . . Sally, what like chap is he,
saysto?"

"Well," replied she, "he's a tallish man,—an' rather a
thin un,—but not so thin, nawther."

"Now, my opinion is," continued the landlord, "that
he's rather of a full-bodied turn of mind."

"Well," said the girl, "he *is* rather full-bodied,—but
not so varra. He hes blue een, and I should think he was
a nice man bi t' look on him."

"I think t' same mysen," said he, "though I never set
een on him i' my life. But, I'm sartin o' *one* thing,—there's
naebody can say that he's a man as hes nowt in him."

"I hope he'll not stop lang i' these parts,—with his blue
een," said the landlady.

"Oh," said Adam, "I could put up wi' t' lad's een, if his
stomach was ony bit like. . . . Didto say he was a
gentleman or a simple body, Sally?"

"He looks like a gentleman," replied she.

"Well, that's a blessin' ; for no poor body could maintain sich a wolf as he keeps in his cote. A man like that should hev somebody runnin' a day's march afore him to scrape his proven together. . . . Will he want ony tea, think ye?"

" I think not," said the landlady. "Thoo hears, he wants to knaw what he hes to pay."

" Well, an' what willto charge him? Thoo cannot charge him less nor t' price o' t' goose. Now, if he'd drunken at t' same bat as he etten there'd ha' bin some sense in't, but he's had no drink mich. He hasn't had enough to wesh that brid down onyway. Thou mun charge him for 't goose."

"One would think he'd not grumnle at that, hooiver," replied she.

" Grumnle or not grumnle, thou mun try it on. What! he's t' reason of a man, sure-ly,—if he's t' stomach of a horse."

" One would hope sae. But I niver heard tell of a horse eatin' goose."

" Well, never thou mind that. Call it a lion i' tho likes. . . . Sally, gan thi ways, an' tell him it'll be seven shillin'. That's about t' size on't, isn't it, Matty?"

"Yes, that's about it. I could hev hed seven shillin' for't, time an' time again."

" Then tell him it's seven shillin'! He's nawther chick nor chylt o' mine,—thank God! Let him pay! Say seven shillin'! Dang it, let's try it on!"

CHAPTER V.

Landlady, count the lawin',
An' gies a cogie mair.
BURNS.

HE traveller was eager to know the upshot of his
message. He sat by the window, smoking, and
chuckling to himself; for his mind was full of
humorous speculation about what was going on in the
kitchen all this while. Hearing the door open, he hastily
assumed an unconcerned air, and as the girl came in, he
quietly blew the smoke from his mouth, and said,—
" Well? "

The girl blushed, as she answered in a timid tone, " Please
sir, t' missis says it'll be seven shillin'."

" All right," replied he, laying down a sovereign ; " and
you may tell your mistress that I think the charge very little
for the dinner that I have had."

The tone and manner in which he received the change
relieved Sally's mind of unpleasant apprehensions.

" Thank ye, sir," said she, blushing again, as she picked
up the sovereign.

" But stay," continued he, " perhaps you had better send
your mistress in."

" Thank ye, sir," replied Sally, looking back from the
doorway.

"Now then," said Sally, as she handed the money to her mistress; "he paid me in a minute, without a word: an' he said it was varra little,—an' he wants to speak to ye."

"Come noo," said the landlord, knocking the ashes out of his pipe, "I like that! There's nae mafflement aboot it! There's nowt licks straight-forrad wark! He's a terrible trencherman,—there's no denyin' that,—but, all's one, if he pays for't. Let a man hev his fill, say I! . . . Matty, lass, tak him his change, an' tell him he shall hev a couple o' ducks to his supper, if he'll stop. I'm rather partial to a man o' that stamp—if he puts it into a good skin, God bless his belly, say I,—for he's a clipper!"

.   .   .   .   .   .

There was a smile on the landlady's face when she entered the parlour. Giving a sly look at the traveller's waistcoat, she held out the tray to him, and said, "There, sir, that's your change."

"Thank you;" said he, taking up the money, "but I really think the charge is too little. Suppose we make it ten shillings? There it is, see, and there's a shilling for the waiter."

"Well, sir," replied she, "it hardly looks right to take it. . . . But ye know what things belongs,—an' I'm sure we're varra much obliged to ye. Now, I hope your dinner was to your likin'."

"Thank you," answered he, "everything was very good, and I have enjoyed it very much. I liked the goose particularly; it was nicely cooked."

"Well," said she, "I'm varra glad. I thow't ye'd like it. Ye see, we're thrang i' t' fields, or else we could have attended to ye better. But I hope we hevn't stinted ye! Now,—if there's anything else ye'd like,——"

"No, thanks," replied he, "I have done very well indeed. If there had been a second goose on the table. I don't think I should have have cut into it."

"Indeed!" said she. "Ay, well, sir. I'm very glad. Mebbe ye'll be stayin' for tea?"

"No, thank you. I'm going on, up Duddon Vale, and over the hills, into Langdale. . . . Oh,—can you tell me anything about the route?"

"No; but my husband can. Ye see, sir, he was born a little aboon Seathut (Seathwaite), an' he knows all t' countra-side between here an' Carlisle,—hill an' hollow, wood an' watter-stid, foot-gate, an' bridle-gate. Ye see, he's a farmer, an' his fadder afore him was a farmer, an' all his fore-elders were farmers, an' cattle-breeders, livin' on their own land, on t' fell-side, ower-lookin' Duddon Vale. If ye'd like to see him, I'll send him in."

"Do, if you please," replied he. "Tell him I shall be very glad if he'll come and take a glass of wine with me."

"Thank ye, sir," said she; "I'll send him in."

. . . . .

"There now," said the landlady, as she entered the kitchen; "it's just as I thowt! He's as civil a man as ever put foot intul a shoe! Yon's nane o' your throssen-up rabblement, not he. He's an awsome guttlin'.—nae doot o' that—but ye wadn't think it, bi t' leuk on him; for there's nowt at a' coorse nor brawsen aboot him (nothing bloated, nor over-fed about his appearance). He's a well-leukin' clear-skinned, healthy man ; an' a varra genteel man, too."

"Well," said the landlord, "he's meat-hèal (meat-whole), whether he's genteel or not,—I'll onswer for that. Thoo cannot say that he's a genteel stomach, ony way."

"Well," replied she, "I'll say nowt about that. He can eat his meat, there's nae doubt. But yon man's worth his meat.—as what he eats. An' then, thou knaws, folks aren't all made alike."

"Nawe, bi t' mass, they aren't," said he ; "an' it's a good job, too ; for if everybody were made like yon genteel divul i' t' parlour there'd be a famine i' t' lond afore t' week end."

"That maks nae matter," replied she. "But, what d'ye think? He said seven shillin' was too little ; an' he made me tak *ten*,—whether I would or not."

"Did he now?"

"He did nowt else."

"An' thoo didn't want to hev it, I guess?"

"Well,—I took it, ony way."

"I thowt sae."

"Well, an' wadn't thou?"

"I doubt I should. . . . But, nae matter. He's a Christian,—if he never said a prayer ; an' I hope he'll never be stinted as lang as he's wick. But, he'll ha to mind an' keep amang fat pastur, or else he'll be nipt."

"An, oh, Sally," cried the landlady, "there's a shillin' for thee, too. That's thy share. Now, thee mind an' put it by. an' save it,—doesto hear? Thou doesn't knaw what thou may come to need ; an' it's a good thing to hev a few pounds laid by to fall back on, if owt should happen.

13

Thou sees how folk are nipt, an' snubbed, an' trodden on,
that have to beg, or to borrow, an' connot help theirsels.
An' there's nobody knows what may betide 'em i' this
world,—no, not th' best on 'em. An' then, thou sees, if
thou has a few pounds i' t' bank, it'll always be makin' a bit
moore. Money i' t' bank's like t' poor man's horse ; it'll
fatten i' t' neet-time, when folk are asleep. Thee tak care
o' thi bit o' money, lass."

" Matty, lass," said the landlord, " thou'll ha' to hev a
surplice made, if thou'rt for goin' on this road."

" Come, don't thee mak fun on it," said she. " I said
nowt but what's reet ; an' thou knaws it."

" Hod thi' tung, lass," replied Adam ; "it's a good advice :
an' I wur sayin' ' Amen ' to every word."

" Well, then," continued she, " about this gentleman i' t'
parlour. I tell tho, he made me tak ten shillin' ; an' he
said he was quite satisfied."

" Quite satisfied, is he ? " replied the landlord. " Well,
come now ; that's a blessin' ! But, if there's ony doubt
about it, thou'd better tak him yon saddle o' mutton in,—
an' let him flirt wi' that a bit. If there's ony empty nooks
laft,—it'll help to fill up,—as far as it goes."

" Do talk to some sense, I pritho," said she. " 'I' man's
reight enough, now. . . . Oh,—thou'rt to go into t'
parlour to him. He's goin' on, up Duddon way, into
Langdale ; an' he wants tho to tell him aboot t' road. Gan
thi ways in. He wants tho to hev a glass o' wine with him.
He towd me to tell tho."

" I'll ax nowt nae better," answered Adam, rising from his
seat.

" Here," said she, laying hold of his sleeve, " thoo's not gannin' in that figure, sure-ly ! *Do* wesh thi hands, an' tidy thisen a bit, hooivver."

" Well,—as thoo says," replied he.

" An' now," said he, when he had put himself into better trim, " I'm his man, ony minute !"

CHAPTER VI.

Come, sit down, my crony, an' gie me your crack.
SCOTCH SONG.

ADAM Ritson was a fine specimen of the heather-bred yeomen of the north of England. Descended from a race of sturdy freeholders,—or "states-men," as they are called in the border counties,—who had for centuries farmed their own land, upon the lower slope of Seathwaite Fell, he inherited the simple habits, the clear vigorous constitution, the manly virtues, and independent bearing of his hardy forefathers,—men of frank, daring temper, brought up, generation after generation, among the wild hills and lonely dales, — men who, in the rough old times of "rugging and riving" had been ever ready to go forth, in battle array, with bills and bows, with lance and good broadsword, to repel the assailing Scot, or to make

a raid across the border, under the banners of their own
country lords. Adam was more than six feet high, as
straight as a pike-staff, and of a remarkably powerful build.
In his youth he had been a famous wrestler, in a country
famous for wrestlers; and he treasured with pride many
trophies of his prowess, in the shape of belts and cups, won
in many a tough struggle among the stalwart lads of Cumberland. Adam was now sixty years of age, and his strong,
bristly hair, that once was a thick mass of crisp, auburn
curls, had become iron-grey; but he was still a hale, and
cheerful man, in the full enjoyment of life, and capable of
extraordinary physical exertion ; and he was, withal, endowed
with a kindly nature, and a rich vein of humour, which made
him a welcome guest wherever he went. When young, he
used to accompany his father to the cattle-fairs of the north,
where his manly figure, and his frank and genial bearing
won him friends among high and low. And, even now, at
" Falkirk Tryste," there was no man more heartily welcome
than Adam Ritson, as a bright, brave, open-tempered, and
generous man, and an upright dealer in cattle. Adam had
five brothers, all living, and all, like himself, tall, strong
men ; and, sometimes, when speaking of his family, he would
say that his parents had "browt up twelve yards and a
hauf o' strang lads, an' five yards an' a hauf o' daycent
lasses,—an' nane on 'em hed ever come to ony ill, yet,—
thank God for't !" Adam's associates, through life, had
been almost entirely rustic, fell-side folk,—farmers, cattle-
dealers, and the like ; yet he was remarkably fond of books ;
and he was a thoughtful reader of such books as fell in his
way ; and he was looked up to, by the simple dalesmen of

the Duddon, as a man of extraordinary gifts,--which,
indeed, he was,—for his nature was more than usually
susceptible to the influences around him; and his mental
capacity was far above the common order. He had
treasured up, with great tenacity, the unwritten traditions
of his native hills; and he was delighted when he could
meet with anybody who had sufficient romance in their
nature to listen to them. More than once, according to the
cherished legends of his own family, had the ancient homestead of his fathers been pillaged by the Scots, in the rough
old days. Even so far back as the time when the Cumbrian
Abbey of St. Bees was plundered by the soldiers of Robert
Bruce, and when the prior, according to Sir Walter Scott,
"was compelled to say mass, with a hollow oak for his stall,"
Adam Ritson used to tell how the story had descended from
father to son. that, then, the scattered inhabitants of Duddon
vale had to flee for shelter down to the old tower of the
Broughtons, at Broughton. But, almost unconsciously to
himself, Adam was gifted with some still higher qualities of
the mind,—qualities which certainly were not fully appre-
ciated by his simple neighbours. Born and reared in a land
of mountain and glen, he found beauty in every common
sight; and he inhaled a sense of freedom from every
breeze that blew. In the plastic time of childhood, he loved
to rove, alone, by the side of the stream that watered his
native vale, watching, with simple-hearted wonder and
delight, the changes of the seasons, and the free play of
Nature, in all her moods of temper, and varieties of form.
To him, the heavens and the earth, the lonely vale. and the
wild hills that folded it in, were peopled with forms of

ever-varying beauty; and, amongst the sequestered scenes
of his youth, he loved

> To stray his gladsome way,
> And view the charms of nature ;
> The rustling corn, the fruited thorn,
> And every happy creature !

An inchoate, germinal genius in his way,—had his lot fallen
among higher spheres of human action,—who knows what
his complete development might have been ? But the vale
of Duddon was dearer to Adam than all the world beside ;
and he never cared to wander far from the pastoral solitude
where he was born.

> Content to live without pretence,
> And earn whate'er his needs require :
> An honest name, with competence,
> All his desire.

As Adam went into the parlour, his old dog, "Laddie,"
slipt in with a rush behind him. "Laddie" was Adam's
constant companion ; and Adam was proud of his fine old
collie. On winter nights, sitting by the fire, with his hand
upon the dog's head, he would talk by the hour about
strange adventures they had gone through together, upon
the fell-sides ; and, all the while, "Laddie" would gaze up
into his face, with a steadfast look of affectionate regard,
and profound attention, as if he knew every word that was
said, and longed to be able to say something about the
matter himself. Well,—the dog rushed in at Adam's heels
that day. Adam would fain have let the dog in freely, if he
had been alone ; but, in deference to the stranger, he held
the door in his hand for an instant, and said, " Now, Laddie,

I doubt thoo'rt not wanted here, my man!" The dog
seemed to know that this was spoken more by way
of experiment than command; and he stood wagging his
tail, and looking up, with a kind of beseeching enquiry, when
the traveller said, "Oh, let him come! I'm fond of dogs!
Let him come in,—he's a fine fellow!" "And so are
you," thought Adam, as he closed the docr; for the saying
pleased him well. "Laddie" wagged his tail again, when
he saw the door closed; and he waited by the wall, that he
might follow at the heels of his master. The stranger rose
from his seat, with easy grace, and a genial smile, as Adam
advanced from the doorway, with long, swinging stride,
stroking the iron-grey bristles upon his brow. "How d'ye
do, sir?" said he, holding out his great horny hand; "How
d'ye do? Are ye keepin' your health well?"

"I'm all right, thank you," replied the traveller. "See;
take a chair."

As soon as Adam had taken his seat. "Laddie" rested
his long nose quietly upon his master's knee, and fixed his
eyes upon his face; and Adam laid his hand upon the dog's
head, as usual.

"You'll take a glass of wine?" said the traveller, filling
Adam's glass.

"Well, thank ye, sir," replied Adam. "I've nae strang
objection to that. Here's your good health, sir! I hope
it'll not be lang afore we see ye again."

"Thank you," said the traveller. "Good health to you!"

"Thank ye," replied Adam; and then, shifting his chair
a little, he continued, "Well, sir; I understand from our
mistress, that you're goin' on, up into Langdale."

'Yes," said the traveller; "and, as I am quite a stranger in this part, I thought you would be able to give me a little information about the road."

"Well, of course I can;" replied Adam; "of course I can; an' I'll do so, with all the pleasure in the world. . . . Oh, I know your way very well. Ye'll hev to travel by the side o' the river Duddon, up into the very hills where it springs fra. An' Duddon's a bonny stream, mind ye! Ye'll say so, when ye've seen it! Oh, I know it right well, ye see, Duddon's my native vale. I was born o' t' fell side, a bit aboon Seathut (Seathwaite); an' ever sin I was quite a lile lad I've bin accustomed to rammle ovver all the country that ye'll hev to go through. Ye see, we hed a deal o' sheep, an' yan thing an' anudder to look after; but, sheep or nae sheep, to tell the truth, I was varra fond o' rammlin' for rammlin's sake, an' that's where it is. I dare say I wandered, by mysen, into nooks o' those hills that few people had ever bin in afore, except t' fox dogs, mebbe, in a hard run, now an' then. . . . Well, now,—we'll begin at t' beginnin'. . . . When ye leave this house, ye'll hev to travel northward on the Bootle road, for about a mile, till ye come nigh to Duddon Brig,—that's where the river Duddon rushes down fra t' tail end o' Duddon Vale, and begins to flow on towards the sands, in a quieter way. Well, now; if ye went ovver Duddon Brig, it would lead ye on by t' north side o' t' sands, up by Buckman's Hall, and down through Millom, an' so by the foot o' Black Coomb, to Bootle, an' Ravenglass, at the sea-side. But, instead o' takin' that road, ye leave Duddon Brig, an' t' Bootle road, an' ye tak a road on the right hand, that leads

up into Duddon Vale. So far, so good. Well, now, as
ye're a stranger, no doubt ye'll want to look about ye, an'
see what there is to be seen."

"That's the very reason why I am wandering about on
foot," said our hero.

"I thowt sae," replied Adam; "an', mind ye, if anybody
wants to see a country like this well, they must tramp it, an'
tak their time, then ye're independent, an' ye can go where
ye like; an' ye can stop when ye like. Oh, there's nought
licks Shanks' pony! . . . Very well. For the first
mile or so, the road winds up an' down t' hill-side, an' in
an' oot among shady trees, that ovver-hang t' way; an' here
an' there ye meet with an old-fashioned cottage, with a
garden in front,—sloping to t' road-side. This shady length
is very pretty in summer-time; an' at this point, the river
runs deep down i' t' gullet o' t' vale. Ye may hear it; but
ye can't see it, for t' bank's varra steep, an' t' trees are thick
between ye an' t' watter-course. Oh, I know that shady bit
o' the way varra well; for I've travelled it i' all wedders, an'
i' all sorts o' leet; aye, an' i' pitch-dark an' all,—oft enough.
But, mind ye, I knaw folk up i' t' vale 'at would rayder gan
twenty mile round than travel that bit, i' t' dark. It's a
flaysome spot i' t' dead time o' t' neet, there's nae doubt,—
not because of owt that's wick, for there's varra seldom onybody stirrin' at sich a time,—though I hev knawn an ugly
trick or two done there, a few years back. Why, about
fifteen years ago, my awn brudder John was ridin' home
fra Broughton, yan stormy neet, an' just as he gat into t'
loneliest part o' this lonesome spot, a man darted out fra
under t' trees, and seized his bridle, an' cocked a pistol at

14

him. Now oor John was not easy daunted. He was a
terrible strang fellow, an' he was a gay bad un to lick. Oor
John got a grip o' this chap's collar, as he was trying to
drag him down; t' pistol went off, an' t' bullet lodged in a
tree by t' road-side : ye may see t' mark on't, yet. Then
John fetched him a clout o' t' heead, wi' t' butt-end of his
whip, an' draggin' him on to t' crupper, he browt him back
into Broughton, at full gallop, as dateless as a clod. It
turned out to be "Black Dick," a Bewcastle gipsy; well
known all over Cummerlan', as a poacher, a smuggler, an' a
robber. Well, it was a bit afore "Black Dick" gat round;
for his wrist was brokken, an' he was a bit maul't udder
ways. Oh, he tackle't t' wrang man when he tackle't oor
John ! Howivver, t' country-side was rid on him for a gay
while; for he was sent ovver t' sea for ten years. . . .
Well, as I was sayin',—t' road winds in an' oot among over-
hangin' trees; but, noo an' then, ye get a peep o' Duddon
Grove, on t' opposite side o' t' river. It's a fine house; but
I suppose ye'll hev mony grander places o' that kind, where
ye come fra?"

"Oh, yes," replied the traveller; "we have many fine
buildings; but the great attraction here is the wild beauty
of the country !"

"Aye, aye," said Adam; "that's just where it is; ye can
build fine houses, and ye may fill 'em wi' fine things; but
ye cannot build Wallabarrow Crag, an' Seathut Fell,—ye
cannot make a vale like Duddon Vale, an' ornament it with
a stream like the Duddon ! To my thinkin', there never
was, nor never will be, a house i' the world to compare wi'
Duddon Vale, on a fine day !"

"I quite agree with you, my friend," said the traveller.

"I can assure you," continued Adam, "I can assure you that I've stood mony a time, upo' Seathut Fell, on a clear winter neet, tracin' the stream far down the vale, an' lookin' round at the mountains, an' then up to the starry sky,—an' I couldn't help but feel that God was t' greatest builder on 'em all!"

"The grand Architect of the universe!" said the traveller.

"'Who meteth out the heavens with a span,'" said Adam.

"'Who walketh upon the wings of the wind,'" said the traveller.

"'Who holdeth the sea in the hollow of his hand,'" said Adam. . . . "Aye, aye," continued he; "this grand world of ours was never built by mortal man. . . . But,—as I was sayin',—Duddon Grove's a fine place o' t' kind. T' house an' grounds cover a great part o' t' lower slope o' Stainton Fell wi' lawns, an' groves, an' windin' walks,—as rich an' fine, in their way, as owt I ever set een on. An' then, reight above all this, t' wild fell rises far up, steep, an' rocky, wi' nowt but black-faced sheep wandering among t' heather, as free as the wind that blaws ower t' tops,—an', mind ye, when there is ony wind, it *does* blaw ower t' top o' Stainton! Oh, Duddon Grove, an' t' fell-side, together,—they're not sae bad, I'll assure ye. . . . Well,—when ye lose sight o' Duddon Grove, ye leave t' shady end o' t' vale behind ye; an' ye're enterin' fairly into the open wild; an', to my thinkin', ye now begin to see the real beauty o' Duddon Vale. The hills begin to shew theirsels,—reight afore ye,—Corney Fell, an' Stainton Fell,

an' Hest Fell, an' Birker Fell,—an', as ye travel on, ye see
mair o' them, an' they grow grander an' grander. Ye meet
wi' varra few trees after this. Its all wild heather, an'
stunted bush, an' moss-grown rock ; but, ye hev the Duddon
with ye, all the way! The road winds, in an' out, by
Duddon side,—never mony yards asunder,—an' mind ye,
every time ye look at that river, ye'll find something new in
it. I've wander't by it, mair or less, all my life, an' its
always fresh to me. It sartinly is a bonny stream,—I will
say that for't! I don't know another to compare wi' t'. I
know mony a stream that hes mair watter in't ; but never a
one 'at's sae full o' pretty frisk as the Duddon is! An',
mind ye, ye're just goin' the reet way to see it well. If ever
ye want to see a mountain stream,—gan upwards,—an' meet
the fallin' watter ; an' there ye hev it, at every stride,—there
ye catch every frolic, an' every little glittering fall,—there
ye hev it, in all its glory,—as one might say !"

"That's perfectly true, my friend," said the traveller.
" I've always found it so. . . . Drink up!"

Adam drank up his glass. The traveller filled again, and
rang for another bottle. The wine was brought in, and
when the door was closed, Adam continued.

"Oh," said he, "ye'll find that I'm right, sir. An', if I'm
not varra mich mistaken, ye'll stop mony a time to look at
that river ; an' ye'll think it bonnier an' bonnier all the way."

" I have no doubt of it," said the traveller.

" Well, now then," continued Adam, "when ye get about
five miles on the road, ye'll come to "Oopha Kirk," (Ulpha
Kirk),—a little country village, close by t' watter-side ; an' I
should advise ye to stop on t' brig a minute o two, an' look

at the river. It's well worth lookin' at. . . . An' now,
sir,—if ye happen to want owt to eat an' drink, when ye get
to "Oopha Kirk," ye'd better try 'em there; for, I doubt
ye'll not find 'em well provided for ye farther on. I should
strangly advise ye to tak some'at wi' ye, when ye leave here."

"Oh, said the traveller, laughing and drinking off his
glass; "I dare say I shall manage very well."

"Oh," replied Adam, "I not quite sae sure about that.
Ye see, I knaw the country well. Ye'll not meet wi' mony
houses on your way; an' it'll all be scrammlin' luck whether
ye get what ye want or not. But we'll see about it afore
ye start. I shouldn't like ye to be ony way stinted, ye
knaw,—that's all."

"Thank you, my friend," said the traveller, "I think I
dare risk it."

"Varra well," replied Adam. "Let's see,—I was at
Oopha Brig? Yes. Well, now, when ye get about a mile
past that, ye come to what we call 'Low, i' Oopha,' an' there
ye see a grand cluster o' hills gatherin' round, wilder at
every stride,—Cove, an' Blakerigg, and Walna Scar, an'
Seathwaite Fell, and Dow Crag, an' Wallabarrow Crag,—all
reight afore ye! Ye see, ye're approachin' the head o' the
vale, where the mountains muster, like a parliament o'
giants, makin' laws for the world. It's a fine part o' the
valley that, an' so ye'll say. . . . Well, ye travel on for
about three mile, an' all the way the river an' the road keep
takkin' a bit of a clip at yan another, and then dartin' away
for a lile rammle by theirsens, an' then creepin' back to
peep at yan another again, like bairns, playin' at hide-an'-
seek amang t' trees,—ye travel on for about three mile, till

ye come to Seathut Chapel.   But, stop,—when ye're within
about a mile o' Seathut Chapel, at a place called Hall
Brig, i' Pendle, it would be better for ye to leave t' high
road, an' tak a bye-way, up t' watter-side, an' ower t' 'Hippin
Steans,' an' on, through t' wood, to Seathut Chapel.   At t'
Hippin Steans ye get a varra beautiful view o' t' river.
.   .   .   Well,—now, we're at Seathut Chapel,—my native
place as I may say, for it's t' nearest village to where I was
born ; an' I dar say I think a good deal mair on it than a
stranger would.   There's nowt honsome in it i' t' way of
buildings,—why, it's just a lile, rough, stragglin' lot o' grey
cots, cluster't togidder, at t' foot o' t' hill, grown ower wi'
moss, an' greenery o' yan sort an' another, as if it were
hauve field an' hauve village, wi' here an' there a thatch wi'
posies on't, like a field wi' a chimney ;—wi' t' bits o'
gables, stannin' yan this way, another that way, or ony
way, just as 't leets, as if they'd all been tummle't out
of a bag, at t' foot o' t' fell, an' laft theer, for t' grass
to grow ower 'em,—or like a lot o' aad cronies, huddle't
round a fire, tellin' tales.   An' t' river's close to.   Neet and
day it goes singing by.   I've knawn mony a ane leave Seathut
Chapel, an' never return.   But neet an' day, the bonny
Duddon still goes singin' by.   Oh, to me it's a varra sweet,
an' a homely spot,—an' homely's just the word, too.   Beside,
ye see, my fadder an' mudder lies buried there,—an' my
gran-fudder, an' my great gran-fadder, an' I knaw not hoo
mony mair o' my awn kin,—ye knaw, that mak's yan feel a
bit tender tull it.   But, nae matter.   Mebbe ye've heard
tell o' Robert Walker,—'Wonderful Walker,' as he was
called ? "

"The Reverend Robert Walker?"

"Yes. He was t' parson at Seathwaite Chapel."

"Oh, yes; I've heard of him."

"Come, now; I'm glad o' that! Well, he lies buried i' Seathut Chapel-garth ; and I thowt that, mebbe, ye'd like to look at t' place where he lies, before ye went ony further on your way."

"That's one of the places I intended to see," said the traveller.

"Ah, well," continued Adam, "it's varra remarkable. He was parson at Seathwaite sixty-seven years. He was ninety-three when he died ; his wife was ninety-three when she died ; an' their eldest daughter was eighty-one when she died. Ye'll find 'em all lyin' together, side by side, i' Seathwaite Chapel-garth, hard by t' aad yew-tree. . . . But, now, we'll wander on towards Langdale, if ye please. . . . Soon after ye leave Seathwaite Chapel ye come to Nettle-slack Bridge, where two roads meet. The right-hand road goes to Coniston, the left-hand road to Langdale. Of course you take the left, which leads up, through a narrow gully, between Harter Fell an' Grey Friars, wi' t' river roarin' deep below. When ye come out of this pass, ye'll think ye're at t' end o' t' world,—for it looks as if it hadn't bin finished ony farther. That upper part o' t' valley sartinly looks varra wild, and desolate. Grey Friars rises up o' one side, and Harter Fell an' Hardknot o' tudder,—an', i' t' vale between, there's not a livin' thing, not a tree, not a house to be sin. Well, yes, there's yan farmhouse,—that's John Tyson's, at Cockley Beck,—but ye'll not see that till ye're near a-top on't, and that house is seven miles fra a mill and five miles

fra a shop, and mair than four miles an' a hauve fra a
church. Now, when ye get there, if ye feel tired, or
hungry, or inclined to stop all neet, I should advise ye to
tak a thowt and consider, for that's your last chance. There
isn't another house till ye get reight ower the top o' Wrynose
Pass, and far away down into Little Langdale ; and ye'll
find that a stiffish walk, if ye intend to do it before neet-fo' ;
but ye'll see how ye are when ye get to Cockley Beck. It's
nobbut rough looking : but if ye happen to be stagged up,
or if ye want oather bed or board, ye'll find that's not a bad
house to call at, for a country nook. An' they're glad to see
ony decent person look in, I con tell ye ; though John has
had some rackle visitors in his time, that made theirsens
mair free than welcome. Ye see it's a varra lonely place.
But ye'll find yersel' quite at home, when ye get there,—if
ye like to ca' an' tak pot-luck : an' they're never short o'
good rough mountain provender, I can tell ye,—if ye can
put up wi't. It's a good meat house, is John's. Ye can
mention my name if ye like. But, if ye like to go on, without callin', well an' good. You'll find it a goodish clim fra
Cockley Beck up to t' top o' Wrynose Pass ; and when ye
git ower top o' that, there ye hev the whole o' Little Langdale, stretchin' far away down, afore ye, as reight as a
ribbin! It's a fine sight, is that, I can tell ye. But,—mind
ye,—it's a lang way frae t' top o' Wrynose to where ye can
get owt to eat. But, when ye do get down into t' vale,
they'll find ye summat or anudder, nae doubt. Now, a good
leg o' fell side o' mutton wadn't come amiss, I warn'd
(warrant), after sic a tramp as that. They'll find ye that,
hooivver. .   .   But, I'll tell ye what, sir,—afore ye

start, ye'd better let our folk cut ye a bit o' summat to tak
wi' ye,—for fear o' mishap."

"Oh, you're very kind," said the traveller, laughing; "but
I don't think there will be any need for that."

"Ay, ay," said Adam; "but ye'll find it's a stiffish walk.
But it depends how far ye've come to-day."

"Oh, about twelve miles," replied the traveller.

"Well, then," replied Adam, "it is as I say,—ye'll find it
a stiffish walk. . . . Now, we've as prime a saddle o'
mutton, yon, as ever knife cut intull. Let our folk cut ye
about two or three pound o' that; we'll put it up nicely for
ye; an' it'll be a bit o' some'at to help out wi',— if ye
happen to find yersel' short."

"Oh, no, thank you for your kind thought," said the
traveller, laughing heartily again; "I think I'll just take
my chance. Surely, as you say, I shall be able to get
a leg of mutton, or something equal to it, in a country
like this."

"Oh, nae doubt o' that," replied Adam, "but then, ye
see,—they mayn't hev it ready cooked for ye."

"Ah, well, then," said the traveller; "I must just wait
patiently; or else take pot-luck, as you say, of anything that
happens to be ready."

"Varra well," said Adam; "ye owt to know best. I'm
only anxious that ye shouldn't be famished in a Christian
country, ye knaw."

"Oh, no fear of that, my friend," said the traveller; "I'm
an old campaigner."

"Come, that's right, sir; I'm glad to hear it," replied
Adam. . . . "Well, now, as you're goin' up Duddon

15

Vale, I shouldn't like ye to pass by Seathwaite without
seein' t' chapel-yard where Robert Walker lies buried."

"I certainly shall stop to look at that," said the traveller.
"He was a very remarkable man."

"He was,—he was, indeed," said Adam. "We've varra
few sic parsons now-a-days."

"There are very few such men in the world at any time,"
said the traveller."

"I suppose not," replied Adam.

CHAPTER VII.

He gloor't, an' glendur't, reet an' lift:
   He twisted to an' fro';
He stopt,—he skriked,—an', in a snift,
   He darted through 'em o'!
LANCASHIRE SONG.

"COME, my friend," said the traveller; "you don't
drink. Finish your glass; and allow me to fill
for you."

"Well, thank ye, sir," replied Adam; "but ye're not
takin' much yersel'."

"Oh, no fear, my friend," said the traveller. "I'll keep
pace."

"Well, now," said Adam, as he laid down his glass again;
"talkin' about parsons,—it reminds me of a comical thing

that happened a long time ago, at a little chapel somewheer
Kes'ick way on. It was yan o' my gran'-fadder's cracks.
Ye s.e, my gran'-fadder lived till he was near ninety; an',
when I was quite a lile slip of a lad, he use't to sit i' t'
corner tellin' his bits o' tales aboot things that happened
when he was young,—for, ye see, t' aad man kept his
faculties to the last, in a maist wonderful way; an' he died
sittin' in his arm-chair, as usual. He seem'd to be asleep;
an' his pipe dropped from his hand; but when they went to
wakken him, they found that it was all over. An' his face
was as quiet as the face of a sleepin' child. Oh, I remember
it well; for I was there at the time. . . . Well, this
thing that I was going to tell.—it's yan o' my gran'-fadder's
bits o' merry tales. It's aboot an aad parson that live't
somewheer up amang t' fells, aboon Kes'ick, when my gran'-
fadder was a young man. It seems that this aad parson
was as poor as a craw; an' he'd nobbut yan suit o' clooas
for both Sunday an' war'-day. Ye see, that's a lang time
ago,—when knee-breeches an' buckle't shoon were common
wear. Well,—yan Setterda' neet, when t' aad man was
undressin' hissen for bed, he fand that his breeches were
getten so sadly aat o' gear that they wadn't be decent for
him to wear at sarvice, t' next mornin'. So he flang 'em
down t' stairs; an' he called out to his son to run with 'em
to t' taylior i' th' village, an' tell him to be sure an' mend 'em
t' same neet, so as to be ready for him to put on t' first thing
i' t' mornin', as he had nae other. An' so, away they went
wi' t' breeches. Well,—as it was Setterda' night, t' taylior
was sittin' drinkin', amang his cronies, at t' ale-heawse; an'
when they browt t' breeches to him, he said 'All reight.

I'll attend to 'em. I knaw that he's nobbut yan pair.
I'll do 'em afore I gan to bed; an' he shall hev 'em
back afore he's up i' t' mornin'!' Well,—what does
t taylior do, at after that, but he goes an' gets blin'
drucken amang his mates, an' away he gans home, an'
reel off to bed, without touchin' t' parson's breeches at all.
Well,—"

"Fill, my friend," said the traveller; "and pass the
bottle."

"Aye, aye; I beg ye pardon, sir," said Adam, as he
passed the bottle "Now, sir; I hope I'm not tirin' ye wi'
these aad-warld cracks o' mine."

"Oh, not in the least," replied the traveller; "go on, I
pray! I'm quite delighted with the story. I only stopped
to grease the wheels a little. Go on, I beg!"

"Well, sir," continued Adam, "when t' taylior wakkent
up, o' th' Sundiy mornin', it was getten lateish on, an' he
had a sair head; an' as he lee i' bed, yawnin', an' gruntin',
an' considerin' what hed taken place t' neet afore, all at
once, he unbethowt him about t' parson's breeches; an' he
bounced out o' bed. 'Bi t' mass,' said he, 'I forgetten t'
parson's breeches! T' aad chap has nowt but these to cover
hissen wi'! An' he'll never go to sarvice baat breeches,
sure-ly! That would be a bonny seet!' Wi' that, t' taylior
jumped upo' t' bench, an' stitched away like a two-year-aad,
till he'd getten t' aad lad's breeches put reet, an' then he
called of his lad Simeon,—a lile careless cowt, ye knaw, as
lads are, afore t' world begins to straddle upo' their shoothers'
'Here, Simeon,' says he, 'thoo mun run off t' parson's wi.
these breeches, as hard as thoo can pelt! They're all that

he has to put on.—an' it's getten hard upo' sarvice time, as
thoo sees ! Away wi' tho, noo, like a good lad ; an' dunnot
stop a minute upon t' road. or thou'll be too lat,—an' there'll
be sic a scrowe as nivver ! If thoo doesn't get theer i' time
for t' parson to go in with his breeches on, 1 nivver dar shew
my face i' t' chapel again ! Noo off wi' tho, an' mak sharp !'
An' away t' lad went, full scutch, wi' th' parcel under his arm,
till he'd getten aat o' seet,—an' then, he began to slacken a
bit, d'ye see. Ye know, do what ye will, lads will be lads,—
like all oather young things that's full o' life ; an' this
taylior's lad wur neither better nor waur than his maks.
Well,--it was a fine summer's mornin', t' sun was shinin' ;
an' t' brids were singin' ; an' t' watter was wimplin' an'
glitterin' ; an' t' trees were rustlin' thick an' green by t' wayside ; an' all around, fra earth to sky, was as bonny as t'
flower-time o' t' year could mak it ; an' before t' lad had
gotten far on his way, he was quite beguile't ; an' he
began o' twitterin', an' tootlin', an' gazin' round, wi'
wide een, as if he was in a world that he'd never sin
afore,—just as a child would, ye knaw. An', for my part,
I can quite excuse t' lad ; I've done t' same thing mysen',
mony an' mony a time. Well, as I was sayin',—he hadn't
gone far afore t' parcel under his arm had clean slidder't
out of his mind ; an' he wander't on, happy an' thowtless,
stoppin' here an' there, bi' t' wayside,—like a bummle-bee
rovin' amang posies. An', now an' then, when he came to
a hole i' t' hedge-side, he popped his stick intull it. But,
mind ye, he hedn't gone far afore he happen't to bob his
stick intull a bit of a hole where there was a wasp-neest.
At after that, I'll awarnd ye, it wasn't lang afore t' lile divul

was wakken't up, to some guage! His bonny dream was
all over, fra that blessed minute; an' he had to begin o'
stirrin' hissen! Out they cam,—ten thousan' strang,—an'
at him they went, tickle-but,—buzzin' about his head, like
little fiery dragons! Well, t' lad was a pluck't un,—an'
he shouted, an' fowt wi' t' parcel to keep 'em off,—till t'
parcel flew loose,—an' then, he fowt on, wi' parson's
breeches, till they gat full o' wasps. But, while t' lad an' t'
wasps were hard at it, i' the very heat o' the battle,—hammer
an' tungs,—up strikes t' chapel-bells,—there was nobbut two
o' them, d'ye see,—up strikes t' chapel-bells,—'tinkle-tum,
tankle, tunkle, tinkle; tunkletum, tinkle, tankle, tunkle.'
So, wi' that t' lad bethowt him that it was sarvice-time; an'
let t' feight go as it might, he must quit the field ; so he rolled
t' breeches up, in a hurry,—wasps an' all,—an' he took to
his heels up t' road, as hard as he could leather at it,—wi'
t' enemy after him, i' full wing! There was nae grass grew
under his feet, till he got to the vestry door, I'll awarnd ye.
Well, bi this time t' parson had about gan t' breeches up;
an' he stood i' t' vestry, buttonin' his lang coat, to see if he
could manage to cover his legs with it, as far down as t' top
of his stockins, when a rap came to t' door. It was t'
taylior's lad, wi' t' breeches, an' as soon as t' parson opened
t' door, he shot into the vestry, like a bullet fra a gun. He
was hot fra the field o' battle ; an' he was quite out o' breath.
His een were starin' wild ; an' his face was as red as a new-
painted wheelbarrow. The minute he gat in, he banged t
door to behind him,—to keep all out that was out,—an', as
he sat down, pantin' to get his breath, he gev a fearful glent
at t' lockhole, to see if owt was coming through. 'Ah,

Simeon, my boy,' said the parson, 'it's you, is it? You've
been a long time. Well, I'm glad you've come. So, they're
all right, are they?' 'Yes, sir,' said Simeon, for he was just
beginning to get his breath. 'Well, you're only just in time,
my lad,' said the parson; 'you're only just in time. I ought
to be in the church, now.' 'I think I'll go in,' said Simeon.
'Yes,' said t' parson: 'go in, my lad; go in. It's past the
time now.' Simeon needed nae mair tellin',—for he'd just
sin a wasp come in at the lock-hole; so he bowted into t'
church, an' pulled t' door to behind him. Then t' parson
pulled his breeches on, in a hurry: an', the minute he'd
getten' 'em on, he darted off into t' church, an' up into t'
pulpit; an' he began o' readin' t' sarvice:—'When the
wicked man turneth away from his—'. He stopped suddenly,
an' changed colour; and then he gev a bit of a cough, an'
began again:—'When the wicked man turneth—.' He
stopped again. 'Oh, by—! What's that?' (*It was a wasp.*)
He wiped his face with his handkerchief, an' began again.
'When the wicked man turneth away from his wick— Oh,
God—bless us all,—there it is again!' Well, the folk stare't
like mad, ye knaw; for they thowt t' aad man was gettin'
wrang in his cock-loft. But, however, he at it again.
'When the wicked man turneth away from his wickedness,
and doeth the thing which is lawful and—a-a-h!' (*Another
wasp.*) 'My friends,' said he, addressin' t' congregation,
'I've been suddenly——a-a-h!' (*Another wasp.*) 'It's
no use, my friends, no mortal man can stand this! I
must,——Oh!' (*Another wasp.*) An' he flang down his
book, and ran back into t' vestry. . . . Now there was
a caper for ye!"

"It's a touching story," said the traveller.

"Aye, aye; it's very touching, as ye say," replied Adam; "it's touching,—to the quick! But ye may guess how the congregation would stare."

"They might well," said the traveller. "It would be quite a new version to them."

"Oh, bless ye; they were all upset! A few o' them ran into t' vestry, to see what was the matter; but,—mind ye,— before they could get in, t' parson had whipt his breeches off, an' he stood under t' window, examinin' his wounds."

"Poor old fellow; it was too bad!" said the traveller.

"Aye, but mind ye," continued Adam, "they weren't lang afore they found out what it was. . . . Simeon had bin sittin' reight i' t' front o' t' pulpit,—wi' his e'en bunged up,— when sarvice began. Of course, ye knaw t' lad was i' terrible pain, for he'd just come through St. Peter's needle his-sen. But when t' sarvice began, he kent in a minute what was t' matter, an' he was forced to let t' cat oot o' t' bag."

"Well," said the traveller, "there would be more laughing than crying about the matter."

"Aye, aye," replied Adam, "of course there would— amang them that wasn't stung. There always is. But, however, that was all t' sarvice they had that mornin', for they sang, 'We praise thee, O God!' an' went their ways, to spread the news."

"Yes," said the traveller, "an' some of them would be better pleased than if they had heard the finest sermon in the world."

"No doubt, sir," replied Adam, "no doubt; for if ye've notice't, t' maist part o' folk i' this world would rather be tickled than taught."

"You're right, my friend," said the traveller. "But, at all events, they wouldn't object to the parson being tickled."

"Of course, not," replied Adam; "but I think there's one thing sartin,—they wouldn't begrudge him of ony fun he gat out of his ticklin'."

" I dare say not," said the traveller.

CHAPTER VIII.

Sacred Religion! "mother of form and fear."
Dread arbitress of mutual respect,
New rites ordaining when the old are wrecked,
Or cease to please the fickle worshipper.
Mother of Love! (that name best suits thee here)
Mother of Love! for this deep vale; protect
Truth's holy lamp, pure source of bright effect,
Gifted to purge the vapoury atmosphere
That seeks to stifle it; as in those days
When this low pile a Gospel teacher knew,
Whose good works form an endless retinue:
A pastor such as Chaucer's verse portrays;
Such as the heaven-taught skill of Herbert drew;
And tender Goldsmith crowned with deathless praise.
WORDSWORTH.

N' so ye've heard tell of our old parson that used to be at Seathwaite Chapel?" said Adam.

"What, you mean the Reverend Robert Walker," said the traveller.

" Yes," replied Adam, "Wonderful Walker, as our dalesfolk call him."

"Oh, yes," answered the traveller; "I've read something of his story, and I shall be glad to know more of it."

16

"Ah, well," said Adam, "it's a story worth reading. . . The old man's gone to his rest many years ago. He lies asleep close by the little chapel, where he worked sae lang. . . . . He was a good man. . . . . To me, his varra gravestone seems to be preachin' a quiet sermon by neet an' day; an' t' little grey chapel that heard his voice sae oft, seems as if it was listenin' to catch a sound that it can never hear again. If ye believe me, sir, I seldom pass that grave without feelin' disposed to take off my hat an' linger a while. He was our minister lang ago; an' he'll be our minister for a lang time to come; for he's well remembered amang us; an' that quiet grave of his seems to fill the whole air with a kind o' divine sarvice. . . . He was a good man, was Robert Walker. He was a friend to me when young, an' he's a friend to me yet. I knew him personally, d'ye see; an' though it's a lang time ago, I've remembered him with a better remembrance as years rolled on. . . . Let me see now. I shall be sixty two come Michaelmas day. Robert Walker was ninety-three years years old when he died. I remember it well. I was at his funeral. There was mair fell-side folk at that funeral than at ony funeral there ever was at Seathwaite Chapel. At that time I should be little mair than fifteen years of age. I went to school till him. Ye see, ours is but a simple mountain village, as you may say. There was nae regular schoolhouse; an' he kept school i' the little chapel where he had gone to school when he was a lile moor-end lad like mysen. . . . . I believe I was a bit of a favourite wi' t' aad man; for he used to lend me books, an' he drilled me, an' taught me mony things, at by-times, out o' school hours,

when he's bin sittin' at his awn fire-side, cardin' wool, or
mendin' his shoes, or makkin rush-dips for winter, out o'
melted mutton fat. There's one thing sartin,—ony bit o'
larnin' that I hev,—such as it is,—I was indebted to Robert
Walker for't,—aye ; an' for mony a good thing besides,—
that you cannot reckon up on a slate. I can assure you, sir,
that it rather pains me when I think about it now, sometimes,—for I feel as if I hadn't given a proper thowt to the
thing when he was livin',—I feel as if I hadn't bin thankful
for't when I had a chance o' bein' thankful for't. . . .
But, what can you expect? What is youth? It's just a
butter-flee, flickerin' i' t' sun! An' young things, runnin ower
wi' life,—what,—let 'em frolic out their frolic-time! An'
lads, ye knaw, they're like wild birds, i' summer, flittin'
about amang t' sunshine, fra tree to tree, fra field to field,
careless, an' thowtless, an' fain that they're wick ; peckin'
fruit here, an' grain there, an' twitterin' the shiny hours away,
without feelin' at all beholden for owt they get,—as if all
that was given to 'em, and all that was done for 'em, was
nowt but what they had a reet to,—or like a child in his
mother's lap, croodlin', an' crowin, an' nozzlin' up to his soft
nest, an' drinkin' his drink, in a happy doze, without knowin'
or carin' where it comes fra."

"Ah, me!" said the traveller; "it's one of the happiest
privileges of childhood!"

"It's a bonny dream, nae doubt," said Adam.

"It is, indeed," said the traveller :—

> 'Tis odour fled as soon as shed ;
> 'Tis morning's wingèd beam :
> 'Tis a light that ne'er will shine again
> On life's dull stream !

" But the world soon begins to waken us up from that
delightful reverie, my friend.'

" It does, indeed, sir," replied Adam.   " We soon find
oursels driftin' out o' the playground into the warkshop o'
life.   An', I can assure you that, as years rolled on, I thowt
mair an' mair o' what Robert Walker hed done for me when
I was a lile, mettlesome, wilful bairn."

" He must have been a fine, homely, pure-hearted old
country parson," said the traveller, in a musing tone.   " I
have been trying to recall some lines that were written upon
him by a great man, and a kindred spirit :—

> The great, the good,
> The well-beloved, the fortunate, the wise,—
> These titles emperors and chiefs have borne,
> Honour assumed or given ; and him, the " Wonderful,"
> Our simple shepherds, speaking from the heart,
> Deservedly have styled.—From his abode
> In a dependent chapelry, that lies
> Behind yon hill, a poor and rugged wild,
> Which in his soul he lovingly embraced.—
> And, having once espoused, would never quit :
> Hither, ere long, that lowly, great, good man
> Will be conveyed.   An unelaborate stone
> May cover him ; and, by its help, perchance,
> A century shall hear his name pronounced,
> With images attendant on the sound ;
> Then shall the slowly gathering twilight close
> In utter night ; and of his course remain
> No cognizable vestiges, no more
> Than of this breath, which frames itself in words
> To speak of him, and instantly dissolves.

" Gowden words !" said Adam ; " gowden words about a
noble man !   Well, well, perhaps his name will be clean for-

gotten some day; but the good he did will not be lost for
all that. The fruit that ripens on the tree may forget the
sun that has helped to ripen it; but the ripeness is there,
after all. . . . But Robert Walker will be lang remembered i Seathut.—Ye see our dales-people are simple, thrifty
folk. They're hardy, an' they're hearty. They spend their
lives, fra year to year, tentin' sheep upo' th' fells, or farmin'
down i' th' vale; an' they see varra little o' t' world outside
o' their own hills, except what they see at a country cattle
fair now an' then. Ye'll hardly ever find owt like downreet
stint amang 'em; for they work hard, an' they live in a plain
homely way; an', as a rule, they're of a savin' turn. But
even amang simple-hearted shepherd folk, like them, Robert
Walker's life was a fine example to all t' country side. Oh,
it was like a lamp in a dark neet! . . . Let me see.
He was born at Under-Craig, i' Seathwaite, i' the year 1709.
That would be when Queen Anne was upo' t' throne. He
was't young'st o' twelve; an' as he was rather of a delicate
frame, they agreed to mak a schoolmaster on him. . . ·
Now, ye knaw, that seems to me but a simple sort of a
reason for makkin' a lad into a schoolmaster; but it's not
uncommon. Why, if a young man happens to lose an arm,
or a leg, it's not an unusual thing to set him up as a schoolmaster, just because he's unfit for owt else, an' not because
he's ony particular brains for t' job."

"That's quite true," said the traveller. "I have often
noticed that in choosing for the young what is to be the
occupation of their future lives,—yes, even in cases where
circumstances allow a free chance of choosing,—parents are
often more influenced by some little consideration of private

and immediate expediency than by any special natural
capacity for the pursuit selected. Hence we have many
blind guides in the world, who, misled themselves, mislead
others, and waste their time; hence we see, here and there,
men limping and blundering through life in employments
for which they are wholly unfit, or have no special love for—
unless they happen to be men of a rare genius, and endowed
with a rare strength of character which enables them to
break away from the ill-fitting harness, and strike out in the
direction to which their own natural gifts incline. History
shows here and there an instance in which a man of
remarkable natural endowment has forced his way up
through the hard crust of untoward circumstance; but the
struggle is often very painful, and sometimes fatal. If all
mankind could be thrown into a riddle, and men could be
shaken out and selected, and each set to the work he was
best fitted for, how much happier each man would be, how
much better for the world at large!"

"It's a hard thing for a lad to be tether't through life to a
job that he cannot do well,—an' doesn't like," said Adam.

"It's a cruel foolishness," said the traveller. "It's wrong
both to the lad, and to everybody else. It robs and injures
both; and fills the world with miserable pretenders. I have
seen poor musicians who ought to have been stonemasons;
wretched painters, who would have made good mechanics ;
and indifferent parsons, who would have been clever com-
mercial men, and not bad fiddlers."

"Ay," said Adam; "an' tayliors that should ha' bin
soldiers."

"Yes," replied the traveller; "and soldiers that should

have been tailors. And poets, too,—so called,—who would have been better at work making shavings in a joiner's shop, or weighing soap behind a grocer's counter. These, however, generally take up the trade of themselves; and their first crude efforts at pithless rhyme are so bespattered by the praise of the ignorant, that,—if the poor fledgling happens to have more vanity than judgment,—the mistake of youth becomes the chronic misfortune of a lifetime."

"Aye, aye," said Adam ; "an' they suffer for't."

"They do, indeed," said the traveller ; "and they make everybody else suffer."

"How comes it," said Adam ; "how comes it, think ye, that they get such encouragement ? "

"Encouragement !" replied the traveller. "As a rule the best of them. who are foolish enough to depend on rhyming-ware for an existence, live poor, scrambling, trampled lives, and die in neglected corners."

"Aye," said Adam ; "an' their works die before they are dead themselves."

"For the most part they are still-born," replied the traveller.

"There's a great many of 'em now-a-days," said Adam.

"For one nightingale there are a thousand sparrows," replied the traveller.

"Well, now," said Adam ; "don't ye think that even the chirp of a sparrow is worth something ? "

"No doubt of it," replied the traveller. "Even the chirp of a sparrow must have some fitting place in the grand harmony which embraces all created things,—and is beyond the range of our mortal comprehension."

" That's true, sir," said Adam thoughtfully ; "that's quite
true. . . . An', t' most o' folks would rather have their
own sparrow than onybody else's nightingale."

" Yes," replied the traveller ; "and it's a very natural
mistake, with those who don't know the difference between
the one and the other. . . . But, we're wandering away
from the story of Robert Walker, my friend. Pray go on."

" Yes, yes," replied Adam. " Well, as I was saying,--
when Robert Walker was a child, he was rather delicate, an'
so his parents agreed to bring him up a scholar. An' i' this
case, it turned out what yan may call a happy choice ; for,
ye see, he was of a thowtful nature, an' all through life he
was about as well-livin' a man as ever stepped shoe-leather ;
an', if I've ony skill about such like things, I consider that
the reight sort o' stuff to mak parsons on. . . . Well,
now, when ye get to Seathwaite, ye must go by all means
into t' chapel-garth ; an' there ye'll find his gravestone. It's
a large blue slab, supported by two upright stones ; an' on it
ye'll find these words :—' In memory of the Rev. Robert
Walker, who died on the 25th of June, 1802, in the 93rd
year of his age, and 67th year of his curacy at Seathwaite.
Also of Ann, his wife, who died on the 28th of January, 1800,
in the 93rd year of her age. Also Elizabeth Robinson, their
eldest daughter, who died 3rd of February, 1829, aged 81
years.' Now, there's a great deal said on that gravestone, in
a few words. I've read it scores o' times, just as if I'd never
seen it afore. Ye see, there's fadder, mudder, an' dowter
lyin' together i' yan grave ; an' their three ages come to two
hundred an' sixty-seven years. . . . But, Robert Walker's
way of life was the maist wonderful thing of all. . . . Ye

see, when Robert was a lile lad, t' parson at Seathwaite kept
school i' t' chapel, an' Robert went there, to larn to read an'
write, amang other fell-side lads, little dreamin' at that time,
mebbe (may be), that he would have to preach, an' teach
school, i' the varra same place, afterwards, for sixty-seven
years of his life-time. Well, at after he had larnt to read
an' write, he went away, ower t' hills, to be schoolmaster at
Lowes-watter; and whilst he was there, teachin' readin',
writin', an' arithmetic, to t' lads an' lasses o' Lowes-watter,
he went to schoo' hissen, at neets, an' at bye-times, to Mr.
Forest, who was the curate o' Lowes-watter. Well, I believe
t' curate took to Robert Walker fearfully : an' he spare't no
pains to get him on ; for he saw that he was made o' good
stuff. An' they studied varra sair togidder ; till, at last,
between the two, Robert was qualified to take holy orders ;
an' it ended in him being ordain't as a parson,—which was
the varra thing he'd set his heart on. Well,—it fell out that
two curacies happen't to be vacant at that time : an',—like
as if it must be,—Robert was the varra man waitin' for t'
job. Yan was at Torver i' Coniston Vale, an' tother was at
Seathwaite, where Robert was born,—the varra chapel where
he'd gone to scnool when he was a lile lad, sixteen year
afore. Well,—ye may guess for yersen,—it was nobbut thin
pikein', noather at t' yan place nor tudder, for Seathwaite
was just worth five pound a year, with a lile bit of a cottage
for t' parson : an' Torver was worth five pound a year,
without ony mak of a place for t' parson to put his yed
intull,—so, there was nae fat to be had noather way. But,
ye see, Robert had always a warm side to his native place ;
beside, mind ye, he had some thowts o' gettin' wed, an'

17

that made him think about t' cottage, ye knaw. Well,—t'
end on it was that he took Seathut,—which was varra
natural. An' then he got wed to a canny, decent sarvant
lass, i' Seathut, that had about forty pound i' t' bank : an' a
lang and a happy life they hed together, them two. Robert
would be about six-an'-twenty when he entered on his lile bit
of a parsonage, at Seathut Chapel, an' his wife would be
about twenty-eight ; an' t' place where they began life
together, they never left it again till he died. His wife died
first, at ninety-three years of age ; an' he died about two years
after, at ninety-three years of age. They're laid together, now,
i' Seathut chapel-garth ; which is within a few yards of their awn
door. During his lifetime he had mony offers o' better places,
where mair money was to be made ; but he was a man of simple
mind, an' nothing could tempt him fra his little chapel at
Seathut, an' his country way o' life, amang his old neighbours
i' Duddon Vale. . . . Well, now, ye'll naturally wonder
how he managed to mak ends meet, an' bring up a large
family in comfort an' decency, an' save two thousan' pounds
out o' such scanty means, —an' well ye may. I've bin browt
up in a plain way mysen' ; an' I've sin mony folk that were
force't to mak a little go a lang way. But Robert Walker's
life was a marvel. There never was a man that made better
use of a poor pastur'. There never was a man that did sae
much good out o' such poor means ; for he was nae niggard,
mind ye : he was a generous man, an' he lived well, too, in
his simple way. Dainties an' finery were out of his line
altogether ; he couldn't afford 'em ; an' if they'd bin within
his reach, he cared nowt for 'em. Of course, he had sair
scrattin' for a lang time ; for though the income o' Seathut

Chapel did rise at last to about seventeen pounds, all told,
it was nobbut a fleabite ; an' he hed to mak out wi' a lock
o' odds an 'ends—teachin' school, writin' letters an' agreements, hay-makin, sheep-shearin,' gardenin',—owt that he
could mak an honest penny by. But, for yan thing, he was
blest with as good a wife as ever man had. They'd a hard
tug, but they were content amang it ; an' they both pulled
yan way, an' that's a great matter. They lived good lives ;
they spared nae pains ; an' they waisted nae time. Eight
hours a day, for five days i' t' week, an' four hours on a
Saturday, he kept school i' t' little chapel—for there was nae
school-house. Whilst he was teachin', he used to sit inside
t' altar-rails, with the communion-table for his desk, an' a
spinnin'-wheel by his side,—for he span whilst he taught.
. . . I think I can see him sittin' there now, with his
fine, lang face, an' his grey hair ; drest in a rough blue frock,
wi' great horn buttons on it : a check lin shirt, wi' a leather
strap round his neck for a stock : a coarse apron ; knee-
breeches o' rough blue cloth ; thick ribbed stockin's ; an' a
heavy pair o' wooden clogs, plated wi' iron. That was his
common week-day wear. But Robert Walker's wark wasn't
done when t' school-hours were over. Till t' time came for
evening prayer afore they went to bed, every hand was at
work in his little cottage, an' he was the busiest o' them all,—
cardin', an' spinnin' flax an' wool ; or makin' rush-dips : or
dressin' hides ; knittin'; readin', writin', mendin' clothes, or
makin' shoes,—an' he sat there, workin' among 'em, an'
guidin' 'em a', with a kind word here, an' a kind word there,—
for he was a varra gentle man. An' I've often heard 'em say
that he was quite a dab at a bit o' tailorin' ; or shoemakin'.

Such things as these he could turn his hand to when there was nowt else to call him off. But he worked hard with his pen, too, at makin' wills, an' drawin' up deeds, an' agreements, an' writin' letters, an' sic like, for t' farmers, an' fellside folk, round about ; particular about Christmas an' Candlemas, when he had sae much wark o' that kind to do that he was sometimes force't to sit at his desk all neet through,—an mind ye, it never made nae difference to what he had to do t' next day. . . . He had a garden, too ; an' he always kept it i' good trim, with his own hand. An' then, he kept a few sheep, an' a couple o' cows ; and these needed attendin' to day by day. Beside this, he rented three acres o' lond ; an' he had about three-quarters of an acre o' glebe lond, an' this he farmed his-sen, without ony help out of his own family. He fed an' looked after his own cattle ; he cleaned his own byre ; he weshed an' shore his own sheep ; an' there was nae kind o' wark about his bit o' lond that was too hard or too humble for him. He looked after it his-sen, an' he took a pride in it. T' parson's lond was about as weel done to as ony i' Duddon Vale. . . . But I hav'nt quite done yet. . . . When t' time o' year cam round, he used to help his neighbours wi' their hay-makin,' an' their sheep-shearin' ; an' mind ye he was reckon't yan o' t' deftest honds at sheep-shearin' in all our country-side. T' farmers didn't pay him for his wark i' money. They all gev him a cleease o' wool, an' a sheet o' hay a-piece, yance a year. T' hay was to be as mich as he could carry away fra t' field in a blanket. T' wool was carded an' spun at his own house for sale ; an' when it was ready, he'd tak thirty or forty pound on't on his back, an' trudge away wi' 't seven or eight miles to market.

I sometimes think it'd mak a good picter o' owd times to see t' parson muckin' his byre out, or trampin' down Duddon Vale to market, wi' his wool on his back. We see nowt o' that mak now-a-days. . . . Now, tea was a thing that he never used—neither him nor his wife. They'd bin browt up o' oatmeal porridge an' milk, an' they stuck to t' owd diet to the last, though, toward t' latter end o' their time, when tea was gettin' common, they kept it i' t' house for t' use o' visitors. Their only firin' was peat, an' dried heather, an' sic like. T' peat he gat out o' mosses his-sen, an' he stacked it his-sen; an' he made his own candles out o' rush-pith an' mutton-fat. For flesh-meat they killed ane o' their own sheep now an' then; an' about t' back end o' t' year they generally killed a cow, an' salted it, an' dried it for winter use. It was a common practice for them to boil all the week's meat at yance, on a Sunday, so that they could give a mess o' broth a-piece to ony o' t' congregation that cam fra a lang distance; an' then they had the meat cold through the week. The family's clothes were mostly made up amang theirsens, out o' stuff o' their own spinnin'; an' they were always comfortably clad, in a simple, homely way. An' this was how he lived an' wrought, for the sixty-seven year that he was our parson at Seathut Chapel. An' out o' this he browt up a large family, i' decency and respectability; an' he trained 'em up carefully i' good ways. He was a man that never would owe anything. He paid everybody their own; he was good to the poor, an' the sick; an' he left two thousand pounds when he died. . . . Ay, I often think of Robert Walker.

. . . . I remember him well. . . . He was a
thowtful man; but whatever happened, he was never
crabbed nor sour. In his quiet way, he was always of a
cheerful turn; and yet, there was something about him that
nae mortal man could tak liberties with. When he was i' t'
chapel, on a Sunday, he looked like some grand owd
patriarch, with his noble face, an' his grey hair, an' his tall
figure. He had a fine voice, too,—deep-toned, an' mellow,—
though it began to tremble a bit after his wife died. I've
heard my fadder say that he never listen't to t' parson after
his voice began to fail, but it browt watter to his een. Ye
see, he was ninety-one when his wife died. I remember her
funeral. She was carried to her grave by three daughters,
an' a grand-daughter. An' they tied a napkin to t' coffin,
an' t'aad man took tother end into his hand, an' so he
followed t' corpse into t' church,—for, ye see, he was nearly
blind; an' there wasn't mony dry een that day. After that,
he began to fall away fast. He had to be led into t' sarvice;
an', sometimes, when he looked at t' seat where his wife
used to sit, his voice began to tremble, an' tears ran down
his cheek, whilst he was preachin'. He lived about two
years after the death of his wife; but he needed care, for he
was hastenin' to his end. The night before he died, his
daughter led him to t' door, as usual, to look at the sky,
before he went to rest. He gazed quietly round for a
minute or two, and the only words he said were, 'How
clear the moon shines to-night!' They put him to bed;
an' t' next mornin', they found him cold an' still; an' his
face was as calm as t' face of a sleepin' child."

"An' so died that fine old country parson," said the traveller. "Oh, that my last end may be like his!"

"Ay," said Adam; "we may all say 'Amen' to that. . . . . He lies i' Seathwaite Chapel-garth, now; but if ever man went to heaven, I think Robert Walker did."

"Even so," replied the traveller; "for that man's life was the life of an angel upon earth:

> As some tall cliff that lifts its awful form,
> Swells from the vale, and midway leaves the storm,
> Though round its breast the rolling clouds are spread,
> Eternal sunshine settles on its head.'"

CHAPTER IX.

They say there's but five upon this isle: we are three of them; if th' other two be brained like us, the state totters."

THE TEMPEST.

IN the meantime, news of the arrival at the King's Head of a strange traveller, who had eaten a whole goose to his dinner,—bones and all,—had filtered out into the little town, chiefly through the medium of Sally, the servant lass, with whom it lost nothing. In that sleepy country nook, where every man knew the number, and kind, and cost of the buttons upon his neighbour's coat,—and where the even tenor of life crept on the same, from day to day, through uneventful years, —even such an incident as this was a kind of god-send, which raised unwonted bubbles upon the stagnant pool. The

news flew from mouth to mouth, with a rapidity only found
in places where life is so still that everybody seems to stand
waiting to hear of something new.   Little Broughton was in
a great ferment that day.   The butcher leaned upon the
half-door of his shop talking to the baker ; the saddler slipt
into the grocer's with the news ; and the villagers stood in
twos and threes, in close conversation at the cottage-doors.
The barber,—who was the two-legged newspaper of the
town,—was in his glory that day ; and he published edition
after edition of the news, with amazing rapidity : and
scarcely an hour had elapsed from the time of the first
issue, before the gastronomic feat originally attributed to our
hero had swollen to alarming dimensions, by the addition of
an apple pie, a pound of cheese, three pints of ale, and two
bottles of wine ; and, according to some accounts the meal
was still going on, as everyone might see who liked to look
in at the parlour window of the King's Head.   Indeed,
several village idlers, impelled by irresistible curiosity, had
already begun to creep towards the front of the hotel, in the
hope of catching a glimpse of our hero.   The first intimation
he had of the state of things outside was the noise made by
a drunken fellow who came reeling up to the front of the
house, shouting and tossing his arms wildly about, attended
by a little circle of admiring tormentors.

Floundering up to the front door, he cried out, " Where's
t' man 'at's etten t' goose?   Turn him out !   I'll oather
eight (eat) him or feight (fight) him for a thaasan' paand,—
brass daan !   What, we're not to be ower-face't wi' show-
folk, are we ?   Turn him out !   I'll have a penk at his
piggin, if I ha' to pay for t' garthin' on't !   Here's a lile

Browton lad 'at'll tackle him ony minute,—if he *has* a goose in him! Turn him out! I'll worry him, just as he stan's,—goose an' all! Turn him out, I tell ye,—or I'll rive him out, bi' t' scuft o' t' neck!"

Here he was staggering in at the doorway, when he was stopt by the landlady, who pushed him back into the street.

" Now, gan thi ways out," said she; "gan thi ways out, thou rackle fool! I'll not ha' tho in here; so I've tell't to! Away wi' tho, now, an' mak nae bodderment, or I'll fetch t' constable to tho,—thoo bledderin' ninny!"

" Ye'll fetch t' constable to mo, will ye? Well,—fetch him then,—an' bring a big un while ye're at it! Ye'll fetch t' constable, eh? An' what'll he du, when he comes? Will he gobble mo up, think ye? Fetch him,—an' be sharp,—he'll find mo somewheer aboot his lug, when he londs! Shaff; ye under-size't foo-mart! If ye bring ony constables to me I'll mak smiddy-smudge on 'em! What,—is there nae drinkin'-shops i' t' taan but yaars? 'Marry, come up,' said Clincher!

> ' Our dame's for gurdle-ceake an' tea;
> Our Betty's aw for thick pez-keale;
> Let ilk yen fancy what they will,
> An' my delight's i' guid strang yell!'

If ye've ony consate o' yersen,—turn out! I'se here! Elebben stun ten,—of a good sooart,—saand, wind an' limb! Whoop, Dragon, mi darlin'. Wag thi left ear!

> ' We went ower to Davie Clay Daubin,
> An' faith a rare caper we had:
> We'd eatin', an' drinkin', an' dancin',
> An' roarin', an' singin' like mad;
> We'd——'

18

Turn out, I say! . . . I had fourteen raands wi' a monkey in a dust-hole, yance,—at White'aven! Come up,—an' be rubbed!

> ' Wa, John, what manishment's tis,
>   At tou's gawn to dee for a hizzy!
> Aw hard o' this terrable fiss,
>   An aw's cum——'

It makes nae matter; I'll hev a gill afore I goo,—or, I'll poo t' slate off!"

Some of the mischievous bystanders encouraged him; and, first one, then another cried, " In wi' tho, 'Tum!"

And away he went reeling in at the doorway, where he was again stopped by the landlady.

" Thoo cums nane in here; so I've tell't to!"

" I owe ye nowt, du eh?"

" Nae matter whether thoo does or not. Thoo's o' t' reet side for runnin',—an' thoo mun stop theer! It'd seem tho better to be at thi wark! What arto thinkin' on?"

" Think! I'll think no more! There's nowt in it! Let them think at's beheend i' their rent,—like ye! I'll think no moore, I tell ye! I wur thinkin' when I upset t' horse an' cart, at Buckman's Ho'. Let them think at' likes; I'll ha noan; it cums to nowt! . . . Turn him out!"

The traveller heard all this through the open window; and he rose from his seat to look out.

"Bless thee, Bottom! bless thee! thou art translated!" said he, gazing steadily at the boisterous reveller outside; and, turning to the landlord as he took his seat again, he said, " That's a fearful wildfowl, my friend! Do you know him?"

" Know him?" replied Adam. " Aye, aye; we know him

well enough. He's a neighbour lad. Poor fellow; he's had bad luck at top end."

"How do you mean?"

"Well,—his cock-loft's in a scrowe."

"What's that?"

"Well,—to tell ye truth, he's not quite all there."

"Oh,—I see. Poor fellow!"

"Yes," said Adam; "yen cannot blame the lad for natural misfortin. He's a bit boddersome, now an' then, poor lad, when he gets drink,—but he's nae harm in him. I blame folk for givin' him drink; it sets him wrang directly. . . . Tak nae notice. Our mistress knows how to manage him better than we. Ye see, I've langish legs, but I've nobbut a short temper,—and that doesn't do. Tak nae notice; Matty'll get him off."

"What's his name?"

"Well,—he's mair names than one,—Tommy Dickson, Red Tom, Flitter—an' yan or two forby. - . . He'll be off soon, now. It generally taks him about a quarter of an hour to finish,—if naebody meddles on him."

.   .   .   .   .   .

Meanwhile Red Tom was still raving in front of the house, with a knot of village idlers about him.

"Ware hawk!" cried he. "I wur born at t' chime hours! I can tell fortin'! Bring a pot,—wi' some'at in it! Bowd Slasher is my name! Ware hawk! I live by suction!

> Deuce tak the clock, click-clackin' sae,
> Still in a body's ear.
> It tells—"

"What's to do wi' thi nose, Tommy?"

"Go look ; barn owl !" replied Tommy.

And away he went staggering down the street, followed by the village rabble, and singing,—

> Aa ! Nichol's now laid in his grave.
> Bi t' side of his fadder and mudder ;
>   The warl not frae deoth could yen save,
> We a' gang off,—teane after tother.

.   .   .   .   .   .

During the time Red Tom was raving in front of the house, an old haymaker, overdone with drink, sat crooning drowsily, all alone, in the taproom, with his chin upon his breast. Hearing the din outside, he said to the servant lass,—

" Who's that ? "

" It's Red Tom," said she ; " he's drunk again."

" Take him off !" said the old man ; " take him off an' send for a fiddler !"

" He's goin' now !" said the lass, looking through the window.

" Bring me another, then," replied the old man, handing the empty pot to her.

.   .   .   .   .   .

After Red Tom had gone his way, the street quietened down to its usual stillness, except that a little whispering went on close by the window, where a few curious villagers had crept slyly up, to get a peep at the strange traveller. Every word was distinctly audible, both to our hero and to the landlord, as they sat talking together.

Adam began to feel uncomfortable.

" Hadn't I better shut the window ?" said he.

"No, no," replied the traveller; "leave it open, please. I like the fresh air."

The whispering went on outside; and Adam fidgeted upon his seat, whilst he tried to drown the sound by speaking in a louder tone.

But the traveller's ears were bent on the talk outside, which amused him exceedingly, although he made no sign of his secret enjoyment.

"He's not an ower-size't man, considerin' t' bugth (bigness) of his meals," said one.

" He's not such a fat un, nawther," said another.

"Nawe," replied the first; " he looks as if he wur a' bone an' pax-wax. . . . But, there's a terrible nippin' machine somewheer i' that lad's inside, I'll awarnd ye."

"He's a rare crop of his awn, hooiver," said the next.

"He has that," continued the first. " It's my opinion that with a little encouragement that man would turn out a glutton."

"I'd give an odd shillin' to see him feed," said another.

"Why; does he do it for brass, think ye?"

" I'll awarnd he does. There'll be a callyvan here in a bit."

"What girth will he be raaand t' chest, think ye?"

" Oh—mair than ye'd think, now."

"I wonder where he's bin browt up."

"Somewhere, I awarnd ye, where there s nae stint. He's nae mountain-grazer, that yan."

"No, no; not he. A thin pastur would be nae use to a crayter like that."

"I'll tell ye what, lads; he'd be a terrible piece o' furniture in a poor man's house."

"Ay, ay, by th' mass! Talk about keepin' t' wolf frae t' door. Somebody would ha' to dee i' that hole!"

"I wonder if he has ony childer."

"I hope not. A generation o' that mak would never do for this country."

"Well, well—I care nowt who he is, nor where he comes fra; but, this I will say, he's gotten *one* inside passenger this time, drive where he will."

"Thoo means t' goose?"

"Ay, the goose and trimmin's; for I understan' that he put as mich stuff out o' seet as would fill a hamper, after he'd finished t' brid. T' barber has a list on't, an' he says it's as mich as man could poo in a hond-cart,—an' a' dainties, too."

"Well, I've bin i' t' carryin' line a good while, mysen, but I never had mich traffic o' that mak."

"Nor me nawther; mine's bin chiefly poddish an' peas-kale, an' blue milk cheese, an' sic like; an' noo an' then I've starken't my kite wi' bacon an' cabbish, an' lythey yel, at a kirn supper, or on a haliday."

"Ay, ay; that's aboot my kitchen, too, Joe, lad. . . . Here, tak thi nose oot o' t' leet, an' let's have another peep at him afore I goo. . . . Well, he's not a faal-lookin' chap; but I'se be fain when he's gone; I've a wife an' nine childer at heám."

"I wish he'd dee," said Joe.

"Oh, give him time, his turn's comin'," replied the other. And then they trickled away from the window.

.   .   .   .   .   .

Adam felt relieved when the whisperers outside had gone away. The traveller, however, had been greatly amused; for he knew right well that he was the theme of their talk, and he knew why. But now there came a lull, and his thoughts began to revert to the journey before him. He looked at his watch. The day had crept on.

"Well, now, my good friend, said he, "another half-hour or so, if you can spare the time, and then I must take the road."

" I can assure ye, sir," said Adam, "I've had great pleasure in your company; an' I shall be glad to have another half-hour on't; but, if ye *are* for goin' into Langdale this after-noon, it wouldn't be wise to linger here mich langer. If ye start in about half-an-hour, ye'll hev six hours good daylect— an' ye'll do it comfortably—that is, if ye don't stop too lang upo' t' road."

" Oh, no fear," said the traveller.

"Ye've the pleasantest part o' the day afore ye," con-tinued Adam : "an't' country 'll look fine as evening comes on."

" Yes," replied the traveller. "Twilight travelling is very beautiful at this time of the year, in a country like this."

" Ah, sir," said Adam, " I've had more pleasure sauntering alone by Duddon side, when dusk was stealing ower the vale, than mortal man can utter !"

" Ah, my friend," said the traveller, "it is only the beautiful mind that sees the beautiful . . . And, now, for a farewell bottle !" said he, rising to ring the bell.

" Excuse me, sir," said Adam, laying his hand upon the traveller's arm, "the stirrup-cup must be mine this day !

It's an old custom. I'm speakin' freely, as if ye was an old friend ; an' I hope ye'll tak it kindly."

The traveller looked at Adam, and saw that he meant it.

" Then, so let it be," replied he.

CHAPTER X.

Good master mine, good mistress, pray
Let me in quiet go my way,
And wander.

GERMAN SONG.

HE traveller and his host sat down to their farewell bottle like old friends who had been happily associated all their lives. By some fine instinct ease and confidence had sprung up with wonderful rapidity during their short acquaintance ; and now they began to feel quite at home with one another. And yet with all Adam's liking for his guest, the remembrance of the extraordinary meal he had eaten still hovered about his mind, and puzzled him exceedingly. There was so much quiet dignity mingled with the genial bearing of the strange traveller,—there was so much unobtrusive refinement about him,—and there was such an utter absence in his manner and appearance of anything like the coarseness, or the lethargy, usually associated with gluttony, that Adam could not help still secretly wondering what manner of man this mysterious wanderer could be.

The traveller saw it all in the frank looks and ill-concealed bewilderment of his host; and, with a keen relish for the humour of the thing, he made up his mind to play out the play.

"Come," said Adam; "here's your good health, sir! an' good luck t'ye, wherever ye may go!"

The traveller lifted his glass.

"Here's to our next meeting!" said he; "and I hope it is not far off,—if God spares our lives!"

"So mote it be!" replied Adam. "I can assure ye, sir, that it's a great pleasure to meet with a man of good capacity, in a country nook like this."

There was a sly ring of sarcastic wit in the words, which made the traveller's eyes twinkle with glee.

Adam was still thinking of the stranger's noontide feat, and he gave a physiological turn to the conversation,— which our hero quietly encouraged.

"Now, I hope ye'll not think me too personal," said Adam; "but, judging from appearances,—you ought to live a lang time."

"I dare say you are right,—so far as appearances go," replied the traveller.

"Now," continued Adam; "a man of an open temper and a good disposition will live langer than a man of an evil, designin' turn o' mind."

"And happier, too," said the traveller.

"Ye see," continued Adam, "whatever happens, his mind's free, an' sweet, an' full of fresh air; an' he's not

19

hamper't neet and day with a nasty burden o' jugglin'
anxieties that he cannot unload."

"It's one of the greatest blessings in life," replied the
traveller.

"It is indeed," continued Adam; "it goes a lang way
towards health of body, too. . . . Ay, with common
care, ye ought to live a good while. . . . But don't ye
think now that ye're rather inclined to a full habit of
body?"

"Perhaps so."

"Ay," said Adam, in a slow and thoughtful tone; "ay!
. . . D'ye sleep well, now?"

"Well—yes."

"Ay," said Adam; "that's better. . . . Now, I suppose, ye've no particular failin' spots i' yer inside?

"Well, I feel a kind of craving, sometimes."

"Ay, I see. . . . Where does it take ye mostly?"

"About here," replied the traveller, laying his hand upon
his stomach.

"How oft d'ye feel it?"

"Two or three times a day, generally."

"Do ye use pills, now?"

"Very seldom."

"Ye tak nowt then?"

"Oh, yes,—at meal-times."

"Ay, ay,—no doubt o' that," replied Adam; "ye'll want
a bit o' some'at then, of course. . . . I suppose oatmeal poddish is not much i' your line?"

"Not much."

"I thowt sae. . . . Capital stuff, now, for regulatin'

your machinery! . . . Now, I'll tell ye what's a good
thing for creatin' an appetite."

Here the traveller could contain himself no longer.
Bursting into laughter, he cried—

"Oh! my dear fellow, if you had recommended something to lessen the appetite I have, it would have been
more to the point!"

Adam began to think he had carried the thing too far,
and the conversation gradually drifted into general themes,
till the half-hour had run out, and the traveller rose to go.

"Now, my friend," said he, "the time is up; and I must
bid you farewell!"

"Well, now, good-bye to ye, sir!" said Adam; "an' God
bless ye! We shall be right glad to see ye if ever ye come
our way again!"

"Good-bye; an' God bless you!" replied he. "If ever
I come within ten miles of Broughton, the distance shall
not divide us!"

The sun was still high in the heavens, and, as he went
his way, with light step and renewed vigour, out at the
town-end, the village folk looked after him from their
cottage-doors, and cried, "That's him!—an' a canny-like
chap, too, he is!"

And long after he had gone away the strange man who
ate the goose at the "King's Head" was the theme of many
a fireside tale in little Broughton town.

.   .   .   .   .   .

Three years had glided after the stranger's visit to
Broughton, and again the summer sunshine filled the air

with golden glow. The woodland leaves were large and
long, and orchard boughs were bending with fruit. The
wild flower gladdened the dusty wayside once more with its
simple beauty : and the wayworn traveller's weary step was
cheered by the song of birds and the scent of the hayfield.
The green earth was gay with new flowers, and every living
thing rejoiced in the general joy of nature.

It was in this sweet season of the year that our hero once
more wandered afoot through pleasant Furness, towards the
romantic lakes and mountains of northern England.   The
chirrupy glee of haymakers in the fields fell pleasantly upon
his ear as he walked in at the lowmost end of Broughton
town, and up towards his old quarters at the "King's
Head." He paused before entering the inn, and looked
around.   There was no visible change in the drowsy little
town, and the old inn looked sleepy, sweet, and comfortable
as before.   With a lively remembrance of his former visit,
he entered the house, and walked into the parlour he had
occupied three years ago.   The window was open again ;
the same sun was shining upon the same quiet street : and
all was the same.   The three years' interval looked like a
dream.   He examined the furniture ; it was exactly the
same, and in the same order ; and the table looked as if he
had only just finished the dinner he had eaten three years
before, and the cloth had been removed whilst he had taken
a nap.   He almost imagined that the room smelt of the
same goose still.   He rang the bell, and in came the same
servant lass,—the same "Sally,"—though more stout and
womanly in appearance.

"Can I have some dinner ?" said he.

She paused,—she stared,—she blushed, and stood stock still. . . . "Dinner," said she; "I'll see, sir." And, closing the door, she ran back into the kitchen.

There was nobody in the kitchen but the landlady.

"He's here again!" cried Sally.

"Who's here again?"

"T' man that eat t' goose!"

"Thou never says!"

"He's yonder!"

The landlord was in the cellar. The landlady shouted down to him.

"Adam!"

"Well!"

"He's here again!"

"Who's here again?"

"T' goose chap!"

"I'm comin'!"

Adam came running up the cellar steps. "Where is he?" said he, rolling down his shirt-sleeves.

"He's i' t' parlour."

"Are you sure it's t' same man?"

"It's the same 'at eat t' goose," said Sally; "an' he wants another."

"The divul he does," said Adam. "Well, he shall have as much as he can eat, if we have to rob a shop for't! . . . Here, gi' mo mi coat. I'll go an' speak tull him."

The traveller advanced to meet Adam, as he came stalking in.

"Well, my old friend," said he, grasping his hand; "I'm here again, you see! And how are you?"

"Well, I'm right glad to see ye, sir," said Adam. "I've often wondered whether I should ever have the pleasure of meetin' wi' ye again. I'm downright fain to see ye. . . . But, stop now. Afore we go any farther. We can talk after. About dinner. We haven't a goose for ye this time ; but——"

"Stop, my friend," said the traveller ; "my appetite has fallen away since I was here last."

".Ay," said Adam. How's that?"

"Take a seat, and I'll tell you."

And when our hero had explained the truth of the matter, and how the gipsy woman had carried away the remains of the goose, Adam sprang to his feet, and, grasping his hand, he cried, " I wouldn't ha' missed this for a thousan' pound ! Bi t' mass ; ye've takken a load off my mind."

And the two were good friends to the last.

But, in spite of the traveller's confession, the people of Broughton still prefer the story of the man that ate the goose,—in its original form.

Th' Barrel Organ.

I CAME out at Haslingden town-end with my old acquaintance, "Rondle o'th Nab," better known by the name of "Sceawter," a moor-end farmer and cattle dealer. He was telling me a story about a cat that squinted, and grew very fat because—to use his own words—it "catched two mice at one go." When he had finished the tale, he stopped suddenly in the middle of the road, and looking round at the hills, he said, "Nea then, I 'se be like to lev yo here. I mun turn off to 'Dick o' Rough-cap's' up Musbury Road. I want to bargain about yon heifer. He's a very fair chap, is Dick,—for a cow-jobber. But yo may as weel go up wi' me, an' then go forrud to our house. We'n some singers comin' to-neet."

"Nay," said I, "I think I'll tak up through Horncliffe, an' by th' moor-gate, to t' 'Top o' th' Hoof.' "

"Well, then," replied he, "yo mun strike off at th' lift hond, about a mile fur on; an' then up th' hill side, an' through th' delph. Fro theer yo mun get upo' th' owd road as weel as yo con; an' when yo'n getten it, keep it. So

good day, an' tak care o' yorsel'. Barfoot folk should never
walk upo' prickles." He then turned, and walked off.
Before he had gone twenty yards he shouted back, "Hey!
I say! Dunnot forget th' cat."

It was a fine autumn day; clear and cool. Dead leaves
were whirling about the road-side. I toiled slowly up the
hill to the famous Horncliffe Quarries, where the sounds of
picks, chisels, and gavelocks, used by the workmen, rose
strangely clear amidst the surrounding stillness. From the
quarries I got up, by an old pack-horse road to a command-
ing elevation at the top of the moors. Here I sat down on
a rude block of mossy stone, upon a bleak point of the hills,
overlooking one of the most picturesque parts of the Irwell
valley. The country around me was part of the wild tract
still known by its ancient name of the Forest of Rossendale.
Lodges of water and beautiful reaches of the winding river
gleamed in the evening sun, among green holms and patches
of woodland, far down the vale; and mills, mansions, farm-
steads, churches, and busy hamlets succeeded each other as
far as the eye could see. The moorland tops and slopes
were all purpled with fading heather, save here and there,
where a well-defined tract of green showed that cultivation
had worked up a little plot of the wilderness into pasture
land. About eight miles south a gray cloud hung over the
town of Bury, and, nearer, a flying trail of white steam marked
the rush of a railway train along the valley. From a lofty
perch of the hills, on the north-west, the sounds of Haslingden church bells came sweetly upon the ear, swayed to and
fro by the unsettled wind, now soft and low, borne away
by the breeze, now full and clear, sweeping by me in a great

gush of melody, and dying out upcn the moorland wilds
behind. Up from the valley came drowsy sounds that tell
the wane of day, and please the ear of evening as she draws
her curtains over the world. A woman's voice floated up
from the pastures of an old farm-house, below where I sat,
calling the cattle home. The barking of dogs sounded
clear in different parts of the vale, and about scattered
hamlets, on the hill sides. I could hear the far-off prattle
of a company of girls, mingled with the lazy joltings of a
cart, the occasional crack of a whip, and the surly call of a
driver to his horses, upon the high road, half a mile below
me. From a wooded slope, on the opposite side of the
valley, the crack of a gun came, waking the echoes for a
minute; and then all seemed to sink into a deeper stillness
than before, and the dreamy surge of sound broke softer
and softer upon the shores of evening, as daylight sobered
down. High above the green valley, on both sides, the
moorlands stretched away in billowy wildernesses—dark,
bleak, and almost soundless, save where the wind harped
his wild anthem upon the heathery waste, and where roaring
streams filled the lonely cloughs with drowsy uproar. It
was a striking scene, and it was an impressive hour. The
bold, round, flat-topped height of Musbury Tor stood
gloomily proud, on the opposite side, girdled off from the
rest of the hills by a green vale. The lofty outlines of
Aviside and Holcombe were glowing with the gorgeous
hues of a cloudless October sunset. Along those wild
ridges the soldiers of ancient Rome marched from Manchester to Preston, when boars and wolves ranged the woods
and thickets of the Irwell valley. The stream is now lined

20

all the way with busy populations, and evidences of great
wealth and enterprise. But the spot from which I looked
down upon it was still naturally wild. The hand of man
had left no mark there, except the grassgrown pack-horse
road. There was no sound nor sign of life immediately
around me.

The wind was cold, and daylight was dying down. It
was getting too near dark to go by the moor tops, so I made
off towards a cottage in the next clough, where an old quarry
man lived, called "Jone o'Twitter's." The pack-horse road
led by the place. Once there I knew that I could spend
a pleasant hour with the old folk, and, after that, be directed
by a short cut down to the great highway in the valley, from
whence an hour's walk would bring me near home. I found
the place easily, for I had been there in summer. It was a
substantial stone-built cottage, or little farm-house, with
mullioned windows. A stone-seated porch, whitewashed
inside, shaded the entrance : and there was a little barn and
a shippon, or cow-house attached. By the by, that word
"shippon," must have been originally "sheep-pen." The
house nestled deep in the clough, upon a shelf of green
land, near the moorland stream. On a rude ornamental
stone, above the threshold of the porch, the date of the
building was quaintly carved, "1696," with the initials,
"J. S.," and then, a little lower down, and partly between
these, the letter "P.," as if intended for "John and Sarah
Pilkington." On the lower slope of the hill, immediately
in front of the house, there was a kind of kitchen garden,
well stocked, and in very fair order. Above the garden, the
wild moorland rose steeply up, marked with wandering

sheep tracks. From the back of the house, a little flower garden sloped away to the edge of a rocky bank. The moorland stream ran wildly along its narrow channel, a few yards below; and, viewed from the garden wall at the edge of the bank, it was a weird bit of stream scenery. The water rushed and roared here; there it played a thousand pranks; and there, again, it was full of graceful eddies; gliding away at last over the smooth lip of a worn rock, a few yards lower down. A kind of green gloom pervaded the watery chasm, caused by the thick shade of trees over-spreading from the opposite bank. It was a spot that a painter might have chosen for "The Kelpie's Home."

The cottage door was open, and I guessed by the silence inside that old "Jone" had not reached home. His wife, Nanny, was a hale and cheerful woman, with a fastidious love of cleanliness and order, and quietness too, for she was more than seventy years of age. I found her knitting, and slowly swaying her portly form to and fro in a shiny old-fashioned chair by the fireside. The carved oak clock-case in the corner was as bright as a mirror; and the slow and solemn ticking of the ancient time-marker was the loudest sound in the house. But the softened roar of the stream outside filled all the place, steeping the senses in a drowsy spell. At the end of a long table under the front window sat Nanny's grand-daughter, a rosy, round-faced lass, about twelve years old. She was turning over the pictures in a well-thumbed copy of "Culpepper's Herbal." She smiled, and shut the book, but seemed unable to speak, as if the poppied enchantment that wrapt the spot had subdued her young spirit to a silence which she could not break. I do not wonder that old superstitions linger in such nooks as that. Life there is like bathing in dreams. But I saw that they had heard me coming ; and when I stopped in the doorway, the old woman broke the charm by saying, " Nay sure ! What ? han yo getten thus far ? Come in, pray yo."

" Well, Nanny," said I, " where's th' owd chap ? "

" Eh," replied the old woman, " it's noan time for him yet. But I see," continued she, looking up at the clock, " it's gettin' further on than I thought. He'll be here in abeawt three-quarters of an hour—that is, if he doesn't co', an' I hope he'll not, to-neet. I'll put th' kettle on. Jenny, my lass, bring him a tot o' ale."

I sat down by the side of a small round table, with a thick plane tree top, scoured as white as a clean shirt ; and Jenny brought me an old-fashioned blue-and-white mug, full of home-brewed.

" Toast a bit o' hard brade," said Nanny, " an' put it into 't."

I did so.

The old woman put the kettle on, and scaled the fire ; and then, settling herself in her chair again, she began to re-arrange her knitting-needles. Seeing that I liked my sops, she said, " Reitch some moor cake-brade. Jenny 'll toast it for yo."

I thanked her, and reached down another piece, which Jenny held to the fire on a fork. And then we were silent for a minute or so.

" I'll tell what," said Nanny, " some folk's o'th luck i'th world.'

"What's up, now, Nanny?" replied I.

"They say'n that Owd Bill at Fo' Edge, has had a dowter wed, an' a cow cauve't, an' a mare foal't o' i' one day. Dun yo co' that nought?"

Before I could reply, the sound of approaching footsteps came upon our ears. Then, they stopt, a few yards off; and a clear voice trolled out a snatch of country song :—

> Owd shoon an' stockins,
> An' slippers at's made o' red leather!
> Come, Betty, wi' me,
> Let's shap to agree,
> An' hutch of a cowd neet together.

> Mash-tubs and barrels!
> A mon connot al'ays be sober!
> A mon connot sing
> To a bonnier thing
> Than a pitcher o' stingin' October!

"Jenny, my lass," said the old woman, "see who it is. It's oather 'Skedlock' or 'Nathan o' Dangler's.'"

Jenny peeped through the window, an' said, "It's Skedlock. He's lookin' at th' turmits i'th garden. Little Joseph's wi' him. They're comin' in. Joseph's new clogs on."

Skedlock came shouldering slowly forward into the cottage—a tall, strong, bright-eyed man of fifty. His long, massive features were embrowned by habitual exposure to the weather, and he wore the mud-stained fustian dress of a quarryman. He was followed by a healthy lad, about twelve years of age—a kind of pocket-copy of himself. They were as like one another as a new shilling and an old crown piece. The lad's dress was of the same kind as his father's, and he seemed to have studiously acquired the same cart-horse gait, as if his limbs were as big and as stark as his father's.

"Well, Skedlock." said Nanny, "thae's getten Joseph witho, I see. Does he go to schoo yet?"

"Nay; he reckons to worch i'th delph wi' me, neaw."

"Nay, sure. Does he get ony wage?"

"Nawe," replied Skedlock; "he's drawn his wage wi' his teeth, so fur. But he's larnin', yo known—he's larnin'. Where's yo'r Jone? I want to see him abeawt some plants."

"Well," said Nanny, "sit tho down a minute. Hasto no news? Thae'rt seldom short of a crack."

"Nay," said Skedlock, scratching his rusty pate, "aw don't know 'at aw've aught fresh." But when he had looked into the fire for a minute or so, his brown face lighted up with a smile, and drawing a chair, he said, "Howd, Nanny; han yo yerd what a do they had at th' owd chapel yester-day?"

"Nawe."

"Eh, dear! . . . Well. yo known, they'n had a deal o' bother about music up at that chapel, this year or two back. Yo'n bin a singer yo'rsel, Nanny, i' yo'r young days—never a better."

"Eh, Skedlock," said Nanny; "aw us't to think I could ha' done a bit forty year sin—an' I could, too—though I say it mysel. I remember gooin' to a oratory once, at Bury. Deborah Travis wur theer, fro Shay. Eh! when aw yerd her sing 'Let the Bright Seraphim,' aw gav in. Isherwood wur theer; an' her at's Mrs. Wood neaw; an' two or three fro Yorkshire road on. It wur th' grand'st sing 'at ever I wur at i' my life. . . . Eh, I's never forget th' practice-neets 'at we use't to have at Israel Grindrod's! Johnny Brello wur one on 'em. He's bin deead a good while. . . . That's wheer I let of our Sam. He sang bass at that time. . . . Poor Johnny! He's bin deead aboon five-an-forty year, neaw."

"Well, but Nanny," said Skedlock, laying his hand on the old woman's shoulder, "yo known what a hard job it is to keep th' bant i'th nick wi' a rook o' musicianers. They cap'n the world for bein' diversome an' bad to plez. Well, as I wur sayin'—they'n had a deeal o' trouble about music this year or two back, up at th' owd chapel. Th' singers fell out wi' th' players. They mostly dun do. An' th' players did everything they could to plague th' singers. They're so like. But yo may have a like aim, Nanny, what mak' o' harmony they'd get out o' sich wark as that. An' then, when Joss o' Piper's geet his wage raise't—five shillin' a year—Dick o' Liddy's said he'd ha' moor too, or else he'd sing no moor at that shop. He're noan beawn to be snape't bi a tootlin' whipper-snapper like Joss—a bit of a bow-legged whelp, twenty year yunger nor his sel. Then there wur a crack coom i' Billy Tootle bassoon; an' Billy stuck to't that some o'th lot had done it for spite. An' there were sich fratchin' an' cabals among 'em as never wur known. An' they natter't, an' brawlt, an' played one another o' maks o' ill-contrive't tricks. Well, yo' may guess, Nanny——

"One Sunday mornin', just afore th' sarvice began, some o'th' singers slipt a pepper-box, an' a hawp'oth o' grey peighs, an' two young rattons, into old Thwittler double-bass; an' as soon as he began a-playin', th' ttle things squeak't an'

scutter't about i'th inside, till they thrut o' out o' tune.
Th' singers couldn't get forrud for laughing'. One on 'em
whisper't to Thwittler, an' axed him if his fiddle had getten
th' bally-warche. But Thwittler never spoke a word. His
senses wur leaving him very fast. At last, he geet so
freeten't, that he chuck't th' fiddle down, an' darted out o'th
chapel, beawt hat ; an' off he ran whoam, in a cowd sweat,
wi' his yure stickin' up like a cushion-full o' stockin'-needles.
An' he bowted straight through th' heawse, an' reet up-stairs
to bed, wi' his clooas on, beawt sayin' a word to chick or
choilt. His wife watched him run through th' heawse ;
but he darted forrad, an' took no notice o' nobody. 'What's
up now,' thought Betty ; an' hoo ran after him. When hoo
geet up-stairs th' owd lad had getten croppen into bed ; an'
he wur ill'd up, o'er th' yed. So Betty turned th' quilt
deawn, an' hoo said, 'Whatever's to do witho, James?"
'Howd thi noise,' said Thwittler, pooin' th' clooas o'er his
yed again, 'howd thi noise ! I'll play no moor at yon shop '•
an' th' bed fair wackert again ; he're i' sich a fluster. 'Mun
I make tho a saup o' gruel?' said Betty. 'Gruel be —— !'
said Thwittler, poppin' his yed out o' th' blankets. 'Didto
ever yer of onybody layin' the devil wi' meighl-porritch?'
An' then he poo'd th' blanket o'er his yed again. 'Where's
thi fiddle?' said Betty. But, as soon as Thwittler yerd th'
fiddle name't, he gav a wild skrike, an' crope lower down
into bed."

"Well, well," said the old woman, laughing, and laying
her knitting down, "aw never yerd sich a tale i' my life."

"Stop, Nanny," said Skedlock, "yo'st yer it out, now."

"Well, yo seen, this mak o' wark went on fro week to

week, till everybody geet weary on it ; an' at last, th' chapel-
wardens summon't a meetin' to see if they couldn't raise a
bit o' daycent music, for Sundays, beawt o' this trouble.
An' they talked back an' forrud about it a good while. Tum
o'th Dingle recommended 'em to have a Jew's harp an'
some triangles. But Bobby Nooker said, 'That's no church
music ! Did onybody ever yer "Th' Owd Hundred" played
on a triangle?' Well, at last they agreed that th' best
way would be to have some sort of a barrel-organ—one o'
thoose that they winden up at th' side, and then they play'n
o' theirsel, beawt ony fingerin' or blowin'. So they order't
one made, wi' some favour-ite tunes in—' Burton,' and
' Liddy,' an' ' French,' an' ' Owd York,' an' sich like. Well,
it seems that Robin o' Sceawter's, th' carrier—his feyther
went by th' name o' "Cowd an' Hungry ;' he're a quarryman by trade ; a long, hard, brown-looking felley, wi' een
like gig-lamps, an' yure as strung as a horse's mane. He
looked as if he'd bin made out o' owd dur-latches an' reawsty
nails. Robin, th' carrier, is his owdest lad ; an' he favvurs
a chap at's bin brought up o' yirth-bobs an' scaplins. Well,
it seems that Robin brought this box-organ up fro th' town
in his cart o'th' Friday neet : an' as luck would have it, he
had to bring a new weshin'-machine at th' same time for
owd Isaac Buckley at th' Hollins Farm. When he geet th'
organ in his cart, they towd him to be careful an' keep it th'
reet side up : an' he wur to mind an' not shake it mich, for
it wur a thing that wur yezzy thrut eawt o' flunters. Well,
I think Robin mun ha' bin fuddle't or summat that neet,
but I dunnot know : for he's s'ch a bowster-yed, mon, that
aw'll be sunken if aw think he knows th' difference between

21

a weshin'-machine an' a church organ, when he's at th'
sharpest. But let that leet as it will. What dun yo think,
but th' blunderin' foo—at after o' that had bin said to him—
went an' 'liver't th' weshin'-machine at th' church, an' th
organ at th' Hollins Farm."

"Well, well," said Nanny, "that wur a bonny come off,
as heaw. But how wenten they on at after?"

"Well, I'll tell yo, Nanny," said Skedlock. "Th' owd
clerk wur noan in when Robin geet to th' dur wi' his cart
that neet, so his wife room with a leet in her hond, an' said,
'Whatever hasto getten for us this time, Robert?' 'Why,'
said Robin, 'it's some mak of a organ. Where win yo ha't
put, Betty?' 'Eh, I'm fain thae's brought it,' said Betty. 'It's
for th' chapel, an' it'll be wanted for Sunday. Sitho, set it
deawn i' this front reawm here, an' mind what thae'rt doin'
with it.' So Robin, an' Barfoot Sam, an' Little Wamble, 'at
looks after th' horses at Th' Rompin' Kitlin, geet it cawt o'th
cart. When they geet how'd on't, Robin said, 'Neaw lads;
afore yo starten; mind what yo'r doin'; an' be as ginger as
yo con. That's a thing 'at's soon thrut cawt o' gear—it's a
organ.' So they hove, an' poo'd, an' grunted, an' thrutch't,
till they geet it set down i'th' parlour; an' they pretended
to be quite knocked up wi' th' job. 'Betty,' said Robin,
wipin his face wi' his sleeve, 'it's bin dry weather latly.'
So th' owd lass took th' hint, an' fotched 'em a quart o'
ale. While they stood i'th middle o'th floor suppin' their
ale, Betty took th' candle an' went a-lookin' at this organ;
an' hoo couldn't tell whatever to make on it. . . . Did'n
yo ever see a weshin'-machine, Nanny?"

"Never i' my life," said Nanny. "Nor aw dunnot want.

Gi me a greight mug, an' some breawn swoap, an' plenty o'
soft wayter, an' yo may tak yo'r machines for me."

"Well," continued Skedlock, "it's moor liker a grindlestone nor a organ. But, as I were tellin yo—

"Betty stare't at this thing, an' hoo walked round it, an'
scrat her yed, mony a time, afore hoo ventur't to speak. At
last hoo said, 'Aw'll tell tho what, Robert; it's a quare-
shaped 'un. It favvurs a yung mangle! Doesto think it'll
be reet?' 'Reet?' said Robin, swipin' his ale off; 'oh, aye;
it's reet enough. It's one of a new pattern 'at's just com'd
up. It's o' reet, Betty. You may see that bith hondle.'
'Well,' said Betty, 'if it's reet, it's reet. But it's noan sich
a nice-lookin' thing for a church, that isn't!' Th' little lass
wur i'th parlour at th' same time, an' hoo said, 'Yes. See
yo, mother. I'm sure it's right. You must tarn this here
handle, an' then it'll play. I seed a man playin' one yesterday, an' he had a monkey with him dressed like a soldier.'
'Keep thy little rootin' fingers off that organ,' said Betty.
'Theaw knows nought about music. That organ musn't be
touched till thi father comes whoam—mind that, neaw.
. . . But, sartinly,' said Betty, takin' th' candle up
again, 'I cannot help lookin' at this thing. It's sich a
quare un. It looks like summat belongin'—maut-grindin, or
summat o' that.' 'Well,' said Robin, 'it has a bit o' that
abeawt it, sartainly. . . . But yo'n find it's o' reet.
They're awterin' o' their organs to this pattern, neaw. I
believe they're for sellin' th' organ at Manchester owd
church, so as they can ha' one like this.' 'Thou never
says!' said Betty. 'Yigh,' said Robin, 'it's true what I'm
telling yo. But aw mun be off, Betty. Aw've to go to th'

Hollins to-neet yet.' 'Why, arto takkin' thame summat?
'Aye; some mak o' a new fangle't machine for weshin'
shirts and things.' 'Nay, sure!' said Betty. 'Aw'll tell tho
what, Robert; they're goin' on at a great rate up at that
shop.' 'Aye, aye,' said Robin. 'Mon, there's no end to
some folk's pride till they come'n to th' floor; an' then there
isn't, sometimes.' 'There isn't, Robert; there isn't. An'
I'll tell tho what; thoose lasses o' theirs—they're as proud
as Lucifer. They're donned more like mountebanks' foos
nor gradely folk—wi' their father't hats, an' their fleawnces,
an' their hoops, an' things. Aw wonder how they can for
shame o' their face. A lot o' mee-mawing snickets! But
they're no better nor porritch, Robert, when they're looked
up.' 'Not a bit, Betty—not a bit! But I mun be off.
Good neet to yo!' 'Good neet, Robert,' said Betty. An'
away he went wi' th' cart up to th' Hollins."

"Aw'll tell tho what, Skedlock," said Nanny; "that
woman's a terrible tung!"

"Aye, hoo has," replied Skedlock; "an' her mother wur
th' same. But, let me finish my tale, Nanny, an then"—

"Well, it wur pitch dark when Robin geet to th' Hollins
farm-yard wi' his cart. He gav a ran-tan at th' back dur,
wi' his whip-hondle; and when th' little lass coom with a
candle, he said, 'Aw've getten a weshin'-machine for yo'.
As soon as th' little lass yerd that, hoo darted off, tellin' o'
th' house that th' new weshin-machine wur come'd. Well,
yo known, they'n five daughters; an' very cliver, honsome,
tidy lasses they are, too,—as what owd Betty says. An' this
news brought 'em o out o' their nooks in a fluster. Owd
Isaac wur sit i'th' parlour, havin' a glass wi' a chap that he'd

bin sellin' a cowt to. Th' little lass went bouncin' into th'
reawm to him; an' hoo sed, 'Eh, father, th' new weshin'-
machine's come'd!' 'Well, well,' said Isaac, pattin' her
o'th' yed; 'go thi ways an' tell thi mother. Aw'm no wesher.
Thae never sees me weshin', doesto? I bought it for yo
lasses; an' yo mun look after it yersels. Tell some o'th
men to get it into th' wesh-house.' So they had it carried
into th' wesh-house; an' when they geet it unpacked they
were quite astonished to see a grand shinin' thing, made o'
rose-wood, an' cover't wi' glitterin' kerly-berlys. Th' little
lass clapped her hands, an' said, 'Eh, isn't it a beauty?'
But th' owd'st daughter looked hard at it, an' hoo said,
'Well, this is th' strangest washin'-machine that I ever saw!'
'Fetch a bucket o' water,' said another, 'an' let's try it!'
But they couldn't get it oppen, whatever they did; till, at
last, they found some keighs, lapt in a piece of breawn paper.
'Here they are,' said Mary. Mary's th' owd'st daughter, yo
known. 'Here they are:' an' hoo potter't an' rooted
abeawt, tryin' these keighs, till hoo fund one that fitted at
th' side, an' hoo twirled it round an' round till hoo'd wund
it up; and then yo may guess how capt they wur, when it
started a-playin' a tune. 'Hello!' said Robin. 'A psaum-
tune, bith mass! A psaum-tune eawt ov a weshin'-machine!
Heaw's that?' An' he start like a throttled cat. 'Nay,'
said Mary, 'I cannot tell what to make o' this!' Th' owd
woman wur theer, an' hoo said, 'Mary, Mary, my lass, thou's
gone an' spoilt it—the very first thing, theaw has.. Theaw's
bin tryin' th' wrong keigh, mon; thou has, for sure. Try
another keigh. Turn th' weshin' on, an' stop that din, do."
Then Mary turned to Robin, an' hoo said, 'Whatever sort

of a machine's this, Robin ?' 'Nay,' said Robin, 'I dunnot
know, beawt it's one o' thoose at's bin made for weshin'
surplices.' But Robin begin a smellin' a rat ; an', as he
didn't want to ha' to tak it back th' same neet, he pike't off
out at th' dur, while they wur hearkenin' th' music ; an' he
drove whoam as fast as he could goo. In a minute or two
th' little lass went dancin' into th' parlour to owd Isaac again,
an' hoo cried out, ' Father, you must come here this minute !
Th' washin'-machine's playin' th' Old Hundred !' 'It's
what ?' cried Isaac, layin' his pipe down. 'It's playin' th
Old Hundred ! It is, for sure ! Oh, it's beautiful ! Come
on !' An' hoo tugged at his lap to get him into th' wesh-
house. Then th' owd woman coom in, and hoo said, ' Isaac,
whatever i' the name o' fortin' hasto bin blunderin' and doin'
again ? Come thi ways an' look at this machine thae's
bought us. It caps me if yon yowling divvle 'll do ony
weshin'. Thae surely doesn't want to ha' thi shirt set to
music, doesto ? Thou ll ha' thi breeches agate o' singin'
next. We'n noise enough i' this hole beawt yon startin' or
skrikin'. Thae 'll ha' th' house full o' fiddlers an' doancers
in a bit.' 'Well, well,' said Isaac, 'aw never yerd sich a
tale i' my life! Yo'n bother't me a good while about a
piano ; but if we'n getten a weshin'-machine that plays church
music, we're set up, wi' a rattle ! But aw'll come an' look
at it.' An away he went to th' wesh-house, wi' th' little lass
pooin' at him, like a kitlin' drawin' a stone-cart. Th' owd
woman followed him, grumblin' o' th' road,—' Isaac, this is
what comes on tho stoppin' so lat' i'th' town of a neet.
There's al'ays some blunderment or another. Aw lippen on
tho happenin' a siyrious mischoance, some o' these neets.

I towd tho mony a time. But thae taks no moor notice o'
me nor if aw're a milestone, or a turmit, or summat. A
mon o' thy years should have a bit o' sense.' 'Well, well,'
said Isaac, hobblin off, 'do howd thi din, lass! I'll go an'
see what ails it. There's olez summat to keep one's spirit's
up, as Ab o' Slender's said when he broke his leg.' But as
soon as Isaac see'd th' weshin'-machine, he brast eawt
a-laughin', an' he sed : ' Hello! Why, this is th' church
organ! Who's brought it?' ' Robin o' Sceawter's.' ' It's
just like him. Where's th' maunderin' foo gone to?' ' He's
off whoam.' ' Well,' said Isaac, 'let it stop where it is.
There 'll be somebody after this i'th mornin'.' An' they
had some rare fun th' next day. afore they geet these things
swapt to their gradely places. However, th' last thing o'
Saturday neet th' weshin'-machine wur brought up fro th'
clerk's, an' th' organ wur takken to th' chapel."

" Well, well," said the old woman; " they geet 'em reet
at the end of o, then ? "

" Aye," said Skedlock ; " but aw've not quite done yet.
Nanny."

" What, were'n they noan gradely sorted, then, after o?"

" Well," said Skedlock, " I'll tell yo."

" As I've yerd th' tale, this new organ wur tried for th'
first time at mornin' sarvice, th' next day. Dick o'-Liddy's,
th' bass singer, wur pike'd eawt to look after it, as he wur
an' owd hond at music ; an' th' parson would ha' gan him a
bit of a lesson, th' neet before, how to manage it, like. But
Dick reckon't that nobody'd no 'casion to larn him nonght
belungin' sich like things as thoose. It wur a bonny come
off if a chap that had been a noted bass-singer five-and-forty

year, an' could tutor a claronet wi' ony mon i' Rosenda
Forest, couldn't manage a box-organ,—beawt bein' teyched
wi' a parson. So they gav him th' keys, and leet him have
his own road. Well, o' Sunday forenoon, as soon as th'
first hymn wur gan out, Dick whisper't round to th' folk i'th
singin'-pew, 'Now for't! Mind yor hits! Aw'm beawn to
set it agate!' An' then he went, an' wun th' organ up, an'
it started a playin' 'French;' and th' singers followed, as
weel as they could, in a slattery sort of a way. But some
on 'em didn't like it. They reckon't that they made nought
o' singin' to machinery. Well, when th' hymn wur done, th'
parson said, 'Let us pray;' an' down they went o' their
knees. But just as folk wur gettin' their een nicely shut,
an' their faces weel hud i' their hats, th' organ banged off
again, wi' th' same tune. 'Hello!' said Dick, jumpin' up,
'th' divvle's off again, bith mass!' Then he darted at th'
organ; an' he rooted about wi' th' keys, tryin' to stop it.
But th' owd lad wur i' sich a fluster, that istid o' stoppin' it,
he swapped th' barrel to another tune. That made him
warse nor ever. Owd Thwittler whisper'd to him, 'Thire,
Dick: thae's shapt that nicely! Give it another twirl, owd
bird!' Well, Dick sweat, an' futter't about till he swapped
th' barrel again. An' then he looked round th' singin'-pew,
as helpless as a kittlin': an' he said to th' singers, 'Whatever
mun aw do, folk?' an' tears coom into his een. 'Roll it '
o'er,' said Thwittler. 'Come here, then,' said Dick. So
they roll't it o'er, as if they wanted to teem th' music out on
it, like ale out of a pitcher. But the organ yowlt on; and
Dick went wur an' wur. 'Come here, yo singers,' said
Dick, 'come here; let's sit us down on't! Here, Sarah;

22

come, thee; thou'rt a fat un!' An' they sit 'em down on
it; but o' wur no use. Th' organ wur reet ony end up;
an' they couldn't smoor th' sound. At last Dick gav in;
an' he leant o'er th' front o' th' singin'-pew, wi' th' sweat
runnin' down his face; an' he sheawted across to th' parson.
'Aw cannot stop it! I wish yo'd send somebry up.' Just
then owd Pudge, th' bang-beggar, coom runnin' into th' pew,
an' he fot Dick a souse at back o' th' yed wi' his pow; an'
he said, 'Come here, Dick; thou'rt a foo. Tak howd; an'
let's carry it eawt.' Dick whisked round an' rubbed his yed,
an' he said, 'Aw say, Pudge, keep that pow to thisel', or
else I'll send my shoon against thoose ribbed stockin's o'
thine.' But he went an' geet howd, an' him an' Pudge
carried into th' chapel-yard, to play itsel' out i'th' open air.
An' it yowlt o' th' way as they went, like a naughty lad bein'
turn't out of a reawm for cryin'. Th' parson waited till it
wur gone; an' then he went on wi' th' sarvice. When they
set th' organ down i'th' chapel yard, owd Pudge wiped his
for-yed, an' he said, 'By th' mass, Dick, thae'll get th' bag
for this job.' 'Why, what for?' said Dick. 'Aw've no
skill of sich like squallin'-boxes as this. If they'd taen my
advice, an' stick't to th' bass fiddle, aw could ha' stopt that
ony minute. It has made me puff carryin' that thing. I
never once thought that it'd start again after th' hymn wur
done. Eh, I wur some mad! If aw'd had a shool-full o'
smo' coals i' my hond, aw'd ha' chuck't 'em into't. . . .
Yer tho', how it's grindin' away just th' same as nought
wur. Ay, thae may weel play th' Owd Hundred, divvleskin!
Thae's made a funeral o' me this mornin'! . . But,
aw say, Pudge, th' next time at there's aught o' this sort

agate again, aw wish thae'd be as good as keep that pow o'
thine to thysel', wilto? Thae's raise't a nob at th' back o'
my yed th' size of a duck-egg; an' it'll be twice as big bi
mornin'. How would yo like me to slap tho o' th' chops
wi' a stockin'-full o' slutch, some Sunday, when thae'rt
swaggerin' i'th front o' th' parson?'"

"While they stood talkin' this way, one o'th singers coom
runnin' out o' th' chapel bare yed, an' he shouted out,
'Dick, thae'rt wanted, this minute! Where's that pitch-
pipe? We'n gated wrang twice o' ready! Come in, wi'
tho'!' 'By th' mass,' said Dick, dartin' back; 'I'd forgetten o' about it. I'se never seen through this job to mi
deein' day.' An' off he ran, an' laft owd Pudge sit upo'
th' organ grinnin' at him. . . . That's a nice do, isn't
it, Nanny?"

"Eh," said the old woman, "I never yerd sich a tale i'
my life. But thae's made part o' that out o' thi own yed,
Skedlock."

"Not a word," said he; "not a word. Yo han it as I
had it, Nanny : as near as I can tell."

"Well," replied she, "how did they go on at after that?"

"Well," said he, "I haven't time to stop to-neet, Nanny:
I'll tell yo some time else; I thought Jone would ha' bin
here by now. He mun ha' co'de at 'Th' Rompin' Kitlin';
but, I'll look in as I go by.'"

"I wish thou would, Skedlock. An' dunnot go an' keep
him, now : send him forrad whoam."

"I will, Nanny I dunnot want to stop, mysel'. Con yo
lend me a lantron?"

"Sure I can. Jenny, bring that lantron; an' leet it. It'll

be two hours afore th' moon rises. It's a fine neet, but it's dark."

When Jenny brought the lantern, I bade Nanny "Good night," and took advantage of Owd Skedlock's convoy down the broken paths, to the high road in the valley. There we parted; and I had a fine starlight walk to "Th' Top o' th' Hough" on that breezy October night.

After a quiet supper in "Owd Bob's" little parlour, I took a walk round about the quaint farmstead, and through the grove upon the brow of the hill. The full moon had risen in the cloudless sky; and the view of the valley as I saw it from "Grant's Tower" that night, was a thing to be remembered for a man's lifetime.

Told by the Winter Fire.

CHAPTER I.

Now all our neighbours' chimneys smoke
  And Christmas logs are burning;
With baked meats all their ovens choke,
  And every spit is turning.
Outside the door let sorrow lie,
  And if for cold it chance to die
We'll tomb it in a Christmas pie,
  And evermore be merry.   GEORGE WITHER.

                By the crackling fire
We'll hold our little, snug, domestic court.   SHAKESPEARE.

HIGH upon the southern slope of Waddington Fell, in the midst of a few green fields, an old country inn stands, with its gable-end close to the road-side, and the heathery moors rising wild behind it. Its comfortable shelter was well known to all who travelled across those storm-swept heights; and when the shades of night had folded up the wide landscape, its cheerful light gleamed like a star upon the dark breast of the moorland hill, far down into the vale, whilst an inviting ray from the little window at the end of the building threw a beam of

bright welcome across the lonely road to every passer by.
The front of the house looked down upon one of the finest
expanses in all the famous valley of the Ribble—a region of
clear rivers and pure air, remarkable for the natural beauty
of its scenery; abounding in historic memorials of the
olden time, and in sweet pictures of rural life. . . . At
the foot of the fell, where the bleak but beautiful heather-
land dies away into rich meadows and pastures green, the
blue smoke curls up from the chimneys of the hamlet of
Waddington, the old town of Wada, a famous chieftain of
Saxon times, whose stronghold in those rude days occupied
a remarkable conical eminence still called "Waddow,"
about a mile south of the hamlet, and hard by the banks of
the Ribble. Waddington is still a quaint, quiet, sweet-
looking rustic village, through the heart of which a limpid
stream comes wimpling down from the moors. It still
retains many features of bygone days. Its ancient church
is an object of interest to the antiquary; and close by the
little stream—which trails its pleasant undersong through
the quiet air of the village, by night and day—stands
Waddington Old Hall, the last shelter of Henry the Sixth,
after lurking, from place to place, for years amongst these
northern wilds. It was from this ancient manor-house that
he fled at last, and was pursued and overtaken by Talbot, of
Bashall, and his men, whilst crossing the river at Brunkerley
hipping-stones, about a mile south of the village. This
sealed the fate of that feeble and unfortunate monarch; for
he was conveyed thence, a prisoner, to London, where he
fell into the hands of his enemies. . . . Looking still
from the front of the old inn, upon the fellside, into the

23

beautiful valley which spreads far and wide at its foot, the
sweet old town of Clitheroe stands upon a gently rising
ground, about three miles to the south, with the ruined
Norman castle of the Lacys—lords of the Honor of Clitheroe
— upon a bold rock over-frowning the market-place. Beyond
that, the scene is bounded, on the south, by the grand ridge
of Pendle, stretching five miles, from the "big end" of the
hill, near the pretty village of Downham ; on the east, to
the wooded slopes ; on the west, where the hill declines
into green holms, and rich meadows, amongst which the
ancient hamlet of Whalley, and its ruined abbey, rest by the
side of the river Calder.   Altogether, the landscape seen
from the front of the old inn—which is the scene of our
story— is a glorious sight.   In the Saxon period of our
history, this beautiful valley is said to have been one of the
most remarkable battle-grounds in all the north, between
conflicting Saxon chiefs, and between the Saxon and the
Dane.   The landscape has certainly been wilder, and more
thickly wooded, then ; but grim old Pendle—the heather-
crested monarch of the scene—stands there yet, in silent
and solitary pride, untouched by change, through all the
lapse of centuries ; and the whole country, as seen from the
wild side of Waddington Fell, must retain much of the same
general aspect that it had a thousand years ago ; for,

> Though much the centuries take, and much bestow,
> Most, through them all, immutable remains,
> Beauty, whose world-wide empire never wanes,—
> Sole permanence in being's ceaseless flow.

It was Christmas Eve ; and every lonely homestead
upon the wild moors was touched with the cheerful temper

of that blessed festival which warms the heart of man with
the kindliest remembrances of all the year.   During many
days past the weather had been keen and clear, delighting
every eye, and rejoicing the hearts of the young and strong
with its bracing beauty,—for old winter was wearing its
brightest robe, and hill and dale, and "every common
sight," in all the wide landscape was lovely to the view.
The heathery slope of Waddington Fell was all white over
with a shining robe of seed-pearls; and every leafless tree,
and rough thorn hedge—every little winter-nipped bush, and
fern-clad wayside well, was festooned with fairy frost-work,
which twinkled in the sun.   Even the rude-built walls and
fences, the lonely "rubbing stoops," in the midst of the
frozen fields, and the farm gear about the yard of the old
inn, were all decked in the glittering enchantment of
cunning nature's happiest wintry mood.   The rugged rut-
worn moorland roads were hard as iron; and the crisp snow
by the roadside crackled under the traveller's foot.   As
twilight deepened down, and the distant landscape began
to fade from view, the blue smoke curled up thicker than
usual from the chimneys of the old house, into the pure
mountain air, for the landlord and his wife were preparing
for a jovial night for their own little family, and for any
stray travellers who might chance to cross the fell that night,
from the Trough of Bolland into Ribblesdale, after the sun
had gone down.   The ordinary business of the solitary
household was all arranged for the night.   The horses in the
stable had been fed and foddered down; the two cows had
been milked;

> The sheep were in the fold,
> And the cattle were in shed;

Little Liddy, the housemaid, had finished her work in the
dairy, and was in her chamber trimming herself up, after the
ruder labours of the day ; " Amos o' Lumpyed's," the hostler,
and general servant-man upon the farm connected with the
inn, had gone down to Clitheroe on an errand ; and old
George, the landlord, known all over the Forest of Bolland
by the name of " Judd o' Sheep Jamie's," old George and
his wife, Betty, had the lower part of the house all to themselves ; for, in those days, that wild fell was not much
travelled, and there had not been a customer in the place
since two hours before the sun went down. But it was
Christmas Eve , and the hearty old couple knew it was a
time not unlikely to bring strange visitors over from Newton-
in-the-Forest, on their way to Clitheroe, after nightfall.

Day was declining ; but the candles were not yet lighted ;
for old George and his wife felt an unconscious delight in
the mystic charm of the lingering twilight hour, which filled
the sweet old house with such a dreamy beauty, at the close
of a fine day. The kitchen looked more bright and cheerful
even than usual. Everything in the place had a holiday
appearance, for the landlady had decorated its walls with
evergreens, amongst which the traditional mistletoe-bush,
hanging from the low ceiling, amongst hams and flitches of
bacon, and great branches of red-berried holly, here and
there, twinkled conspicuously in the firelight. The fire was
piled up high in the wide chimney, and its rosy glow lit up
the whole room, in which everything, great and small, was
radiant with the beauty of perfect cleanliness and order.
The round-topped table was covered with a snow-white
cloth, upon which tea-things were laid for the landlord and

his wife, and Liddy, the servant-girl.   The great kettle hung
upon its usual hook, above the glowing grate ; and a quaint
tea-pot, which rarely made its appearance, stood upon the
hob.   Betty had brought her best old china out, too, for the
occasion ; and, in addition to the usual simple fare of home-
baked bread and sweet mountain butter, of her own making,
with a dish of fried eggs and bacon, several dainties of the
season, amongst which were spice cakes, and cheese, and
mince pies, occupied the board ; and upon the great oak
dresser, under the window, a cold chine of beef stood ready
for all comers.   It was a pleasant sight ; and the good old
couple looked around with quiet delight, as they went to and
fro.   Everything seemed to wink and chuckle with glee ; and
the antique eight-days clock, in the corner, ticked more
blithely than usual as the ruddy firelight played upon its
polished mahogany case, across the white-scoured floor of the
kitchen.

The landlord had sat down in his armchair by the fire,
and was enjoying the luxury of a quiet smoke, whilst looking
contentedly around.

"Come, George," said the landlady, drawing her chair up
to the table, "come an' get thi baggin'!"

The old man laid down his pipe, and rising slowly from
his seat, till his tall figure seemed almost to touch the low
ceiling of the kitchen, he yawned, and said, "Well, I'm
willin', lass ; but afore I begin, I think I'll stretch my legs a
minute or two."   Then, with a slow and heavy footstep, he
sauntered out at the doorway, to look at the night.

By this time the full moon was up ; and it was as light as
day.   The frost-pearled moorside was one glittering expanse

of silvery brilliants, under the soft radiance of the queen of
night; and the clear blue sky was thickly "fretted with
golden fires." The cold seemed to strengthen as the night
came on, and the snow, which had lain freezing for many a
day, was now so hard that the foot left no mark upon its
surface.

"Betty, lass," said the old man, calling to his wife, "come
here a minute! I never seed a finer neet i' my life! This
is gooin' to be one o'th' grand owd-fashioned wintry Kes-
masses—with a bit o' howsome (wholesome) nip in it—sich
as there use't to be when I wur a lad! Look here, mon!
It's full moon; an' it's as leet as noonday! I could see to
read th' almanac very near! An' th' stars are as thick i'th'
sky as a swarm o' gowden midges!"

The old woman came to the doorway, and looked out.

"Ay," said she, gazing round upon the bright scene, "it
is a bonny neet, for sure! But come thi ways in; thou's no
hat on, an' thou'll get coud, i' tho stons theer much lunger!
Come thi ways in, an' let's get er baggins!"

The old man came slowly back into the house, muttering
that a bit o' frost would do nobody no harm.

"Come, Liddy," said the old woman, shouting upstairs to
the servant girl, "whatever arto doin' so long up theer?
Come thi ways down! Th' baggin's ready!"

The girl—a rosy little rustic Hebe—came downstairs,
looking sweet and tidy, from top to toe, and the three sat
down to the table together.

CHAPTER II.

Some say, that ever against that season comes
Wherein our Saviour's birth is celebrated,
The bird of dawning singeth all night long :
And then, they say, no spirits can walk abroad ;
The nights are wholesome ; then no planets strike,
No fairy takes, no witch hath power to charm ;
So hallow'd and so gracious is the time. '   SHAKESPEARE.

'Twas Christmas broached the mightiest ale ;
'Twas Christmas told the merriest tale ;
A Christmas gambol oft would cheer
The poor man's heart through half the year."

                                        SIR WALTER SCOTT.

"NOW then," said the landlady, beginning to fill the cups, "let's fo' to. It looks as if we wur gooin' to ha' th' house to ersels—Christmas Eve as it is—so we may as weel try to make th' best on't. Now, Liddy, lass ; reitch to—an' do not be shy. Here, George ; thou'll sweeten for thisel'. I lippen't o' some of our Jonathan's childer comin' up, fro' Waddin'ton,—an' to tell th' truth, I feel raither disappointed."

"Thou doesn't need." said the old man "It's Christmas Eve,—as thou says,—an' folk are o getherin' round their own hearthstones,—among theirsels."

"Well ; an' aren't they our own gront-childer? George, thou talks silly."

"Never mind, lass. They known th' gate,—if they wanten to come. But, give 'em time, mon,—give 'em time. . . . Now, when I wur a lad, my faither wouldn't ha' had one on

us away fro' whoam at Christmas time, upo' no 'count. We
were a great family,—an' a bit scatter't, mony a mile
asunder,—but he said that he like't to gether o his flock
together into th' owd fowd, upo' Longridge Fell, every Yule-
time, so that he could reckon 'em up, an' see their faces once
more, bi th' leet of a roarin' winter fire. He said it did him
good ; an' it did, too. As for my mother,—I don't think hoo
could ha' poo'd through th' winter if hoo hadn't sin her
childer, an' her childer's childer about her,—fro' o sides,—
owd an' yung,—an' there wur a grand swarm on us,—little
an' big,—when we wur o together ; for two o'th' lads an'
three o' my sisters were wed, an' they brought th' yung uns
wi' 'em. I can remember us musterin' thirty i'th' owd
kitchen, the very Christmas afore my mother deed ; an' a
heartier family I never clapt een on,—for there weren't one
on 'em that wur oather sick, or soory, or sore—an' that's
sayin' a good deeol, i' sich a world as this is."

"Well, George," replied she, "I think that we'n a reet to
expect our own childer to come an' see us i'th' same way.
They'n never missed yet ; an' it looks very strange. They're
o that we han left ; an' I shan't feel reet if they don't come.'

"Don't fret thisel' to soon, lass. There's time enough.
What, th' cawf-leet's noan o'er yet. Make thisel' comfortable. Thou'll see this kitchen turn't th' wrang side up afore
th' neet's o'er. I shouldn't wonder if they aren't comin'
gigglin' up th' fellside this very minute, as merry as ingle-
crickets."

"Well," said the old woman, wiping her eyes, "we's see.
. . . . I could like to yer their feet."

"Nay, nay, lass," said he, "don't goo an' fret thisel' about nought. Thou'll have 'em among these mince-pies afore aught's lung. I'll be bound that th' childer are as anxious to come up as thou art for 'em to come. Dri thi een, lass, do! . . . Here, afore I begin o' mi baggin' I'll put some moore dry eldin' upo' that fire. We'n make a shine i th' hole, whether onybody comes or not."

And the stalwart old fell-ranger—for in his younger days he had been by turns a shepherd and a gamekeeper—rose from the table and fetched a great tree-root from the out-house, which he planted fairly upon the glowing fire. The well-dried log ignited at once, and the flame went roaring up the wide chimney, filling the kitchen with a ruddier light even than before.

"Theer," said he, "that looks like Kesmass, doesn't it? We's need no candles for a bit. That'll make this house shine down th' dark moorside like a great lantron! I'll be bund little Nelly's clappin' her honds just this minute, an' sayin', 'Look yon! I can see my gronny's window! . . . Hello, Liddy; who's left this spade i'th' nook here?"

The girl rose from her seat at the table.

"It's Amos," said she. "He left it when he coom in to his baggin', afore he set off to Clitnero."

"Well, tak it into th' shippon. It's no business here. Let's ha' th' house as tidy as we con, as it's Kesmass Eve."

The girl went out with the spade, and the old man sat down again to his evening meal.

"I'll tell tho what, George," said the landlady, as she filled his cup, "yon lad's raither of a careless turn. How does thou get on wi' him?"

"Well," replied he, "Owd Bill wur worth a dozen on

24

him! Poor owd Bill—he wur a great loss. I miss him as if he'd bin my own brother—he'd bin wi' us so lung."

"Well," said the landlady, "we han th' satisfaction o' knowin' that we made him as comfortable as we could as long as he wur bedridden."

"Aye," said he, "it's an ill thing to have to look back— when folk are laid by for ever— an' remember that yo didn't do as yo should to 'em while they wur alive."

"It is," said she, "it is. . . . But we ha'not that on er minds, George—as how 'tis."

"Nawe, we ha'not, lass." replied he. . . . "As for this new lad this Amos—he's nobbut a shiftless, sham-mockin' sort of a craiter, as far as he's gone. He's sin nought—an' he knows nought—an' he'll not do so mich, if he can help it. I doubt th' lad's had an ill bringin'-up, an' he's some idle bwons in his pelt. He's a lither lump o' stuff— except at catin' an' drinkin'. At dinner-time he'll count four; but, when it comes to a bit o' solid waik, he isn't abuon th' hauve of a gradely chap. But he'll happen mend— we's see in a bit."

"I wonder what's keepin' him i' Clithero till now?"

"Bother thi yed noan about th' lad. He'll turn up of hissel'. I dare say he's let (alighted upon, met with) o' some of his owd cronies. Thou knows it's haliday time, an' yung cowts are jumpin' th' fences a bit; an' one connot expect th' lad to keep his feet just th' same as if it wur a common wortchin'-day. I guess he'll ha' bits o' runs of his own th' sime as other yung craiters—an' he may run a bit, as far as I am concarn't."

"He should be in afore bedtime."

"What does it matter? We're noan boun to bed yet. Never mind th' lad. If he comes, he comes; an' if he doesn't it'll make little odds, for there's nought mich for him to do to-morn."

"Willto have another cup?"

"Nawe, I've done very weel. Poo up to th' hob, an' let's make ersels comfortable. Liddy'll side these things."

He then rose from the table, and taking the arm-chair in the corner, he lit his pipe; and, for the next hour or two, the time glided by in quiet chat with his wife, who sat rocking herself on the opposite side of the fire, the kind old man trying all the while to divert the mind of his good dame from the unusual solitude of their hearth on Christmas Eve.

Whilst they were thus conversing together, a loud sough of wind went moaning round their solitary dwelling, and the doors of the outhouses began to rattle.

"Hollo," said the old man, "th' wind's risin'! What's comin' now?" and looking up at the window he saw that the sky had become overcast. Then, rising from his chair, he went to the door, and found that a sudden change had come over the scene. The wind swept fiercely in at the open doorway. The moon had disappeared, and the sky, lately so bright and clear, was now one wild scene of commotion. Dark clouds were flying across the heavens, and wild-driving mist and sleet filled all the air. Not a star was now in sight. Every moment the air grew thicker; the wind grew wilder: and the flying sleet began to be mingled with thick flakes of snow.

"What a change!" said the old man, closing the door.

"We're gooin' to have a snowstorm; an' not a little un, noather. We don't need to expect onybody up fro Clithero to-neet now, if this howds out. . . . Liddy, goo an' put a leet i' yon end window that looks upo' th' roadside, so that onybody may see it that happens to come o'er th' top o'th' fell."

CHAPTER III.

In winter's tedious nights, sit by the fire
With good old folks, and let them tell thee tales.

SHAKESPEARE.

Then came the merry maskers in,
And carols roared with blithesome din ;
If unmelodious was the song,
It was a hearty note, and strong.   SCOTT.

HE storm grew wilder, and the snow fell faster every minute. The air was thick with flying flakes, and the whole landscape was, now, one ghastly sheet of white. As the snow increased, the wind sank down to a steady, sullen moan, as if overladen, and the usual stillness of the moorland solitude deepened to a death-like hush, which added to the appalling aspect of the scene.

A light, planted in the little window at the gable-end of the house, now threw a cheerful ray across the lonely road which led down the fell-side. The doors and shutters were all fastened. The old landlady and the little household settled down, in full expectation of passing this Christmas Eve in quiet seclusion amongst themselves; and another hour had glided by, during which the snow came down faster and thicker, when somebody lifted the latch, which was followed by a loud knock at the door, and voices heard in conversation outside.

"There's somebody here at last," said the old man, going to the door just as the knock was repeated louder than before. "Who's theer?" cried he, before drawing the bolt of the door.

"There's three on us," replied a merry voice in the storm outside; "there's me, an' Jack o'th' Tinker's, an' Alick o' Cauve-lickt Antony's. We'n com'd o'er th' top, by Wallapa Well, out o' Newton-i'-Bollan.' Oppen th' dur. We connot get no fur (further)."

The landlord threw the door open at once, and in rushed the three travellers, muffled to the chin, and all white with snow.

"Lads," said he, glancing at the wintry storm before he closed the door again, "yo'n brought a wild neet wi' yo'!"

"Nay," replied the spokesman of the three, looking round the kitchen, as he shook the snow from his clothing, "we'n left it beheend us,—an' between yo' an' me, maister, I'm fain to get under cover,-- for we're just about done up. Con we stop o neet?"

"Yo' may, if yo'n a mind—an' welcome!" said the old landlord.

"That's th' mak! (make, sort.)"

"Here," said the landlady, setting three chairs around
the hearth, "draw up, an' warm yo' : for yo' mun have had
a terrible trawnce o'er th' fell i' this storm."

"Thank yo', mistress," replied the rattle-pate who had
first spoken, "I like th' look o' this side o' th' house, I con
tell yo'! An' its a good job we geet in, too,—for Alick
here's noan weel."

"What's th' matter?"

"He's a terrible pain in his inside."

"Eh dear! Does he tak' nought for it?"

"Yigh,—three or four times a day,—an' sometimes moor."

"Some mak' o' bottle, I guess?"

"Nay; it's mostly pills?"

"What mak' o' pills?"

"They're for th' stomach."

"Oh! that's wheer it tak's him, is it?"

"Aye, aye," said the landlord, laughing; "I'm a bit
trouble't wi' th' same complaint mysel'. But yo'n com'd to
th' reet shop for bein' cure't this time. We're seldom short
o' hunger physic i' this house, thank God! . . . . . .
Liddy, set th' cowd beef upo' th' table, an' let these lads
thwite (to cut with a thwittle) at it a bit."

The table was quickly spread with substantial Christmas
fare, and the hungry travellers sat down. For about half-an-
hour every man of the three "played a good stick," as the
old saying goes, chatting blithely together all the while;
and when they had eaten their fill they rose and took their
seats around the hearth again, in merry mood. They had
hardly got well settled before a whining and scratching was
heard at the door.

"Hello, Alick," said Billy o' Mall's o' Jumper's, the

"ready-mouth" of the party, 'thou's laft thi dog out! Oppen th' dur!"

Little Liddy opened the door, and in rushed the dog, whisking the snow from his hide all over the floor.

"I'll tell tho what, Alick," said Billy, "that dog o' thine's a quare-lookin' craiter. What breed doest o co' it?"

"Nay, thou fastens me now," replied Alick. "It's a mixtur o' maks (kinds). Sometimes I think it's a tarrier, an' sometimes I think it'll turn out a foomart-dog; but th' yure's to short. It's a bit o' bull about th' nose; but it looks as if it had bin clemmed at t'other end, for th' hinder-quarter's nipt in like a greyhount whelp. I doubt it's had moore faithers than one. But I like th' dog, for o that; it's sich a feaw un. It's good to nought mich but for a bit o' company. It followed me whoam fro' th' fair about a month sin', an' I didn't like to send it away in th' wide world, to be starve't, an' punce't, an' knocked about fro' window to wole."

"Well, yo're a good pair, Alick," said Billy, "an', as far as I'm concarn't, I'se be sorry if ever yo're parted. . . . But it reminds me," continued he, "of a dog that I bought one Whit-Monday. When I took it whoam my wife stare't at this thing a bit; an' at last hoo said, 'Now, then, what hasto getten this time?' 'Well,' I said, 'it pretends to be a dog.' 'A dog, eh?' said hoo. 'I shouldn't ha' thought it; for it's feaw enough for a corn-boggart. What, thou'll turn this house into a gradely menagerie soon, what wi' th' hens, an' th' pigeons, an' th' poll-parrot, an' two canaries. Thou'rt nought short but a camel, an' two or three monkeys, an' thou'll be set up for life. But I'm noan boun to ha' that

thing i' this house, I can tell tho.' An' I said hoo should,
an' hoo said hoo wouldn't; an' we fell out about it. But
while we wur at it ding-dong, th' cat coom in an' settle't o
disputes wi' a rattle.   Th' cat had just kittle't that mornin',
an' as soon as it seed th' dog it flew at it, an' for a
minute or two I couldn't tell which wur which, they wur so
mixt up together. An' they whuzzed round like a fizz-gig.
First I geet a wap o'th' dog, then I seed a bit o'th' cat; but
I couldn't sort em at o; an' between yeawlin', an' scrattin',
an' spittin', an' squeakin', they kickt up sich a din that it
made mi yure ston o' one end. At last th' cat jumped onto
th' table, wheer th' dinner wur set out, an' th' dog jumped
after it. Then they set th' pots agate o' flyin'; an' amung
th' rest, a dishful o' bacon collops went to th' floor. Our
Sall flew at 'em wi' a quart pot in her hond; but, as hoo
wur gooin', hoo happen't to set her foot onto a bacon
collop, an' away hoo went across the floor in a great
slur (slide), wi' her legs a yard asunder, an' hoo never
stopt till hoo coom bang again th' edge o'th' clock wi'
her nose, an' down hoo went, back'ards, upo' th' floor,
wi her nose bleedin'. 'Oh, I'm kilt!" cried Sall, 'I'm kilt!'
an' I went to help her; but, just as I wur bendin' down, hoo
up wi' her foot and took me bang between th' een, wi' sich
a welt that sparks flew i' o directions: an' down I went
staggerin', th' hinder-end first, into a mugful o' dough, that
stood at th' end o' th' dresser—and there I stuck fast. By
this time hoo'd getten to her feet; and while I wur busy,
tryin' to wriggle mysel' out o' th' mug, hoo flang an' owd
birdcage at mi yed, that wur stonnin i'th' nook—an' that
wur followed wi' a mugful o' starch that coom flusk into my

face, an' filled my mouth an' een, till I wur as blint as a bat. I don't know what hoo sent th' next, but I kept feeling one cloat after another, as thick as leet, an' when I coom to reckon mysel' up. I found that I'd a pair o' prime black een, an' a cut o' mi foryed, an' four or five fresh lumps o' my yed—for hoo had me fast, an' hoo kept hommerin' at it like a nail-maker i' full wark. After I'd getten the starch out o' mi een, I wur a good bit afore I could rive mysel' out o' th' mug—an' then I fund that I'd as mich bakin'-stuff stickin' to th' thick end o' mi breeches as would ha' made a couple o' four-pond loaves. While this wur agate, th' cat had run up to th' top o'th' eight-days clock, an' th' dog had gone yeawlin' out at th' dur, wi' a quart pot after it. I know not where th' dog's londed, but it took off toward Yor'shire, an' I've never sin it fro' that day to this; an' I don't think I ever shall—as lung as our Sall's alive. . . . Well, when I'd poo'd mysel' out o'th' mug, I fund our Sall rear't up again th' dresser, strokin' her nose, an' tryin' to get her breath; an' I believe, to th' best o' my remembrance, that I said some words that I never yeard in a chapel—but I'll not mention 'em again. An' hoo left me nought short, for hoo towd me more about my private character than ever I knew afore. It made my yure ston up, I con tell yo. But let that drop; for I don't like to think on't; an' I don't want it to goo ony fur. . . . Well, as I stoode i'th' middle o'th' floor, tryin' to poo this stuff off mi breeches, we looked at one another for a minute or two. At last, I said to her, 'Now, then, owd lass; what does to think o' thisel'? Thou'rt a bonny baigle (beagle, dog), for onybody to look at!' 'Ay; an' so art thou,' said Sall. 'Thou'd make

25

a rare alehouse sign if thi pictur' wur takken as thou
stons!' 'Well,' I said, 'I should look a bit different,
owd lass, for thou's takken some pains wi' this face o'
mine this last twothre minutes.' 'Sarve tho reet, thou
greight idle rack-an'-hook!' said Sall. 'Where's that pratty
dog o' thine? Thou'd better look after it! It's a pity
to lose sich a thing as yon. It should ha' stopt, an'
had a bit o' some'at to eat. I doubt th' poor thing's noan
satisfied wi his maister. Go thi ways, an' look for it, or
else somebody'l be steighlin it. Poor thing! Folk shouldn't
be rough wi' things that connot speak for theirsels.' 'Never
thee mind, owd lass,' I said; 'I'll ha' that dog back here if
I'm a livin' mon—whether thou likes it or not.' 'I would,
lad,' said Sall; 'an' bring a wild craiter or two, at th' same
time; an' let's set up a show!' 'Nay,' I said, 'there needs
no moore wild craiters where thou art. An', as for a show,
that nose o' thine would fotch brass just this minute,—if I
had tho in a caravan. But, I'll be gooin',—an' th' next
time I come thou'll be fain to see me.—whether I've a dog
or not.' ''Tak thisel' out o' mi seet,—an' keep thi heels
this road on!' cried Sall. An' as I went out at th' dur-hole,
a rollin'-pin flew close by my ear-hole, an' broke a weshin'-
mug that stoode at tother side o'th' road. . . . I coom
off, an' left her to it a bit."

Billy's dog story put all the company into a merry temper;
and the night wore on in cheery chat and story. As it
drew near midnight, the storm gradually abated, and the
heavens grew bright again.

"Now then," said the old landlord, looking up at the
clock, "it'll be Christmas Day i' two minutes! Fill up, lads!"

The old clock in the corner struck twelve; and every body listened to the last stroke.

"Stop!" said the old man. "Husht! . . . Ay, yon's Clithero Church bells!"

The merry peal, mellowed by distance, came floating up the fellside, with the glad tidings of the happiest feast of all the year.

"A Merry Christmas and a Happy New Year!" cried old George, rising to his feet; and as the toast went blithely round the kitchen, a burst of music arose under the window. It was the Christmas waits, who had wandered up from Clitheroe to salute old George and his wife.

Sweetly into the wintry air arose Dr. Byrom's fine carol, "Christians awake, salute the happy morn" sung to the well-known, glad old tune, which was composed for it by Wainwright, the organist of Manchester Old Church.

The landlord threw the door wide open, and cried, "A Merry Christmas to yo o'! Come in, an' let's look at yo! I'm fain to see yo, by th' mass! Come in. But who han we here?" said he, laying his hand upon the shoulder of a little figure, muffled in a red cloak. The child threw its cloak off, and held up its laughing mouth to be kissed.

"Eh, it's our Nelly!" cried the old landlady. "Eh, my darlin', my darlin'!"

"Yes," said the child, "an' my father's here; an' our George, an' our Mary; an' Kate an' Annie are comin' up, beside!"

"Eh, my darlin's—my darlin's!" cried the kind old matron, bursting into tears of joy, as she clasped her children to her breast, again and again, one after another.

And it was a blithe Christmas morning in that old house upon Waddington Fell Side.

Tattlin' Matty.

CHAPTER I.

Aw'm not a woman at' oft speaks,
Or sings folk doleful sungs,
But aw con tell my mind to thee,—
Thae knows what things belnngs.

NATTERIN' NAN.

"FO' Edge," or Fall Edge, about five miles north of Bury, is one of the wildest moorland ridges in Lancashire. It is a little lower than "Whittle Pike," the bleak cone of which stands about half a mile to the south-west, more than sixteen hundred feet above the sea. The view from "Fo' Edge," looking westward, is very striking. A deep, lonely clough, green only on the lower grounds, and almost treeless, save where some cherished bit of shade overhangs the gables of a solitary farm-house, or where scanty patches of young plantation fringe the banks of the stream, which murmurs in many-mooded cadences down the rocky channel, hidden from view. The clough is bounded on each side by wild hills, which, though not of immense height, have a solemn and imposing aspect, sloping and swelling down in grand billowy sweeps, and in some places falling away abruptly in steep bluffs of barren crag. For about two miles the clough has a desolate appearance ; and the only habitations visible are four or five moorland farm-houses, perched here and there, on green "coignes of vantage," far apart, upon the scene. The plaintive bleat of scattered sheep, and the clucking cry of startled grouse come wildly from those lonely wastes. Further down the hills die away in gentler slopes of greener land, into the rich valley through which the Irwell runs in freakish windings on its way to the sea, between banks studded with tall chimneys, that tell the busy tale of Lancashire industrialism. The landscape then closes on the west with the steep side of Holcombe Hill, well cultivated, far up ; streaked with white and winding roads, and sprinkled with farm-houses, little clustered folds, churches, and mansions ; but crowned all along the summit with a dark tract of heathery desolation. It is a fine moorland landscape, well known to those earnest students of botany and geology, who, not content with a lazy reliance upon other men's theories, go forth, with loving hearts and hungry minds, to "read, mark, learn, and inwardly digest" here a leaf and there a leaf of nature's old book for themselves.

A little below the rocky crest of " Fo' Edge," on the west side, there is a quaint farmstead, where a family of kind-hearted, simple folk live. It is the highmost, the last and loneliest dwelling upon the mountain side. A little companionship of friends—men of varied tastes and acquirements, who love to roam the moors together, " when summer

days are fine," we have often wandered up to that old farm-
house, and always found a welcome there: none the less
because we were always accompanied by an old scientific
friend who had been nursed in his infancy by the farmer's
wife. The last time we were there was in the pride of the
year. We had spent some three hours of the sunniest
part of the day in rambling up the rocky bed of the stream,
toward its source on "Fo' Edge," stepping from stone to
stone, slipping into the brook sometimes, and resting oft in
cool nooks to chat, and watch the water play. In that
pleasant river-ramble we lingered by many a delicious pool
and by many a silvery fall. But, when we got into the wild
gorge, at the head of the clough, we had to clamber up
slippery crags, and through watery crevices festooned with
mist powdered ferns, and cushioned with beds of the greenest
moss, glittering with pearly spray. Up the ragged ravine
we clambered, from rock to rock, till we came out, at last,
upon the unshaded moorland, a little below the "Edge,"
where the gables of "Bill o' Johnny's" mountain nest met
our eyes, and we felt at home. As we drew near the house
the dogs rushed forth, barking furiously, till some familiar
face met their eyes, when their fury died away, first into low
growls, then into a whimpering welcome, as they came
slowly up, wriggling their bodies and wagging their tails, in
recognition of old friends ; but, that done, they walked quietly
round among the company, snuffing slily at the legs of those
least known to them, as if they were not willing to fondle
every new comer without due examination. The dogs had
roused the family. Out they came, one after another, and
heartily glad they were to see us. Why hadn't we sent them

word that we were coming? They were sure we were
hungry, and so we were. And then a cheery bustle arose in
the house, and we loitered about the farm till dinner was
spread for us upon a green knoll, by the side of an old well,
fed by a rindle of cold spring water. And there, under the
blue sky, we feasted, with wild plovers wheeling about us;
and, high over head, the skylark raining down his glad song
upon our green table. Black-faced sheep upon the mountain
side stared at us with wondering eyes; and our noisy merriment startled the grouse from his heathery cover. It was a
hearty meal. Oat-cake and "Oon-cake," new baked that
day by homely old ".Ann;" sweet moorland butter, cheese,
crisp young onions, dripping with well-water, new milk,
warm from the cow, fried ham, and home-brewed ale. It
was a delicious feast, eaten in the grandest room man ever
entered. Fun, and song, and sage discourse went round
freely; and that banquet under the blue sky will be long
remembered by us amongst little things that light the past
with gleams of joy.

Long before sunset, we came down the mountain side,
halting in twos and threes, now and then, to share some
burst of merriment; or to listen to some snatch of learned
discourse upon the testimony of the rocks; or to ask our
friend, the "Antiquary," a question about relics of Roman
occupation in the district. It is three miles from "Fo'
Edge" to "Mercer's" comfortable hostelry, at the foot of
the hills, at Edenfield. Here we rested and regaled for an
hour or so; after which we came away: some to take the
train at Stubbins, and some to walk along the high road,
five miles, to Bury. My route was different to the others:

and at the south end of the village I parted from my friends,
taking a road on the left hand, which leads into the old
highway from Burnley to Manchester. This old road is
lonely now, and a great part of it is rugged and watery, and
grown over with grass and weeds. In some places it dives
down steep banks, into deep cloughs, and crosses brawling
streams, and then climbs again in slippery, toilsome windings, that make one think that if the horses of these days
only knew what their ancestors had to go through, they
would be thankful for railways. In some parts of the road
there are holes, and pools of water : in others great masses
of rock crop out, laid bare by heavy rains, and kept so by
long neglect ; and in others the banks have slipped into the
path, leaving it so narrow that "two wheelbarrows would
tremble if they met." There is many an old house by this
road side, now roofless and ruined, which fifty years ago
was a flourishing country inn, or some other brisk haunt of
a great thoroughfare. But, the lone highway has long since
forgotten what a four-horse coach was like ; and there is an
air of desolation and decay all along, except down in the
cloughs, where mills have been built by the water sides.

The rosy rays of evening fell grandly upon the silent road
as I walked along, musing whether or not I should call to
see "Owd Grunsel," the gardener, whose house I was
approaching. Owd Grunsel's little cot stands in a snug
green nook, at the foot of a little ridge of woodland. The
rustling trees tell every changing mood of the wind to it all
day long, and the ends of the wooded ridge curl in towards
it lovingly, as if they wished to protect it from the troubles
of the outer world. All day long the birds sing jets of song

to the old gardener's cottage; and, when night comes, and
the household lights are put out, the trees seem to whisper
to one another. "Hush! Sing low! It is asleep!" And
when, before the first lifting of the morning latch, the blue
smoke begins to curl up from the chimney into the clear
air, the leaves of the wood clap their little hands with glee
to see it waken up again. The old man's nest looks up at
the wild moors; and a garden divides it from the lonely
road. About a mile down the hills, there is a busy manufacturing village; but the intervening ridge of woodland
hides that cosy cot from the noisy side of the world.

As I drew near the place, I saw the door was open, as
usual; and the cat was sitting at the threshold, looking
dreamily out into the twilight. And I could see Matty
and her grand-daughter moving to and fro inside. The old
woman was a little deaf; but, before I had opened the gate,
I heard little Jenny say, "Hey, gronny! See yo who's
coming!"

"Well, if ever!" said the old woman, turning round as
she wiped a basin which she had just washed. "Well, iv
ever! Is that yo? Come fonnd, prayo! It's good for
sore e'en, is this. . . . Jenny, bring him a cheer, lass.
Thae stons theer as gawmless as a boother-stone! . . .
Yo known this woman, dunnot yo?" continued she, pointing
to a stout, sweet, apple-faced body, who sat at the opposite
side of the fire, with a basket upon her knees, and a choco-
late-coloured silk kerchief tied upon her head. "It's Jim
wife, at th' Nod. They'n bin killin' a pig; an' hoo's brought
me a bit o' spar-rib,—an' a link o' black puddins,—an' a
bit o' swine's graice to rub mi bakin'-tins wi'. Aw say, aw

26

dunnot know heaw aw'm to pay 'em, for they're al'ays
bringing summat or another."

"Eh, never name it, Matty," said the woman, shifting,
uneasily upon her chair, and the colour rising into her
ruddy cheek; "Never name it! It's nobbut good will an'
ill, mon; a bit of a thing like that."

"Well, Mary," said the old woman, "aw con nobbut
thank tho, thae knows. But yo see'n," continued she,
turning to me," "I nurs't her, when hoo wur quite yung,
at after her mother dee'd : an' hoo like taks to mo, as if
hoo're a lass o' my own,—doesn'to, Mary?"

"Yigh, aw do," replied the woman; "an' so does
eawr Jim."

"Ay, he does," replied the old woman, sighing, as she
opened the oven door and shut it again; "ay, he does.
. . . Yo see'n, aw'm bakin'," continued she, turning to
me. "Our Sam 's gardenin' deawn at 'Thistley Knowe';
but he 'll not be long afore he 's here. Sit yo deawn a bit,"
and then she scaled the fire, and set the kettle on.

"Well, Matty," said I, pulling up my chair, "and how
are yo gettin' on?"

"Why," replied she, setting one hand upon her side,
"but poorly, bless yo,—but poorly. This rheumatic troubles
me so. An' my e'e-seet 's gettin' warse. Mon. age will tell,
— it will tell. . . An' aw feel quite knocked up to-day.
. . . Eh, aw've had sich a trawnce !"

"Why, where han yo bin?"

"Stop a minute," said the old woman, "I'll put th' dur
to. . . . Come, puss! Ch-ch-ch! . . Jenny, fotch
yon mug in."

When the door was shut, she hobbled up to the oven,
and taking a cake out, she tapped upon it with her finger,
and turned it over. As she put it in again she muttered to
herself, " Ay, it 's doin' nicely." Closing the oven, and
setting her hands upon her hips, she gave a long sigh as she
looked slowly round the house, and said, " I think I 'll e'en
drop it for to-day; for I 'm e'en done o'er. Oh, this pain !
It taks me across th' smo' o' my back. Jenny, reitch that
knittin'. An' poo th' cheer up to th' hob, for I 'm as wake
as a kitlin'."

The old woman sat down ; and, as she arranged her
needles, she said, " I 'm fain yo co'de, for it gets *one-ly* at
neet, wi' nobody to talk to. An' I like a bit of a chat.
Our Sam says he wonders how it is that th' rheumatic
never touches my tongue. But I 'll tell yo where aw've bin
to-day."

" Do," said I, hutching my chair near to the hob.

" I will," replied Matty, disentangling her worsted, and
settling herself once more, in a way that convinced me she
was going to begin a long story.

" Yo see'n," she began, " yo see'n, our Sam went out
yesterday a gettin' a burn o' nettles for th' owd mistress at
Th' Split Brid, yon. He never cheep't a word to me. But
I knowed what he wor after, bless yo. Yo see'n hoo wur
very good to him at th' time that he lee ill so long. Why
hoo 's good to onybody,—an' that 's where it is. That
woman 's like as if hoo taks a pride i' helpin' folk that are a
bit hamper't—hoo does for sure. Doesn't hoo, Mary?"

" Yigh ; hoo does."

" Ay. Hoo 's a very feelin' body, is Nanny,—hoo is for

sure.   An' as for our Sam; why, he's very thoughtless abeawt some things. reet enough; but Lord bless yo, iv onybody does him a good turn, he never forgets it,—never. .   .   Thae knows that; doesn'to, Mary?"

"Yigh, aw do."

"When he's th' sober side eawt, neaw," continued the old woman, "he's not a mon 'at's g'in to talkin' at o'. He'll sit by the fire, hour after hour, an' never cheep. . . But, eh, yo should yer him when he's had a gill or two! Lord in heaven bless yo; he's as soft as my pocket. An' he comes eawt wi' sich nonsense as one would expect that a mon at his time o' life should ha' forgetten. . . Aw say to him, sometimes aw say, 'Sam, do houd thi tung, aw pritho! That mak o' talk may do for yung folk 'at's new wed,—but it's noan becomin' in an owd body.' An' then he will ha't that he's as yung as ever he wur. . . But, aw known better, bless yo. . . . But then, what's th' use? One's like to humour him a bit, yo known.   Thae's yerd him, Mary, when he's bin agate ov his bother, hasn'to?"

"Sure, aw have, mony a time."

"Ay, thae has. . . . But yo'd be astonished to see heaw nee the wayter lies to his een, when he's o' that shap. Iv aw happen to mention somebry 'at's been good to him, or some poor body 'at's ill off, aw con have him cryin' in a minute. . . . But, aw cannot find i' my heart to try him wi' sich things, for aw connot help thinkin' 'at it's a sign 'at he's breighkin up.   He al'ays wur a feelin' mon; but he gets war, he gets war. . . . It's me 'at knows. We'n been teed together forty year come Ladymas; an' yo' known, owd wed folk finden one another's bits o'

ways eawt, wi' livin', an' tewin', an' pooin', an' feightin' th'
world together. They're so like. Jenny, th' cat's
at that milk, sitho !"

"Scat !" said Jenny, jumping up. And then she put the
bowl upon a shelf in the buttery, and closed the door.

"Aw've my weddin' things i'th kist up stairs : an' there
they mun stop to mi deein' day. . . . Aw go an' look
at 'em sometimes, an' aw turn 'em o'er, an' air 'em, an put
fresh neps among 'em,—an' it brings owd days to mi mind,
very strung. . . . Mary, reitch that tother bo' o' wustid
off th' table, willto ?"

"Aw see noan," replied she, turning round. "Oh, it's
here," said she, picking it up from the floor, and handing it
to the old woman.

"Aye, aye," continued Matty, sighing as she took the ball
of worsted. "Aye,—aye. It isn't to tell what folk han to
go through i' this world ! Sometimes, ov a Sunday mornin',
when he's been donned in his haliday things,—at after aw've
brush't him, an' teed his hankeycher on, aw've watch't him
as he walked eawt at that very gate, an' aw've thought to
mysel' that he wur the nicest mon 'at ever trode upo' God's
greawnd ! An' he wur too. . . But come, winnot
yo have a droight o' ale ? . . Jenny, fill him a tot.
It's noan so very strung ; but it's my own brewin', an' there's
no mak o' prowt in it. Maut an' hops, an' nought else,—
nobbut spring wayter. . . . But, eh, bless my life !
Aw'm maunder—maunder—maunderin' an' clean forgettin'
what aw meant to tell yo. Aw have sich a memory ! . . .
Well, but—see yo. Th' last neet, good Sunday an' o' as it
wur,—eawr Sam coom in abeawt six o'clock, just as th'

chapel bell below yon wur tollin' in for the latter sarvice,
an' he'd two blue lin hankeychers wi' him, cromfull o' green
stuff. Yo' known what a chap he is for yarbs. Jenny took
'em on him, and laid 'em upo' top o'th drawers. An' as he
hanged his hat up a-back o'th door, he says to me, 'I've bin
gettin' some nettles for Owd Nanny, at Th' Split Brid, yon.
I wish thou'd tak 'em up i'th mornin'." 'Eh, Sam,' I said ;
'thou's never bin nettlin' of a Sunday again, hasto?'
'Why, what for?' he said, as nattle as could be. 'They
groon of a Sunday, donnot they? Thou'll want to stop th'
smo' drink fro wortchin' of a Sunday in now. I believe if
th' house wur a-fire thou wouldn't sleck it out if it wur
Sunday. It's forty years sin thee an' mee geet wed
one Sunday. I wish, now, that I'd put that off while
Monday.' Eh, yo never yerd how he went on ! 'Owd
Limper's wife geet her bed th' last Sunday,' he said.
'How leets thou didn't go an' stop that?' Eh, he
did talk ! He axed me if I'd ony notion who it wur
that made Setterday. An' he as good as towd me that
I wur a Sunday saint an' Monday divvle. But I took no
notice. Lord bless yo, we'n had mony a scog about th'
same thing. Men han ways o' their own, an' they winnot
be said by sich as me. They thinken they'n o'th wit i'th
world. So aw leet it drop, an' set th' tay out. . . . Well,
I made a bit of a fat cake, as it wur Sunday ; an' aw went
into th' garden an' poo'd some sallet ; an' nice an' crisp it
wur. As soon as he set een on it, he begun a-laughin', an'
he says, 'Eh, thou's never bin pooin' sallet ov a Sunday,
hasto?' But I took no notice. So, when we'd getten th'
tay o'er, he poo'd up to th' fire, an' began a-smookin' ; an'

I donned my spectacles, an' read th' Bible while bed-time. An' there wur no moor about it that neet."

The old woman bent down to pick up her worsted ; and whilst she was doing that, Mary rose, and said that she must be going home.

"What's o' thi hurry ?" said the old woman.

"Well, yo known," replied Mary, "aw shouldn't like to be eawt when he comes whoam."

"Nawe, nawe, thae'rt reet, lass," answered the old woman. "Go thi ways. . . . An' thae mun do as weel asto con, thae knows. Everybody's summat to meet wi' i' this world. . . . An' mind thae keeps yon chylt warm, whatever thae does. It'll get o'er it, thae's see."

"Ay, aw will."

"Well, good neet to tho, Mary ?"

"Good neet !" said Mary, wiping her eyes. " Aw'll come o' Sunday."

CHAPTER II.

Heaven bless thee, woman ; what a heap of stuff hast thou been twisting together, without head or tail.

SANCHO PANZA.

THE sun had gone down behind the western hills, and the hum of life from the village in the valley had died away. In the wood a few throstles were still tossing their rich gushes of responsive song from side to side, like choristers in an old cathedral ; and they seemed

to sing louder than ever, as if they had been neglecting their
music till the last thing ; or, like schoolboys at a late game
of cricket, wished to crowd as much fun as possible into the
lingering light, before they were called home to roost. The
wind was playing a quiet tune on its green harp behind the
cottage, by way of gentle hint to all around that it was bed-
time ; and the voices of day were gradually giving place to
those mysterious minstrels who fill the dreamy midsummer
night with melodies too fine for the ear of the sunlit hours.

Mary's way home led up into the wild moors, which rolled
away from the front of the cottage in great heathery billows
of silent solitude. As she slowly ascended the rugged by-
path the old gardener's wife stood in the doorway watching
her ; and she lifted her hands, and slowly shook her head as
she said, in a low plaintive tone, "Aye, aye ; go thi ways,
Mary, my lass ; go thi ways. Thae's getten thi wark bi th'
hond. God help tho !" The old woman stood till Mary
disappeared round a craggy knoll, and then she turned and
came into the house. Taking up her knitting she sat down
by the fire again ; and, as she arranged her worsted, she
heaved a sigh and said, "Aye, poor Mary! Hoo's tried to
some tune—hoo is that ! An' a better lass never stepped
shoe leather—never. God help her ! An' God help us o',
for we needen it, we done so." The old woman went on
knitting in silence for a minute or two ; and I was wondering
what painful story was smouldering under this sad soliloquy
when little Jenny broke the stillness by asking her grand-
mother whether she should mend the fire or not.

"Nawe, nawe," said Matty ; "it's warm enough ; but thae
may put th' dur to."

Jenny closed the door and sat down; and, as the old woman showed no disposition to speak further upon the subject that so evidently troubled her, I reminded her that she had broken off at the beginning of the story which she had promised a little while before.

"Aye, aye," said she, "so aw did, so aw did. Well, as aw wur tellin' yo, this mornin' as soon as th' breakfast wur sided aw teed a bit o' stuff up for eawr Sam's dinner, an' off he seet to th' 'Thistley Knows' a doin' some gardenin' jobs. Well, he hadn't bin gwon mony minutes afore who should come in but eawr Jonathan's daughter. . . . Sarah's getten a fine strung lass, neaw. Hoo wove at Scutcher's while they wur agate; but, sin they stopped hoo's helped her mother wi' th' clooas. Her mother taks in weshin'. Eawr Jonathan's a greight family. The Lord knows heaw he manages to scrat for a livin' these times, for he's bin eawt o' wark nine months, an' Nanny's nee th' deawn-lyin' again. . . . But, as aw wur tellin' yo, Sarah's a fine, hearty lass. Hoo'll be nineteen come Rushbearin' Sunday. But, what thinken yo? That monkey ov a lad o' Snapper's is after her, as yung as hoo is. . . . Eh; but iv aw wur her mother, see yo, aw'd tak that pouse at top o'th' yed wi' th' fire-pote iv ever he darken't my dur-hole upo' sich an arran' as that—aw *would*.' . . . He'll never do her a smite o' good; for he thinks o' nought i' th' world but race-runnin' an' wrostlin', an' pigeon-flyin', an' single-step doancin', an' sich like sleeveless wark as that. An' he's as mischievous a little twod as ever broke brade. . . . One neet aw sit knittin' at th' table under th' window theer, as it met be to-neet, nobbut it wur darker, an' o' at once my ear

27

gated o' ticklin' like hey-go-mad, an' weet began o' runnin'
eawt on it. Well, aw shaked my yed, an' aw wiped my ear,
an' better wiped it ; but it made no mends. At last aw geet
freeten't, for aw began o' thinkin' some new ailment had
taen howd on mo. So aw laid deawn my knittin' and aw
said, 'Jenny, run for thi gronfayther. There's summat
uncuth agate i' this yed o' mine. Aw believe aw'm beawn
to have a fit.' But as soon as hoo oppen't th' dur there wur
a great crack o' laughin' an' a scutter o' feet i'th' garden.
. . . An' what wur it, thinken yo? . . . It wur
nought i'th world but that ill-getten whelp o' Snapper's that
had bin squirtin' wayter into my ear through a hole i'th
corner o'th window. . . . Eh, aw wur some mad ! . . .
But, that's nought, bless yo. . . . Aw'll tell yo heaw he
sarv't owd Ailse 'at keeps th' toffy-shop deawn i'th fowd yon.
Yo known Ailse is a lone woman. Hoo lives in a little low
cot 'at stons by itsel', a bit past 'Th' Noon Sun Well.' It's
a less heawse nor this. Why, yo may touch th' bottom o'th
chamber window wi' yo'r hond nearly. . . . Well, as
this ill-mixt cowt o' Snapper's wur trailin' whoam late one
winter's neet, when he'd bin drinkin' an' doin' wi' a rackety
swarm 'at gwos to th' sign o'th ' Twitchelt Boggart ' a-playin'
at dominoes, an' sich like, he sees a mug 'at Ailse had laft
eawt o'th' dur 'at after hoo'd getten to bed. O', wur dark
an' still; an' there wur nought stirrin' but sich like rackless
neet-crows as his-sel'. . . . Well; what does he do,
but starts a-roggin' at th' dur, as iv th' heawse wur a-fire.
Well; Ailse coom to th' window in her neet-geawn; an' hoo
code eawt, 'Whatever's to do?' 'Mistress,' he said, 'dun
yo know 'at yo'n laft a mug eawt?' 'Eh, ay,' hoo says

'aw have.' 'Well,' he said, 'hadn't yo better tak it in?
There's a rook o' chaps bin cloddin' at it. Aw thought aw'd
tell yo.' 'Thank yo, maister,' said Ailse; 'thank yo mony
a time. Aw'll come deawn an' fotch it in.' Well; th' ill-
contrive't divvle—'at aw should say sich a thing,—he see'd
that th' chamber-window wur a very little un; so he said,
'Here, mistress; yo'n no 'casion to come deawn. Aw'll
reitch it up to yo.' So without givin' it a thought, hoo
thanked him again, and hoo leant forrud eawt o'th window,
while he hove th' mug up to her. An' as soon as hoo'd
getten howd on't, he bad her good neet, an' walked off.
'Good neet, maister!' said Ailse; 'an' thank yo!' an' then
hoo began a twistin' an' twinin' to get th' mug in. But th'
window wur too little,—dunnot yo see; an' theer hoo wur,
in her neet-geawn, th' hauve road eawt o'th house, ov a
snowy neet,—grinnin' an' gruntin' an' feightin' wi' th' mug,
till her arms warch't again. . . . But it wur no use.
So at last hoo sheawted after him, 'Hey! Maister! Aw say!
Tak th' mug deawn again! Aw connot get it in!' But
there wur no onswer. . . . Th' pousement wur watchin'
her off at th' hcawse-end o th' time, bless yo; but he never
cheep't. Well; yo known, hoo couldn't ston shiverin' theer
o' neet, wi' th' mug in her arms. An' there wur nobody to help
her. So, at last, hoo leet it go to th' floor wi' a crash.
'Thire!' said Ailse, lookin' deawn after th' mug, 'that's
ninepence! . . . But th' felly's noan to blame. He
did it with a good thowt.' 'Ay, aw did, Ailse,' said he,
peepin' off at th' corner. 'Good neet, owd crayther!'
Ailse see'd in a minute that hoo'd bin taen in; an' hoo gav
him a good tung-lashin' as he walked off. 'Thae'rt some

mak ov a mismanner't waistril,' hoo said, 'that theaw art.
But, i' thou'll reitch me a good-sized lump o' that mug up,
neaw, aw 'll tay tho a-top o'th nob wi't, scawndly; an' soon,
too; for theaw 'rt an ill whelp o' sombory's.   But aw 'll fot
law on tho, iv aw live while mornin', see iv aw dunnot!'
An' so hoo went on.   But hoo met as weel ha' talked to a
stoo-fuut, bless yo.   He took no moor notice nor iv it had
bin an owd cat meawin'! . . .   Eh, he 's an ill un,—
pile't-up an' deawn-thrutch't.   He desarves floggin' fro
teawn to teawn at a cart-tail,—an' he 'll get it yet,—iv he 's
luck. . . .   But aw'm missin' my tale.   As aw 're tellin'
yo,- -this mornin', cawr Jonathan daughter coom to th' dur
wi' a basket-full 'o clooas ov her yed, an' hoo code cawt,
' Is my Aint Mattie in?'   An' aw said, 'Ay; come in witho,
what arto stonnin' theer for?'   So hoo set th' basket deawn
at th' dur, an' coom in; an' hoo said 'at her mother had
towd her to co' a-seein' heaw aw wur.   An' aw said to her,
' Well, lass; thae mun tell her 'at aw'm nobbut thus an' so.
Tell her 'at aw've had a smatch o'th rheumatic again.   An'
th' spine o' my back troubles me badly.   An' aw'm ill o' my
yed betimes.   This weather's again me. . . . .   Thi
Uncle Sam's wortchin' up at th' Thistley Knowe. . . .
Hasto had thi breakfast?'   An' who said, ' Eh, ay.   Lung
sin.' . .   At th' same time aw know that they're clemmed
like wedge-wood. . .   Aw don't know heaw it is.   That
lass would ha' had a bite wi' us, neaw an' then, when times
wur good; but aw connot get her to taste, neaw.   Hoo like
as iv hoo shames to own 'at they're ill off.   An' hoo looks
hungry; an' her face is nipped wi' stomach-frost.   But,
hoo's preawder nor ever, aw believe.   An' they're o' alike,

except th' very little uns. . . . Eawr Sam sent two
shillin' up tother day; but Jonathan sent it back, an' said it
wur a —— shame iv they could'nt feight through beawt lyin'
upo' two owd folk like us. . . . My heart bleeds for
'em, see yo,—for aw know they're ill pincer't. But. aw geet
th' brass to Nanny at after, beawt lettin' Jonathan know,
dunnot yo see. Well; hoo're nearly as ill as tother; for
hoo cried, like an owd foo'. an' hoo said hoo would'nt ha'
touched it, but for th' sake o'th childer. . . But, Lord
bless my life! aw'm maunderin', an' missin' my tale again.
This yed o' mine isn't worth a row o' pins. . . . As
aw're tellin' yo abeawt eawr Jonathan lass :—' Well. Sarah,'
aw said to her; 'an' wheer hasto bin?' So, hoo towd mo
that hoo'd bin up to th' Ho' for some weshin'. an' hoo're
gooin' whoam wi't. So, aw towd her aw had to go deawn
to th' fowd wi' a burn o' nettles, an' iv hoo'd watch two or
three minutes, we'd go together part o'th gate. . . . .
Well; in a bit we set off,—hur wi' her basket. an' me wi' my
nettles; an' a bonny marlock hoo played upo' th' road.
But yo'st yer. . . . When we geet to th' corner o'th
lone, at th' side o' Amos o' Rapper shop, there wur some
stone-carts gooin' by; an' th' owd mistress at th' Parsonage.
an' two young ladies, very nicely donned, stoode upo' th'
foot-gate, waitin' till they'd getten by. As soon as Sarah
see'd 'em, hoo said, ' Aint Matty; aw'm tire't.' So I said,
' Put thi basket down, then.' Well, see yo, hoo'd no sooner
set th' basket upo' Amos dur-step, than hoo begins a-starin'
at these dresses, an' hoo made no moor ado but went
an' geet howd o' one o'th young ladies' skirts, an'
hoo says, 'See yo, Aint Matty! Come here! That's

same mak o' staff as we use't to weighve at Owd Scutcher's.
Aw could like one off it mysel'.   It's nobbut chep stuff.'
Well; yo should ha' sin that young woman turn round!
Her face wur as red as a yetter!   Hoo nipt th' skirt out o'
Sarah's hond, an' hoo says, 'Well, I'm sure!   Sich im-
pidence!' an' then, they o' three whiskt off to th' tother side
o'th' road,—as peeart as pynots.   Eh, I wur sum mad at
Sarah,—th' little snicket!   Aw didn't know which gate to
turn my een.   To be sure, th' lass did it without a thought;
but then folk like thoose dunnot look at things th' same as
sich as me does.   ' Eh, Sarah,' I said, 'thou shouldn't ha'
done so!'   Well; hoo looks at me as innocent as a flea, an'
hoo says, 'What's to do, Aint Matty? It's quare if one mun
go by their own wark beawt oppenin' their mouth to't.'   But
I pike't up my nettles, an' Sarah took th' basket, an' we geet
out o' seet as fast as we could.   An' I gav her a good talkin'
to as we walked away.   When we coom to th' corner where
I had to turn up, hoo wiped her een with her brat, an' hoo
said, 'Well, Aint Matty; yo dunnot need to sauce mo so
mich.   Aw want noan of her clooas.   But, aw couldn't help
speighkin when aw see'd that stuff,—for aw'm nearly sure
aw've woven it, iv hoo wears it.'   . . .   An', raylee o' me;
aw felt soory for th' lass after o',—for th' chylt thought
nought wrang,—not hoo.   But, they han sich awvish ways
in a country place, mon. . . .   When we parted at th' corner
o'th road, aw said, 'Neaw, Sarah, thae'll be a good lass,
winnot tho?'   An' hoo said hoo would.   An' then hoo took
off whoam, an' aw went forrud to th' sign o' Th' Split Brid
wi' my nettles.——"

And now, to my great relief, the old woman paused and

rose to stir the fire. Her little grand-daughter, who had
been turning over the pictures in an old copy of Culpepper's
Herbal, had dropped asleep, with her head on the book.
"Come, my lass," said Matty, patting her on the head; "thi
gron-dad winnot be lung, neaw. Thae's go to bed as soon
as he comes." The kettle was boiling furiously; and as the
old woman lifted it on to the hob, I took advantage of her
momentary silence, which I knew would not last long—and
I rose to go home.

"Nay, what's yo'r hurry?" said Matty. "Stop till eawr
Sam comes. I haven't towd yo heaw aw went on at Th'
Split Brid, yet."

But, "enough is as good as a feast;" and I had heard
more than enough of old Matty's twaddle for one sitting;
so I told her that I would hear it at some more convenient
time.

"Well," said she, following me to the door, "drop in
some day th' next week, iv yo'r this gate on. Yo known
aw 've no neighbours to have a bit ov a cample to. An' aw
connot talk to eawr Sam; for it mays him as crampt as a
wisket. It wur nobbut tother day, aw begun a-tellin' a tale
'at's getten eawt abeawt Tummy Clapper an' his wife, an' he
said to that lass, he said, 'Jenny, run deawn to Billy
Peighswad's as fast as tho con for some wool to put i' my
ears. An' tell 'em 'at thi gron-mother's in a scandil-fit.' He
like as iv he connot abide to yer one speighk, sometimes.
An' it's very awker't, for aw've nobry to talk to, nobbut this
bit ov a lass ov eawrs; an' hoo's noan like an up-groon body,
yo known. But, one's like to humour him."

It was a cloudless summer night; and the moon was

beginning to tinge the moorland hills with silvery light. I
should not have known that there was any wind astir but for
a sleepy rustle in the grove behind the cottage, which
sounded distinctly in the deep stillness around.

"Good neet, Matty," said I, walking out at the garden
gate.

"Good neet to yo!" replied the old woman. "Iv yo
leeten ov cawr Sam upo th' road, hasten him whoam."

Owd Cronies.

THE face of nature has been so much changed in Lancashire during the last eighty years that it is hard to conceive what the country was like three or four centuries ago. Almost within the memory of living man, the rise of modern industrialism, and the combination upon the same spot of the elements essential to success in manufacturing enterprise—coal, stone, clay, iron, and water; the great energy of the old inhabitants; the vast influx of population from other quarters, and the rapid growth of wealth and towns—these things altogether have overwhelmed the ancient features of the land like a sudden deluge; and now the county which, up to a century ago, had seen least of change, has, since that time, undergone greater alteration in its appearance and way of life than any other part of the kingdom. In ancient days, when men never dreamt of the slumbering wealth beneath the surface, its soil was reckoned among the poorest in England, and its people among the hardiest; its range of hills rolled across the country in stormy waves of lonely moorland; its cloughs were impassable

28

swamps; its forests were wild hunting-grounds, kept for the
pleasure of the king and the nobles of the land; its roads
were chiefly ancient bridle-paths; and upon its plains there
were vast tracts of wild heath and spongy moss. Sterile,
remote, and unattractive, it held little communion with the
rest of the kingdom, except when stirred by some great event
which roused the whole land to war. Then, indeed, the
strong-bred bowmen and billmen of Lancashire mustered
from their leafy nooks and followed the banners of their
proud aristocracy to many a well-fought field, where their
stern front and deadly shafts have spread dismay amongst
the boldest foes. In those wild times Lancashire was famous
over all England for its terrible bowmen. In many of its
ancient towns—as at Rochdale and Bury—there are places
which, though now covered by modern streets, still bear the
name of "The Butts," where the ancient population practised
archery, then the warlike sport of the yeomanry of England.
Some parts of Lancashire cherish the old love of archery to
this day: and on the south-eastern border of the county the
legends of Robin Hood are still associated with the land.
Upon the wild western slope of Blackstone Edge an immense
crag stands alone—the rugged monarch of the moorland—
in the lowmost part of which there is a small cave, known all
over the country side by the name of " Robin Hood's Bed,"
and upon the opposite hills there are great boulders, which
he is said to have flung across the valley. Ancient Lancashire was a comparatively roadless wild; and its sparse
population—scattered about in quaint hamlets and isolated
farm-nooks—were a rough, bold, and independent race,
clinging tenaciously to the language, manners, and traditions

of their fore-elders ; and despising all the rest of the world, of which they knew next to nothing. Its simple life was singularly self-contained, and what little traffic it had was carried on by strings of pack-horses, upon rugged tracks, which had been the pathways of the ancient inhabitants of the land from the earliest historic times. These facts leak out in all that we read of Lancashire in the olden time. The learned Camden, after travelling over the rest of the kingdom, implored the protection of Heaven before entering on a region so little known and of such wild repute as Lancashire was in those days; and Arthur Young, the famous Suffolk agriculturist, writing about the end of the last century, complains in vigorous, old-fashioned English about the state of the Lancashire roads at that time. He lived long enough, however, to see the beginning of a new state of things in that county.

CHAPTER I.

MIDDLETON IN THE OLDEN TIME.

O' crom-full o' ancientry.
OUR FOLK.

IN the time of the Plantagenets, when the woods of Lancashire were wild and thick, when its air was pure, and its rivers clear, and all the country wore the livery of nature, Middleton must have been one of the most picturesque villages in the county. In those days, when the neighbouring hamlet of Blackley was deep in the heart of a forest —when " Boggart Ho' Clough " was a "deer leap," and " Th' White Moss " was a lonely waste of evil repute, little Middleton, with its fine old manorial hall, its moated rectory, its timber-built houses, and its venerable church upon the hill, must have been a pretty nest of rural life in the midst of a green and quiet country.   Even now, when the land has been stript of its ancient woods, and all nature seems to have been pressed into the service of modern necessiti:s, the country around is prettily varied in feature, and the little town is pleasant to the eye.   The history of the place is obscure until the beginning of the thirteenth century when Henry the Third was king, in whose reign a church existed, upon the site of the present one.   In the same reign the manor was held, "by military service," by a family bearing the local name—the Middletons of Middleton ; one of whom, Sir James Middleton, is associated with the founda- tion of a chantry chapel in the ancient church of Rochdale, five miles off.   From the Middletons this manor passed, in the reign of Henry the Fourth, into the hands of the Bartons, then a famous family in Lancashire.   From the Bartons the lordship of Middleton passed into the possession of the Asshetons—men of great renown in their day.   Baines says :—

Margaret, the daughter of John Barton, Esq., having married Ralph Assheton, Esq., a son of Sir John Assheton, knight, of Ashton- under-Lyne, he became lord of Middleton in her right, in the seven- teenth of Henry the Sixth, 1438, and was the same year appointed a page of honour to that king.   He was knight-marshal of England, lieutenant of the Tower of London, and sheriff of Yorkshire, 1473— 1474.   He attended the Duke of Gloucester at the battle of Haldon or Hutton Field, Scotland, in order to recover Berwick, and was created a knight *banneret* on the field for his gallant services. 1483. On the succession of Richard the Third to the Crown, he created Ralph vice-constable of England, by letters patent in 1483.

And thus it was that the little town of Middleton emerged from its old historic obscurity, and became associated thenceforth with the great events of the times, through connection with the Asshetons, in the person of Sir Ralph Assheton— the terrible "Black Lad" of Lancashire story—one of the most ambitious and active members of a powerful family, of whose tyranny tradition still preserves the remembrance. Dr. Hibbert, in his history of Ashton-under-Lyne, says of this famous favourite of a cruel king :—

He committed violent excesses in this part of the kingdom. In retaining also for life the privilege of *guld riding*, he, on a certain day in the spring, made his appearance in this manner, clad in black armour (whence his name of "Black Lad"), mounted on a charger, and attended by a numerous train of his followers, in order to levy the penalty arising from neglect of clearing the land from *carr gulds*. The name of the "Black Lad" is at present regarded with no other sentiment than that of horror. Tradition has, indeed, still perpetuated the prayer that was fervently ejaculated for a deliverance from his tyranny :—

> Sweet Jesu, for thy mercy sake,
> And for Thy bitter passion,
> Save us from the axe of the Tower,
> And from Sir Ralph of Assheton.

The present church seems to have been built upon the site of the previous edifice, by Sir Richard Assheton, a grandson of the "Black Lad." On the south side of the church is the following inscription, which indicates both the rebuilders and the date of the present edifice : " Ricardus Assheton et Anne,

uxor ejus, Anno D'ni MDXXXIIII." This Sir Richard was,
for his valour and bravery at the battle of Flodden Field,
knighted by Henry the Eighth, and had divers privileges
granted within his manor of Middleton. An ancient window
of stained glass commemorates the death of sixteen of the
band of Middleton archers, who fought under Sir Richard in
that famous fray. The church contains numerous monuments
of the Asshetons ; and part of the armour of the same "Sir
Richard," dedicated by him to Saint Leonard, of Middleton,
is still preserved in the church. These Asshetons seem to
have been a stirring race of men through many a century,
and it is curious to speculate upon what kind of life was led
by the obscure tenantry of these warlike lords of Middleton,
in those

> Dear lamented times
> When theft and homicide were jokes, not crimes :
> When burning peels and towns were acts of merit,
> And red revenge became a lad of spirit ;
> When every eye saw fairies, ghosts, and devils
> Frisk in the moonbeams in their midnight revels.

The life of the aristocracy is recorded in many ways, but of
the undercurrent of human existence we know very little.
We have still a curious picture left of what kind of life was
led by the ancient gentry of Lancashire in the "Journal of
Nicholas Assheton, of Downham, in Ribblesdale," who was
a scion of the knightly family of Middleton. It is a singularly
minute record, full of graphic details, and of "touches which
make the past more than present." In Dr. Whitaker's
analysis of its contents we get a vivid glance of this charac-
teristic memorial. He says :—

Thus ends the journal of Nicholas Assheton, then a young and active man, engaged in all the business of, and enjoying all the amusements of the country. What he might in a rainy day and a serious mood have done for himself I will now do for him, or rather for his readers—analyse this curious fragment, and assign every portion of time accounted for to its proper occupation ; premising, however, that there are great chasms in the journal, one of three months at least ; and that the days which are marked " home," &c., are passed over as blanks, though perhaps better spent than many which are more strongly characterised. In this period, then, he accounts for the hearing of forty sermons, three of them by as many bishops, and one for communion. On the other hand he records sixteen fox chases, ten stag hunts, two of the buck, as many of the otter and hare, one of the badger, four days of grouse shooting, the same of fishing in the Ribble and Hodder, and two of hawking. Shooting with the long and crossbow, horse matches, and foot races were the other means of consuming time without doors. Stage plays and cards are never mentioned. As a scale by which the writer measured his own degrees of intemperance, and a catalogue of his excesses, let the reader attend to the following : " Merrie" eleven times, " verie merrie " once, " more than merrie " once. " merrie as Robin Hood " once, " plaid the bacchanalian " once, " somewhat too busie with drink " once, " sick with drink " once, " foolish " once, and lastly, " fooled this day worse " once. With all these confessions we hear of neither resolutions nor attempts at amendment. In this short period he saw four deaths of the Asshetons ; he attended the king at Hoghton Tower ; he assisted in quelling a private quarrel in Wensleydale ; attended the king's commission in the great cause of the copyholds of Blackburn Hundred ; and took two journeys to London on business with the Court of War ls and Star Chamber. A man more largely connected, or extensively acquainted with his county, there probably never was.

Such was Nicholas Assheton, of the time of James the First, who, in the course of his Journal, mentions, again and again, his visits to "Cousin Assheton, of Middleton." A little nearer our own day we find these Asshetons still abreast with the events of the time. In the Cromwellian war, Ralph Assheton, of Middleton, was an energetic adherent to the Parliamentary cause. On the 24th of September, 1642, about one hundred and fifty of his tenants, in complete arms, joined the forces of Manchester in opposition to the Royalists. He commanded the Parliamentary troops at the siege of Warrington. He was engaged at the siege of Lathom House, and led the Middleton Clubmen at the siege of Bolton-le-Moors. In 1648 he was a major-general, and commanded the Lancashire soldiery of the Commonwealth, on the marshalling of the Parliamentary forces to oppose the Duke of Hamilton. His son Ralph, however, espoused the cause of Charles the Second, and was created a baronet in 1663.

The old hall of the Asshetons at Middleton must have been a fine specimen of an ancient manor house. It was situated in a park, hard by the town, "but having been modernised about the latter part of last century, and afterwards deserted by its owners, it was entirely demolished in 1845." Canon Raines says of it :—

Middleton Hall was a timber-built house, surrounding two spacious courts, and approached by two bridges over a moat. The great entrance hall was described, about the year 1770 or 1771, as "resembling a ship turned upside down," from which it might appear that it had rested upon crooks, and was probably built in Edwardian times by the Middletons. the then material owners. This ancient hall was hung round with two or three hundred heavy matchlocks, with buff-coats and some half suits of armour, which have all been removed and dispersed within living memory. Some of this armour is now in the collection of George Shaw, Esq., of St. Chad's, Saddleworth.

This memorable old house saw many generations of strong Englishmen. In Samuel Bamford's "Early Days" I find the following notice of it : -

The Old Hall was perhaps one of the finest relics of the sort in the country. It was built of plaster and framework; panels, carvings, and massy beams of black oak, strong enough for a mill floor. The yard was entered through a low wicket, at a ponderous gate, the interior of the yard was laid with small diamond-shaped flags; a door led on the left into a large and lofty hall, which was hung round with matchlocks, swords, targets, and hunting weapons, intermingled with trophies of the chase.

The site of the hall is now occupied by a cotton factory, and no traces of its ancient park remain. Speaking of the old parsonage, as it appeared in his youth, Bamford says :—

The rectory was then an old irregular-looking edifice, built partly of brick and partly of stone, with a moat round it, and shot-holes in the walls for musketry or cross-bows.

Bamford dwells lovingly upon the ancient features of his native town, and the pleasant appearance of the country around, when he was a boy—that is, about the end of the last century. He speaks of the old stained-glass window in the northern aisle of the church, representing "a band of archers, kneeling, each with his bow on his shoulder, his quiver at his breast, and his name above his head," commemorative of Middleton men who were slain at the battle of Flodden Field, under the command of Sir Richard Assheton. He says :—

On the north side of the churchyard wall stood an old thatched timber and daub house, which we entered down a step, through a strong low door with a wooden latch. This was "Old Joe Wellins's," the church alehouse, a place particularly resorted to by rough fellows when they had a mind for a private drinking bout. It was a current tradition that gentlemen roadsters, who lived by levying contributions on the northern highways, made this their "boozing-ken," or place of concealment, after their foraging expeditions. Nevison and Turpin are said to have frequented this old secluded alehouse.

29

He speaks plaintively of the days when "few of the lonely, out-of-the-way places—the wells, the by-paths, the dark old lanes, and solitary houses—escaped the reputation of being haunted by boggarts, feeorin', witches, fairies, clapcans, and such like beings of terror, who were supposed to be lurking in almost every retired corner or sombre-looking place, whence they came forth at permitted hours to enjoy their nocturnal freedom." He babbles pleasantly of the green fields and shady dingles of his youth ; and he tells us of the old haunted "Owler Bridge" over the Irk, where his father used to sing hymns as he crossed in the dark when on his way to take lessons from "th' wise mon o' Hulton-fowd ;" and of the haunted Grammar School; and of " Boarshaw," where, in ancient days, a boar of great size having been killed by one of the Asshetons, of Middleton, the boar's head was thenceforth borne as the family crest ; and of " Doom Cloof," a deep clift or gully, "darkened by timber and underwood, and haunted by fairies and clapcans ;" and of the ancient house at the head of " Blomley Cloof," which was haunted by the ghost of "Owd Blomley," a fierce re-tainer of the Hopwoods, of Hopwood, during the civil wars. With the plaintive delight of a romantic second childhood, he tells over the old superstitious country tales of an age gone by, and lingers lovingly among the lonely woods, the green rambling-grounds, and shady dingles of his youth, and closes his graphic " glimpse of auld lang syne " with these words : " But the cloughs and hollows in the neighbourhood of Middleton are now as bare as if they had been swept by a fire. The woods, the shelters, the bosky dingles, the pleasant summer shadows are no longer there ; nay, the hedgerows are stinted; the wild roses and honey-bines are nearly all gone: "The glory has departed." They are gone, as he himself now is gone, and as all things on earth must go. The old man sleeps in peace, close by the church of St. Leonard, almost the only relic of ancient Middleton now left, except the rectory, and the old timber-built inn called the Boar's Head, which is the scene of our story.

—

CHAPTER II.

THE OLD BOAR'S HEAD.

Where greybeard mirth and smiling toil retired,
Where village statesmen talked with looks profound,
And news much older than their ale went round.

GOLDSMITH.

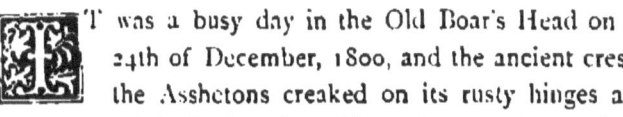'T was a busy day in the Old Boar's Head on the 24th of December, 1800, and the ancient crest of the Asshetons creaked on its rusty hinges as it swung to and fro in the wintry blast. It was a famous house at that time, for all the coaches that ran between Manchester and York called there; and this alone made it the centre of the village life and of village loungers seeking news. In addition to which the old inn was remarkable for its cleanliness and the general geniality of its appearance inside and out. Its accommodation was excellent; its fare was bountiful, and of the best quality; its charges were reasonable; and its home-brewed ale was renowned for strength and purity. The host and hostess, too, were of the good old, strong, deep-

blooming breed of country folk—genuine descendants of the
stiff, unbridled Saxon race—the very pair to keep a substantial
wayside inn sweet, and sound, and homely. Genial, generous,
and business-like, with a thorough hatred of dirt, disorder,
and injustice, they had a warm side for poor humanity in all
its forms, and a natural love of the busy varieties of roadside
life. Giles Buckley, the landlord, was a stalwart, large-bodied
specimen of an Englishman. In the old time of bills and
bows he would have been a formidable antagonist upon the
battle field. With a mind free from all underhand dealing,
he was happy-hearted, humorous, kind, and naturally of an
obliging disposition ; a foe to riotous excess, he was yet able
to stand any amount of drink, which enabled him to entertain
by his presence any number of successive guests. Naturally
intelligent, and fond of fun, his way of life had acquainted
him with great varieties of mankind ; and he was an inex-
haustible storehouse of tale, anecdote, and song. Such was
the usual simplicity of his life and the strength of his constitution that, when any extraordinary occasion called for
special indulgence, a night's rest brought him forth again as
fresh as a daisy and as firm as a rock. With these attractions
no wonder that the Old Boar's Head was one of the best
accustomed inns for miles around. Many a weary traveller
hastened onwards in the dark to gain the shelter of that
famous inn ; and many a forlorn wanderer's heart was made
glad in its glowing kitchen. Here, too, when twilight came,
the village folk met to enjoy the company of their neighbours,
to tell old tales, and to discuss the news of the day and the
gossip of the village.

It was a busy day, for, in addition to the usual bustle of

the place, the landlord had invited a few friends to supper on Christmas Eve ; and the whole house was astir to do honour to the feast, which had been the talk of the village for a week. In the kitchen the stout old landlady bustled about among her servants, looking anxiously after the preparation. "Now, lasses," said she, "do stir yoursel's! Yo' known what we han to do. Get this place sided up ; th' coach 'll be here directly. There's three dinners i'th front parlour, an' th' men 'll be in fro' th' stable afore long. Sally, go into th' nooks an' corners wi' that brush o' thine, an' be sharp. If I've ony clennin' done, I mun have it done thrugh-an'-through. I cannot abide your scamblin', sham-smart ways. I like to *be* clen, as well as to *look* so. I wish to the Lord thou'd manage to do thi wark beawt so mich tentin'. Thou'll make a bonny dossy of a wife for sombry, when thou comes to be left to thisel'. It 'll be weary deed for ony poor lad 'at gets thee, if thou doesn't awter."

Sally blushed and nettled up. "I never seed sich a house as this for clennin'," said she ; "yo're al'ays agate—th' day to an end. My mother never——"

"Keep thi tung between thi teeth," replied the landlady ; "an' dunnot tell me about thi mother. I mun ha' th' wark done as I want it, an' not as thi mother wants it. Come, stir thoose shanks o' thine ! Thou'rt gettin' to fat and to full ! I'm talkin' to thi for thi own good. But thou'd raither sit by th' fire fro' mornin' to neet, countin' cinders, an' up to thi een i' dirt, if folk would let tho live an idle life. I declare it seems as if some poor craiters were born to be miserable theirsel's, an' to make everybody miserable about 'em. I've no patience wi' sich like slotchin' wark. Do try some bit like,

lass; an' dunnot need so mich talkin' to. . . . Martha,
I'll chop that suet; go thi way up stairs an' help to make
th' beds. . . . Nanny, how's that beef gettin' on? . . .
Tell Bill to mend these fires. . . . What's yon bell?"

It was a bright, cold winter's day. The wind came
steadily, with cutting keenness, from the north-east. The
snow-drifts by the wayside were crisp and hard : the hoar-
frost glittered, but did not melt in the sun; and the high
road rang under foot like a metal plate. The old church
clock had struck twelve, and a knot of grammar school lads
were "sleddin" down the brow which leads to the church,
whilst others stood by the footpath, watching them, and
blowing their nails; whilst their gleeful clamour sounded far
into the little town. In front of the "Boar's Head," a stiff-
built, old, grey-haired hostler was puffing and blowing as he
curried and brushed the hide of a traveller's horse, whilst
another was briskly engaged in whistling "Britons, strike
home!" as he swept the coble-pavement before the doorway.
A dense flock of sparrows, flitting from the road up to the
eaves of the house, and back again, filled all the air in front
of the inn with a gleeful twitterment; whilst a redbreast
chanted, by fits, his pretty, plaintive winter song from the
leafless thorns on the opposite side of the road. Two or
three villagers were lounging about the doorway, as usual,
talking to the hostlers.

"Jack," said one of them, "that's noan an ill mak of a tit"

"Nawe, bi th' mass," replied Jack; "there's some comfort
i' hondlin' a thing like this. It's as bonny a bit o' horse-flesh
as ever I clapt e'en on. Nevison, th' heeway-man, had one
the very marrow o' this. I can remember it as if it were
to-day."

"By Guy, Jack ; this is happen it."

"It's hectum as like ! What the dule arto talkin' about? Both him an' his horse were laid low afore thou were born. Beside. Nevison's tit had a white star upo' th' for-yed ; an' it were raither of oather finer i'th leg nor this. Oh, nawe ; Nevison's were never sin upo' this side at after he robbed th' vicar o' Rachda', at ' Th' Slattocks.' Let's see ; that'll be forty year sin' come peigh-cod time."

"Well ; him an' Dick Turpin,—they'n played some bonny marlocks upo' these roads, bi o' accounts."

" Aye, aye ; now thou talks. They wur two lively cowts, for sure. But they seldom tried their pranks long together upo' one spot. Old Joe Wellins says ' 'at they dropt in at th' church ale-house yon, one back-end, at after they'd robbed th' York mail, and they lee theer a whole week, as snug as two mites in an owd cheese ; though th' hue and cry were out all o'er England.' Well, they crope off one mornin', just afore skrike o' day ; an' in about two year after they turn't up again, i'th deeod time o' th' neet ; but they were so swapped that no mortal mon could ha' towd 'em. . . . Hasto bin up at owd Jim's, at Goom Cloof, latly ?"

" Aye ; I code th' last week about a cauve he had to sell. But I coom off at th' edge o' dark ; for I may no 'count o' stoppin' i' that nook after delit (daylight); 'Owd Blomley's' agate war than ever."

" What, th' boggart ?"

" Ay; an' th' warst boggart there is upo' this country side for flaysome deed, an' powlerin' about i'th neet time ! I'd back it again oather witch, fairy, clapcan, Nut Nan, Jenny Green-teeth, Baum Rappit, Radcliffe Dog, or the dule hissel' !

I wouldn't live i' that hole, sitho, if I met wear red shoon !
I wur sittin' i' that kitchen a twothre week back, just as th'
owl-leet coom on, an' o' at once there were a great yeawl
room down th' chimbley, an' th' arm-cheer shifted out o' one
nook into tother, an' never mortal soul laid finger on it !
But, bi th' mass, my yure began o' stonnin' straight up, an' I
crope out o' that cote as if I'd been steighlin' summat. I
gav a bit of a glent o'er my shoolder as I went out, an' th'
tungs an' poker were just startin' o' doancin' a three-hond
reel wi' th' churn. But, by th' mon, I never looked beheend
me again ; for I thought it'd be my turn th' next. An' I're
in another township in a twothre minutes."

Just then a snatch of song came from the open window of
the taproom :—

When they snapen your heart, an' they stinten your fare,
   It's time to be joggin' away :
When th' pitchers are empty, an' th' pouches are bare,
   It's time to be joggin' away.

" Hello, Jack ; who's yon ?"

" It's Craddy o' Batters," replied Jack. " He's sittin' i'th
tap-reawm be hissel' yon, singin' an' talkin' to his pint pot,
as usal. Go thi ways in to him."

Here the landlady looked out at the doorway.

" Bill," said she, " when thou's done sweepin', come in to
thi dinner ; an' then fill yon boighler up, and look to th'
fires. Jack, come to thi dinner."

" I'm comin' as soon as I've put th' horse up," replied the
oll hostler. " Jone," said he to his village crony, " thou
looks starve't ; how leets thou doesn't go inside an' get a
saup o' summat warm ?"

"Well, Jack; if thou thinks I'm partial to starvation thou'rt off at th' side. But I'm one o' thoose chaps 'at hasn't mich to stir on, thou knows. I've been rootin' up an' down mi clooas a good wile to find brass for another gill: but I can leet o' nought but two gallows-buttons an a 'bacco papper."

"Come; I'll lend tho a shillin'."

"Fork out, owd brid! Thou talks like an angel!"

"Theer it is, sitho. Now creep into the tap-reawm at th' side o' owd Craddy yon, an' I'll come to yo in a bit."

CHAPTER III.

THE LANDLORD'S GUESTS.

The winds wh'stle cold;
The stars glimmer red
The sheep are in the fold,
And the cattle are in the shed.

OLD GLEE.

Man, wh't changes come o'er us. I mind when master and servant sat a' at ae table; and, if ye'll bel'eve me, I've seen mair wit playe'l off at a dinner time than ye'll gather now in half a year.

SCOTS COMEDY.

THE winter sun sank down behind the snow-clad hills; and as night crept on, clear and cold, the bustle of village life died away into stillness, save where the fire of the blacksmith's forge threw a broad, red glow upon the glittering highway, and the chime of his busy

hammers rang loud and clear in the deepening silence all
over the little town, mingling now and then with bursts of
laughter from a knot of loungers, who were whiling away
the winter evening among the fun that gathered round the
dusky smithy's genial glow. The cloudless sky was thick
with stars, and their solemn light filled all the frosty air with
a subtle radiance, which strengthened as the sunless hours
stole on. It was a hearty, hardy, old-fashioned winter night.
The village doors were closed, for the frost was intense, and
the north wind blew keen and wild, whistling weird melodies
in the lock-holes and crevices of many a lonely grange,
whose inmates shuddered as they huddled closer round the
fire, listening with superstitious fear to the rattle of doors
and windows, and the wild sough of the blast outside. All
signs of life in quaint little Middleton were stilling down,
except where a cottage candle threw a flickering gleam into
the night, or the shrill voice of a woman cut through the
cold air as she called home her truant lad, who had lingered
behind his mates "sleddin'" upon the steep below the
church. All else was deepening down into starlit silence,
save where the bright windows, and open, straw-strewn doorway of the Old Boar's Head attracted the shivering traveller
with its cheerful glow.

Amongst the guests invited by old Giles to his Christmas
supper there were Randal Holt, or "Rondle o' Raunger's,"
an old schoolmaster, who was looked up to by his neighbours
as a kind of "hamel-scoance," or lantern of the village;
"Jem o' th' Har-barn," a sturdy yeoman, who reckoned
among his ancestors one of the band of Middleton archers
who followed Sir Richard Assheton to Flodden Field; "Jim

o' Dauber's,' a village painter; "Jone o' Gavelock's," a humorous old weaver; Henry Shaw, better known as " th' wool chap," a well-known traveller in the flannel trade, and an old customer at the Boar's Head. These, with the principal tailor and the principal shoemaker of the town,—all old cronies together,—made up Giles Buckley's Christmas party.

Of course the news of the feast had spread over the town long before the time; and when the eventful evening came on, the lads of the village, as they returned from their wintry games, lingered about the doorway of the Boar's Head, yammering, and sniffing at the odours of the kitchen; and then ran home with the savoury tale.

"Eh, mother," said the tailor's lad, as he darted into the house with his wooden "sled" upon his back. "there's moore beef up at th' Boar's Yed than there is onywheer else i' this world! I've bin a-smellin'! Eh, I wish I live't at yon house! An' there's goose amung it, too, mother,—I can tell goose. . . . Eh, I am some hungry! Wheer's my supper?"

"Thou'rt al'ays hungry. Sit tho down an' warm thisel' a bit, like a good lad; till I've finished my ironin'. I shan't be mony minutes. An' put that "sled" o' thine out o' th gate."

"Eh, mother, couldn't yo' gi' me a lump o' oon-cake to be gooin' on wi'?"

"Make a less din for a minute or two, I tell tho! Thou fair moiders me! Bless my life, thou met (might) be clemmed!"

"Eh, mother, I wish I wur gooin' to my supper wi' my faither to-neet. Dun yo think he'll bring ony goose back wi' him?"

"Not he, marry. Whatever arto camplin' an' talkin' about?"

"Mun I sit up till he comes whoam?"

"Nawe; thou mun do nought o'th sort. Thou mun get thi porritch, and go to bed like a good lad; an' thou shall ha' some goose to-morn. It's hanged up i' the buttery yon. It's Kesmass to-morn thou knows."

"Eh, mother; I wish it wur Kesmass every day,—dunnot yo?"

"Marry, choilt, how thou talks," said she, setting a bowl of milk and a thick piece of bread before him; "get that into tho; an' let it stop thi mouth."

About six in the evening Giles's guests began to trickle in at the doorway, and a tailor was the first man up on the ground.

"Hello, Snip," said Giles, as the tailor came in at the front door, drest in his Sunday clothes, with a fruited sprig of holly stuck in his button-hole; "by th' mass, thou'rt as grand as Thornham rushcart! A merry Christmas to tho, owd craiter! I' gadlin, we's never look beheend us after this. Come thi ways in!"

"A merry Christmas to yo, Giles!" replied the tailor, rubbing his hands. "Here; don't put th' door to; Lapstone an' owd Rondle are upo' th' road,"

"That's reet," replied Giles; "th' moore an' th' merrier!"

"They're here now," said the tailor, as the two old cronies came up to the door, laughing noisily.

"Roll up, an' buy 'em alive!" cried Giles, slapping old Randal on the back. "Tops o' trees, an' shinin' daisies! Buy 'em or lev 'em,—I'll bate nought at mi stuff! Come in, lads! I hope yo're i' good fettle! Wheer's tother?"

"There's three or four on 'em upo' th' gate; an' I pept in

at th' painter's as we coom by. He're agate o' rubbing his yed wi' toppin'-fat."

"Here, Giles," said the landlady, "tak 'em into this room till th' supper's ready. There's a good fire."

"Come in here, lads," said Giles, "an' sattle yo'rsels a bit, while they setten th' table out. Here, I'll buttle for yo'. Cowd ale afore supper, lads, an' aught 'at yo'n a mind for at after. Tak howd, and weet yo'r whistles, for a start."

As the servant entered with another jug, a snatch of song came from the tap-room hard by :

> Peighs-porritch whot, peighs-porritch cowd,
> Peighs-porritch in a dish, nine days owd.

"Craddy o' Batters, for a crown," cried Randal.

"It's nought else," replied Giles ; "he's been here mony an hour. Th' owd lad's started Kesmass o'ready ; an' it'll last him till 'Th' First Market,' I'll uphowd. By th' mass, let's have him in ! What, he's somebody's choilt, an' he'll do wi' his supper as weel as ony on us. What say'n yo, lads ?"

"Fot him in ; he's rare company,' said Randal.

"So said, so done," replied Giles. "Mary, tell owd Craddy to come here."

"Win yo ha' th' whole lot in ?" said the landlady.

"Why, who is there beside ?"

"There's owd Bonny Mouth ; an' Jem o' Pratty Strider's."

"Well ; what the hangment, they're neighbours' childer. Let's have 'em o'! This is no time to make fish o' one an' flesh of another! Let's have 'em o'!"

In came Craddy and his friends, all in their working gear, which contrasted strangely with the holiday garb of the rest of the company ; but everybody was in good humour, and everybody made them welcome; although Craddy was getting merry with the drink he had taken during the day. " Never mind, lad," said Giles, slapping him on the shoulder, ' thou'll be as reet as a ribbin when tho gets a bit o' beef into tho !" They had hardly got well seated amongst the rest before the landlady came in to say that supper was ready ; and away they steamed in the wake of old Giles, towards the place where the feast was spread.

The quaint room was profusely decorated with evergreens ; a great bush of mistletoe hung from the centre of the ceiling; and there was a huge log burning in the fire-grate, which filled the place with a ruddy glow. The long table was spread with bountiful piles of roast and boiled meats, and with pies, and savoury country messes : and all the house was redolent of good cheer.

Giles took the chair at the head of the table, in front of a noble sirloin, which became his presence well.

" Here, owd craiter," said he, to Jem o' th' Har-barn, "go thee to th' tother end, an' try thy thwittle upo' yon goose. Thou use to be a rare hond at mowin'; an' I've sin tho thwite very hondsomely at a goose afore now. Come, off with tho, an' bother noan."

The burly yeoman smiled quietly, and took his seat at the other end of the table ; and two finer specimens of the old English breed rarely faced one another.

" Now, lads," said Giles, "are yo getten sattle't into yor boozes ? "

" Ay, we're o' reet," said Jone o' Gavelock's, "we're o' reet, if I can get Craddy, here, to hutch a bit fur off."

" Craddy," said Giles, " hutch up lower, mon ; an' draw

nar to th' table. Thou looks as if thou were beawn to fire a
gun. Thou's no 'casion to be fleyed. I want yo to have fair
elbow-reawm, for yo'n a deeol to do. . . . Come, that's
better."

" Now, then," said Giles, knocking upon the tal le with his
carving-knife, "are yo ready?"

" O' ready," replied Jone o' Gavelock's.

" Well, then," said Giles, rising from his seat, " God bless
everybody 'ats i' this house,—an' everybody o'th outside
on't,—for a start! Lads, yo're as welcome as th' flowers o'
May! Yo seen what there is afore yo. I hope yo're in good
fettle; an' I hope it'll agree wi' yo! Fo' to,- an' spare
nought! . . . Who says beef?"

" Britons, strike home!" said Jem o' th' Har-barn, at the
other end of the table, seizing his carving-knife. " Who says
goose? It's as prime a brid as ever I clapt e'en on! Come,
Craddy, owd lad; I'll gi' thee a leg to begin wi'. Jone, help
him to some potitos."

" Buttle out, free!" cried Giles to the servants, "an' look
after these plates!"

And to it they fell, all round the jovial board,—hammer
and tongs; and for the next hour or so there was a ceaseless
clatter of knives and forks and plates; and the servants were
kept in continual motion among the guests.

" Come, Lapstone," said Giles, "back thi cart up.—an' fill
again!"

" Stop, an' rosin a minute," replied Lapstone; " I'll be
theer again directly."

" Now, Craddy, my lad, how arto gettin' on?"

" O' reet," said Craddy, " I'm nobbut wyndin' (taking
breath) a bit."

"Don't stop short of up, lads," said Giles; "let another reef out, an' start again! . . . Jem, thou'rt lookin' after thisel', I guess, among th' rook."

"We're doin' weel here," replied Jem. "If thou'll mind that end o' th' table, I'll keep 'em goin' here."

"Giles," said old Bonny Mouth, "I'll trouble yo for a bit moore o' that under-cut."

"Ay; an' thou'st have it, my lad," replied Giles; "thou'st have it, if this knife hondle stops on."

"Come, Gavelock, owd brid, wakken up; thou'rt noan sto'in' (getting tired) arto?"

"By th' mon, it's gettin' time, I think. Thou doesn't want to see mo brawsen, doesto? I measur't a hond-bradth off between my singlet an' th' table, afore we started, an' they're welly met. I've done very weel, Giles,—I've done very weel."

"What! thou'll have a bit o' cheese, sure?"

"Well, aye, aye,—a bit o' cheese, as thou says. I think I've an odd nook laft for that."

At last the festive fray sank down into peace; the hungriest of the hungry had eaten his fill, and the knives lay at rest.

"Come, Jone," said Giles to Jone o' Gavelock's, "say a word or two afore we gettin' up."

The old weaver rose slowly from his seat, and looking quietly round the board, he said: "Lads, we'n had a rare supper. I've played a good stick mysel', an' I'm thankful. We dunnot leet o' sich a do as this every day. It's a bit o' Kessmass sunshine! Giles, here's good luck to thee an' thine! I wish we may never do ony wur nor we'n done this n·et; an' I wish that everybody i' th' world may do as weel; for there's a deeol o' folk 'at's noan so weel off, an' one connot help but think about it at a time like this, yo known. But, as far as I'm consarn't, I feel fain 'at I'm wick, an' yo looken as breet as rook o' squirrels o' round,—except Craddy, theer; I think he'll repent to-morn 'at he hadn't a bit moore o' that beef."

"Oh, nay," cried Caddy; "I've done very weel! I couldn't bant another smite!"

"Well then, that'll do," continued the old weaver. "God bless yo o'! Giles, owd lad, here's luck to tho again! An' now I think that'll do."

And the old man sat down, amidst cries of "Amen to that!" and "Bravo, Jone!"

When they had drunk the health of the host and hostess, with "three times three and one cheer more," which made the mistletoe-bush twirl round upon the ceiling, as if it enjoyed the fun, old Giles returned thanks in a few hearty words, and then said, "Now, lads, let's go out an' stretch er legs a bit till they siden these things. It'll help to sattle your suppers. An' when they'n getten o' reet, we'n come back an' have bit of a frisk."

CHAPTER IV.

Come all ye weary wanderers
Beneath the wintry sky,
This day forget your worldly cares,
And lay your sorrows by.   CHRISTMAS SONG.

HE supper things were cleared away, the room was trimmed up and swept, the fire had been mended, and the guests were seated once more around the board with their glasses before them. Pipes and tobacco lay about. At the head of the table Giles sat, with an old-

31

fashioned silver ladle in his hand. in front of a great bowl of
punch, chatting cheerfully as he served the steaming liquor
out right and left. At the other end "Jem o' th' Har-barn"
presided over another bowl of the same inspiring compound.
"Bith heart, lads," said he, "this is a grand brew! Talk
about posies! It's making my yure curl! Here. Craddy,
tak howd! That'll tickle tho up, owd brid,—wi' thi rags, an'
jags, an' tinkerin' bags!"

"Now, lads," said Giles, rapping the table with his ladle,
"as we're getten meeterly weel saddl't again, I propose that
every mon round th' board oather tells a tale or sings a sung.
What say'n yo?"

"I'll agree to that," said Snip, who was a good singer; and
"Agreed,—Agreed!" was the general cry.

Turning to the shoemaker, who was a notable budget of
country story. Giles said "Lapstone, what says thou?"

"Oh," replied the shoemaker, "I'm never again a good
thing!"

"Well, then," said Giles, "we couldn't do better nor start
wi' thee!"

"Nay, nay," replied the shoemaker, "let somebody else
begin. I'm noan at concert pitch yet."

"Thou shall be, afore thou'rt mich owder," said Giles.
"Here, let's fill for tho. Thou'rt hanging fire terribly. Theer,
sitho. Sup, an' then brast off."

"Giles, I think thou should set us agate, thisel'."

"Me! nought o' th' sort. Rats afore mice! Come, gi'
mouth.— an' bother noan."

"Well, well," replied the shoemaker, "I've oft yerd that
force were physic for mad dogs. What is to be mun be,—
there's nought else for it."

And quietly trimming the bowl of his pipe, the old man oegan the tale of

THE WICK SECK.

"It's a bit of a crack o' mi' faither's," said he. "I've yerd him tell it time an' time again, when I wur a lad; an' it isn't a week sin I wur tellin' it mysel, up at owd Mistress Taylor's yon, at th' sign o' 'Th' Trumpeter.' . . . It's about an owd farmer, known by th' name o' 'Judd o' Jers.' He live't upo' Chadderton side, yon, an' he wur reckon't very weel off. His wife had been deeod some time, an' he'd nought but hissel' an' an only daughter,—as hondsome a lass as ever stept shoe-leather. Hoo wur th' pride o'th country side, an' hoo commonly went bi th' name o' 'Th' Rose o' Chadderton.' Well, gentle an' simple, an' rich an' poor, they'rn cockin' their hats at this lass of owd Judd's, on o' sides. Two or three fine lads listed through her; an' I believe one poor divvle fro' Owdham drown't hissel' becose hoo'd ha' no truck wi' him. It matter't nought to Mary who coom,—silk or fustian,—they had to fo' back,—every one on 'em but *one*,—an' that wur a limber, weel-mettle't yung farmer, co'd 'Dick o' Rattler's,' 'at coom out o' Thornham. As fine a lad he wur, I believe, as ever bote off th' edge of a cake,—an' he turn't out as weel at th' end of o',—but he'd bin raither of a rackle turn up to that time. Well, o' somehow, this lass of owd Judd's an' him geet terrible thick, an' come what would, hoo were like as if hoo couldn't bide to clap her een upo' nobody else nobbut him. But owd Judd thought there were nought i' th' world good enough for his daughter; an' there were so mony ill tales flyin' about this Thornham cowt that he

wouldn't yer tell on him at o', an' he swore mich an' moore,
that if ever he catch't him about th' house again he'd tan
his hide for him ; an' he would ha' done, too,—for he wur a
great strung chap, an' he'd a very strung temper.   Hall Ben
o' Blakeley were a lusty fellow, an' as swipper as a kitlin ;
but owd Judd thrut him o'er th' hedge, one Middleton
rushbearin',— just like a bit of a catch-bo'.   Well, i' spite of
o' 'at could be said an' done, this lad stuck to th' lass, an'
th' lass stuck to th' lad,—-for they were gradely fond o' one
another,—an' th' moore they were sunder't th' moore they
crope together. . . .   Well, th' owd chap never wur
rough wi' his daughter, but he wur anxious about her,—for
hoo wur th' leet of his e'en,—an' he'd getten it into his yed
that this Dick wouldn't behave weel to her; beside, he
didn't like th' notion of his hard-getten brass bein' squander't
bi a fast-gated spendthrift, sich as he thought him at that
time.   So he talked to Mary about it again an' again; but
hoo did nought nobbut fret ; an' when hoo began o' cryin'
th' owd lad couldn't ston it at o', an' he use't to walk off wi'
a sore heart, for he lippen't o' nought but ill to th' poor
lass. . . .   Well, o' wur no use.   These two wur so ta'en
up wi' one another that they still met at by-times i' odd
nooks an' corners, as they weren't allowed to meet i'th
oppen ; an' owd Judd couldn't go to noather market nor
fair, but, o' somehow, Dick geet to know on it aforehond.
Well, things went on o' this ill fashion till, at th' end of o',
Dick played one bit of a marlock 'at brought th' upshot on,
an' put o' to reets.   It seems that he wur determin't, if Mary
couldn't get out o' th' house to him, he'd goo into th' house
to Mary, o' somehow ; so he made it up wi' two of his mates

that they should put him into a seck, an' co' at owd Judd's
wi' th' cart, just afore lockin'-up time, an' ax if they could
lev it i'th kitchen till mornin'. Well, they put a lot o' saw-
dust into th' bottom of a lung seck; an' then Dick geet
into 't; an' they packed him nicely about wi' hay, so as to
make it look round, an' shapely; an' they laft two or three
peep-holes at th' top, so that he could get his breath, an' see
what were gooin' on; and he'd a bit of a knife in his hond,
so that he could let hissel out when th' time coom. Well,
when neet coom on, Mary sit bi th' kitchen fire, mendin'
stockin's, an' hearkenin' for th' sound o'th wheels, bringin'
this seck of hers,—for hoo wanted to get it snugly in afore her
faither coom whoam fro' th' market. Well, it wur gettin' nee
bed-time, an' still owd Judd hadn't londed. . . . . But
stop: I'm missin' my tale. . . . . . . It seems that
one o' these cronies o' Dick's had bin tattlin' at th' owd
alehouse i' Chadderton Fowd, an' he'd letten cat out o'th
bag; and somebry that wur theer happen't to leet of owd
Judd at th' market th' same day, an' he towd him th' whole
tale about this seck, what there wur in it, an' when it wur to
lond. Well, th' owd chap wur terribly put about; for he
see'd that it wur no use strivin' ony lunger; and he went up
and down th' market frettin' and mutterin' to his sel', 'I
met as weel give in, an' let 'em have it to theirsels; and try
to make a good job of an ill un. . . . But I'll sattle wi'
yon seck this neet!' So he hung about later than usual, to
gi' th' seck time to get londed. Well, it wur gettin' nee bed-
time when these cronies o' Dick's set off wi' th' cart wi' th'
seck in it; an' they knocked at owd Judd's kitchen dur, and
axed if they could lev th' seck till mornin', as they weren't

gooin' whoam. An' Mary said: 'Ay; they could lev it an'
welcome :' an' hoo towd 'em to rear it up at th' side o'th
owd clock, 'at stoode in a nook nearly out o' seet. So they
rear't it nicely up, an' then they bad her 'Good neet,' and
crope out, sniggerin' an' laughin' to theirsels. Mary watched
'em off, out o'th yard, an' down th' lone ; an' then hoo
barred th' dur beheend 'em. Hoo hearken't a minute or
two, till o' were still ; an' then hoo went quietly up to th'
seck, an' said, ' Dick !' An' th' seck gav a bit of a wriggle,
an' said, ' Mary !'

"' Eh. Dick,' said Mary again, talkin' to th' seck ; ' this
is quare wark !'

" Th' seck stirred again a bit, an' said, ' Let mi yed out !'

"' Stop a minute,' said Mary. An' hoo went an' hearkened
at th' dur. O' wur still, an' there wur nought comin' ; so hoo
crope back, an' unteed th' seck-mouth ; an' out popped
Dick's yed, wi' his yure full o' hayseeds.

"' Wheer's thi faither?' said Dick.

"' I expect him every minute. Get in witho' till I've
getten him to bed.'

"' Give us a kussin' !'

" An' hoo gave him one : an' hoo said, ' Eh, Dick, whatever mun I do if my faither finds this out ?'

"' Thou mun do as I towd tho, an' let me put th' axins
up. Mon, th' owd chap 'll come to, if we getten wed. . .
Gi' mi another !'

"' Eh, Dick, I wish he would let tho come into th' house,
an' see one daicently. I don't like this mak o' wark. It'll
come to no good.'

"' Well, let's get wed, I tell tho ! He connot get o'er

that! An' I'll come where thou art as lung as I live,—if I
have to come down a chimbley! . . . Come, give o'er
cryin', lass! I can ston aught but that! I wish th' owd
chap didn't think so ill on me,—so as things could go on
straight-forrad an' gradely. . . . . . Wipe thi een,
lass, an' gi' me another; or else thou'll ha' me cryin' too.
. . . . I wish my honds wur free! . . . .
Com a bit nar! . . It's first time i' thi life thou ever
clipt a seck, isn't it, lass?"

"'Eh, Dick, pritho, don't talk! I connot bide to think
about it! . . Husht! . . . Put thi yed in, put thi
yed in! Mi faither's comin'!'

"Dick needed no moore tellin'. Down went his yed:
an' Mary's hands flutter't as hoo teed him up again. Then
hoo ran an' unbarred th' dur; an' hoo'd hardly getten nicely
sit down bi th' fire to her stockin's again afore her faither
walked in.

"'Faither,' said Mary, 'yo're very late.'

"'Ay,' said Judd, givin' a sly glent round th' kitchen:
'I've stopt too lung.'

"'Win yo have ony supper?'

"'Nawe.'

"'Yo'd better ha' summat. It's ready here.'

"'Nay; I've no stomach for supper to-neet.'

"Well, th' lass felt soory for him; an' hoo could hardly
help for cryin'; an' hoo kept hur yed down at her wark.

"'Thou may go to bed, Mary,' said Judd; 'I'll lock
up.'

"'I've a lot o' stockin's to mend yet,' said Mary.

"'Well, then,' said Judd, 'I may as weel have a bit of a

smoke ;' an' he lit his pipe, an' planted his cheer so that he could see o' round th' kitchen.

"For th' next quarter of an hour there weren't a word spokken ; but there wur three folk i' that hole that wur about as ill thrutched i' their minds as ony poor craiters i' Christendom could be,—partickilar th' seck. That began o' wishin' it wur a whoam again.

"In a bit owd Judd knocked th' dust out of his pipe, an' said, 'Well : I may as well be goin.' Thou'll not be long, I guess?'

"'Nawe,' said Mary, 'I'll not be long.' But hoo never lifted her yed when hoo spoke.

"Then owd Judd geet up, an' stretched hissel', an' began o' saunterin' about kitchen, till he coom up to th' nook where th' seck wur rear't again th' clock, an' theer he made a full stop. Mary tremble't from yed to fuut ; an' th' seck began o' feelin' poorly.

"'Hello,' said Judd ; ' what's this seck ? '

"Well, th' poor lass wur i' sich a flutter that hoo could hardly get a word out ; but hoo managed to tell him that two o' Stakehill Robin lads had co'd wi' th' cart, at th' edge o' dark, an' axed if they could lev this seck till mornin'.

"Owd Judd gav a surly sort of a grunt ; an' he said, ' I think they'd better ha' takken it where it belungs,—or else ha' put it into th' shippon, yon. This is no place for sich like things. . . . . . I wonder what there is in it?'

" An' he gav a rough punce at th' seck, where it bulge't out a bit.

"Th' seck jumped, an' said, 'Oh !',—an' weel it met, for th' owd lad had a sayrious fuut.

"Mary dropt th' stockin's to th' floor, an' went as white as a sheet.

"'It's happen barley,' said Judd; an' he punce't at th' seck again : an' th' seck jumped, and said 'Oh !' again,—for this time it let upo' th' shins.

"Then Judd nipt up a knobstick, an' began a weltin' at th' seck as he said, 'to penk th' dust out on't a bit,' an th' stick happen't to come across summat tender, for th' seek gav a grate yeawl, an' started o' swearin' like a drunken tinker.

"'Hello, said Judd, 'what han we agate now? This seck's of a feaw-mouthed breed! There's some mak o' jumpin'-stuff in it too. . . . . Here ; I've shot mony a queer thing i' mi' time ; and I'll have a bang at a seck, for once!'"

"An' he nipt th' gun down.

"When th' seck yerd that, it tumble't out o' th' nook, an' began o' rollin' up an' down th' floor; an' it skrike't out 'Howd, howd! D—— it, howd a minute! Untee this bag,—an' let's have a chance for mi life! Cut this bant ; I'm noan beawn to dee in a poke !'

"'If ever seck deed i' this world,' said Judd, 'thou dees this neet !'

"Well, th' seck roll't, an' wriggle't, and skrike't 'Murder!' an' Mary dropt on her knees, an' cried 'Eh, faither ; for God in heaven's sake, don't shoot! It's Richard !'

"Owd Judd grounded th' gun, as if he wur fair dumfounder't,—though he knew o' about th' job—th' hare an' th' hare-gate.

"Bi this time Dick had cut a bit of a hole i' th' seck, an'

32

he'd getten his yed out at th' top ; an' theer he lee upo' th'
kitchen floor, starin' up at Judd, an' Judd starin' down at him.

"Mary had dropt into a cheer i'th corner, cryin' as if her
heart would break.

"When these two had stared at one another a while, Judd
said, 'Well, an' what does to think o' thisel'?'

"'I think I'm a —— foo',' said Dick.

"'Thou'rt as like one,' said Judd, 'as aught 'at ever I
clapt een on.'

"'I dar say,' said Dick, hagglin' at th' seck to get hissel' out.

"'Well, an' what dost to want here?' said Judd.

"'Yo'n known that a good while,' answered Dick ; 'I want
yo'r Mary.'

"Owd Judd gav a turn or two about th' kitchen ; an' then
he said, 'Here, I'll hae this job settle't afore thou comes out
o' that seck. I've gan thee th' bag mony a time, but thou's
taen it thisel' at last. An' now, I think we'n try what a noose
'll do for tho,—as there's nought else for't. . . . Here :
get out o' that seck, an' let's see what thou'rt like, for thou'rt
a weary sect at present.'

"Well, Mary weren't a minute wi' helpin' Dick to get out
o' th' seck ; and they sattle't th' whole concarn, straight off.
Dick went liltin' back to Thornham that neet, as leet as a
layrock ; an' Mary crope off to bed i' better heart nor hoo'd
bin for mony a year afore. Well, about a month after that
they geet wed at Middleton Church here ; an' they live't wi
owd Judd till he deed. Dick wur a good-hearted lad, an' he
turned quite stiddy ; an' they'd as fine a family as ever sun
shone on. One o'th grondsons lives upo' th' same lond
now ; an' they han' th' owd seck by 'em to this day."

CHAPTER V.

I love a ballad but even too well, if it be doleful matter
merrily set down, or a very pleasant thing indeed and sung
lamentably.   CLOWN, IN THE WINTER'S TALE.

THE shoemaker's story was received with a buzz of
approbation all round the board.

"Well done, Lapstone!" said Giles; "that's a
good tale; an' thou's towd it weel! . . . Push thi glass
here; I'm sure thou'rt dry. . . . Now, lads; yo'n had
a start. Who's th' next? . . . But stop; afore we gwon
ony fur, let's buttle out an' pipe up, an' have a bit of a chat.
Send yo'r tots up! . . . Now then; is their nobody at
th' table 'at can give us a bit of a ditty, for a change? . .
Here, Snip; thou use't to be a good hond at a sung. Brast
off, owd brid!"

"Well," said Snip, "I'm willin' enough; but my supper's
noan sattle't yet, mon; an' it's hard wark singin' through a
pile o' beef. Beside, I haven't a memory worth a hep now.
I know lots o' bits o' sungs. They done weel enough for
one to wortch to; but I don't think I could waggon through
a sung of ony sort fro end to end. Th' fact is, Giles, I
known nought at o' about aught i' this world, nobbut bits."

"Well, let's have a bit then," said Giles. "Come, get
agate; an' give o'er preachin'."

"O' reet," said Snip: "I'll try my hond at 'Tum Pobs!'"

"Tum Pobs," said Giles, rapping on the table with his

ladle. "Snip's beawn to give 'Tum Pobs.' . . . Now then, gi' m juth, owd brid !"

With his pipe in one hand, an' his glass in the other, Snip turned his face to the ceiling, and began :—

> Tum Pobs wur a good-nature't sort of a lad ;
> He wove for his livin', an' live't wi' his dad :
> He wur fond o' down-craiters. an' th' neighbours o' said,
> That he're reet in his heart. but he'd nought in his yed.
> > Derry down.

> Nan o' Flup's wur a lass that wur swipper and strung :
> Hoo'd a temper o' fire, an' a rattlin' tung ;
> Hoo're as hondsome a filly as mortal e'er see'd,
> But hoo coom of a racklesome, natterin' breed.
> > Derry down.

"Now, then," said Snip, "I towd yo I should be fast. . . But, stop. . . . This Nan o' Flup's wur gettin' thirty year owd ; and hoo thought it wur about time to look round, an' tak a chance o' some mak ; so hoo began o' settin' her cap at this lad :—

> An' hoo coodle't, an' foodle't, an' simper't, an' sken'd,
> Till Tummy geet maddle't clen up i' th' fur end.
> > Derry down.

> He're so lapt up i' Nan, both i'th heart an' i'th yed,
> That I doubt he'd ha' dee'd if they hadn't bin wed :
> So at last they stroke honds, an' agreed to be one ;
> An' hoo tice't him to church,—an' poor Tummy wur done.
> > Derry down.

> An' when th' news o' this weddin' geet down into th' fowd,
> Folk chuckle't an' laughed. an' thought Tummy wur sowd ;
> An' th' women o' said, " Nan's to mich for yon lad ,
> He'd better ha' stopped till he deed wi his dad."
> > Derry down.

But they buckle't together, for better an' wur ;
An', at first, things wur reet between Tummy an' hur ,
An' they'rn meeterly thick, both by dayleet an' dark,
Till th' wayter o' life cool't 'em down to their wark.
                    Derry down.

Then Nan lost no time, but coom back to hersel' ;
An' hoo cample't, an' snapt, as no mortal can tell ;
An' poor Tum o' Pobs soon fund out that his wife,
Though an angel at first, wur a divul for life,
                    Derry down.

Here the singer stopped again, and hemmed, and coughed,
and played with his pipe.

" It's no use," said he, " there's another hole i' th' ballet."

" Hark back," said Giles.

" Rom a bit o' talk in," said Rondle o' Rogers, " an' get
end-way."

" Come, I'll try," said Snip, trimming his pipe again. . . .
Well, Tum o' Pobs soon fund out that he'd dropt in for a
boighlin-piece ; but he determin't to make th' best on't ; so
he gran' an' bode, fro' day to day ; an' he'd a decol to bide,
for Nan went wur an' wur ; till, at last, hoo hector't an'
natter't o'er him to that degree that he hadn't a minute's
comfort bi neet nor day. But still Tum took it quietly ; an'
that made her wur nor ever,—for hoo'd bin brought up
amung o' maks o' racket,—an' hoo couldn't ston a quiet life.
So,—to make ill wur,—hoo began o' hittin' him, and scrattin'
his nose-end wi' forks, an' flingin' things at him :—

It wur sometimes a pitcher, an' sometimes a pon,—
Nan didn't care what,—if it let o' th' owd mon.
                    Derry down.

An' if that didn't vex him, her temper wur ich,
Hoo'd nip up a tough-lookin' lump of a switch ;
An' sometimes it lapt round his yed wi' a bend,
An' sometimes it coom across Tummy's nose end.

Derry down.

"An' so they toart't on, o' this ill fashion, year after year,
till, at last, Nan wur ta'en ill,—

An' hoo flang no moor pots at owd Tum for a while.

Derry down.

"Well, at th' end of o', Nan dee'd,—th' same as other
folk, -an', o' somehow, poor owd Tum missed her just as
mich as if hoo'd bin an angel ; for, after o' 'at he'd gone
through, Tum wur a good-nature't chap, an'

As Nan wur laid down he hove mony a sigh,
An, o' somehow, th' owd lad made a shift for to cry.

Derry down.

"Theer," said Snip ; "that's end o' mi sung. It's been a
mixture of a trot and a canter ; but I've done as weel as I
could."

"Thou's done very weel, Snip," said Giles, "but it's
nobbut a bit, after o'. I think thou should give us another
bit of a stave, to make up wi'. Bang off again,—while thou'rt
warm under th' saddle."

"Here, here," replied Snip ; "I'll have a bar's rest, if
yo'n a mind. Let Craddy try his hond. He knows a
ballet forty verses lung. I'll come in again, at after he's
done."

"Forty verses, eh?" said Giles. "By Guy, that'll last
Craddy till to-morn at noon ; for he al'ays sings as if he're a

a funeral. It'll tak' him hauve-an-hour to get through one verse. . . Bi th' mass, he's asleep ! . . . . Come, Craddy, my lad ; let's see what thou'rt made on !"

But Craddy had been boozing all day, and he was fast sinking into a state of maudlin helplessness ; and flourishing his pipe in the air, he said :—

"Ay,—fill it up ! . . . . Robin at th' Crowshaw Booth has a lad 'at can creep through a cat-hole !"

"Here ; I think we'n let him alone," said Giles. "It's gettin' time for him to be gooin' up yon broo. . . . . . Come, Snip, owd lad ; fill this bit of a gap up, an' then we'n co' o' somebody else."

"Stop," cried Jem o' th' Har-barn, "we'n a volunteer at this end. Rondle's beawn to give us a stave. . . . Silence ! . . Goo on, Rondle."

And old Rondle struck up,—

> Bill o' Sheepsheawter's ;
>   Robin o' th' Dree ;
> Rondle o' Sceawter's ;
>   Twilter an' me ;
> We made Mall o' Sleet's
>   Owd pewter pots ring ;
> That neet wur a neet
>   To comfort a king !

> Rondle sang keaunter ;
>   Robin sang bass ;
> Twilter sang o' maks
>   O' comical ways ;
> Th' tenor wur fine,—
>   Bill took it up well ;
> An' th' tribble wur mine,—
>   I sang it mysel'.

Th' first we'd a psaum,
  An' then we'd a sung;
An' then we sang glees,
  Till th' rack-an'-hook rung :
An' merry owd Mall
  Chim't in like a brid,
As hoo tinkle't to th' tune,
  Upo' th' owd kettle-lid.

" Weet yo'r whistles," said Mall,
  " It makes better chime."
" Stop, an' rosin," said Bill,
  " It's gettin' hee time."
" A tot-a-piece, bring,"
  Said Rondle, " an' then.—
Like layrocks o' th' wing,
  We'n tootle again."

We tootle't an' sang
  Till midneet coom on ;
We caper't down th' broo,
  Bi' th' shinin' o'th moon ;
As we wander't o'er th' moss,
  Bill lap shoolder-hee ;
An' " I'm fain at I'm wick !"
  Cried Robin o' th' Dree.

" Well done our side !" said Jem o' th' Har-barn.   " Thi
ballis-pipes are i' fine fettle, Rondle, owd lad ; good luck
to tho !"

CHAPTER VI.

Three-man-song-men all, and very good ones; but they are
most of them means and basses; but one Puritan amongst them,
and he sings psalms to hornpipes.   WINTER'S TALE.

HE clatter of applause which followed old Rondle's
song woke up poor Craddy, who had been sitting
in a kind of doze, with half-shut eyes. He started
to his feet; and waving his pipe in the air, he cried out,—

Reet leg, lift leg, under-leg, over-leg;
Th' little bird sings in a mornin'!

"Owd Ben, at 'Th' Slattocks,' had a daughter wed, an' a
keaw cauve't, an' a mare foal't, an' a cat kittle't o' in one day.
There, nought i' Englan' can lick that!"

Then he dropt on his seat again, and closing his eyes
again, his pipe fell from his fingers.

"It's time for that lad to go whoam," said Jem o'th
Har-barn; "he con ston nought."

"Poor Crad," said Giles; "he's hard wortch't an' under-
fed; an' he's noan o'er paid; an' when he comes to a hearty
feed, an' a warm fire, he's sooner done up than sich as thee
and me, Jem. . . . But he's asleep. Let him rest a
bit; an' we'n see how he goes on. I'll see him safe londed."

"Well, Giles," said Jem, rising from his chair, with his
glass in his hand, "here's good health an' good hearts,—an'
milk and meighl enough for us o'!"

33

"Th' same to thee, Jem!" said Giles.   And the toast
went heartily round the board.

"An', now then, Giles," said Jem, "as I'm no hond at
tellin' a tale,--If thou's nought again it,—I'll do a bit of a
stave mysel'."

"Bravo, Jem." said Giles, "get agate, owd lad!" . .
Silence," cried he, rapping the table with his ladle.

And, in a deep but melodious voice, Jem o' th' Harbarn
began this song :---

It's of three jolly hunters, an' a-hunting they did go :
An' they hunted, an' they halloo'd, an' they blew their horns also.
     Look ye there!

An' one said, "Mind yo'r e'en, an' keep yo'r noses reet i'th wind,
An' then, bi scent or seet, yo'n leet o' summat to yor mind."
     Look ye there!

They hunted, and they halloo'd, an' the first thing they did find
Was a tatter'i hoggart, in a feelt, an' that they left behind.
     Look ye there!

One said it was a boggart, an' another he said " Nay :
It's just a drunken tinker that has gone an' lost his way."
     Look ye there!

They hunted, an' they halloo'd, an' the next thing they did find
Was a turnip in a stubble-field, an' that they left behind.
     Look ye there!

One said it was a turnip, an' another he said "Nay :
It's just a cannon-bo' at owd Noll Crummill thrut away."
     Look ye there!

They hunted, an' they halloo'd, an' the next thing they did find
Was a cratchinly owd pig-trough, an' that, too, they left behind.
     Look ye there!

One said it was a pig-trough, but another he said " Nay
It's some poor craiter's colfin," an' that caused 'em much dismay.
Look ye there!

They hunted, an' they halloo'd, an' the next thing they did find
Was a jackdaw, lyin' cowd an' still, an' that they left behind.
Look ye there!

One said it was a jackdaw, an' another he said " Nay ;
It's nobbut an' owd blackin'-brush 'at somebry's tbrut away."
Look ye there!

They hunted, an' they halloo'd, an' tbe next thing they did find
Was a gruntin', grindin' grindlestone, an' that they left behind.
Look ye there !

One said it was a grindlestone, another he said " Nay ;
It's nought but an' owd frozzen cheese 'at somebry's roll't away.
Look ye there !

They hunted, an' they halloo'd, and the next thing they did find,
Was a bull-cauve in a pin-fowd, an' that, too, they left behind.
Look ye there !

One said it wur a bull-cauve, an' another he said " Nay ;
It's just a painted jackass that has never larnt to bray."
Look ye there!

They hunted, an' they halloo'd, an the next thing they did find,
Was two young lovers in a lane, an' these they left behind.
Look ye there !

One said that they were lovers, but another he said " Nay
They're two poor wanderin' lunatics —come let us go away.
Look ye there!

So they hunted, an' they halloo d till the setting of the sun ;
An' they'd nought to bring away at last, when th' huntin'-day was done.
Look ye there !

Then one unto tbe other said, " This huntin' doesn't pay.
But we'n powler't up an' down a bit, an' had a rattlin' day.
Look ye there!

"Jem, owd lad," said Giles, "thou's a rare voice,—an'
thou al'ays had.—I've yerd it mony a time, when thou's bin
after th' dogs, up i' Thornham Heights, yon ; but, if I wur
thee, th' next time I sang a sung I'd pike one 'at had oather
some sense or some fun in it. There is'nt mich o' noather
on 'em i' that thou's just gan us."

"I'll tell tho what, Giles," replied Jem, "I doubt this bit
o' supper hasn't agreed wi' tho very weel, for thou'rt gettin'
cam'd as a crushed whisket ; an' I think it's hee time thou
tried thi' hond thisel. . . . Come, get agate, and let's
see what thou can do !"

"Thou has me theer, owd lad," said Giles ; "but bide a
bit, bide a bit,—I'll come in i' my turn, thou'll see. . . .
Come. chaps, buttle out ; yo're doin' nought."

"Ay, come," said Jem o' th' Har-barn, flourishing his
ladle, "drink up, and no heel-taps. Here, send yor glasses
this road on. Come, Henry, straighten that face o' thine ;
arto beheend i' thi rent, or is th' wool trade out o' flunters ?
Cheer up, owd lad ; all things has but a time. It's a poor
heart that never rejoices, mon. Cheer up."

"I'm o' reet, Jem," replied th' wool chap.

"Well, then," said Jem, "what arto lookin' so rivven about?"

"God bless thi life, Jem," said th' wool chap, "I'm noan
rivven. I'm as happy as a cat in a tripe shop ; but I've bin
watchin' owd Craddy theer, as he sits chunnerin' to hissel',
wi' his e'en shut, till I feel as drowsy as if I'd bin hearkenin'
a lung sarmon after a hearty meal."

"He's sound asleep now, I see," said Jem. "Thee wakken
up, ony how. Thou's sin a deal i' thi time : come tell us
summat or another."

"Nawe, nawe ; I'll come in a bit fur on. Try th painter, here ; he's as lively as a cricket, an' his tung's as limber as a lamb's tail. Try th' painter."

"Ay, ay," said Giles, at the other end of the table. "Ay, ay, an' nought but reet noather. Come, Dabble, old craiter, get into thi looms. Thou's generally a bit o' summat to say. Thou mun oather sing or tell us a tale."

"Well," said the painter, "I don't know many songs, but——"

"Howd, howd a minute," said Giles. "Don't sing, that's a good lad,—don't sing. Now I remember th' last time thou tried to sing i' this hole it stopt th' clock, an' turn't th' ale sour ; an' it made us o' ill for a week after. If I wur a house, an' thou tried to sing i' my inside, I'd fo' a-top on tho. So, as far as singin' gwos, we'n let tho off."

"Well," said the painter, "just as you've a mind : but I used to be reckoned a very fair tenor up at th' owd chapel, yon."

"Husht, Dabble, my lad," said Giles, "husht ! Not another word about singin' ! Keep thi tenor to thisel' this neet ! If they wanten it up at th' owd chapel, let 'em have it, an' welcome ; but keep thi tenor to thysel' this neet, I pritho ! . . . Let's see. didn'to paint a sign or summat once, co'de ' Th' Turk's Yed ' ? I remember some mak of a tale about it. Tell us that."

"Very well," said the painter, "if you think I'm not intrudin', I'll tell it as I can."

"Come, come," said Giles, "get agate o' thi tale, an' don't make a barn-owl o' thisel'."

CHAPTER VII.

THE PAINTER'S STORY.

I wol yow telle a litel thing in prose,
That oughte like yow, as I suppose,
Or elles certes ye be to daungerous.
CHAUCER.

OW the painter was a natural genius in his art,
although in other respects he was a man of no
especial mark, and of very little culture. Under
an air of uncommon simplicity, he concealed great shrewd-
ness in worldly affairs ; and his conversation was a quaint
mixture of artistic insight, cunning innocence, dry humour,
and maundering inconsequentiality.

"Come, Dabble," said Giles, "get forrad wi' thi tale."

The painter screwed up his mouth, as usual, and began
with an air of school-boy hesitation.

"Well, ye know, Giles, I've painted a good deal o'
portraits in my time——'

"Ay, ay," said Giles ; "I know thou'rt a clivver chap,
Dabble. Get eend-ways wi' thi tale. Thou talks as if thou'd
a fish-hook i' thi tung."

"Well, ye know, Giles," replied Dabble, "I'm not a man
as has been used to talkin' among sich like glib-tongued
people as you ; so you must excuse me bein' so slow. For
my mother used to say when I was a boy——"

"Get eend-ways, I tell tho," replied Giles; "or I'll fling th' ladle at thi yed!"

"Very well, then," said Dabble, "if you'll promise not to fling th' ladle at me, I'll try to go on. . . . Well, as I wus saying, I've painted a good deal o' portraits in my time,— that is, when I wasn't engaged in somethin' as had rather more weft in it. Though,—mind ye,—a man as has any power in him, he may put a good deal into a portrait,—if he likes,—for, mind ye, Giles, there's a great deal in the very commonest face as you can meet when ye come to consider it properly. Sir Joshua Reynolds, now, he knowed all about that, as well as any man livin'. . . . Well but, this that I was going to tell about—. . . . But, stop. You may fill this glass again, if ye please; an' then I can go on comfortably. . . . There; thank ye! Now, I'm all right! . . . Well, I should happen to be about five-an'-thirty years of age when it happened. I remember my birthday was on the fourteenth of November, owd style, at a quarter-past three in the morning: an' both me an' my mother had a very hard time of it, I can tell ye. But never mind that; we got over it in the end, an' that's more than some can say. . . . Well, at this particklar time I was livin' in a town not above a hundred miles from here,—but I'd better not tell ye where it was, or else ye might know the man. His name was John somethin,—I forget just now,—but I remember that people as didn't admire him much used to call him "Jone o' Blunders." He was very well off; but when you've said that you've done, for he hadn't much else about him, except his paunch; an' I can assure you, Giles, that that was a thing which would ha'

made ye look at him a second time,—that is, if ye'd never
seen his face; for, to tell ye truth, he was ugly enough to
make into a corn-boggart. The very dogs used to bark at
him, an' then run away, when they met him on the street.
But never mind. The fact is, Giles, that at time I had very
little to stir on, an' I was right down glad of any sort of a
job as would help to make both ends meet; for, don't ye see,
Giles, I was a married man, an' there's always somethin'
wantin' where there's a wife an' children about. Well, one
gloomy day, when I was sittin' by myself in my room,
potterin' away at somethin' or another, the latch was lifted
an' all at once a great big ugly fellow comes walkin' right in,
with a bandy-legged dog at his heels. He didn't knock nor
nuthin', but he came right in : an' the look of his face made
me shake in my shoes. . . . I remember I used to
wear shoes at that time. I wear boots, now, ye see. Well,
I thought at first that he must be a bum-bailiff; for he was
the very cut o' one o' that breed : an' I began o' feelin'
rather queer; for, don't yo see, Giles, I owed a little money
at that time, an' when I looked at this surly-lookin' chap an'
his dog, I thought to mysel, 'It's all over; I'm in for it
now!' But I thought it was best to keep a civil tongue in
my head, so I said, 'How dy'e do, sir! It's a fine
mornin'!' Well, ye know, I'm not generally given to
lyin',—not as a rule,—but that was a sneezer for
a start; for, between you and me, Giles, it was
anything but a fine mornin'; for it was damp an'
drizzly, an' as dark as a fox's mouth; but the fact
is, Giles, I hardly knew what I was sayin' just at
the time, don't ye see. However, I might have been

talkin' to a milestone, for he took no notice, but kept
standin' there, i'th middle o' th' floor, with a cudgel in his
hand, starin' round as if he was goin' to mark my goods
for rent. I didn't half like it, I can tell ye. Besides, there
was this ugly dog of his; it stood just behind him, lookin'
through his legs, with its eyes fixed right on me, as if it was
choosin' a spot to fly at as soon as the word was given. I
can assure you, Giles, that the general state of affairs made
me feel bad in my inside for a minute or two. At last
I managed to pluck up my spirit a bit, and I asked him if
he would take a chair. Well, ye see, Giles, in the first place
that was a queer thing to say to a bum-bailiff, to begin with.
Besides, it was wrong in another way, for I hadn't a single
chair in the place. The only thing I had to sit on was two
three-legged stools. I wonder now that the fellow didn't
hit me with his stick. But, however, as I was tellin' ye, I
was in such a flustration that I pulled up one o' these stools,
and I said, 'Will ye take a chair, sir, if ye please?' But it
was no use, bless ye. He still kept agate o' takin' no
notice. An', between you an' me, Giles, it was a good job ;
because the stool was such a little un that he wouldn't have
been comfortable, for he was three times as broad as top o'
th' stool, an' that leaves rather too much margin outside, ye
know, Giles. Don't ye think it would, now?"

"I think nought at o' about it," said Giles. "Get
forrad witho,—an' get done witho,—for thou'rt makin' me
as mazy as a tup. I doubt there's moore clout than dinner
about this tale o' thine. . . . Here; grease thi wheels,
an' start again."

"Thank ye, Giles," said Dabble; and drinking off his

34

glass he said, "Now then; I shall soon be at it, if you'll not hurry me. When I was a boy at school, my mother used to say——"

"Here, come, come," said Giles; "we'n ha' noan o' that. Get forrad wi' thi tale, an' bother no moore about thee an' thi mother."

"Stop a minute!" cried Jem o'th Har-barn; "hadn't we better have a bit of a sung or summat, between; an' then he can go on again?"

"Nawe, by th' mass!" said Giles; "we'n let him get it o'er,—if ever he will get it o'er! . . . Come; get forrad! . . . Silence, for Dabble!"

"I'm ready," said the painter, trimming his pipe. . . . "Let's see; where did I leave off? . . . Oh! . . . Well, as I was sayin', this man as I took for a bum-bailiff stood a while in the middle o'th floor, lookin' round without takin' a bit o' notice of anything that I said to him. At last he gave a surly sort of a grunt, and he said, 'I underston' thou'rt a sort of a painter.'

"An' I said, 'Yes; I have painted a good deal in my time.'

"'What mak?'" said he.

"'Well.' I said, 'some of my work's not so bad—though I say it myself.'"

"'That's nought to do wi','" said he, groundin' his cudgel, with a bang; 'arto a sign-painter, or what mak o' paintin' doesto do?'"

"An' I said, 'Oh; all sorts.'"

"'Conto do faces?'" said he.

"'Of course I can,'" said I.

"'Doesto think thou could paint mine?'"

"'Certainly,' said I. 'Whereabouts?' I saw, yo know, that one of his-eyes was a great deal darker than the other; and having had a little experience in the art of restoring certain departments of the human countenance to the original tone of colour, which had been lost by the sudden application of injurious external influences,—ye know, Giles,—I began to think this was another job of the same kind, and so I gave him a bit of a smile, and I said to him again, 'Certainly, sir. Whereabouts, please?' Ye know, Giles, I didn't like to mention his eye, because I thought he mightn't like it.' 'Whereabouts, please?'" said I.

"'Whereabouts?' cried he. 'What arto bletherin' about? I want it paintin' all o'er!'

"'Oh, I see,' said I; 'you're gooin' to a masquerade ball, or something. All right. I'll soon make ye so as nobody'll know ye.'"

"'Gooin' to what?' cried he."

"'By the living Jingo,' thinks I, 'I'm wrong again;' so I said to him, 'I hope you will excuse me, sir, but I thought perhaps you might be going to a masquerade ball, or something.'"

"'Bith hectum!' cried he, grappling his cudgel, 'if thou talks to me about masquerades I'll rub tho down wi' a wooden towel, tightly!' And his dog began to grin."

"Thinks I, 'This is goin' to turn out an ugly customer,' and I gave a sly look round: but there was no chance of escape, bless ye, for this fellow and his dog stood right between me and the door. Well, you know, Giles, I saw at once that there was nothing for it but to keep as thick

with him an' his dog as possible. An' it made me sweat,
I can tell ye, for I began to think that he was a lunatic, or
something, don't ye see, Giles. So I took my hat off; an'
I wiped my forehead again; an' I said, 'Well, sir; I
should be very glad to oblige ye in any way that I possibly
can, I'm sure, but, just now, I can't say that I quite
understand what it is that you want exactly.' "

" ' Well, then,' said he, ' thou'rt a leather-yed.' "

" I was going to say, ' Thank you, sir,' but I thought I'd
better not, because it might vex him ; so I only grinned a
little, and wiped my forehead again."

" Well, he gave another look round the place, and he
said, ' Hast nought to sup i'th hole ? ' "

" And I said, ' No, sir, I have nothing at all in the place
in that line except some copal varnish, and a little drop o'
ginger cordial, that I take now an' then when I'm seized
with a pain in my inside. Will ye try a little ? You're
quite welcome.' "

" He grunted again, an' he said, ' I'd as soon ha' tone as
tother. But I'll ha' noather on 'em ; mix 'em together, an'
sup 'em thisel'. . . . But come,' said he, ' I didn't
want to ston botherin' here o' day. Didto never yer tell of
a portrait ? ' "

" ' A portrait ! ' said I ; ' Oh, that's it, is it? Ah, well,—
now I begin to comprehend.' "

" ' Thou's bin a good while about it,' said he."

" ' Well, yes,' said I, ' that's true. But it's better late
than never, ye know, isn't it ! ' "

" ' I don't know whether it is or not,' said he; ' it just
depends.' "

"'Well, ye know, Giles, I thought I'd better not contradict him : so I said, 'Oh! a portrait is it? Ay, very well, sir. See ye, take this chair, please ;' and I pushed the stool towards him again."

"'Well, he just gave the stool a touch with his foot, an' away it went spinning to the other side of the room."

"'Thou met as weel gi' mi a fire-potter nob to sit on as that,' said he. 'Hasto nought bigger?'"

"'Well, ye see, sir,' said I, 'I'm not overstocked with furniture ; but, if ye like, I'll clear the things away from this table; and, judging by the naked eye, I should say that would be about the size required for your convenience.'"

"'Let thi bits o' tanklements stop where they are,' said he ; 'I can ston.'"

"'Very well. sir,' said I, 'and what size d'ye think as you would like this portrait of yours to be?' said I."

"'Oh, th' yed,' said he ; 'nought nobbut th' yed. I don't think tother's worth botherin' about.'"

"'And between you and me, Giles, he was right there ; for though he was a tremendous size of a chap, at the very least three parts of him was paunch, and such like; and he was terribly knock-kneed, and he was a queer shape altogether. He looked like a packsheet full o' tripe badly tied up. And yet, ye know, Giles, he would have made a very striking picture, in a certain sense, for he was what ye may call beautifully-ugly from top to toe. But, however, he seemed to have taken a particular fancy to his own face,—some people, do, you know, Giles,— his face he would have, an' nothin' else,—an', God knows,

that wasn't handsome. However, it was no business o'
mine; an' it was a thing that couldn't be helped; for the
man wasn't his own father,—nor I wasn't his father; and,
between you and me, Giles, I should have been sorry if I
had been. I dare say his mother thought him nice, once,—
women do get such things into their heads,—but I question
whether anybody else would think so that had good eye-
sight. I remember an old rhyme that says :—

> Although I'm feaw, despise me not,
>   The truth to you I'll tell ;
> I'm of another's hondy-wark,
>   I didn't make mysel'.

And it's quite true. Beside, if he had made his-sel', it's
just possible that he might have been uglier than ever.
But that's neither here nor there. Let every tub stand on
its own bottom, say I. The man was as God made him,—
and he was a customer,—and that was enough for me. So
I spoke him fair, for this dog of his was keeping its eyes on
me all the time."

"'Very well, sir,' said I; 'you want just the head, and
nothing else. . . . Kit Cat, I suppose ?"'

"'Kit what?'" said he.

"'Kit Cat,'" said I.

"'I noather want Kit Cat, nor Kit Dog,' he said. 'I
want a gradely pickter !'"

"'Well, sir,' said I; 'if you'll leave the thing to me, you
shall have a gradely pickter.'"

"'Well; get agate o' thi paintin', then,' said he; 'get
agate o' thi paintin'. Brass is no object to me.'"

"Well, ye see, Giles, I was a bit flurried, so I said that it
was no object to me neither."

"He took me up in a minute, and he said, 'That's o' reet, then. Thou connot begin to soon.'"

"Thinks I to myself, 'This'll not do;' so, for fear of any further mistakes, I said, 'Well, sir, you'll excuse me, but I've noticed several times in the course of my chequered existence that money comes in very handy when one wants to buy things; and, as one's always needin' something or another, perhaps it would be as well to name a price, if you've no objections.'"

"Then he banged his cudgel on the floor again, and he said, 'How lects thou didn't say so at first? Come, what's it to be? Oppen thi mouth, an' ha' done wi't.'"

"So at last we agreed that this portrait was to be ten pounds; and when we had struck the bargain, he said, 'But mind, it mun be a good un, or else I'll not have it.'"

"'Well, sir,' said I, 'when the portrait's finished, if you don't like it, I'll leave it to any respectable judge to decide the matter.'"

"'Well, then,' said he, 'we'n lev it this dog o' mine. If it wags it tale at it I'll pay for it; but if it barks at it thou'll have it thrut o' thi honds.'"

"'Very well, sir,' said I, 'agreed. I'll leave it to the dog.' It was a foolish thing to do, ye know, but I did it. Beside, ye see, though I didn't like th' dog, nor th' dog didn't like me, I thought it couldn't object to a genuine work of art; for if I've noticed, Giles, that, as a rule, dogs are as good judges of these things as the ordinary run of Christians are, though they don't say as much about it.'"

"Well, to make a long story short, we agreed. . . . But before I go any further I must tell ye that this customer

of mine had a great wart playfully planted on the left side
of his nose, and it was a very unsightly thing. So I laid
my finger on my nose-end, and I said to him, 'Well, but
how about the wart? I hope you'll not consider me impertinent. but you'll not have that in, will ye?'"

"'Wart,' cried he ; 'what business has thou wi' th' wart?
It's noan o' thine ! I'll have it in !'"

"'Well, my friend,' said I, 'I hope you'll excuse me ; but
if you was to touch it every morning with a little vitriol, it
would be gone in a few days.'"

"'Vitriol !' cried he ; 'put thi vitriol into thi porritch !
I'll ha' no vitriol ! I've had this wart ever sin' I wur born,
an' I'll not part wi' it now ! I'll have it in ! I shouldn't
look like mysel' beawt it !'"

"So I hinted to him that, taking everything into consideration, perhaps it mightn't be an advantage to look like one's
self sometimes."

"Well, that made him roar again ; and, grappling his
cudgel by the middle, he cried, 'I'll have it in, I tell tho !
It's my own, an' I'll have it in !'"

"'Very well, my friend,' said I ; 'far be it from me to
infringe upon the rights of private property. It's your own,
as you say : and you *shall* have it in. . . . Be content,
my friend,' said I, laying my hand on his shoulder like
that,- just to quieten him. ye know, Giles,—'be content, my
friend. you shall have it in, an' I'll put another on the
opposite side, if you like, just to make an even balance.'"

" Well, that set him roaring worse than ever, and he made
such a din that this dog of his seemed to get it into his head
that we were fighting, and all at once he made a dart at me,

and got fast hold of the calf of my leg. I hadn't much of a calf, to be sure, but it made free with what there was, I can tell ye. Well, ye see, Giles, that set me agate o' roarin' too, and I danced up an' down a bit, wi' th' dog hanging to my leg, and I kept cryin' out 'Tak' it off,—tak it off!' Well, he was in no hurry about the matter. To tell ye the truth, Giles, he seemed rather to enjoy it. However, he did take it off at last, and the moment I got loose I jumped on to the table, and I said, 'My friend, are you the proprietor of that animal?'"

"And he said, 'Ay; I've had it sin it wur a pup. There isn't a better dog i'th town for varmin?'"

"'Oh, thank you,' said I; 'then I suppose you take me for varmin, do ye?'"

"'Well,' said he, 'this dog's noan a bad judge about sich like things as that.'"

"So I thanked him again."

"'Come off that table.' said he. 'What arto' doin' up theer? Arto beawn to sell up, or summat?'"

"'I'm much obliged to you, my friend,' said I; 'but I prefer my present position, so long as that dog's in the room.' Then I rubbed my leg again, and I said, 'What d'ye feed it on, as a rule?'"

"'Shin o' beef, an' garbage,' said he."

"'Ay, then,' said I, 'I suppose the brute takes me for a stock you've been layin in.'"

Here Giles rapped the table with his ladle.

"Stop, stop, Jemmy," cried he. "How long's this maunderin' nominy o' thine gooin' to last? I can make noather top nor tail on't. Thou's bin agate o' buzzin' for

35

this last hauve hour, like a hum-a-bee in a foxglove, about
dogs an' pickters, an' warts, an' warts, an' pickters, an' dogs,
till I'm gettin' as mazy as a tup. Thou'rt as ill as a maut-
mill.—wuzz, wuzz, wuzz, grind, grind, grind. Cut it short !
What the dule, thou'll have us o' asleep. Thou's done for
'Bonny Mouth', a good while sin. Look where he is,
theer,—wi' his een shut, an' his mouth wide oppen, as if he
wur catchin' fleas. An' Craddy's noan so mich better ; he
keeps droppin' off, an' startin' up again,—like a goose wi' a
nail in it yed. Cut it short, I pritho,—or else drop it
o'together,—an' let someb'dy else start. By th' mass, I'd as
soon be at a berrin', as sit hearkenin' thee. . . . Come,
lads ; wakken up ! Jem ; nudge owd Bonny,— he's a mouth
like a breast-hee coalpit."

"Here ; I'll wakken him," said Jem.   "Now then !
Come, Bonny Mouth ! Wakken up, my lad !"

Bonny Mouth gave a great yawn ; and then, looking round
with half-wakened eyes, he said, "O' reet ! has he getten it
o'er ?"

"Not quite," said Jem.

"Well then," said Bonny Mouth, dropping his chin again,
"I'll have another bit of a nap, yo can wakken me up when
he's done."

"Here, here," cried Giles ; "we'n ha' no sleepin' ! Beside,
thou snoors like a reawsty trindle ! Prop thoose foggy e'en
o' thine a minute or two, till we se'en what he's for doin'."

Then turning to the painter, he said "Now, Jemmy, my
lad, thou's had a fairish do,—an' it's knockin' us o' up.
How long's this tale o' thine beawn to last ?"

"Well, Giles," said the painter, "if you keep stoppin' me

this way, it'll last till about three o'clock i'th afternoon o'
New Year's day; but if you'll let me go on in my own way
I'll wind it up in a few minutes."

" Then wind it up,—an' soon!" said Giles; "wind it up,—
that's a good lad!"

"Ye know, Giles," said the painter, "you set me gooin'
yourself."

"Come, come," said Giles; let's ha' no preichment! Get
end-ways! I know I set thee gooin'. I've that to answer
for, among th' rest o' mi sins. But, never mind, get end-
ways, an' get it o'er."

"Very well, then," said the painter, "I will get it over.
. . . Let me see. Where was I? Oh,—the dog. . . .
Ah, well; I'll say no more about that. But the end of the
thing was that I painted this portrait; but when it was
finished I could'nt get him to say whether he liked it or he
didn't like it. All that I could get out of him was, 'Wait
a bit till I see what th' dog thinks about it.' Well, he set a
day; and he brought his dog to criticise the portrait. And,
mind ye, Giles, I've seen worse art critics than a dog in my
time. But, as it happened, this turned out rather unfortunate
for me, and it was this way. He took th' dog in his hands
on th' floor, and he said, 'Now then; set th' pickter i'th
front on't, and let's see.' Well; I reared the portrait up
against the table, in what I considered a good light."

"'Now then, Pinch,' said he to the dog, 'doesto see
that?'"

"'Now for it,' thinks I; 'death or glory!' and I kept
myself ready for action; for, ye know, Giles, I had a lively
remembrance of the animal's last visit to my leg; and I

thought it just possible that it might take a fancy to another mouthful."

"'Now, Pinch,' said he, 'doesto see that?'"

"Well; the dog began to snarl savagely, the very first thing; and put me into such a sweat, that I knocked a bottle over; and then th' dog darted straight at me. But I was on th' table again in a jiffy; and there I stopt till the whole thing was ended."

" Well; when the dog began to snarl, he said, ' Come, that sattles it!'"

"'My friend,' said I, 'you d'n't give the picture a fair chance. If you'll let the dog alone, it'll be quiet enough.'"

"'Th' dog noather likes thee nor thi pickter,' said he, 'so thou may keep thi pickter, an I'll keep mi dog.'"

"And away they went together."

"Well, the end of it was that I had this portrait left on my hands for months; and it was a dead loss, for I didn't know what to do with it. But 'it's a long lane that never has a turn,' yo know, Giles: an' one fine morning, when I was sitting at my work, a man came in and said that he wanted me to paint him a sign for his public-house. And so I asked him what sign?"

"'Th' Turk's Yed,' said he."

"Well, I was turning over in my mind whether to accept the job or not, for I didn't half like it—though I'd hard strugglin' at that time to make ends meet. Well, while I was turning the thing over in my mind, the man stood in the middle of the floor, looking round; and his eyes happened to light on this rejected portrait, that had been reared up i'th corner so long."

"'Hollo,' said he, 'what's this?'"

"So I told him the whole tale about this portrait."

"'Oh, I know him,' said he: 'Owd Jone o' Blunder's. . . . Ay, an' it's like him, too—he's as feaw as a fried dromedary.'"

"'Well,' said I, 'he certainly isn't handsome.'"

"'Hondsome,' said he; 'nawe, bi th' heart—he's noather hondsome face nor hondsome ways! . . . But, by th' mass, I'll tell tho what,' said he, 'thi pickter of owd Jone's would come in grandly for my sign, with a bit o' touchin' up. An' it wouldn't need much, noather,—for he's as ugly as ony Turk i' this wide world,—an' as savage.'"

"Well, to make a long story short, I agreed to touch his portrait up, and make it into the sign of 'The Turk's Head.' I put him a turban on, and I made him a black beard, and I put rings into his ears; and a very good Turk he made, I can tell ye. It was a kind of a godsend to me, for the man was pleased with his sign, and he paid me a good price for it. . . . Well, this sign hadn't been up a week before the whole story had got out about Jone o' Blunder's portrait being turned into the Turk's Head sign; and from that day to this, Jone has gone by the name of 'Th' Owd Turk.' But, mind ye, before the sign had been up a month it disappeared one dark night, and was never heard of afterwards. . . . And that ends my tale."

"'That's reet, my lad,'" said Giles. "Here; let's fill thi tot again. I'm sure thou'rt dry."

"An' now then, Giles," said the painter, "the next time you ask me to tell a tale I'll either sing a song, or stand on my head, instead."

" Well, my lad," said Giles, "oather'll do,—though thou'rt
nobbut a poor hond at singing'—but oather 'll do."

"I know you think I'm very simple, Giles," said the
painter.

"Thou knows nought o'th sort, Jemmy," replied Giles ;
"thou knows nought o' th' sort ; for I think thou'rt as deep
as th' north star. If onybody bruns thee for a foo', James,
they'n waste their coals. But never mind, my lad, thou's
done as weel as thou could, an' that's as much as one can
expect i' this world,—an' a good deal moore than we getten'
sometimes. Here, let's gi tho another thimblefull."

"Come, lads," said Giles, "time's gettin' on. It'll be
Kesmass Day afore we known where we are. Let's be
gettin' on. Here, Harry, old buzzart, keep th' backstone
warm. What arto dremin' about ? Thou looks as if thou'd
bin stonnin' o' one leg under a pump o' day for a wager.
Wakken up an' keep th' backstone warm ! Thou's done
nought yet. What conto give us ? "

"I'll be there when I'm wanted, Giles," said th' wool chap,
smiling.

"Now's the time, then," said Giles, rapping the table with
his ladle. "Order, for th' wool chap. . . . . . Now,
Harry, what's it to be ? Arto for singin' or doancin', or
tellin' a tale ? "

"I think I'll try an old song, Giles."

"That'll do, my lad. Pipe up, an' good luck to tho.
. . . Silence, for an owd sung ! Goo on, Harry."

And Harry struck up at once, in a melodious voice, and like a man who had been used to that kind of thing :—

> If I live to grow old, for I find I go down,
> Let this be my fate in a country town :—
> May I have a warm house, with a stone at the gate,
> And a cleanly young girl to rub my old pate ;
> May I govern my passions with absolute sway,
> And grow wiser and better as strength wears away,
> Without stone or gout—by a gentle decay.
>
> CHORUS.—May I govern my passions, &c.

> In a country town, by a murmuring brook,
> With the ocean at distance, on which I may look ;
> With a wide green plain, without hedge or stile,
> And an easy pad nag for to ride out a mile.
>
> CHORUS. May I govern my passions, &c.

> With Horace and Plutarch, and one or two more
> Of the best wits that lived in the age before ;
> With a dish of roast mutton, not venison or teal,
> And clean, though coarse, linen at every meal.
>
> CHORUS.—May I govern my passions. &c.

> With a pudding on Sunday, and stout humming liquor,
> And scraps of old Latin to welcome the vicar ;
> And a hidden reserve of good Burgundy wine,
> To drink the King's health in as oft as I dine.
>
> CHORUS.—May I govern my passions. &c.

> When the days are grown short, and it freezes and snows,
> May I have a coal fire as high as my nose ;
> A fire which, when only stirred up with a prong,
> Will keep the room temperate all the night long.
>
> CHORUS.—May I govern my passions. &c.

> With courage undaunted may I face my last day ;
> And when I am dead may the better sort say—
> " In the morning when sober, in the evening when mellow,
> He's gone, and he leaves not behind him his fellow."
>
> CHORUS.—May I govern my passions. &c.

The wool chap's song was received with a clatter of applause.

"By th' mon, Harry," said Giles, "thou's a gowden throttle, owd brid! Good health to tho!"

"Good health to th' wool chap!" cried Craddy, who had wakened up again by the din; "good health to th' wool chap!

> ' Bravo—bravo—very well sung ;
> Jolly companions, every one.''

"To order!" cried Jem o' th' Har-barn ; "to order, lads. We'n plenty to go on wi'. . . . Giles, we'n another sung at this end if thou'll keep 'em quiet a bit."

"Good again!" said Giles. "Order for another sung. . . . Here, let's buttle out first. . . . Now then, Jem, we're o' ready. Who's beawn to sing?"

"Well, I'll try another bit of a ditty mysel', Giles ; if thou's nought again it."

"Then tootle away, old layrock ; till th' welkin rings ! . . . Silence, lads, Jem's gettin' his top-lip ready. Brast off, Jem!"

> Now, since we're met, let's merry, merry be,
>   In spite of all our foes ;
> And he that will not merry be,
>   We'll pull him by the nose.

CHORUS.

> Let him be merry, merry there,
>   And we'll be merry, merry here ;
> For who can know where he shall go,
>   To be merry another year ?

And he that will not merry, merry be,
With a generous bowl and a toast,
May he in Bridewell be shut up,
And chained unto a post.
Let him be merry there, &c.

And he that will not merry, merry be.
And take his glass in course,
May he be obliged to drink small beer,
Without money in his purse.
Let him be merry there, &c.

And he that will not merry, merry be,
With a lot of jolly boys.
May he be plagued with a scolding wife,
To confound him with her noise.
Let him be merry there, &c.

And he that will not merry, merry be,
With his sweetheart by his side,
Let him be laid in the cold churchyard,
With a head-stone for his bride.
Let him be merry there, &c.

"Bravo, Jem," said Giles. "By th' mass, thour't i' grand fettle. Thou mends as thou gets owder."

"Stop a minute," said Jem, "we'n another volunteer at this end. . . . To order! . . . Goo on, Snip!" And Snip began:—

Wassail! wassail! all over the town;
Our toast it is white and our ale it is brown;
Our bowl it is made of a maplin tree;
And we are all good fellows—I drink to thee!

Here's to our horse, and to his right ear,
God send th' owd lonlort a happy new year;
A happy new year to thee and to me;
With my wassailing bowl I drink to thee!

Here's to our mare, and to her right eye :
God send th' owd mistress a Kessmass pie ;
A good Kessmas pie as hoo ever did see ;
With my wassailing bowl I drink to thee !

Here's to th' owd cow, and to her long tail,
And God send that th' maister never may fail
To brew us good beer ; I pray you draw near,
And my wassailing song you soon shall hear.

Send hither a maid—you're sure to have one—
That'll not leave us here in the cold alone ;
Come hither, fair maid, an' trole back the pin.
And we'll sing you a song when we do get in.

Come, butler, and bring us a bowl of the best,
And I hope that your soul in heaven may rest ;
But if you do bring us a bowl of the small,
I care not if butler and bowl do fall.

" Well done, Snip !" cried Giles ; and, lifting his glass, he
said, "Come, lads, chorus :—

With my wassailing bowl I drink to thee!

Then each man took his glass in his hand ; and again and
again the blithe burden rang in every nook and corner of
the Old Boar's Head that wintry night.

.

" Giles," said Lapstone, " did'n yo ever yer tell o' Sam o'
Boar-cloof an' his stuffed hare ? "

" I've yerd summat about it ; but what it is I connot
justly remember.   Let's have it."

" Well, yo known that he wur a top-mark shooter ?"

" I know that he thought so ; but he were terribly wrang

.

If he wur to aim at a hay-stack he'd be sure to hit oather a church or a coal-house. I durst let him shoot at me for a shillin'. There isn't a brid i' this part o' the country that would stir a peg for him, if he wur to boke (point) his gun at it a whole day."

"Well, he wur noan quite as ill as that, but he wur terrible fond o' bein' thought a sportsman; an' he're al'ays botherin' wi' guns, an' wearin' leather gaiters, an' shootin' jackets, wi' as mony pockets in as would howd a seck o' potitos. Well, thoose at' knew th' owd lad knew that he wur moor of a freetener than a killer; an' they used to play bits o' marlocks wi' him. . . . Well, one day, two or three mischievous cowts i'th fowd yon, geet a hare skin, an' stuffed it nicely wi' fithers an' bran, an' sich like, an' stitched it up a bit, an' then they went an' planted it slyly in a bush at the bottom o' Sam's garden, so that it showed itsel' a bit fro' th' back window. . . , So far so good. . . . When they'd done that, they crept to th' back o'th trees to see th' gam; an' they sent a lad in at Sam's front dur, wi' th' news o' this hare i' the garden. 'Sam,' said th' lad, 'there's a hare under th' fayberry tree, at th' bottom o' yo'r garden,—ye' mun be sharp;' an' off he darted back again. Well, th' whol house wur up in a second. 'Reitch that gun," cried Sam. 'It's gwon to th' mendin',' said his son Joe. "Then run, thee, like a red-shank up to owd Dick's, an' borrow his gun. Be sharp, now!' An' th' lad darted off to owd Dick's. 'Keep still, every one on' yo'. I see it yon. I'll have that hare if I'm a livin' mon. What the dule's yon lad after 'at he's so lung? I could ha' bin at Rachda' an' back bi' now. Keep off that back dur, I tell

yo. I see it! It's yon yet. We'n ha' that divulskin jugged
to-morn, if yo'n be quiet a bit. Howd,—it's off! Nay, it's
theer yet! What the hectum's yon lad doin'.' Th' owd'st
daughter looked through th' front window, an' hoo said, 'I
see him! He's comin' down th' brow, yon, full pelt, wi' th'
gun on his shoulder.' 'O' reet,' said Sam, rubbin' his honds;
'o' reet. Keep still. This is a grand do.' In coom th' lad,
pantin' for breath, wi' th' gun in his honds. 'Make a less
din,' said Sam, givin' th' lad a souse on th' yed, 'an' gi's
howd o' that gun. If thou speaks a quarter of a word for
this next five minutes, I'll shoot thee wheer tho stons.' Well,
Sam charge't gun, an' o' th' time he wur doin' it he kept
sayin', 'Don't stir, now. Keep still. . . . Now then,
oppen that shut gently, an' I'll teich yon divvle for comin' into
my garden. Ston' fur, o' on yo. Now then, my lad, thou'll
height no moore cabbich after to-day.' . . . Bang went
th' gun, an' bran an' fithers flew i' o' directions; an' Sam ran
to pike th' hare up; but afore he'd getten theer these chaps
'at had been watchin' him began o' shoutin'——."

"Howd!" cried Jone o' Gavelock's, striking the table
with his fist; "I'll not yer another word said against Sam o'
Boarcloof, bi never a mon 'at stept shoe-leather. He's own
cousin to me."

"Well," said Lapstone, "an' if he is own cousin to thee,
he's no better for that."

"Better or wur, it's theer; an' he owes thee nought."

"Nawe, he doesn't," said Lapstone; "an' I'll take good
care 'at he never does do, noather. Doesto yer that, owd
lad?"

"Come, come, lads; let's ha' no fratchin'! Jone, thou'rt gettin' terribly rivven o' at once. Arto potter't i' thi inside about summat?"

"Not I. But I don't like to yer folk co'de beheend their backs."

"Who wur co'in' him beheend his back?" cried Lapstone.

"Why, thou wur," replied Jone; 'and I know how it is, too. It's o' because thou made him a pair o' shoon 'at didn't fit, an' he thrut 'em 'o thi honds."

"I'd as soon make a pair o' dancin' pumps for a camel as make shoon for him at ony time; for his feet arn't both of a size; an' his yed's wur to fit than his feet."

"Come, come, lads; drop it!" said Giles. "We'n ha' no foin' out to-neet, but what I do mysel'! Keep yo'r tempers, an' sup again! We'n ha' no fratchin',—not till Kessmass is o'er as how 'tis. . . . Here, Lapstone, as thou didn't finish th' tother, thou'd better give us a bit o' summat else."

"I'm willing," said Lapstone.

"Let hur went, then!" cried Giles; "let hur went! as th' Welchman said."

"Well," said Lapstone, "didn' yo ever yer a tale about Dan o' Nelly's,—better known bi th' name o' Scutter-slutch,— ridin' fro' Owdham to Bill o' Jacks, i' Saddleworth, in a coach beawt horses?"

Here Jone o' Gavelock's struck the table again, and sprang to his feet.

"I'll ston this no lunger!" cried he. "That's another cousin o' mine! He's doin' this o' purpose; an' he's no 'casion, for his gronfather wur hanged for sheep-steighlin'!—

let him crack that nut! Dan o' Nelly's is own cousin to me o' th' mother's side; and I'll not yer a word said again him bi mortal mon! Now, what have I towd yo?"

And the old man sat down again, foaming with passion.

"By th' mass! Jone," said Giles, "thou seems to be akin to o' th' foo's o'th country side."

"Well, then;" replied Jone, "thee an' me should be relations, Giles; an' I didn't know it afore."

This raised a general laugh round the board; in which Giles joined as heartily as the rest.

"Thou had me theer, owd lad," said he. "Well, well,—come, never mind. I'm content to be a cousin o' thine amung th' rook. As far as foolishness gwos, I doubt we're o' sib-an'-sib, rib-an' rib. But bridle yo'r tempers, lads; an' let's get on as weel as we con."

"Gi mi thi hond, Giles!" said Jone o' Gavelock's; "gi mi thi hond! I've nought again Lapstone, theer, if he'll let mi relations alone. Blood's thicker nor wayter, thou knows, Giles,—blood's thicker nor wayter."

"Ay, ay; it is, owd lad," said Giles; "an' a great deeol dirtier, too, sometimes."

This raised another laugh among the company; and they melted into jovial amity again.

"By th' mon," said Jone o' Gavelock's, thumping the table, "I've a good mind to tell a tale mysel'."

"Do, owd brid," said Giles; "an' I'll let tho off for o' at ever thou did again mi i' thi life!"

"It'll be about th' Owd Volunteers," said Lapstone to Snip, in a whisper; "It'll be about th' Owd Volunteers, for a crown. He generally tells that about this time at neet. Husht! he's coughed twice; he'll be ready directly."

"Ay, but he'll sup first," said Snip.

"That's sartin," said Lapstone, taking hold of his glass; "an' so will I."

CHAPTER VIII.

THE KING AND THE VOLUNTEER.

> " I wol yow telle as wel as *my* kan,
> A litel jape that fell in our cite."
>
> CHAUCER.

OW, Jone, my lad," said Giles, "what arto beawn to give us?"

"If yo'n wait a minute, till I've charge't this pipe, I'll gi' yo' summat, yo'st see," said Jone.

"That'll do, my lad," said Giles, "but mind thou mentions nobry's relations this time."

"Come, come, Giles," cried Jem o' th' Har-barn, "we'n had enough o' that! Thou'll not let 'em be quiet when they are quiet."

"It's o' reet, this time, Giles," said Jone, trimming the bowl of his pipe with his finger, "it's o' reet this time. This is about mysel'."

"Thou couldn't do better," said Giles, "off witho!"

"Well, then, here goes," said Jone. . . "When I wur i' th' Volunteers,——"

" Didn't I tell tho?" said Lapstone to Snip. " Didn't I
tell tho it would be 'th' Volunteers?'   He's sure to begin
that about this time at neet."

Jone overheard the half whisper on the other side
of the table, and, stopping in his story, he looked
mazily round, as if searching for the speaker, and said,
" Here, come ; if we're o' gooin' to talk at once, like
Rossenda' churchwardens, I'll wait a bit till there's a
better chance."

" Silence," cried Giles, " silence for Jone ! We'n not have
a word fro' nobry till th' owd lad's done his do ! . . .
Start again, Jone, my lad," said Giles, " I'll keep 'em
quiet."

" Well : I'll try again, then," said Jone. . . . " When
I wur i' th' Lancashire Volunteers we wur summon't up to
Lunnon to a review, an' we geet a bit of a glent at a different
mak of life while we were theer.   An' mind yo, they were a
lot o' th swipper'st, stark'est lads in Christendom, wur th'
Lancashire Volunteers.   They'd'n a foughten a lion a piece
for a quart of ale ! Well, th' King were very fond of us
Lancashire chaps ; an', when he were at a loose end, he
passed as mich time wi' us as ever he could spare.   Him an'
me geet terribly thick, an' when he'd knocked off for th' day,
we powler't up and down Lunnon together, i' o' mak o'
nooks an' corners ; an' this is how I let on him first of o' :—
We lee down at Chelsea at that time, an' one day when I
wur walkin' th' sentry, a fattish owd chap coom up to th' gate,
wi' a ash plant in his hond ; an' he wur walkin' straight in,
beawt sayin' a word.   But I stopt him wi' mi gun, an' I said,
' Here, owd mon, keep o' thi own side ! Thou munnot go

in here! We can do beawt thee when we're busy!' Wi'
that, he up wi' his stick, an' he said, ' Thee keep thi gun to
thi'sel, an ston out o' mi gate, or else I'll tak tho a-top o'th
nob once or twice ! I'll hae thee to know I'm th' maister o'
this cote !' Well, wi' that, I brast out a-laughin', an' I said,
' Come, that's a good un ! Thou's done it this time, owd
brid ! Who arto, if I mun be so bowd !' ' Well, he said,
' I'm th' King,—that's o'.' Well, that made me oppen my
e'en a bit, yo known, so I said, ' What, thee a king ! By th'
mon, I thought thou'd been hawkin' stockin'-yorn ! Arto
reet i' thi yed, thinksto ? . . . Wheer's thi crown ?'
' Well,' he said. ' I haven't it on to day, becose it's off at th'
mendin'. I happen't to lev it upo' th' table one day th' last
week, while I went out for a bit o' bacco, er Charlotte wur
busy wi' th' weshin',—an' th' childer geet hold on't, an began o'
rollin' it up an' down th' floor, till th' revits coom out. I had
to send it off to owd Ben, th' whitesmith. He promis't to
have it done bi yesterday, at baggin-time : an' he said he'd
send it down bi th' lad ; but I doubt he's getten upo' th'
fuddle again. Th' last time it went to th' mendin' he popt
it : an' er Charlotte had to go four or five times afore hoo
could get th' ticket out on him ; an' then hoo had to go an'
get it out for me to go to' church in o' Sunday.' Weel, yo
known, when I yerd that, I began o' pooin' my horns in ; an'
I put my gun o' one side, an' I said, ' Well, thou may go in,
owd lad, as it's thee. But, if I wur thee, I'd al'ays ha' mi
crown wi' me, or else nobry'll know 'at thou'rt a king.' . .
Well, at after that th' owd lad an' me geet thicker nor ever :
an' he wur like as if he never were comfortable but when we
wur together. Well, time went on a bit ; an' one day, when

37

us lads were upo' th' parade, th' sarjan' comes up to me, an'
he says, 'Howd that gun straight!' An' I said, 'I am
howdin' it straight!' An' he said, 'Thou artn't howdin' it
straight!' An' I said, 'Thou lies, I am howdin' it straight!'
An' wi' that, he knocked th gun straight out o' my hond ;
an' then he said, 'Pike that gun up!' An' I said, 'Nawe,
I'll not pike it up! It is wheer thou's put it, an' thou'll ha'
to pike it up thi'sel'!' An' he said, 'Pike that gun up, or
else I'll ha' tho put i'th guard-house!' Well, I towd him
'at I didn't care for noather him nor th' guard-house! An'
that set him agate o' bletherin' an' gosterin' up an' down like
mad. An' while he wur agate of his din, who should come
up, bi' th' mass, but th' king hissel'; an' when he see'd th'
gun lyin' upo' th' floor, he said, 'Jone, is that thy gun?'
An' I said, 'Ay, it is, owd lad!' An' then he said, 'What's
it doin' upo' th' floor?' An' I said, ' I'h' sarjan' theer's just
knocked it out o' mi' hond,' an', wi' that, he up with his foot
an' puncee't that sarjan' up an' down th' yard till he skriked
like a jay; an' if I'd spokken hauve a word to owd George
just then, I could ha' had him shot; but I thought I'd see
how he went on. . . . . Well, th' king an' me geet
thicker than ever ; an' one day I axed him up to his baggin';
an' he coom. Our Betty an' th' childer wur up i Lunnon
wi' mo, an' we had er baggins together. Well, th' king kept
lookin' at these childer of ours, an' he said, 'I'll tell tho
what, Jone, thou's a lot o' th' finest, fresh-colour't childer 'at
ever clapt e'en on. Mine are o' as yollo' as marigowds. What
dun yo feed 'em on!' An' I said ' Porritch.' ' Porritch,
porritch,' he said : ' what's that?' ' Why,' I said ; ' hasto never
had noan?' An' he said, he'd never yerd tell on 'em afore.

'Come,' I said. 'Our Betty's make us a pon-full.' So hoo made
'em, an' we o' fell to, an' when th' owd lad had ta'en two or three
spoonful, he said, 'By th' mass, Jone, I'll tell tho what,—this
is grand stuff!' If our Charlotte knowed how to make these,
we'd have 'em regilar!' 'Well,' I said, if thou's a mind, our
Betty's go down an' larn her!' An' he said, 'Agreed on,
owd lad! Gi' us thi hond! Agreed on!' So we set a time,
an' our Betty went down : an' owd Charlotte an' her wur up
an' down th' kitchen a whole day, among this porritch ; an'
I believe that, fro' that day to this, they'n never had a meal
i' that house but they'n had a bowl o' porritch upo' th' table.
An' when th' Lancashire Volunteers left Lunnon, th' owd lad
coom a-seeing me off, an' he made me promise to send him
a stone or two o' gradely meighl fro' whoam, an' he'd send th'
brass at th' end o' th' month, when th' pay-day coom. An'
I sent him a lot, an' he sent th' brass in a week or two after
bi a chap 'at wur comin' down to Manchester a-buying a bit
o' fustian for a suit o' clooas for th' Prince o' Wales. I've
never sin him sin', but he's sent word now an' then ; an' I
believe thoose children o' th' king's han never looked
beheend 'em sin' they started o' aitin' porritch. . .
An' that's o'."

"Jone, owd lad," said Giles, "thou's towd us a tale, an'
its a good un o' th' mak. Lads, here's to Jone o' Gavelock's
an' owd King George!"

The health was drunk with boisterous glee.

"An' now," said Giles, rising from the table, "that clock's
just upo' th' stroke o' twelve. It'll be Kesmass Day in a
two-thre minutes, an' afore we parten, I should just like——
Hush! What's that ?"

It was a sweet, childlike voice, that seemed to hover about them in the air, singing—

> Long time ago in Palestine,
>   Upon a wintry morn,
> All in a lonely cattle shed,
>   The Prince of Peace was born;
> His parents they were simple folk,
>   And simple lives they led,
> And in the way of righteousness
>   This little child was bred,

The last stroke of twelve rang out from the clock before these words were ended. Up struck the bells of St. Leonard's church upon the hill in front of the house; and from a band of "waits," who had gathered beneath the window of the inn, there arose into the starlight wintry air the glad old carol of the day :—

> Christians awake, salute the happy morn,
> Whereon the Saviour of this world was born.

Giles ran and flung open the door. ".A Merry Christmas to yo, lads !" cried he. " Come in out o' th' cowd !"

The Dead Man's Dinner.

CHAPTER I.

Now fades the glimmering landscape on the sight,
And all the air a solemn stillness holds.

GRAY.

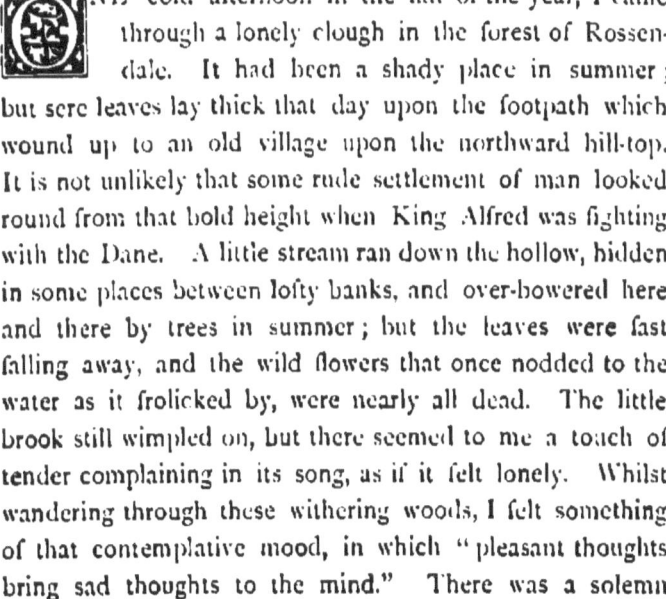

ONE cold afternoon in the fall of the year, I came through a lonely clough in the forest of Rossendale. It had been a shady place in summer; but sere leaves lay thick that day upon the footpath which wound up to an old village upon the northward hill-top. It is not unlikely that some rude settlement of man looked round from that bold height when King Alfred was fighting with the Dane. A little stream ran down the hollow, hidden in some places between lofty banks, and over-bowered here and there by trees in summer; but the leaves were fast falling away, and the wild flowers that once nodded to the water as it frolicked by, were nearly all dead. The little brook still wimpled on, but there seemed to me a touch of tender complaining in its song, as if it felt lonely. Whilst wandering through these withering woods, I felt something of that contemplative mood, in which "pleasant thoughts bring sad thoughts to the mind." There was a solemn

charm in the tempered harmony of autumnal hues that
clothed the scene ; and there was something unusually chill
and hushed in the appearance of the sky, where streamy
cloudlets, wild as a Druid's hair, were gliding southward,
with subdued motion, as if impressed with the thought that
they too were drifting—they knew not whither. The
thinning trees had a starved look, and all the landscape
was preaching the funeral sermon of the year. The bleak
hills stood like mourners round the scene, and the finger
of silence lay upon the lip of nature as in the chamber of a
dying man, save that now and then a low wind came with
dirge-like sough through the glen, bringing down another
shower of dead leaves from " bare ruined choirs where late
the sweet birds sang." Trailing my solitary way through
these rustling relics of the summer's green I came up from
the clough just as twilight was beginning to dusk the woodland hollows into deeper gloom. As I crossed the sloping
field near the old church the chimes rang out sweet and
distinct upon the evening air. The thin crescent of a new
moon was bright in the sky ; and, between flying clouds,
the evening star looked down with steady gleam upon the
folding world. The old church wore an unusually solemn
aspect at that contemplative vesper-hour. I lingered a few
minutes in the graveyard. The tenants of . that silent
ground were sleeping soundly, " after life's fitful fever."
Here was a storied monument ; there, a pauper's undistin-
guished mound ; but the closing event, that comes to all
alike, had laid them side by side in the peaceful companionship of common decay at last. They had crossed the edge
of the great forest,—" the undiscovered country, from whose

bourne no traveller returns." I tried to read some of the
epitaphs upon the gravestones, but the shades of night had
begun to shroud those brief records of the poor inhabitants
below, so I took my way out by the great gate, where
withered leaves from the trees about the entrance rustled
audibly around me in the fading light.

A little street, mostly of old-fashioned cottages, with
gardens in front of them, led from the church gates into the
village. There was a quaint irregularity about this little
street. It looked pretty and picturesque, and full of sweet,
nest-like simplicity. The houses seemed to have each a
story and a will of its own. On both sides they stood a
little in and out, here and there : some leaned forward,
some backward, and one or two had got a paralytic twist,
that threw the gable end curiously out of the line, as if the
window round the corner was trying to see what time it was
by the church clock at the end of the street. They were a
" good deal out of drawing," as painters say ; but there was
a clean, cozy air about them, that was pleasant to the eye.
Taken altogether, with the bit of trailing greenery about the
doors and windows, they looked like two lines of old people
advancing to each other in a country dance at holiday time,
with three or four smart young sprigs, more gaily dressed,
joining in the fun, and eyeing the wavering string of ancient
caperers with a kind of patronising admiration. Many of
the doors were open. Pot-plants peeped through almost
every window ; and here and there I saw bright utensils
winking upon the walls inside. In one cottage I heard a
cheerful jingle of tea-things : in another a lad sat near the
open door playing " The Sicilian Mariner's Hymn " upon

an accordion. At the threshold of the next there stood a
comely woman, wearing a clean white cap and a print bed-
gown, and with suds upon her stout arms, as if she had just
left the washing-mug. Her cap-strings fluttered in the wind
as she leaned with one hand against the door-cheek, calling
her children in from play, in a shrill, long-drawn cry, that
rang all over the neighbourhood. "Martha! . . .
Mary! . . . Come in this minute! . . . 'Lijah!
Come in to thi porritch! Eh, I'll warm thee, gentleman,—
I will! Look what a seet thae's made o' thi cloas!" She
gave the ruddy lad a motherly love-tap as he ran by her
into the house, and then she closed the door upon her little
fold. I knew that these cottages were the homes of working-
people, most of them weavers, and, in addition to their
handicraft, some of them students of science,—botany,
music, or mathematics. A gray-haired man, with his shirt-
sleeves rolled up, and stocking-legs drawn upon his arms,
leaned upon a garden gate, smoking, and looking drowsily
round. The village gossips were gathering to their old
lounging-place at the far corner of the street ; and I met
tired workmen sauntering homeward with their cans and
dinner-baskets. A bright fire filled the front room of " Billy
Wimberry's " ale house with a cheerful glow. The " Duke
o' York's March" rang merrily from the hand-bells inside :
and an old weaver was sidling up to the door with his hands
in his pockets, and looking slyly round, with a face as
innocent as a kitling,—the first drop before the shower of
nightly revelry came on. The evening grew wilder as daylight died away ; and a little further up a swing sign creaked
rustily in the wind in front of the "Old Bull." " Blind

Jerry," the fiddler, had taken his seat in the tap-room corner
for the night : and as no customers had yet arrived, he was
playing " Roslin Castle " for his own pleasure. The beautiful
wail streamed forth upon the moaning wind in fine accor-
dance with the hour and the whole mood of nature outside.

The " Bull " was one of the homeliest inns a mortal man
could put his head into. An old wood-and-plaster house—
but sound and substantial still—like a good constitution
well preserved. Many a fine oak fell to supply the timber
for that quaint-gabled hostelry. It had an inviting look. even
outside. Something frank and generous beamed through
those chequered walls and diamond-paned lattices, that
warmed the whole neighbourhood. The white and black
that distinguished the wood from the rest of the building
were clean white and clean black. The windows, the
blinds, the clean pavement in front, the well-filled watering-
trough, the old horse-block, and everything about the open
doorway, hinted that all was right inside. A good old-
fashioned inn, glowing throughout with genuine comfort.
There was neither stint, nor extortion, nor dirt, nor disorder
of any kind, allowed therein. Some of its rooms were
wainscotted with black oak. It was full of cosy nooks, too :
and stored with many a rare piece of furniture, inlaid
cabinets, and carved oak chairs and tables, that shone like
dusky looking-glasses. On the shelves of the bar there
were several quaint gilt vases, and two mighty old China
punch-bowls, which were only taken down three times a
year, on certain red-letters days, when the " Old Bull " was
alive from the cellar to the ridging with the flowing revel of
some annual holiday, long and regularly " kept up " under

38

that many-chimnied roof. The kitchen, too, had a charm
of its own. Its snowy walls glittered with bright dish-
covers, warming-pans, ladles, and other shining metal
utensils. The vast firegrate was always clean, and hardly
ever cold. The grand oak clock in the corner beat time
with slow and solemn sound, as if it had authority to keep
order in that place. The delf-rack was full of crockery, and
the thick plane-tree top of the long dresser was as white as
scouring could make it. And then, the ceiling! Ah! the
ceiling of that bright little kitchen world was a firmament
studded with cheerful things! It was hung with great hams
and flitches; and rounds of spiced beef, sewed up in brown
holland; and bundles of dried herbs; with here a copper
kettle, and there a brass pan for boiling preserves. In the
middle there was a large stringed frame, or "brade-fleigh,"
covered with crisp oat-cakes, the ends of which hung down
in inviting curls,—free to all hands. "It snowed of meat
and drink in that house," as Chaucer says; and a good deal
of that snow, like the snows of heaven, fell quietly upon the
poor; for the old landlady and her daughter had womanly
hearts within them, and were always glad to do a good turn
to the needy; and they liked to have people of the same
disposition about them. . . . But who can tell how
many famished wanderers may have halted at meal times,
and looked wistfully in at that cheerful doorway for a
moment, and then crawled forward into the cold world
beyond, unknown to the kind hearts within those quaint
walls. . . . On one of the beams an antique halbert
hung; and on another there was a long fowling-piece—a
cherished relic of the landlord, who had been laid at rest,

many a long year since, in the churchyard. Everything in
the "Old Bull" betokened long-continued care and success-
ful housekeeping. Ay, even the cats in the kitchen, so
portly and sleek, and so magnificently lazy, that they looked
as if they had to lean against the wall to mew. They glided
about with a slow, serene majesty, as if they had no need to
be in a hurry about things. They had made a position in
the world, and you could see at a glance that they knew it,
Their bread was baked. There was a full-fed, self-satisfied
calm about them, as if they had been aldermen a good
while, and were going to be mayors next year. They looked
as if they owned a good deal of valuable scrip, and sub-
scribed to things, and had "two coats, and everything
handsome about them." It was very clear that they had
long since retired from the mouse line, or, at least, that the
business was now managed entirely by junior partners.
They had nothing to do but to sign cheques, and eat and
drink, and doze, and be grand. If ever cats aspired to a
pedigree, and coats of arms, and things, these were the cats
I could almost imagine them taking a bath every morning,
and then ringing the bell for breakfast and the newspapers.
. . . The poultry in the yard, too, were all well off. They
were plump, comfortable-looking fowls, who had less scratching to do than their neighbours. Their plumage was rich and
clean, and glossy with good living. They slept soundly
o'nights. and they rose in a morning with minds at ease about
the day's peck. In fact, everything about the "Old Bull"
seemed healthy and prosperous, and well-cared for; ay,
even to the loud-chirping crickets on the hearth. . . . .
At the rear of the house there was a pretty little parlour,

with a bow-window, that commanded a view of the clough
and the hills beyond. It was pleasant to sit by that open
window on a summer evening, when birds peeped in and
sang; when the roses, clustering by the wall, filled the room
with a sweet smell ; and when the voices of the bowlers at
play upon the old green came clear upon the air. I thought
of this little parlour as I drew near the door of the " Old
Bull " that cold night, and—I went in.

As I walked up the lobby, crooning to the sound of
Jerry's fiddle, the house seemed to me unusually still. I
peeped through the bar-window. There was nobody in ;
but I met the landlady's daughter, Mary, coming from the
kitchen with a cup of tea in her hand. She was in haste, and
I thought she looked anxious. Pointing towards the little
parlour, she said, " You'll find the doctor in there, sir. My
mother's not well." And then she ran upstairs with the tea.

I was glad to hear that the doctor was in. It was a
pleasure and a benefit to meet with him, for he was a fine
old man,—a gentleman in heart and thought ; and a man of
rare cultivation. In youth he was an active politician ; but
his whole life had been marked by a catholic respect for all
shades of sincere opinion, even whilst warmly advocating his
own. Singularly child-like in his trustful simplicity, there
was yet a natural dignity about him, arising from the goodness of his heart and the noble tone of his mind—a dignity
that could bear the shock of free contact with his kind, and
needed no outworks of frigid mannerism to defend it from
impertinent familiarity. He was a genial man too, and
could crack his joke with the best, at the right time. Strongly
attached to his profession, the long practice of it had

brought him into contact with a great variety of human life,
and his sympathies were wider even than his experience.
The poor loved him well ; and they had a good reason for
it. I found him sitting by the fire, with the *Times* in his hand
"Good evening, doctor," said I.

"Good evening, sir," replied he. "I'm glad to see you."

"Thank you," said I, shaking his offered hand. "Mary
tells me that her mother is unwell. Do you know what's
the matter, doctor?"

"Well," replied he, "the old lady has had an excellent
constitution, but she has reached that time of life when
nature begins to whisper to the best of us that the inevitable
hour is not far off. She is seventy-five, and a very sensitive
person by nature ; and she has had a great shock to-day.
Have you heard of the accident?"

"Not a word. What is it, sir?"

"Oh, a very sad thing," replied he, taking a pinch of
snuff, and laying his old tortoise-shell box upon the table :—

"For the last twelve years I have attended the family of a
labourer of the name of Greenhalgh, but better known among
his neighbours as ' Solid Jimmy.' I never knew a more comfortable couple, in their humble way, than Greenhalgh and
his wife. I don't think his wages averaged more than
seventeen or eighteen shillings a week, the year round ; but
they managed to pay their way, and live respectably upon it ;
and their little cottage was as sweet a nest as any poor man
need wish for. They have had nine children, too. The
youngest is not quite ten months old, and Matty's in what
country folk call ' th' expectin' way' again. Jenny, the
eldest, is about eleven, and she lies dangerously ill of

inflammation. I called to see her this forenoon; and, as I
was about to leave the house, Matty took me aside, and
said, 'Doctor, eawr James axed me to go wi' his dinner
to-day, an' tak word heaw Jenny's gooin' on. Ile's quite
unsattl't abeawt her.' So I told her that I was going partly
the same way, and, if she was ready, we would walk
together. She seemed pleased, and she began to hurry the
dinner things into her basket; and it was touching to see
her flutter about the house, as if half loath to leave it.
Pointing to a young woman, who was busy about the fire,
she said, 'This is my sister Nelly; hoo's comed to look after
th' childer while I'm away.' Then she went to the cradle,
where the youngest child lay asleep, and, tucking the clothes
in tenderly, she croodled over it in a dove-like way, as only
a mother can do. They had brought a bed down into the
next room for the girl who was ill. The door was open, and
the child lay there watching her mother as she went to and
fro. Matty went to her bed-side, and softly smoothed the
pillow; and, as she straightened the clothes about her, she
whispered, 'Neaw, my lass, I'm gooin' wi' thi father's
dinner. I'll not be long. Thae mun lie still, an' thae'll
soon be weel, thae's see.' Then, as she closed the door in
coming away, she looked back again into the room, and said,
'Thi father 'll bring tho some posies when he comes fro his
wark.' . . . When we had got a few yards away from
the cottage, Matty gave a great sob, and she said, 'Eh,
doctor, I'm fleyed we 're gooin' to lose her!' But I
reassured the poor woman as well as I could; and when I
parted with her at the corner of the orchard she was in good
spirits again, and she went forward up the road with her

husband's dinner. It was then about ten minutes to twelve."

" And now," continued the doctor, taking another pinch of snuff, and ringing the bell, "'Lame Jonas,' the old servant man here, can tell the rest of the story better than I can, for he saw more of it."

" Fanny," said he, when the servant entered, " if old Jonas is at liberty, send him here for a few minutes."

She closed the door, and I heard her tell a lad in the lobby to fetch " Owd Jonas."

" What Owd Jonas ?" inquired the lad. " Is it Limper ? "

" Yes. He must come directly."

Away went the lad shouting through the back yard, " Limper's wanted i'th bar this minute !"

The house was so still that we could hear the old man reply gruffly from the stables. " Hello ! What arto makin' that din abeawt? I'll may thee limp if I get howd on tho ! "

In a minute or two he came stumping up the lobby.

" Neaw, then," said he to Fanny; " what's to do again ? "

" Th' doctor wants yo i'th parlour, Jonas."

" Oh," replied he in a softer tone, as he rolled down his shirt sleeves in a hurry. " Bobby, go thee fot my jacket cawt o'th kitchen. Be slippy !"

In another minute he stood in the doorway, with an old crushed milking hat in his hand. " Dun yo want me, doctor ? "

" Yes," replied the doctor ; " if you've time, I want you to tell us about the accident to-day. Sit down, Jonas. How's your leg?"

"Well," said Jonas, "it gi's bits o' steawnges neaw an' then ; but it's no wur, upo' th' whol."

" Well," said the doctor, "before you begin, Jonas, what will you have to drink? I know you don't like to sit dry-mouth."

"A saup o' rum, if yo plezzen, doctor, said Jonas. "It's good for th' rheumatic, isn' it?"

The old doctor smiled, and rang the bell.

When the rum came, Jonas laid his hat upon the window-sill, and sat down. "Ay, ay," said he, stirring his glass thoughtfully, ; "it's a bad job for sure—very. . . Come, here's yo're good health, doctor ;" and then, nodding side-way to me, he said, "an' yors an' o." And then, settling down in his chair, with his glass in his hand, he began.

CHAPTER II.

" And will he not come again ?
And will he not come again ?
Ah, no, he is dead :
Go to thy death-bed ;
He never will come again."　　　HAMLET.

"ELL, doctor," said Jonas, still stirring his rum and water, and looking thoughtfully in the glass, "I hardly know heaw to begin my tale. I didn't see it fro' th' first exactly ; but I'll tell yo what I did see, as weel as I con :—

" Eawr mistress sent mo this forenoon wi' a bottle o' red

port an' some bits o' nourishments for Owd Hannah, th'
mangle-woman, that's bin lyin' ill so lung. Th' poor owd
lass—hoo's had a weary time on't; but hoo's welly done wi'
this world. Well, as I coom back, I stopped a minute
or two at th' side o'th main-soof 'at they're makin' up i'th
road, yon. They'n cut happen three yard an' a hauve
deawn; an' Jimmy Greenhalgh, fro' th' Birches—him 'at
they co'n 'Owd Solid'—wur wortchin deawn at the bottom.
I didn't know who it wur till he looked up, an' axed me
what time it wur. I tow'd him that it had just gone a
quarter to twelve; and he said, 'It 's bin a long forenoon,
Jonas; but it's drawin' to an end. I wish eawr Matty'd
come. We'n one o'th childer ill, an' I want to yer heaw
hoo's gettin' on.' I axed him which it wur, an' he said it
wur their Fanny. An' I don't wonder at Jimmy bein'
consarnt abeawt her, for there's summat moor nor common
abeawt that lass; an' I know that hoo's olez bin a sort of
a nestle-brid at their heawse. But I didn't like to say
nought no fur to him at th' time, for he's a very feelin' mon,
is Jimmy. So, he went on wi' his wark, an' I coom deawn
whoam. When I geet into the heawse, eawr mistress said,
'Well, heaw's yon poor owd woman?' But hoo'd hardly
getten th' words eawt of her meawth afore we yerd a fearful
skrike o' women set up, and a strange hurry agate i'th street:
an' folks' feet clatterin by th' front dur at a terrible rate. I
felt a bit of a cowd crill, for summat towd mo that there wur
misfortin' afoot. Eawr mistress dropped her knittin to th'
floor, an' hoo said, ' Eh, Jonas, there's somebory run o'er!'
An' hoo tremble't fro yed to foot. I would ha' gone eawt
to see what were to do, but hoo said, 'Nawe, nawe; stop
here till eawr Mary comes!' An' hoo rang th' bell.

39

" There wur a lot o' carters i'th tap-reaum, and two riders-eawt i'th bar; but they wur off in a minute, an' th' sarvants an' o' went flutterin' deawn th' lobby. Then somebory in a leet geawn ran by th' bar window, an' th' mistress said, " Yon's cawr Mary! Let's go an' see what's th' matter!" An' hoo laid her hond o' my shoolder, an' we followed to th' front dur.

" When we geet theer, folk wur hurryin' fro' o' sides up to the new soof, and theer they stoode, in a greight welter, lookin deawn into th' hole, wi' faces as pale as my shirt. I would fain a-gwon up to th' spot, but th' owd woman would'nt let me stir a peg. Well in a minute or so, there wur a cry set up for 'Moor spades!' an' some ran one gate, some another. Little Jerry, th' stable lad, coom hurryin' up to th' dur, eawt o' breath, an' he said, 'Th' soof's fo'n in! There's a chap smoorin'! I'm beawn for some spades!' an' he dashed through to th' back yard. Owd Sprint, th' taylior, wur runnin' deawn th' middle o'th road, beawt hat, an' I beckon't on him, but he cried eawt that he wur gooin' for a doctor, an' he couldn't stop. . . . It wur a terrible thing to see th' folk cluster't abeawt that soof. . . Onybody 'at's yerd that low buzz 'at a lot o' men makes when there's aught sayrious agate.—they may tell it again as long as they liven. . . . Well, th' next thing, Mary coom to us, and begged of her mother to go into th' heawse; an' hoo said that hoo'd sent Robin up to see heaw they wur gooin' on, an' he'd be back directly. So we helped her into th' parlour, here; an' some an' ill hoo wur, I con tell yo.

" We wur just talkin' abeawt gettin' th' owd woman upstairs, when Robin coom in wi' th' news. 'Eh, mistress,' he said, 'it's poor Jim Greenhalgh! I've sin sich a seet! Just as it stroke twelve, his wife coom off at th' corner o'th road wi' his dinner. Owd Suzy, th' wesherwoman, wur wi' her, an' they seem't to be talkin' very comfortably together. It would ha' been better if somebory could ha' stopped 'em afore they'd gettin' to th' place; but hoo wur too near. When Matty see'd th' creawd, hoo walked up, quite unconsarnt, an' axed a chap 'at stoode at the cawtside what there wur to do. He wur a stranger, and breek-maker bi' th look on him,—an' he onsor't her very snappish an' said, 'There's somebory kilt i'th soof;' an' then he towd her to mind her own business. But summat seem't to strike her o' at once on' hoo gripp't him by th' arm an' said, 'Oh, what's he code?' The chap starc't at her white face; but afore he could say a word, somebory beheend sheawted cawt, "It's Jimmy Greenhalgh, at th' Birches!' an' then, in an instant, th' dinner-basket dropped to th' floor, an' her arms shot up, an' hoo gav a wild skrike 'at startle't th' folk i'th street, like a flash o' leetenin'. They just catch't her afore hoo fell to th' greawnd like a lump o' wood. The neighbour women coom runnin' reawnd when they yerd her cry; an' as first one then another looked at her, they said, 'Eh, it's Marty It's his wife! Eh, poor thing!', . . An' they geet howd on her, and carried her into Sally Grimshaw's, an' laid her upo' th' couch cheer, as dateless as a stone!"

"An' neaw, doctor," continued Jonas, "I've towd th' tale as far as I con, bwoth what I seed, an' what Robin seed. I dar say yo can tell th' remainder better nor me."

" Well," said the doctor, taking another pinch of snuff an l wiping his eyes, under pretence of cleaning his spectacles, "perhaps I can, Jonas. I have seen a good deal of sorrow in my time, but the circumstances connected with this accident have certainly touched me a little. It is very sad.

"I was standing by the sewer, when old Sally Grimshaw came and said that I was wanted in her house directly. I had only just learnt that the poor fellow they were extricating from a living grave was the man whose sick child I had visited about an hour before; and it did not strike me at that moment that his wife was on her way to the spot with his dinner. But when I saw that pale face, as she lay there insensible, I knew her at once.

"She was slowly recovering, when a lad shouted into the house, 'They're gettin' him cawt!' Old Sally closed the door quietly, just as the poor woman opened her eyes. Looking vacantly from face to face, and then at the walls, she put her hand to her forehead, and said, 'Wheer am I?' But when she saw the dinner-basket on the table, she sank down insensible again. Just then I heard an increased bustle outside, and I looked through the window. They were lifting the body up to the bank of the sewer, and two men were coming down the street with a bearing barrow and a sheet. Leaving some instructions with old Sally, I went out, and found the poor fellow quite dead. I directed the men to bring the body down to this house, where they laid it upon the tressle-table in the club room.

"By this time my friend Dr. Lord had arrived, and leaving him with the body, I was hurrying back to the cottage, when I saw a little company of women coming down towards this place. I knew at a glance what was the matter. It was poor Matty, and the women I had left with her at Sally

Grimshaw's. They were trying to persuade her to turn
back; but it was useless. 'I mun go,' she said; 'oh,
I mun go to him!' and her countenance looked fearfully pale and wild. She carried the dinner basket
on her arm, too, and would not let anybody else
touch it. I made no attempt to hinder her, but turned
back with them to the room where he was lying. . . .
Poor Matty! She walked calmly up to the table, and, taking
off the cloth that covered the things in the basket, she lifted
the bowl out containing the dinner, and set it down with the
bread, and knife and fork, beside the dead man. Then she
looked at his cold face, and said, 'Jim!' as if inviting him to
eat. I began to fear for the poor woman's reason. She sat
down by the table, and all was silent for a minute or two.
The stillness seemed to wake her from this fearful calm. She
got up, and looked steadily at the dead man's face again for
a few seconds, and then the flood-gates of nature were
mercifully opened, and she burst into a passionate fit of
tears. I was glad to see this, for I knew it would relieve
her. It was a touching scene. Everybody was moved to
tears. She kissed his pale face, and shading the hair away
from his brow, she said, 'Oh! my poor lad! He'll never
speighk to me again!—never!—never!' And then she sat
down again, and moaned and sobbed bitterly. As she sat
thus, rocking herself to and fro, old Sally touched her arm,
and whispered to her; but the poor creature seemed to take
no notice of her. She rose, and looking at her husband's
face again, she said, 'He towd me to be sure an' come at
twelve o'clock. . . . Oh, Jim!—Jim!—my poor lad!
What mun I say to thi childer?' And then she sank

down upon the seat again, in a kind of stupor. Whilst she
was in that state, I ordered a coach into the yard. Mary
and old Sally led her passively into it; and by the time we
got down to her own cottage, she seemed more dead than
alive,—in fact, I fear that her life is in great danger. They
got her to bed as quietly as possible.

"The news had reached the cottage before we got there.
The door was open, and poor Matty's sister was moving
about the melancholy house in silence, with tearful eyes.
Two neighbour women from the village had brought the
news; but I was glad that they had not told it to the poor
girl who was ill, although she had asked several times if her
mother had come back. A kind widow lady here, in the
village, had provided for the rest of the children in her own
house, for the present, till their relatives arrived, who lived
at some distance.

"I stayed at the cottage till Dr. Lord arrived at five this
afternoon, and I promised to relieve him at half-past eight.
I see it is half-past seven now. It is very likely I may have
to remain there through the night, for I fear, from the
symptoms, that premature labour may ensue; and, if so, it
will be a very dangerous case. I don't know what is to be
done with that family of little children. Poor creatures!
When I think of this day's business, I pray, as I have often
prayed, that I may never forget the unfortunate. The old
lady here, too," continued the doctor, "will need careful
attention. I must see her before leaving," and he rang the
bell. When the landlady's daughter entered, he enquired
how her mother was.

"She is sound asleep, sir," said Mary.

"Then don't disturb her on my account," replied he. "But you know where I am going?"

"Yes," said she, "and if you happen to want anything we have in the house, doctor, somebody will be up all night to attend you. Will you take any supper before you go, sir?"

"Well, I may stop all night. I'll take a few biscuits with me, and a little port wine in one of your small flask bottles."

She brought the biscuits and the wine, and the doctor stowed them away in his pocket. As he rose to go, I told him that. as it was on my way home, we could walk together, if he had no objection. He accepted the offer with pleasure. I was helping him on with his great-coat, when somebody knocked at the door.

"Come in."

It was old Jonas, with a thick red muffler tied round his neck

"Win yo ha' th' lantron, doctor? I've nought else to do. Mary sent me to ax you."

"No, no; thank you," replied the doctor; "it's a clear night, and this gentleman is going the same way."

"Well," said Jonas, following us down the lobby, "If yo chancen to want a bit of an arran or ought doin i'th neet-time, yo'n nought to do but to send somebory, and tell 'em to ring at th' front dur here. I'll beawnce cawt in a minute; for I'm nobbut a leet sleeper. But there's to be somebory up i'th kitchen o' neet, I believe, so yo'n no 'casion to be fleyed o' disturbin' us."

"Thank you, Jonas; thank you." replied the doctor. "I'll not disturb you unless there be serious reason for it, you may depend."

"Eh, never yo mind, doctor," said Jonas. "We're noan tickle at a time like this. I'll go an' sit up o' neet wi' yo, if I can be of ony sarvice,—an welcome."

"No, thank you," answered the doctor ; "I'll send up if there be any need, and I shall be glad to have your assistance. Good night, Jonas."

"Good neet to yo!" said Jonas, looking round. "It is starleet, I see." And he stood in the doorway watching us as we walked down the road.

"Poor old fellow!" said the doctor. "He is a kindhearted, faithful creature. And, simple as he looks, he is a shrewd, clear-headed man ; and his life has been marked by strange events, and more suffering than falls to the common lot of mankind. To me he is a very interesting character, and, when he is in the mood, I am always glad to listen to his artless tales and quaint comments upon persons and things. In fact, I have found all through life that, if one had only the eye to perceive it, there is a charmed circle of good around every man one meets, however humble or obscure, within which he is unique in his service to mankind—a new volume of that great library of human life that fills the world with interesting variety."

There was a solemn grandeur about the night. The stars shone out in unusual numbers and brilliance. The wind was wild and cold, and moaning sounds came up from the woody clough, like the changing surge of the sea, as heard in the distance at midnight. As we drew near the dead man's cottage, the blinds were all down, and lights shone in every window ; but not a sound was audible outside. As I parted with the doctor at the door I caught sight of women moving to and fro, and heard a sound of sobbing. The door closed, and I stood for a minute gazing at the windows where ghostly figures flitted now and then between the lights and the white blinds. The sacred atmosphere of sorrow enveloped that little dwelling, over which such an unexpected change had come since the morning. "No man knows what a day may bring forth." And it is no wonder that, as I walked home in the starlight that night, those noble words should occur to my mind which commend to the fatherly goodness of heaven "all those who are any ways afflicted or distressed in mind, body, or estate, that it may please Thee to comfort and relieve them, according to their several necessities, giving them patience under their sufferings, and a happy issue out of all their afflictions."

Excelsior Steam Printing and Bookbinding Works,
Hulme Hall Road, Manchester.

www.ingramcontent.com/pod-product-compliance
Lightning Source LLC
Chambersburg PA
CBHW060540030726

47498CB00004B/1259